Ever

JESSA RUSSO

For Kristy — Keep chasing your dreams so someday I can get a signed copy of your book! :) Thanks so much — hope you enjoy EVER!

A

A Division of **Whampa, LLC**
P.O. Box 2540
Dulles, VA 20101
Tel/Fax: 800-998-2509
http://curiosityquills.com

© 2012 Jessa Russo
http://jessarussowrites.blogspot.com

Cover design by Alex & Me Design

Cover photo by Face On By Tamara

Edited by Krystal Wade
http://krystal-wade.com

ISBN: 978-1-62007-088-8 (ebook)
ISBN: 978-1-62007-089-5 (paperback)
ISBN: 978-1-62007-090-1 (hardcover)

Table of Contents

For Papa:

You always dreamed of writing your first book, but never got the chance.
I dedicate my first book to you.

I hope you're proud of me and watching my journey unfold.
I love you and miss you always.

1946 - 1996

One

O ne glance at the calendar was all I needed. One quick glance and I instantly realized why my heart felt heavy. Why Frankie kept sneaking sideways glances at me. Why Jessie was more chatty than usual. My eyes widened at the realization. I'd almost forgotten. How could I have almost forgotten? The day was . . . *is* . . . unforgettable.

I lived next door to Frankie my entire life. We played together when we were little. He pulled my pigtails. I tattled; he teased. He's the very best friend I've ever had.

I've been in love with him as long as I can remember.

Today marked the second anniversary of his death. Exactly seven-hundred and thirty days had passed since the car accident took his life, and *didn't* take *mine*. Seven-hundred and thirty days since the only guy I've ever loved died in my arms, followed me home from the hospital, and never left my house again.

How could I have almost forgotten?

As I looked at him leaning against the antique roll-top desk my mom insisted was proper living room decor, he was beautiful, even in death.

I'd never forget holding onto him as the last breath left his body. I cried and screamed, but no one came in time. No one heard me. No one even knew we'd swerved off the road until an hour or so later when I pulled myself from the overturned Chevy and crawled to the top of the hill. Frankie was by my side the entire time. My hands and knees were bloodied and filthy from the climb. He kept telling me to continue when all I wanted to do was close my eyes. At the time, I'd convinced myself he was a figment of my traumatized mind. I knew his body remained pinned under the steering column. I knew he couldn't possibly be walking with me, urging me to survive. I figured I'd simply been unable to let him go yet. Maybe I just needed *time.*

Turned out he couldn't let me go either.

Just a silly square on the calendar. This date signified so much. The earth-shattering feeling of losing him. The shock of finding out he was . . . *is* . . . still here. The solid, devastating fact that he would forever be here, with me, and yet, *never* truly be mine.

I'll never forget it, and yet . . . I almost did.

My heart sank. Part of me wished I *had* forgotten this day. I wished my mom didn't insist on having a calendar hanging in every freaking room.

I hadn't touched him since he died. We hadn't hugged. He hadn't held me. I saw him every day. I woke up in the same house with him every morning. But still, I couldn't touch him. And he couldn't touch me.

When I looked at him now, two years later, I felt a sense of longing I just couldn't shake. A sense of need that couldn't be met. An emptiness grew inside me. I ached for him—I ached for *me*—and all the things I lost when Frankie died. All the what-ifs and the maybes, the hope that one day he'd see me as more than just the silly girl he'd grown up with.

I needed to *feel* again. I needed contact. I needed to be touched and held and loved. I simply couldn't stand it anymore. My loneliness ate away at my insides, chipping pieces away from my soul every day that went by without the physical closeness I craved. I just wanted a normal life, a normal relationship. A boyfriend.

But as I looked at Frankie and he smiled that crooked smile I loved so much, pushing his Buddy Holly glasses up on his nose, my heart clenched, and I knew I had to keep up the facade. I had to remain right where I was, pretending to be happy alone. But if *alone* meant with Frankie, then I couldn't really be anywhere else anyway.

I couldn't be *with* anyone else. I just couldn't.

None of us acknowledged the significance of this anniversary or the car accident it represented. We didn't speak of what we lost that day. We didn't remember the tragedy, or at least, we weren't supposed to. But the memory was always there in the back of my mind, a constant reminder. I'd never be normal again. I'd never have a normal life, a normal relationship.

While my best friend Jessie went on date after date and had story after story of all the good, bad, and ugly of dating high school boys, I just got to listen. I'd never go on an official date. I'd never get to double date with my best friend. I'd never talk to her about sex or exchange embarrassing make-out stories. At this rate, I'd probably never even *have* an embarrassing make-out story—let alone *sex*.

I'd never have a *real* boyfriend.

I couldn't just go date some random guy and pretend I hadn't given Frankie my heart all those years ago. Pretend he didn't still have possession of it.

So we didn't speak about that fateful day. We didn't talk about what today represented. We didn't discuss the future because let's face it: Frankie didn't have one, and mine was pathetic at best.

We didn't discuss how fate left us with nothing more than our friendship . . . and no possibility of anything else.

This day was just another date on the calendar. Just another painful, unspoken reminder that though Frankie was still here, I was very much alone. The ultimate case of loving a boy I could never have.

"Ever! Hello? Are you listening to me?"

Shoot. Jessie was talking to me. I quickly tried to replay whatever she'd last said. Oh yeah. Vampires and werewolves. We were on that subject again, were we?

"Good grief, Jess."

"Oh, *Ever!* How can you doubt what's out there with your own house full of ghosts?" She waved a hand in Frankie's direction, not caring to acknowledge the fact that using the word in plural form was a bit of an exaggeration. "I mean, geez, Ever, he is *right* under your nose!"

Catching Frankie grinning from the corner of my eyes, I shook my head at him and unsuccessfully stifled a moan. *Here we go again.*

Jessie was getting all riled up, her blue eyes wide and her pink-lipped mouth pinched tight. Her cropped blonde hair bounced as she shook her head and delved once again into the exciting world of her beliefs versus my, well, *non*-beliefs. Really, I couldn't help but roll my eyes. I also had nothing to say on the subject that hadn't already been said. We'd been over this before, and logical or not, my arguments were always ignored by Jessie. So why bother?

"Seriously, I happen to believe that in this vast universe there must be a little room for everyone. I mean, if there *really* is a parallel Fae world, would we know about it? No. Probably not. Think on that for a sec. Yeah, so who's to say it does or doesn't exist, right? Certainly not me. I mean, I'm open to whatever." She shrugged, emphasizing her nonchalance.

"Come on, Jess. I'm not debating this with you again. Why haven't we ever seen or heard of a vampire or a vampire attack? Wouldn't word spread pretty quickly if a werewolf were running rampant on the night of a full moon? Or, oh, I don't know, I think someone would have actually *seen* a leprechaun or tooth fairy by now, don't you think? And, don't you think these things would be all over the *news* if they existed?"

I knew I was baiting her by bringing up the news—she's a little bit of a self-proclaimed expert on journalism, being that it's her dream to become the youngest person at KTLA—but I couldn't help myself.

"Oh, Ever! I'm not even going there with you right now! You know it wouldn't be on the news because we"—she was lumping herself in with professional newscasters again—"have duties to uphold a sense of calm. Can you even *imagine* what would happen if Sam Rubin started reporting on vampire bites instead of the Oscars? And furthermore, did *you* know that there was such a thing as ghosts before they took up residence in *your* living room?"

She paused briefly, glancing over at Frankie slouched against the roll-top, and pretended to wait for an answer. I shot her a look, reminding her to watch what she said around him.

"No! You didn't. And don't shake your head at me, Ever, because I know you didn't know. I was there when it happened, remember? I *know* how shocked you were when Frankie followed you home after . . ."

I held my breath, hoping she'd catch herself before saying the words.

"We were *all* shocked. But that didn't change the fact that it happened. So why not open your mind a little and stop being so ignorant!"

Frankie snorted at the last part, amused that Jessie dared call me ignorant, but tightened his smile into a hard line when I glared at him.

"Um, *excuse* me? I am *not* ignorant, Jessie. I'm realistic. There's a huge difference—"

I was about to gladly debate that difference with Jessie when my mom came out of the kitchen and plopped a plate full of fresh-out-of-the-oven brownies in front of us. She gave me that wise warning look only a mother knows how to give, her long dark hair moving as she gave me a quick shake of her head. I shoved a brownie in my mouth, in its entirety, to keep from starting a fight with Jess. My mom winked at me then retreated back to the kitchen.

Yeah, yeah, I get it.

I changed the subject by walking to the DVD player to pop in the next disc we'd planned on watching, but my attention was drawn to the front yard. My view of the street was obstructed on one side by the old magnolia tree and flowering bougainvillea, and a moving truck on the other. The yard was draped in shadows. I had a tiny little tunnel of vision straight into the front yard next door.

The sudden appearance of a moving truck bothered me. I hadn't known anyone was moving into the house next door. It had been empty since Frankie's dad moved away . . . shortly after the divorce, which was shortly before his mom's suicide, which was all very shortly after—and *due to*—the car accident we didn't speak of. Trying to convince his father that Frankie's ghost was still hanging around proved impossible. He thought I had a sick sense of humor, ended up hating me, and left without telling us a thing. No forwarding address, no goodbyes. After knowing me for my entire life, he'd suddenly looked at me as though I were a monster.

There had never been a For Sale sign, or an open house, or even a Realtor.

It irritated me, though I had no idea why it should matter, really. I mean, Frankie's house was vacant. Last we'd been able to uncover, his dad lived somewhere in the mid-west with family. Frankie wasn't going anywhere, so why should I care if another family moved in next door?

But I did. I couldn't pretend it didn't feel like the end of an era or something. I'd practically grown up in that house.

My thoughts were interrupted when I saw the new neighbor. Suddenly it didn't feel like the *end* of anything. More like the beginning. Of what, I didn't yet know. But I wanted to find out.

He jumped down out of the back of the moving truck, instead of using the ramp, and made his way toward the front of Frankie's house.

I would have to stop calling it that.

He carried a box labeled "Toby's Room." I played around with the name in my mind before saying it quietly. "Toby," I whispered. Yes. I liked the way that sounded, almost as much as I liked the way he looked. Wow.

He wore tight black Levis and a snug-fitting, faded black t-shirt, finished with a pair of worn-out black boots. I looked down at my own clothes, amused to see we looked like we could have gone shopping in the same closet this morning. Both of us in all faded black, except I had a tiny touch of red in the form of a glitter skull and crossbones on the bottom hem of my purposely-distressed black-on-black striped tank top. *So he's a snappy dresser. Nice.*

His hair was a bit long on top, and the back curled up just enough that it looked like he was far between haircuts. His bangs hung in his face, and he kept blowing the golden brown hair out of his eyes— without much success. I found myself smiling as he did so, the action making him seem distracted and innocent.

Judging by the way he carried himself, I could tell he was a bit older than me, but I was unsure of how much. Maybe a few years? He had on sunglasses, so I couldn't see his eyes, but boy did I want to. To say that my curiosity was piqued would be a gross understatement. I glanced back at Frankie, guilt-ridden for feeling any inkling of interest in another guy, but he was busy talking to my mom in the doorway of the kitchen and hadn't yet noticed the new neighbor. Or my instant fascination with said neighbor.

The way the two houses were lined up, I had a clear view of the front door of Frankie's—*Toby's*—house from my living room window. It had been a bonus for our parents when we were kids because they could easily watch us playing out front from either house.

I shamelessly watched Toby walk the length of the moving truck and enter the house. Right before he disappeared inside, he glanced over and caught me staring at him.

Shoot!

Before I could look away, I swear I saw a smile turn up the corners of his mouth. Reaching my hand up to my black hair, I remembered with horror the 1982 scrunchie holding the messy ponytail-bun-thing I had going on. My face quickly heated, and I knew I was probably bright red—my trademark blushing. I was suddenly very self-conscious, unable to think of anything but that damned scrunchie. I pulled it out, much too late for it to even matter because he was gone. To my dismay, I slowly realized that the scrunchie was the least of my worries. I still had a mouth full of brownies stored in my cheek like a chipmunk gearing up for the winter. Fan-*freaking*-tastic. Between that and the hair, I'd have to say as far as first impressions go, this one had been a complete fail.

"Ever? Ever?"

Jessie was calling me, but I was shamelessly waiting for another glimpse of him.

"Hellooo . . .. .Earth to Elenoaaaaaarrr!"

Oh hell no.

"*What?*"

I whipped around, prepared to bite off Jessie's head for using my first name, but she giggled and shrank back into the couch. My glare must have been fierce. I don't know what she expected; she knew how much I hate that name. Frankie snorted again and ducked his head, avoiding another glare from me. Instead, he diligently focused on an imaginary hangnail. He obviously hadn't noticed what—or who—I had been staring at. Good.

"Geez, Ever. Chill. What are you looking at?"

"What? Nothing." I glanced at Frankie, worried he'd catch my guilty tone.

"Whatever. Are you going to put in the movie? We better hurry if we're going to watch all three of them tonight. I want to be home before Susan gets there."

Ah yes, Susan. Jessie's mom, in little more than the biological sense. At this moment, she was probably out on yet another date, with yet another random guy, draining yet another bottle of whiskey.

If Jessie was lucky, this current guy wouldn't end up crashing on their couch for God knows how long.

I waited a few more seconds, hoping to catch a glimpse of my new neighbor, but not wanting to draw any attention to what I was staring at. I tore myself away from the window, popped another movie into the DVD player, then curled up on the couch opposite Jessie. My scruffy little terrier mix, Gollum, lifted his head long enough for me to slide underneath it so he could resume his intense resting regimen.

My attention, unfortunately, was not on the movie, and not because I'd seen it so many times before. I couldn't stop thinking about the hot new guy next door. Even more imaginative than usual, my mind started making up all sorts of different things about him, and I found myself creating and playing out scenarios in my head about how the two of us would meet and what would come next.

My fantasizing about Toby was tainted with remorse for Frankie, but the daydreams didn't cease. And really, it isn't like my remorse was even valid. Frankie wasn't *actually* my boyfriend, regardless of how long I'd loved him. He didn't even *know* I loved him in the first place.

"Whoa. Um, Ever? Who is *that?*"

"Hmm?" Still indulging in my fantasy world, I was barely able to acknowledge Jessie when she spoke.

"Dude. Look outside."

I slowly looked up and saw Gollum staring out at the front yard, a low growl starting up in his belly. Following his gaze out the window, I saw the new neighbor again. Before I even realized I was moving, I was on my feet, making my way toward the front door. I vaguely registered Jessie's bewildered voice calling me as I walked outside, frantically smoothing my hair along the way.

He leaned nonchalantly against the trunk of my Magnolia tree, hands in his pockets and completely at home there, as if he'd stood there like that a million times. He watched me through black Ray-Ban Wayfarers as I approached. I tilted my head to one side as I looked at him, and slowly, he did the same. I stopped a few feet from him, and we stood there, silently regarding one another. A soft-spoken voice in my head tried in vain to convince me to turn around and head back into my house, but I've never been very good at listening to that voice.

Up close, my earlier assumptions were confirmed. He had to be at least twenty years old. He had a little bit of scruffy beard stubble, that most guys my age still dreamed about. His mouth had the frown lines of someone who was perpetually deep in thought and the smirk of someone who thinks everything is just one big joke. The combination made him seem annoyed and amused all at the same time, and I'd be lying if I said I didn't like him instantly.

This is bad, very bad. That silly little voice tried to warn me again. *Shh.*

His arms were crossed, but the tightness in his muscles showed he was fit. He wasn't bulky like someone who spent every waking moment in the gym lifting weights, but he was sculpted and lean like a swimmer. Matching the whole swimming notion, his skin was golden tanned.

Unlike Frankie's ghostly pallor. Damn. Frankie. *What am I doing out here?*

My body was stuck in place as I intensely examined the new stranger, and it continued to be completely at odds with the cautionary voice in my head.

He was gorgeous. Where Frankie was the all-American rockabilly musician type, always dreaming of the classic cars he'd never get to own, Toby was total badass, boots and all.

Maybe the complete lack of a normal relationship had caused me to become this crazy person who stands outside, silently examining strangers. Maybe harboring my impossible feelings for a ghost for so long turned me into a socially inept freak. I didn't know why, but I found myself *really* wanting to touch him.

He leaned forward, like he was about to walk toward me, and startled me out of my examination of him. I stepped back a foot or so and realized my hand was outstretched in his direction. *Oh my god! I've actually been reaching for him!* I yanked my hand back to my side, hoping he hadn't noticed, and cursed my own stupidity.

Settling back against the tree, an amused smirk pulled at his face. Of course he'd noticed. He probably thought his new neighbor was a complete nutcase.

I should say something to convince him otherwise.

I couldn't come up with anything. I stood there dumbstruck and unable to speak. *Gah! I am a freak.* But really, what could I say after such a ridiculous gesture as reaching out to touch a total stranger? It occurred to me, too late, that I could have pretended I was going for a handshake.

Idiot.

"Hey."

Oh geez, he was speaking to me. "Hey."

As he watched me, he obviously found amusement in my awkwardness. His smirk slowly curved into a full-blown smile.

Fantastic.

"I'm Toby. I just moved in next door." He hitched a thumb in the direction of Frankie's old house, and my stomach twisted ever so slightly.

"Yeah. Cool."

Ah! I sound like such a tool!

"And you are . . . ?"

My eyes widened. "Oh. Sorry. I'm Ever."

His eyebrows drew together. "Ever? Like, *'forever and ever'*?"

"Yep. Just like that. It's a nickname." *Shoot!* Why had I said that? I knew he'd be tempted to ask what it was short for – people always were. *Don't ask. Don't ask.*

"Oh yeah? That's cool. What's it short for?"

Damn. Um . . . "My initials. E, V, V, R."

"Four initials, huh?"

"Yeah, well, my last name is Van Ruysdael, so two for that." *Please don't ask about my first name.* I was relieved when he didn't. Maybe he saw a silent warning in my wide eyes.

"Cool. So what do you do for fun around here, Ever?"

"Um." I shrugged, trying to figure out what to say. Did I confess, and tell him that I stayed home a lot because I was secretly in love with my best-friend-turned-ghostly-roommate who was stuck inside my house? Probably not. At least, not if I wanted to keep the freak factor to a minimum. "I don't know . . . there's lots of stuff. The mall. The beach. Irvine Spectrum . . . ."

"Can I take you out some time?"

Oh. Well, that was unexpected. I ran my hands through my hair. I wanted so badly to say yes. I wanted so badly to escape my purgatory. Yet I felt so guilty for wanting that. My mouth opened, and for a second, I feared that the word might actually fly out against my better judgment. *Yes.*

"No. I have a boyfriend."

Seriously? I lied instead of just saying yes and letting this hot new guy take me out? Wow. I actually was a freak. He cocked his head, and I swear I saw him look past me to my window as if he knew my "boyfriend" was actually right inside the house. I swallowed hard, hoping Frankie's pale face wasn't at the window.

"Huh. Really? Well, that's a bummer."

Toby stared at me a little longer than necessary, and I felt my heart rate increase before he shrugged casually and walked back toward Frankie's house. *His* house. I swear Toby doubted me, though I couldn't see how. There's no way he could have known anything about me before today.

"See ya 'round, Ever," he called over his shoulder as he retreated.

I turned back to my house to see three faces shamelessly peering out the window. Below them, a fourth face, covered in fur, lost interest immediately and started staring down the street, probably looking for a rabbit to dream about chasing later. I noticed my mom's wide eyes and enthusiastic smile, before she politely turned and pretended to be doing something else.

Jessie had the biggest, most ridiculous grin on her face that I'd ever seen. Before I could even begin to make my way back inside, she was already making her way *outside* to pester me with the first of what I was sure would be a thousand questions. She'd been trying to convince me to get over my feelings for Frankie to no avail, so seeing me interact with someone else was probably the greatest thing in the world as far as Jessie was concerned.

The other face, characteristically pale and translucent, looked even paler—as if he'd just seen a ghost. No pun intended. Frankie looked almost . . . broken. My heart pinched, and my stomach turned over. But why would he look that way? Why would he be . . . sad? Before I had much of a chance to ponder why Frankie would look so disappointed about me talking to the new neighbor, he quickly made his expression one of boredom then headed off to the back of the house. I'm pretty sure that was his way of avoiding me, though I'll admit, I'm not sure why he needed to.

Shaking my head at the absurdity of it all, my ridiculous guilt at the top of the list, I prepared to face Jessie, who was eager to pounce on me with her newscast-worthy interrogation.

Two

Finally in bed, I was unable to rest peacefully because I couldn't stop thinking about Toby. And Frankie. And Frankie and Toby. They would rotate and twist, but they were both equally front and center in my brain, preventing me from my much desired sleep.

I hadn't seen Toby again all evening. I kept sneaking glances out the living room window, hoping for a glimpse of him, but nothing happened. At some point, the moving truck must have left, because when I looked outside a little after ten, the driveway was empty. I hadn't seen Frankie again all night either.

He was mad at me—that much I could tell—but I didn't know why.

Now, thanks to both of them, I was sick with guilt, my stomach in knots.

But on the other hand, there was a spark of something I hadn't felt in a very long time slowly forming inside of me.

Anticipation.

I tried to ignore it, without much luck. I had an intense curiosity building inside me, and I wanted to know everything there was to know about Toby. Of course, being the complete glutton for punishment that I am, my intense curiosity fueled my intense *guilt*, and I figured I'd never get to sleep again.

Luckily, pondering all of my problems proved too boring to keep me awake, and sleep eventually found me. I woke up off and on throughout the night from terrifying nightmares. At some point, I changed out of my pajamas after waking up drenched, stripping off the flannel pants and t-shirt, and exchanging them for black and white checkered hipster panties and a black sports bra.

This time, I was panting and scared, but like the dreams I'd had earlier in the night, I couldn't remember a thing about what terrified me. Only the fear remained, relentlessly gripping me even after I opened my eyes and assessed my position on the floor.

Sweating in a tangle of sheets and blankets, my toes were so cold they felt like they'd been soaking in ice. The strange combination made me feel clammy and gross, and I considered taking a shower. Gollum was nowhere to be found; obviously annoyed by my tossing and turning, he must have left my room for the couch.

The clock blinked in red, the annoying glare telling me it was 4:30 a.m. I leaned back against the frame of my bed and noticed Frankie sitting on the edge of the chair at my writing desk.

I gasped.

He sat with his elbows on his knees and his hands clasped between them, watching me with both concern and . . . something else I couldn't quite place.

Regardless of my mom and dad's rules about boys never being allowed in my room—even *dead* ones—Frankie was a welcome presence, and my heart lifted after the initial shock faded away. Guilt still tried to creep through my mind, and I figured that it must have been the cause of my troubled sleep. But with him there in front of me, I felt only relief. We silently stared at each other in the darkness for a long time while my breathing returned to normal.

"What were you dreaming about, Doll?"

"I . . . I don't know," I answered, shaking my head. "I can't remember any of it." I paused, wondering about something that had nothing to do with my nightmare, and added, "How long have you been in here, Frankie?"

He stood and walked to the side of my bed, reaching out to help me up, even though he couldn't actually make physical contact with me or my bedding, or really be of any help at all. Old habits are hard to ignore, even for a ghost. He clenched his fists and dropped them to his sides.

"Not long. You were calling my name."

"Oh. I was?" Another thought occurred to me, and I wondered if he had a creepy '*watch you while you sleep*' thing going on, but I didn't voice that part. "Do you come in here very often?"

"No, Doll. Give me some credit, please. I'm not a three-hundred-year-old vampire with boundary issues."

I shook my head, unable to suppress my smile. I swore sometimes he read my mind, even though I knew that was impossible. Untangling myself from the sheets on the floor, I stood and stretched before I climbed back into bed. I paused at the sound of Frankie sucking in a quick breath.

The noise registered in my mind as odd because I was well aware that ghosts don't actually need to breathe. I turned to look at him, my eyebrows drawn together and head tilted in confusion—only to realize my lack of clothing was the cause of his sudden intake of breath. His eyes were glued to my chest, which was spilling out of my sports bra.

My own breath caught in my throat as I looked down at myself. Almost all of me was exposed. Part of me felt self-conscious and vulnerable, but only for a second.

My eyes found Frankie's face again, and pushing aside my discomfort, I watched his gaze slowly travel over me. He seemed captivated by my lack of clothing, and took his sweet time before meeting my gaze. When I should have been flush with embarrassment, I wasn't. Instead I was alive, on fire . . . and well, I don't really know what I felt. Brazen. Bold. I was suddenly sure . . . and confident. The way Frankie's eyes took me in made me feel like I was the most beautiful girl in the world. Was I imagining it? I watched him watch me slowly slide back into bed, his eyes lingering on me in a way I'd never seen him look at me before. Something thick and confusing lingered in the air between us. A desire that was just out of reach.

You're imagining this.

I watched him for a few long seconds, holding my breath the entire time, wondering if he was also aware of the heated moment happening between us, or if the feelings were all my own. Was it just wishful thinking on my part? Was I imagining the heated look in his eyes because I *wanted* to see it there so badly?

Once back in bed, and in spite of my lack of clothing, I found that I was feeling very calm with Frankie in my bedroom, as if his presence there wasn't abnormal at all, and was just as it should be. The fear from my nightmare relented, and the strange *intensity* between us was slipping away, back to the safety of my harbored feelings for him. Frankie stood next to my bed like a protective guard, and I sighed, my eyes closing as I did so.

He was my own personal guardian angel.

Three

E ver?"

I slept like a rock the rest of the night, and I would have kept sleeping if not for my mom's voice and a knock on my doorjamb. No more nightmares plagued me in the night, and upon opening my eyes, I found I was in exactly the same position in which I fell asleep. The only difference being that Frankie no longer stood guard.

Frankie! My gaze darted to my mom in the open doorway as I panicked that she'd catch Frankie in my room. A quick glance around showed me I was alone, and I fell back on the pillow in short-lived relief. My cheeks flared up with embarrassment as my next realization popped into my mind: my overly exposed body and the fact that Frankie had seen me almost naked during the night. Oh, wow. What came over me? If he had still been here and seen me like this, *in the daytime*, I would have freaked.

"I'm sorry I scared you, honey, but are you going to sleep *all* day, sleepy head?"

"Hey, Mom. Sorry. I guess I'm just a little tired." *Frankie was in my room all night,* I thought, my cheeks slightly flushing. Like it mattered. Like anything could have happened between us anyway. Ugh, I seriously needed to get a life. Or a real boyfriend. Preferably both.

Mom went straight for the window, and I braced myself as she purposely blinded me with the late-morning sun—which she proceeded to point out, was *already very high in the sky, thank you very much.* Content that she'd blinded me enough to get my butt out of bed, she wasted no time going straight into all the details she'd learned about the new family next door while I'd been *sleeping all day.* Her words, not mine. Eleven was by no means *all day,* especially on a Saturday when I had no work or school to attend.

She followed me around as I went through my morning routine, occasionally trying in vain to shoo Gollum—who had returned sometime in the early hours of the morning—off my bed, and talking incessantly.

She continued talking as I grabbed my bikini and a sundress, and the only peace I was able to obtain was during my ten-minute shower, and only then because I practically pushed her out of the bathroom. Although, if I know my mom, she may have continued talking long after I closed the door in her face.

After I dressed, I replaced my towel on the hook and opened the door to hear she hadn't missed a beat. I was right about the talking going on while I'd been showering. As I brushed my teeth and braided my hair, I barely registered what she was saying because my mind was so jumbled with thoughts. Once done in the bathroom, she followed me back into the bedroom and absently picked up around my room while I checked my emails.

". . . and the *dad.* You should hear Sharon go on about him! Apparently he's quite the looker. She couldn't stop raving about him. She kept saying, 'Oohwee, if I was single!'"

Ugh. This was *so* not the conversation I wanted to be having right now. No offense to Sharon, but hearing about how hot my mom's friend thinks Toby's dad is doesn't rank very high on my meter of important facts. On top of that, talking about Toby's dad was doing absolutely nothing to reduce my thoughts of Toby, throwing him right back to the forefront of my mind. My mom rambled on for a few more minutes, completely oblivious to the glazed look in my eyes. I was only catching bits and pieces of the one-sided conversation going on around me.

". . . no idea where the mom is . . . Sharon says she just up and left one day . . . the dad's a traveling salesman, so they move a lot . . . or wait, maybe she said he was military . . . oh I can't remem—"

"Mom, you know Sharon's a gossip and a busy-body."

She continued right through my interruption, as if I hadn't even spoken aloud. But that was typical too—she loved Sharon, gossip mill or not. I was taking my boots to the closet when she finally said something that warranted my attention. My *full* attention.

". . . and when he came over this morning, he was so polite! Oh, Ever, I just know you two will hit it off! And for him to bring you flowers!"

Um, what? I'm pretty sure I actually heard my jaw hit the floor. Oh wait, that was my boots hitting the floor with a *thud*. Whatever, it could have been my mouth.

". . . seems like a really nice boy . . . Dad will want to know more about him, I'm sure, but . . ."

"Mom, stop. What did you just say?"

"Hmm? Oh, I was saying that *of course* Dad will want to meet him, and . . ."

"No, no, no. *Before* that. He was here? At the house?"

Frankie.

"Oh! That! Yes, silly, don't you listen to anything I say?" She glanced over at me and shook her head before continuing, pulling a chunk of her dark waves behind her ear. "He came by earlier this morning with some flowers for you and some jelly filled croissants for Dad and me. They were store bought of course, but it's the thought that counts. And really, we should have been bringing a welcome gift to *them*, but they moved in only yesterday, and frankly, it hadn't even occurred to me yet . . . ."

I was already out the door and down the hall, running for the front half of the house.

"Ever! He's gone now, honey! That was *hours* ago!"

The flowers were sitting on the kitchen table, staring at me with their big black eyes.

White petals with black centers.

Anemones.

He knew my favorite flower. *How* did he know my favorite flower? The coincidence was more than strange. Anemones aren't your average 'run to the store and pick up some flowers' variety. Roses? Sure. That would have made sense, even if they'd been a little formal and kind of creepy. Daisies? Absolutely. A mixed springtime arrangement of colorful blooms wrapped in plastic? Yup. Definitely.

But not black and white anemones.

"Ever, honey, I know he's cute and all, but I wasn't done with my story!" My mom entered the kitchen behind me. "He said that he and his dad were leaving for the day. Returning the moving truck or something." She paused, looking off into space with an almost dreamy-eyed look on her face. "Can you believe he brought your *favorite* flower? Amazing."

Regardless of how awed my mom clearly was by Toby's flower choice, or how she was so pointedly ignoring the fact that we wouldn't be *hitting it off* anytime soon with my first love still living—or *not* living—in my house, the anemones were a bit too coincidental for my taste. I absently grabbed a Pop Tart out of the cabinet then sat down in front of the flowers. I stared at the anemones as if somehow I could intimidate them into speaking to me if I just stared at them long enough. Maybe I should have just asked *them* how Toby knew my favorite flower.

"Honey? What is it?"

"Nothing, I just . . . I don't know. I've got some stuff on my mind."

"Hmm. Okay. Well, do you want to talk about it?"

"No thanks, Mom. I'm all right. It's no biggie."

"Okay, honey." She grabbed the half-eaten Pop Tart out of my hand and replaced it with an apple. "Hey, I haven't seen Frankie in a while. Have you seen him?"

"What? No! Why would I have seen him? I've been in bed, Mom."

Shit. Way to act normal. You'd think I'd lost my virginity the way I was acting, not just had *one* boy in my room, *one* time. I must have answered a little too defensively because Mom raised one eyebrow and gave me a funny look. As she started to respond, I was saved from further questioning when Dad called to her from the backyard. I watched with relief as she ran out to meet him. To see the way they acted around each other, you'd think they were two people who hadn't just woken up in the same bed together a few hours earlier, like they had every morning for the past twenty years. She ran into his arms as though they were in the opening credits of a love story on *Lifetime.*

Ugh. I turned away to pour myself a cup of coffee when they started kissing. My mind switched back to my silly excuse for a love life.

Frankie was everything a girl could ask for—honest, loyal, funny . . . incredibly good-looking, if I did say so myself. He had such an honest way about him, and he'd always been there for me. He was a part of every important memory I'd ever had. He was protective and compassionate, so who wouldn't fall for him?

Sane people, that's who. Frankie died two years ago. *Sane* people do not fall in love with dead people, plain and simple. Regardless of his many good traits, or his rockabilly good looks, I could never have him. Only a crazy person would allow herself to continue obsessing over someone long after he'd died. *Sane* people focus on things they actually *can* attain, like relationships with *living* people.

Like Toby, for instance. When I thought about Toby, I felt that little spark of anticipation, that excitement of something new. I hadn't let myself feel anything for anyone other than Frankie since even *before* his death. But my thoughts about Toby soon turned to guilt, along with some other feelings I couldn't quite put my finger on yet. What was I going to do with myself?

Honestly, I *really* needed to stop acting like thinking about Toby was somehow cheating on Frankie. You couldn't betray a boyfriend if he wasn't actually your boyfriend and never had been.

After a few minutes, my attention fell back to the flowers—my *favorite* flowers—sitting on the table in front of me.

So, Toby had been here and he brought flowers for me. And this was *after* I was embarrassingly awkward when he tried to ask me out yesterday, turning him down with a lie. I knew I didn't have a ton of experience with guys, but *come on*, that just didn't make sense regardless of what angle you looked at it from. He should have been running for the hills from the girl with the scrunchie and the imaginary boyfriend.

And what kind of guy brings flowers for a girl who has a boyfriend, anyway? I wondered what he was after. Surely I hadn't made such a good impression that he was willing to ignore the boyfriend part.

Clearly, with my confusion about the new guy next door, and my ever-frustrating feelings for my best friend, I had two dilemmas and no answer in sight for either of them. What a big Saturday this was turning out to be, and it was barely twelve o'clock.

A car horn sounded from the driveway, reminding me that I was supposed to be heading to the beach with Jessie. Just what I needed to get my mind off Frankie and Toby. I quickly grabbed my bag, annoyed on Jessie's behalf at my inability to be on time for anything. I stepped out into the beautiful spring day and made my way to her car. I'd barely gotten my cheeks in the seat before she was rolling out of the driveway.

"Geez, Jess, why didn't you just come inside?"

"Yeah right, and add another half hour to our morning? I want to get a good spot by the volleyball courts!"

Jessie's hot pink VW bug was packed full to the brim with coolers, beach umbrellas, towels, a portable iPod player, three different kinds of tanning oils, and about a million other things only Jessie would consider a necessity for a day at the beach—all of them pink, if possible. Of course, on that note, I should probably add that I'd *never* gotten to the beach and wished I had something I forgot at home. Jessie always had me covered.

Her blonde hair was hidden under a bright pink bandana, and her Juicy Couture cover-up was the same pink as her car.

I wore my signature black, of course, with a black and gray argyle print bikini, black sundress and my dark hair pulled back in a messy ponytail. We were quite the pair of mismatched friends.

I'd been staring out the window since we left, not purposely ignoring Jessie, but just trying to make sense of my life. I was obviously totally unaware of anything going on around me, because Jessie had to say my name a few times to get my attention.

"Ev!"

"Huh?"

"You're awfully quiet today. What's up?"

"Hmm, where to start . . . ?"

"Ooh, this sounds good!"

"Slow down, Jess, there's nothing too interesting to talk about." I saw the disappointment forming on her face. Of course, in her world, she probably would have already been on at least one date with the hot new neighbor, found a way to magically turn Frankie back into a human, and by now they'd both be madly in love with her and most likely fighting each other for her heart—and all this after only twenty-four hours since Toby had moved in next door. My having nothing like that to talk about probably *was* disappointing for her. I continued anyway.

"So, you know that new guy from next door? Toby?"

"I knew this would be good! So what, did he ask you out?"

"Yes, Jess, but geez, he only moved in yesterday!"

"And? Oh god. You told him no, didn't you? I knew you were acting funny after you talked to him yesterday! I swear I always know when you're hiding something from me."

I ignored her and kept going, reluctant to outright admit to the innocent little fib I'd told Toby when I turned him down. She'd already figured out the gist of it. She didn't need to know I pretended to have a boyfriend, too. My desire to sound like a total loser only went so far.

"Oh, Ever."

"He brought me flowers this morning, and—"

"*What?* Oh my gosh, Ever, *what* is the problem? And do not say Frankie!"

"They were black and white anemones."

Jessie's faced scrunched up, drawing her blonde eyebrows together. "What? Really? That's weird."

"I know. That's the thing: how did he know, right?"

She pondered this for all of two-point-two seconds, before she was quickly back to being intrigued by the idea that the mysterious new neighbor gave me flowers. Eager to drive me toward a boy I could actually date *for real,* Jessie seemed to push any question from her mind.

"Who cares? He has good taste in girls *and* flowers. Sounds like a keeper to me." She flashed her electric smile, and that was the end of it.

"Yeah, I guess so," I said, though I wasn't convinced. The flower thing was pretty weird.

After driving a few more miles in silence, Jessie picked up on my feelings once again and tried to prod me for more. "What else is it, Ever? I know you can't be this quiet over a weird coincidence about flowers."

She was right, of course. There was so much more on my mind.

"Well, you know, I'm feeling kind of . . . ." I trailed off then, not quite sure what to say. Luckily, knowing me as well as she did, Jessie jumped right in.

"Oh, Ever. Really? Please don't tell me you're feeling all weird because of Frankie."

"Well—"

"No. This has got to stop. Seriously, Ev, it's not healthy! I mean, we are seventeen years old. We are supposed to be dating and having fun. Susan says—in one of the only bits of advice I'll even bother with—that we should be dating *multiple* guys at a time! *Multiple*." She sounded out each syllable, and I worried she'd stop to spell the word for me. Then she winked and continued, "We're young. We're hot. And we're single. You shouldn't be waiting around for Frankie, Ev. It's just . . . it's just a waste."

She lowered her voice at the end, trying to soften the blow of her words, but it didn't matter. I was well aware that my feelings for Frankie were a waste of time—I wasn't a total idiot—but that didn't make them go away, and it didn't make them any less a real part of me. Knowing how impossible a relationship with Frankie would be didn't make me desire one any less.

"Never mind, Jess. I'll figure it out."

I was disappointed by the response she'd given me regarding the flowers, and she obviously didn't have much along the lines of advice about Frankie that I hadn't already heard before. I mean, I get why she tried to get me to move on. It was just easier said than done.

I shrugged it off and tried to enjoy the day at the beach.

Four

I woke up a few times in the night, not because of nightmares—
I had none—but because my inner alarm clock decided I
should wake up and check for Frankie at 12:30 a.m., 2:30 a.m.,
and once again at 5:30 a.m., as if his appearance in my bedroom
would now be a regular occurrence. Was I hoping for that? *Yes.* Like
the ones before it, the 5:30 a.m. room search left me incredibly
disappointed, but this time unable to fall back asleep.

After yesterday's trip to the beach, followed by no trace of Frankie
last night, followed then by a full night of no ghostly visitors, I was
beginning to convince myself that Frankie's visit to my room in the
wee hours of Friday night had simply been a part of the dream world
that had so completely consumed me—a figment of my overactive
imagination. Really, it made a lot more sense that my guilt over my
interest in the neighbor created a dream version of Frankie—one that
I had no qualms about being nearly naked in front of.

Even more important than that was the very existence of a guilty
conscience in the first place. Why I had any guilt was anyone's guess,

but I couldn't seem to shake the feeling that somehow having even the slightest interest in Toby was a betrayal of Frankie.

Annoyed and exhausted, I headed into the kitchen to start the coffee because my brain wouldn't fully function without it.

"Mornin', Doll."

"Shit! Frankie!" My traitorous cheeks flamed bright red in his presence, the memory of Friday night rushing into my mind. I turned to face him sitting on the counter. With one leg folded underneath him, and the other one dangling, he twirled a ghostly unlit cigarette in his fingers like a baton, a wry smile pulling up at his mouth.

My heart stopped for a second as my breath caught in my chest. I hadn't a clue what to say to him. As he stared at me, I couldn't help but remember the intense way he'd looked at me in my room the other night. He was looking at me that way again. I hadn't imagined it. The fact that nothing came from that moment between us was irrelevant. My heart raced, and I wondered if either one of us would look at one another the same way again.

After being able to talk to Frankie about everything and anything for as long as I could remember, I was suddenly, painfully, tongue-tied. I swear he knew it too. He let his gaze slide over my body in a similar fashion as he did before—pausing briefly at my mid-section— and even though I was no longer in merely a bra and panties, I could almost see the gears turning in his head as he thought about my lack of clothing the previous night.

He smiled at me—a mischievous, knowing smile—and my cheeks heated up a bit more.

"I almost didn't recognize you with all of your clothes on."

And then he winked at me. My mouth dropped open on a gasp. He actually winked at me. I wanted to punch him, but I restrained myself. I hadn't figured out the logistics of punching a ghost yet.

"Ugh. You're impossible. I'm going to my room."

"Oh, Doll, come on. I'm teasing you!"

It was hard to resist him when he smiled at me so playfully like that, but I stomped off down the hall, Gollum close on my heels.

Frankie's laughter followed me out of the kitchen. *Well, I'm glad he's enjoying himself. Jerk.*

I was trying to portray an air of nonchalance, when all the while I was torn between wanting to get away from him as fast as I could to keep my silly lovesick feelings for him a secret, and turning around and running into his arms.

His ghostly arms.

His ghostly arms that could never, *ever* hold me.

I didn't have long to stew on that fact, or pout about my depressing lack of a love life because it was time to get ready for work. Lately, my shift at the animal shelter started early on Sundays because of the before-church adoptions my boss really thought would take off. She called them the Early Bird Adoptions and had some tagline I could never remember about the *early bird getting the dog,* or something silly like that. Jessie and I had to be in by seven every Sunday morning. Today was the fifth Early Bird Adoption event, and we'd had only *one* adoption so far.

I grabbed my iPod and my purse then headed for the door, stopping quickly to say goodbye to my mom and dad. They were huddled together over their coffee mugs, talking and laughing about who knows what, barely even noticing my presence in the room. I had to clear my throat to get them to tear their eyes away from each other and acknowledge me.

I didn't see Frankie again, which was fine with me. I didn't honestly know what to say to him, and he clearly found that fact amusing. Apparently, he was about as *unaffected* by seeing me nearly naked as I was *affected* by it.

Jessie was waiting for me when I pulled up to the shelter, leaning against her car, which was parked right in front. Our manager hated when she did that, but Jessie could charm anyone, and somehow she always managed to get her way. She wore a fitted pink tube top with a matching cardigan, both of which were almost the exact same pink of her car. The surprising aspect of her outfit wasn't the shade of pink though, since Jessie only ever wore pink. It was the introduction of another color entirely: cream, not to mention a wardrobe item I had no idea she even owned: leggings. Cream, lace-trimmed leggings to be exact. *Cream.* They must have been brand new since I'd never seen her in *anything* other than variations of pink, and I'd definitely never seen her in leggings. At all.

I parked my green machine in the employee parking lot across the street and sprinted to meet up with Jess. I'd spent so much time in my room feeling sorry for myself that I was almost late. Again.

"Helloo? Late much?"

"Hey, Jess. What's with the leggings?"

"Oh. Yeah, well, I thought it would be fun for spring. You know, switching it up a bit. Nude is *all* the rage right now."

I didn't correct her by telling her that she wasn't actually wearing nude. I just nodded and told her I liked them.

"Well, of course you do. Duh. I know all about your unhealthy obsession with leggings."

Jessie worked in the front office of the shelter, so she could get away with open-toed sandals and light colored clothes. I'm more of a hands-on kind of girl, and I spent my shelter hours in the back with the dogs. Cream leggings on me would have been ruined within the first five minutes. Nothing like muddy paw prints up and down your legs to ruin your brand new springtime fashions. I had on an old pair of dark purple sweats, cut off to be shorts, and a black wife beater with an unraveled hem and a few scattered holes.

Our boss, Jo, reprimanded us for being late, even though we were actually two minutes early according to the digital clock on the wall. But to Jo, late was not being a good five minutes *early* for your shift. We'd come to realize that Jo just complained to hear herself complain, and we were used to it. We offered her our usual "Yes, Jo. Sorry, Jo" in unison, while we bowed our heads to her in mock ascension. I followed Jessie to the break room where we stuffed our lunches into the employee refrigerator then headed off to our respective jobs.

I was so deep in thought that the day flew by quickly. When two came around, and I hadn't shown up at the front desk yet, Jessie came looking for me. I had apparently been spending an *excessive* amount of time washing my favorite Husky-Corgi mix. Spectra's fur had probably never been as clean—and probably will never be again. I was so lost in my thoughts about my frustrating feelings for my ghostly best friend and my curiosity about the new guy next door, that I hadn't even been paying attention to the massive amount of soap suds covering the poor dog. Unfortunately, I too was covered.

Jessie's high-pitched squeal snapped me into the present. "Oh my gosh, Ever! Look at all that soap!"

I broke away from my thoughts about Frankie and Toby, my eyes widening in surprise as I noticed all the bubbles. Spectra sure didn't seem to mind the mess, since it meant she'd been getting my undivided attention for so long. Jessie rushed to my aid, laughing hysterically as she did so, to help me rinse Spectra and get everything cleaned up the best we could. By the time we were ready to go home, we were both soaked and soapy and looking remarkably like the wet dog who was watching the fiasco unfold in front of her.

Jessie followed me home, waving to me emphatically every time I glanced in my rearview. I had to wonder if she looked where she was going at all, or if she just watched for me to look back at her so she could do her ridiculous waving thing. When we got to the house, it hadn't been long enough of a drive to dry off, so we were definitely quite the pair. We looked as though we'd driven through the car wash in a convertible—with the top down.

Of *course* this would be the time Toby chose to try his luck with me a second time. I was sure he'd be rethinking the notion, the longer he had to think about my awkwardness from yesterday. Apparently not. Seeing me now, I was sure he would reconsider.

As I got out of the car, I quickly considered my options. I could bury my head in the dirt and stay there. Forever. Like a sopping wet ostrich stuck in the sand.

I could jump back into my car and drive away like a madwoman. *Hmmm. Nope.* One glance told me that would be impossible since Jessie's bug was parked behind me in the driveway. *Oh! I know!* I could run away on foot since the car wasn't an option. I glanced down the street, pondering the idea.

"Hey."

Aw man, too late. Option D it was then: say hello.

He leaned against the trunk of my magnolia tree, with what I guessed was his trademark nonchalance oozing off him. His dark sunglasses hid his eyes again, much to my dismay. I just wanted a little peek, that's all. I don't think that was too much to ask for.

"Um, hi," I said, self-consciously running a hand over my wet hair. I looked over at Jessie and . . . *uh oh.*

With a sly smile on her face, she looked back and forth between Toby and me, and I just knew I was about to regret not running away down the street. I knew her too well, and I knew I was in trouble. She elbowed me and stepped forward with her hand extended and her beauty queen smile plastered across her face. I glanced down the street once more, considering my escape.

"Hi there! I'm Jessica Lynn Smith—Ever's *best* friend—but you can call me Jessie. And *you* are?"

Not like she didn't already know. I closed my eyes for a second, wishing to be anywhere else.

"Hey, I'm Toby. I just moved in next door."

"Toby . . . ?"

"James. Toby James."

"Fantastic! Well, *Toby James*, Ever was just telling me how much she'd *love* to show you around."

I gasped.

"Wouldn't you, Ev?"

Oh god. Why? Why would she do this to me? Couldn't I go on loving Frankie in peace? I wasn't hurting anyone! So our relationship was weird and fruitless; who cares?

Proud of herself to no end, and no doubt mentally giving herself a high-five, Jessie giggled while she walked backward into the house, leaving me to come up with something more to say to Toby. She'd just started a conversation, volunteered me to show him around, and *left.*

I'm going to kill her.

"So, um, thanks for the flowers. How did you know they were my favorite?"

"I didn't."

Um, okay. That's weird. "Hmm, well, they're not really your run-of-the-mill daisies, so I guess I just thought it was strange, but . . ." I paused, waiting for him to say something that would make the obscure flower choice make sense, but he just stared at me. "Well, um, thanks."

"Sure."

Since that was about the extent of what I could come up with to say, I was just staring at him, and he was staring at me. I swear Jessie's words still lingered out there, threatening to make me commit to a date.

On a side note, and regardless of how much I told myself to ignore it, he was seriously gorgeous. I was completely in awe of him, and again, that anticipation in my belly tried to stretch its fingers and crawl to the surface, right into my carefully guarded heart.

He wore another all-black ensemble, and I couldn't help but swoon over him. This time, he'd topped his t-shirt with a faded black leather jacket, which was completely out of place in the spring warmth, but he looked amazing in it, so why question his choice? He was a few inches taller than me—long and lean, but muscular. The image of seeing his arms for the first time flashed through my mind, and I wished he'd left his jacket at home so I could see them again. *Ah hell. What is happening here? I should go inside.*

His hair was damp, and I figured he'd just stepped out of the shower. My thoughts slipped further out of my control, and I found myself pondering what brand of shampoo he used. From that thought, I headed straight into total creep status and contemplated what kind of soap he used. I wanted to lean in and smell him, but luckily, that little voice inside me warned that doing so would be the end of whatever was hopefully coming my way with my new neighbor Toby. I considered ignoring the voice again, but decided against it.

After a moment, I realized Toby was analyzing me just as much as I was analyzing him. My breath caught in my throat.

"You're all wet."

Shit.

His head tilted slightly to one side, and the smirk returned to his face as he waited for me to explain my appearance. I had forgotten what I looked like—and what I must smell like. *A wet dog,* I reminded myself. Instantly, both hands were in my hair, trying to smooth it out, and he watched with amusement as my car keys tangled briefly in the matted mess. Well, I was glad someone was enjoying my discomfort.

"You work at the Animal Shelter?"

Oh no! I do smell like a wet dog!

My face must have given away my shock, because he quickly pointed to my chest and added, "Your name tag? You're still wearing it. Was there a flood today?"

"Oh, wow. I'm sorry! I don't normally look like this! I was giving one of the dogs a bath, and then, well, you can see what happened. Let me go change! I'll be right back!"

I turned away from him without a second thought, knowing only that I had to get out of the drenched, dog-hair-covered clothing immediately—before I died of embarrassment right there on my front lawn.

I was almost to the door when he caught up to me.

"Hey, Ever, wait," he said, as he reached for my elbow to slow me down.

I may have actually skidded to a stop at the feel of his hand on my skin, but luckily, when I looked down at my feet, my heels weren't smoking, and I hadn't left any grooves in the cement. *Phew.*

He glanced briefly behind me to my house.

I panicked, picturing Frankie's face at the window.

"Can I come in?"

"What? No!" *Easy there, turbo, no need to alarm him.* He looked taken aback by my sharp response, so I tried again, a bit more calmly. "No, sorry, not right now. I gotta go. Sorry."

"Wait up. Was your friend telling the truth about you wanting to take me out tonight?"

"Tonight?" And there they were: Jessie's words coming back to bite me. My hands were in my hair again. I had to force myself to bring them back down to my sides. Damn that nervous habit. My cheeks flared. *Ugh.* Damn that one too.

Why is he asking me out again? I lied to him when he'd asked before, but obviously he had no way of knowing that. I was trying to come up with another lie, another way of getting out of going on a date with him, when my mouth opened up against my control and said the word I was trying to avoid, but deep down wished I'd said yesterday.

"Yes."

"Great," he said with a grin. He was clearly pleased by my response, which in turn left me pleased by his smile, and soon we were both grinning at each other like fools.

I mentally cursed myself. And Jessie. This was all *her* fault.

"You don't have school tomorrow or anything, right?"

"Well, yeah, I do. Wait, no. I don't go to regular school. But, I mean, I don't. I don't have school tomorrow. It's Spring Break anyway. Sure. I can go out, I guess. Let me go change first though."

His smile grew at my choppy, nervous response.

"Cool. Your boyfriend won't mind?"

"Um . . . no. I don't really . . . ."

"It's cool. You don't have to explain. See you here in an hour or so?"

"Cool. Yeah." And, just like that, I was back to those single syllable responses.

I was bursting with excitement, and I couldn't ignore the feeling even though I desperately wanted to. As I walked inside, a huge smile stretched and distorted my face. I imagined I resembled something of a clown. A big, dumb, goofy clown who'd just accepted a date with a guy she barely knew. A guy who wasn't Frankie.

At least Jessie would be happy. I forced myself to walk in slowly, trying desperately to mimic Toby's perpetual nonchalance, but of course, I tripped coming in the door. I didn't turn around to see if he noticed—best to act like it didn't happen. A quick glance around the living room showed me that Frankie was nowhere in sight, but I still tried to act as casual as possible as I walked down the hall, just in case he appeared before I got to my room.

Once inside my room, with the door closed, I could no longer keep my excitement at bay.

"I have a date! I have a date!" I squealed in as close to a whisper as I could muster, not wanting to be overheard. Jessie was sitting on the bed, flipping through a magazine, and she looked up at me with a doe-eyed expression of mock surprise.

"Let me guess . . . you have a date?" she asked with a giggle.

"Shh!"

"Why are we whisp—?" she looked at me and sighed. "Oh, okay. I'll play along. So, I guess we're not having dinner tonight, huh?" Shaking her head and laughing as she gathered her things, she started to head for the door.

"Shoot. I forgot! You're not mad, are you, Jess? I'll cancel if . . . ."

"Oh, *Ever*! Are you kidding me? New Hottie on The Block wants to take you out, and I'm going to make you stay? Yeah right! Please, it was me who had to practically *throw* you at him to even get you to wise up! I knew the second I saw all that *black* . . . and those motorcycle boots"—she grimaced—"he's totally perfect for you. And you know what, Ev, maybe this is just what you need to get your mind off certain *other* things."

She nodded toward my closed bedroom door, though I needed no clarification. I knew exactly what *other things* she referred to because she'd been trying to get me to forget about Frankie for as long as I could remember. She wasn't a big believer in loving a guy you couldn't have *or* pining after a guy who didn't show interest. Both of which applied to Frankie.

As she exited my room, she said, "Don't do anything I wouldn't . . . wait, never mind. Do *everything!*" She winked at me, and I couldn't help but laugh. "And call me the *second* you get home!"

I was starting to undress for my shower when the door opened slightly and Jessie popped her head back through the doorway.

"And do *not* wear those hideous old boots, Ever. I mean it!"

Five

I don't think I've ever gotten ready for *anything* so fast in my life. I showered, put my hair up in a twist, and played a quick round of *What's In Ever's Closet?* in front of my mirror, all the while wishing my pinktastic *human* best friend was still there to help me. I silently thanked my lucky stars my other *ghostly* best friend was nowhere to be found. Somehow, I couldn't picture Frankie being as excited about my date as Jessie had been, even if he didn't see me *that* way, and I really didn't want that guilt knot returning to my stomach.

I applied a bit of makeup, though not much more than the usual mascara and lip-gloss, and remarkably, I was out the door in less than thirty minutes. I was incredibly proud of myself for having a couple minutes to spare, but time to spare or not, Toby was already outside waiting for me. Damn.

Wow.

He rested casually on the hood of a classic Ford Mustang parked on the street, halfway between both of our houses. Sleek and smooth and shiny black, with red leather interior, I had butterflies in my stomach just thinking about getting inside. My Civic was my baby, and though she was old, she was far from a classic—an old beast of a car.

He wore the same outfit from an hour ago, but I noticed, a bit happily, that the jacket was nowhere in sight. He pushed up off the car, glancing briefly past me to my house, and I again had an image of Frankie pop into my mind and a strange, unsettling feeling fell over me. But as Toby approached me, looking me over with an approving smile, that thought was almost instantly forgotten. His smile did funny things to my insides, and the way he kept trying to get his hair out of his eyes made me want to touch it. His V-neck t-shirt was snug-fitting and showed lean muscles underneath it, and my eyes were drawn to the groove in his collarbone.

"Wow. You look great."

Funny, I had been thinking the same thing about you.

"Oh, thanks." I checked my hair with my hands, making sure it was still tucked neatly into a twist, then took my purse off my shoulder to get inside the car.

I had settled on a red tunic, instead of my usual black, feeling a little adventurous . . . though not adventurous enough to skip the leggings. I had my limits. I'd grabbed my favorite red rose earrings, which I'd bought last year at the swap meet from a boutique specializing in Dia de Los Muertos merchandise, as a last minute addition. In the end, I'd somewhat reluctantly swapped my beat-up black boots for some black gladiator-style sandals that my mom *insisted* I buy to be part of my spring wardrobe a few weeks ago. Between Jessie making it a point to forbid me to wear my favorite boots, and since my mom was always getting on me about them as well, I figured wearing the sandals obliged them both, whether or not they were there to see it happen.

"I guess it's a step up from sopping wet and smelling like dog, huh?"

"I kinda liked you sopping wet. And you smell *nothing* like dog."

Cue my red cheeks.

With that comment, he shut the door, and I was in the car alone for a few seconds as he walked around to his side. I took a few deep breaths and ordered my heart to quit racing.

Once he was inside, Toby took off his sunglasses and leaned over the center console, reaching for the glove box. I waited to see what he was doing, when his hand grazed my knee just slightly. I sucked in a quick breath at the slight touch. Reaching past me, he retrieved the case for his sunglasses. I exhaled a bit too loudly, completely unaware I'd been holding my breath, and he stopped what he was doing, turning his head sideways to look at me. That sexy half-smile was on his face again.

With mere inches between us, I looked into his eyes for the first time. They were strikingly dark blue, almost midnight. It was such a contrast from his dirty blond hair that I wouldn't have believed the combination would work.

Oh, it works.

It worked so well, in fact, I was half-tempted to smash his sunglasses into smithereens so he could never hide his eyes behind them again. But that would be weird.

"Where to, Ever?"

I was mesmerized looking into those eyes. I was so used to Frankie's—so translucent and almost far away, even when they were right in front of my face. Toby held eye contact with an intensity that made lightning shoot through my body, clear down into my toes. It felt like every inch of me was alive, and the butterflies in my stomach intensified.

Damnit, I'm holding my breath again.

"Ever?"

With a slight shake of my head, and a sigh I'm sure he heard, I snapped myself back into the here and now. If I kept getting dumbstruck around him, he would definitely decide there was something *very* wrong with me.

"Oh, I don't know, uh . . . ."

"Well, hey, I'm new around here, right? And your friend *did* say you wanted to show me around a bit, right?"

"Yeah, um, okay, let's see . . . where are you from originally?"

"Not around here."

"Yeah, I get that, but where exactly *is* 'not around here?'"

He was still just inches away from me, and I found it hard to focus with his face so close to mine. When he smiled, I was shocked to discover that I had a barely resistible urge to kiss him. *Whoa. Slow down, Ever.* I wondered where the new brazen side of me had come from all of the sudden. *Especially* since I didn't even know the first thing about kissing boys.

"Montana. I'm from Butte, Montana."

"Montana, huh? Okay, so no beaches. Hmm. Have you ever even *seen* the ocean? Like, on a vacation or something?"

"Nope. I guess I'm pretty sad, huh?"

"Yes!"

He leaned back into his seat, looking at me sideways with that perpetual smirk still on his face, and I realized my blunder.

"Oh my gosh. I mean, no! *You're* not sad! *It's* sad! I can't even imagine growing up away from the ocean. Okay, we're heading to the beach. Take Chapman up to the 55 heading west, and it will take us all the way to PCH. That's Pacific Coast Highway, if you don't know."

"Highway 1, right?"

"Yeah. Exactly. Except we don't really call it that. I'll tell you where to go from there."

As we pulled away from our neighboring houses, a flash of something caught my eye from my living room window, but when I looked back there was nothing—or no one—there.

Frankie.

Toby and I talked a little on the way to the coast, and I pointed out a few key places—like all the nearest Starbucks, and my favorite little hole-in-the-wall place for breakfast burritos—but mostly we rode in silence and listened to music. His car had a place to plug in his iPod, and he handed it to me right away to scroll through. The songs were in alphabetical order, so it didn't take me long to find out that, like Jessie and me, he also liked the Black Keys. *It's my lucky day. He's gorgeous and he has great taste in music. Seriously?* I guessed Jessie wasn't the devil incarnate for making me go out with him after all.

Once we hit PCH, I had him head south to Laguna Beach. We found a spot to park on one of the residential side streets that luckily didn't have parking meters . . . since neither of us could find any quarters. Toby parked the Mustang, and we set out to Tablerock Beach on foot. He didn't touch me or grab my hand on the way down to the beach, but I swear I felt his close proximity to me in my entire body. I'm sure that was only due to my nerves and excitement, but I was lit up like I'd been plugged into a wall socket—currents dancing happily just below the surface of my skin. I had the usual Frankie guilt, sure, but everything else about being near Toby was so thrilling that I was a bit annoyed I hadn't followed Jessie's advice before now. If going out on a date with a hot guy was *this* exciting, I'd been missing out.

"So, back at the house, you said something about not going to regular school. Did you drop out or something?"

"Oh no, nothing like that. I'm homeschooled." *Here it comes.* I cringed slightly and braced myself for 'the look,' but it never came. *Weird.*

In fact, he seemed genuinely interested in my homeschooling. I proceeded to tell him all about it, leaving out the part about why it began in the first place. Somehow, I couldn't imagine telling Toby that my mom started homeschooling me after—*or because of*—Frankie's death. I'd been such a mess after he died—and came back—that I'd had an enormous amount of trouble in school. Not like starting fights and smoking, though I did try both at one point, but basically just not being able to focus on anything—or caring to. All I'd wanted to do was get home to Frankie. So eventually, my parents decided to just teach me at home.

We got down to the beach and found a large grouping of rocks. We climbed up to the highest point we could reach, and he sat down, taking my hand in his. As he pulled me down to sit next to him, I couldn't believe how amazing it felt to hold his hand. More of that excited warmth spread through me at his touch. I wondered if Jessie felt this every time she dated a new guy. It could be the reason she chose to go out with a new guy every weekend.

As the sun descended, turning the skyline impossible hues of orange and purple, I found myself able to open up to Toby almost completely. He was good at prompting me to continue, but it was difficult to be one-hundred percent open with him without sabotaging myself by bringing up Frankie. I managed to pay very close attention to my words, and after a few hours, I felt I'd exhausted my life story—all seventeen years of it.

When he asked about my neighborhood, I mean, *our* neighborhood, it became even more difficult to keep Frankie a secret. So instead of talking about anything current, I decided to tell him about my home's embarrassing history of paint colors. We're talking seriously embarrassing aesthetic quirks. I lived in the house that for years was periwinkle—amid a neighborhood of varying shades of beige. As I neared the point in the history lesson where Dad finally convinced Mom to paint over the hideous shade of—

"Oh shoot! My mom!" I jumped up and nearly toppled off the rocks in my haste. He jumped up as well, reaching out to grab me, and steadied me so I didn't plummet to the sand below. My heartbeat was far from steady as I realized I was completely wrapped in his arms, held tightly to his body. *Oh.* His eyes narrowed in on my lips, and I heard myself sigh. Then I cringed. *Ugh.* I had to stop doing that. He donned that knowing smirk of his and released me without letting go of my hand.

"I'm sorry I totally just freaked out, but I realized I never told my Mom and Dad where I was going tonight. Do you have your cell phone with you?"

"No. It's charging on my kitchen counter right now."

"Shit."

"What, you don't have yours either?"

"Um . . . I don't even have a phone with which to charge." Truthfully, I'd never really needed to call anyone before. I was either at home with Frankie or out with Jessie.

He gave me a funny look, "Oh. Okay, so . . . ?"

"I guess I should get home. I don't want them to freak out. I'm sorry."

I had been so caught up in the moment and the excitement of going out with Toby, I hadn't even thought to leave a note. I hoped they weren't too worried about me and that they had thought to call Jessie to ask where I was. There weren't a lot of rules and restrictions in my family, and I never wanted to tempt my parents to change that.

"No apology needed."

We made it home just after nine, and there were no lights on in the house. I saw Gollum's eager little face at the front window, but my parents didn't seem to be home. I hastily ended our date for nothing.

And then it occurred to me what a moron I was, and my head fell back against the headrest. I'd made a huge mistake and ended our date for no reason at all. *I'm such an idiot.* Toby parked the car in his driveway, and I heard him shuffle in his seat, turning to face me.

"Toby?"

"Yeah?"

"Please, tell me it's not Sunday." I peeked at him through barely opened eyes, not turning my head to face him, knowing the answer was not what I wanted to hear.

"It's not Sunday," he said with a grin.

I closed my eyes again, unwilling to accept my defeat. "But it is Sunday, isn't it?"

"Yes. Why? What happens on Sunday?" I heard him smiling without seeing his face.

"Ugh," I groaned. "Sunday is when my mom goes to Bunco at Sharon's house"—I pointed down the street in the direction of

Sharon's house without opening my eyes—"and my dad goes to wherever dads go when the moms are away. Poker. A bar somewhere. Bowling tournaments. Who knows?" I threw my hands up in annoyance.

"So you're saying we didn't have to rush home?"

"Yeah," I said on a sigh. "I'm sorry. I completely forgot."

"Okay, well we're home now. No big deal." He turned the car back on, just enough to play the music again, and while still facing me, grabbed my hand and held it in both of his. Again, that funny feeling warmed me, and I shook my head at the idea that I'd been missing out on this feeling all these years.

"So. Where were we . . . oh yeah, your house. You said it used to be . . . *purple?*"

I opened my eyes and turned in my seat to face him. He remembered right where I'd been in my story, and I was awed he'd been paying such close attention. *Okay, Jessie, he's not so bad.* We picked right back up where we left off, as if I hadn't actually ended the date abruptly. For no reason at all. I planned to never let myself forget that little mishap, but my self-punishing would have to wait. For now, I was going to allow myself to enjoy being with Toby.

We spent the next few hours sitting in the Mustang, talking, or listening to music silently, not feeling the pressure to fill the empty air between us. I was surprised at how easily I could just sit with him. My awkwardness faded, my guilt was tucked down deep, and I was just . . . *content.* I knew my experience with the opposite sex was limited—always pining for Frankie and having nothing more than friendship to show for it—but I had never felt so comfortable with anyone. Except for Frankie.

But Frankie isn't an option, I reminded myself for the millionth time. *Toby is. And he's right here.*

Because of the late hour, and my increasing yawns, I eventually—reluctantly—said goodnight to Toby and headed inside the house with the intense feeling of walking on air. I was half-disappointed that he didn't try to kiss me goodnight, but half-impressed with him for holding back. I was also slightly relieved because kissing Toby with Frankie possibly lurking in the living room would have been terrible. Well, for me at least. Not quite sure if Frankie would even have cared.

Goodnight kiss or not, there was a dreamy smile plastered to my face when I hit the sack. After throwing on a satin cami and short set, I crawled into bed and hoped my dreams would be as happy as my date with Toby had been.

They weren't.

Around two in the morning, I woke up to Frankie saying my name. I was covered in sweat, and my sheets were tangled around one of my feet at the bottom of the bed. My pillow was hugged up against my body, my knuckles white and rigid from gripping it so tightly.

"Ever? Ever? Wake up, Doll."

I sat straight up, scared and confused, and tried to make sense of the dream. Frankie was in my room again, and the immense relief at seeing him there added more confusion to my half-asleep state of mind. It was like I was scared for him, for his safety. As I began to get my bearings, I realized that, once again, I was unable to remember a single thing about my nightmare. The fear still gripped me, and Frankie's face was fresh in my mind, but that was all.

Frankie watched me, his eyes pinched with worry.

"You can't remember this one either?"

I shook my head. No need to tell him I was somehow afraid for him. It didn't make sense anyway. He stood over me, concern drawing his eyebrows together.

I lay back down on my side then scooted my back against the wall, leaving room for another person—*or ghost*—to lie next to me. I looked up at Frankie and patted the bed beside me, just needing to feel close to him to dispel my silly worries and fears from my nightmare. The startled look on his face made me laugh, and I just patted the bed again and closed my eyes.

It briefly occurred to me that I'd never be so brave if I was fully awake, but as I questioned my odd, half-awake behavior, I opened my eyes just enough to see Frankie's translucent figure lying in front of me. My heart felt whole, and it just didn't matter if I'd be lying with him like that fully awake. He was there now, and nothing else mattered but Frankie's face so close to mine. He was curled up in a way mimicking my body—legs bent toward me, almost touching mine, and our heads pulled close together, nose to nose.

I smiled. I was safe with Frankie.

I fell back to sleep almost instantly, my last thought before sleeping: "I wish I could hold him."

"Doll?"

"Hmm?"

"I wish I could hold you, too."

I was briefly alarmed when I realized I'd voiced my thought, but I was too tired to respond to him or think on it further.

Six

I was watching TV on the couch, lounging the day away in a gray wife-beater and my fleece pajama pants—black with little gray skulls and pink hearts; the only pink in my entire wardrobe—when the doorbell rang. I quickly peeked out the window, and after not seeing a car anywhere on the street or a delivery truck pulling away, I assumed the visitor was my mom's friend Sharon or another neighbor dropping by.

Oh, it was a neighbor all right. Just not any neighbor I was expecting to see.

Because I'm a complete idiot, I opened the door to Toby.

Why hadn't I even considered that it could have been *Toby* at the door? I quickly glanced around the living room, hoping Frankie heard the knock on the door and wouldn't choose that moment to walk in.

My hair was pulled back into one of those messy ponytail-bun-things I may as well have trademarked as my own, and I carried a container of yogurt and granola in my hand. Because this must have been my lucky day, the spoon was still sticking out of my mouth.

Mortified wouldn't even begin to describe it.

"Nice PJ's." He smiled as he looked me over, and I felt like dying right then would be a welcomed blessing.

He was not in pajamas, of course. *Probably because it's noon.* That thought made me wonder if he even owned pajamas, and I found myself blushing at the thought of what he might sleep in. Flannel pajama bottoms . . . boxers . . . nothing at all . . . .

He cleared his throat, and I snapped back into the present, my eyes widening as I realized what a perv I was being.

"Oh, hey," I said, smooth as usual.

"Hey," he responded with a small laugh. "How 'bout a second date? Are you free tonight?"

"Yes! Absolutely!" *Oh wow. Real smooth.* I took a deep breath and tried for a more *muted* excitement. "I mean, sure. I'd love to."

Much better.

We made plans to meet out front later that evening.

Around 5:30 p.m., we finished depositing about a million quarters into a parking meter in one of the many parking lots on the peninsula in Newport Beach. I'd made sure to come prepared for this date, and my purse was weighed down with a couple handfuls of change. Luckily, I'd used up most of it in the meter, so the weight wasn't an issue. Being the first Monday night of Spring Break for a lot of school districts in the area meant the peninsula was pretty packed, but not as packed as it probably would have been if it was a Friday or Saturday night.

"You get in trouble last night?" Toby asked, reminding me of my first date snafu.

"No. My parents didn't even come home until after I was in bed. I haven't seen them yet today, but I left them a note this time—just in case."

"Cool. I remembered my cell phone this time, too. Just in case."

He smiled at me and took my hand, letting me lead the way, and making my heart skip a few beats in the process. We headed to Mutt Lynch's, a restaurant that faces west and sits right on the boardwalk. I may have let it slip out to the hostess that yesterday was Toby's very first time seeing the ocean, so she sat us at a tall pub-style table in the front of the restaurant with a view of the beach. She looked at Toby with pity as she handed us our menus, and he just shook his head and smiled. I shrugged, unapologetic for letting the waitress know the true horror of his existence prior to moving here. I couldn't help it. It was weird that he'd never been to the ocean. I mean, how did he live like that all those years? I couldn't even ponder the idea without feeling . . . dried up.

"I'll have a Hef," he said to our server after I'd finished my drink order.

I looked up from my water, slightly surprised at his choice. *So, he's at least twenty-one. Hmm, I wonder what Dad will say.* I tucked that aside to ponder later. He changed his mind almost immediately and settled on an Arnold Palmer instead. Maybe he'd decided against it since I couldn't drink a beer. Then it occurred to me that maybe he'd changed his mind because he realized he'd forgotten his fake ID. Yeah, that could be it.

Then it occurred to me I should just ask.

"How old are you?"

"Twenty-two."

Oh. Wow. I had guessed twenty or so. Hmm. Five years older than me. *Jessie's going to die when I tell her!*

As we waited for our food, I realized that all I wanted to do was enjoy the intense way he looked at me, and the occasional sideways glances that sent my nerves somersaulting. I was in a perpetual state of speechlessness around him. Luckily for us, he was insanely good at prompting me to speak, and I once again found myself spilling my life story to him.

Our food arrived, and I was about to dig into my cobb salad when . . . *Oh gross.* I'd forgotten to ask for no olives. Ugh. Olives. The little cockroaches of the food chain. As I was pushing them off my salad, annoyed by my apparent brain fart, he was eating them one by one off of my bread plate. As if this wasn't the first time we'd eaten together and we'd been through the motion a million times. When I paused to watch him, he stopped mid-bite, his eyes opening wide.

"Oh! Sorry. You weren't saving those for last were you?" It came out muffled around a mouthful of olives waiting to be chewed.

I shook my head side to side, amused by the easy comfort between us.

Throughout the meal, Toby continued his questions, keeping me talking in his usual way, and even when I tried to change the subject and ask him about his life, he appeared so interested in mine that before long, I was rambling on and on again.

When the bill came, I tried to pay for my half of dinner, not really knowing what he was expecting. He looked at me as if I'd said something hilarious and pushed my debit card aside.

I happily admitted to myself that this was, in fact, our second "official" date. I let out a little squeal of delight—that could only be heard inside my head—and silently thanked Jessie for pushing me to go out with Toby.

After dinner, we headed to Balboa and played a few video games in the arcade followed by a few rounds of skee ball because it was the best game ever and one I knew I could win. When we were finally out of quarters, from both video games and the second trip to the parking meter, and we'd used all of Toby's dollar bills, we decided to ride the Ferris wheel. I offered to pay for that as well, and again he shot down the idea, looking at me like I was crazy.

"Really?" he asked with raised eyebrows.

"What? I was just offering."

"Put your debit card away, Ever. It is bad enough we used all of your quarters. I think I can cover the expense of a Ferris wheel ride."

He paid the attendant, and we silently waited in line. His hand was on my lower back as we waited, and I could feel nothing else. Every cell in my body focused on that one spot as if it was the only place on my body with any feeling. The Ferris wheel attendant motioned for me to get in first, and then Toby slid in beside me. I was nervous and excited sitting so close to him. But in all honesty, though half of me felt a bit jittery with anticipation and nervousness, the other half of me felt like I'd known Toby forever, not just for a day or two. An odd combination of dueling feelings. I liked it.

Once we were settled into the rickety old seat, he scooted a bit closer to me so the sides of our legs were touching. My heart rate picked up speed. He rested his left hand on my leg, palm up, and looked at me with those gorgeous blue eyes, both expectant and playful. I looked back and forth from his hand to his face, and placed my hand in his. He wove his fingers through mine, and at the touch of him, the excited feeling shot through me again. I smiled what I'm sure was a too big and too ridiculous, toothy grin, but I couldn't help it. I swear I could almost *feel* my skin vibrating. I was amazed that he couldn't hear my heart thumping away in my chest. It was practically *all* I could hear.

We sat quietly as the Ferris wheel slowly began its ascent. Between last night's date at the beach and all the talking through dinner, I was pretty sure he had learned just about *everything* there was to know about me. Except my biggest secret, of course.

The silence was welcomed because I didn't know if I could talk even if I wanted to with the crazy feelings running through me. I still hadn't gotten much out of him—or anything at all, really—but I planned to turn the tables and grill *him* on our next date. The excitement of that thought set my heart pounding even more. A third date. *Yes, I want that very badly.*

The sun was gone from the horizon, but I could make out most of the coastline's twinkling lights, so since we were delayed for the time being as people boarded the ride below us, I took the chance to point out a few landmarks along the coast.

He took the chance to lean in toward me.

I was mid-sentence, pointing something out to him, when I froze, realizing what he was doing. I inhaled a quick breath as my heart rate increased once again. *Holy shit.*

He leaned over and lightly brushed his thumb against my lips, sending tingles through my entire face. His other hand still held my hand between us, and I hoped it wasn't sweating profusely.

My mouth was open—both from the shock of his touch and the fact that I had been talking just seconds ago—and I quickly shut it, swallowing loudly, and hoping that he couldn't tell how nervous I was. Or how incredibly *excited* I was by the prospect of my very first kiss.

Oh god. What if I'm bad?

My heart raced in anticipation and fear, and the butterflies in my stomach moved from light fluttering to somersaults and back flips. My entire body seemed filled with sensations totally foreign to me. Feelings and worries I'd never experienced.

He licked his lips, leaned in further, and kissed me. He was a bit hesitant at first, kissing me slowly and gently, making sure he wasn't overstepping any boundaries.

I closed my eyes and leaned in to him, my lips parting just a bit, mimicking his, and following his lead. It felt both strange and exciting to kiss him, our tongues slightly touching, and his lips moving around mine. He kissed me delicately and each change in the movement of his lips sent intense shivers down my spine. Warmth built deep in my belly, and I feared I might laugh from the nervous excitement of it all.

After a moment that was far too short, the Ferris wheel began its descent, and Toby pulled away to look at me with those velvety blue-black eyes. I couldn't help the smile that pulled fiercely at my lips.

He smiled, and this time I was *sure* he could hear my heart beating. How could he not? I sure could. It thumped away rapidly in my ears, deafening in its excitement. It was a feeling I hoped would never go away.

Frankie's face popped into my mind again, and the moment was ruined. He'd never be my first kiss. I shook my head, trying to push my thoughts of Frankie far, far away. Toby, catching the slight movement and seemingly feeling uncertain, looked at me with a question in his eyes. His smile faltered ever so slightly, and I silently cursed Frankie for making me feel that way and for his terrible timing, popping into my head so unwarranted.

"Was that okay?"

"Oh, yes, *definitely* okay! *More* than okay!" *Whoa. Slow down, girl.* I was rambling again, my awkwardness back with a vengeance. I reached up and smoothed my hair, trying to gain some composure as I felt my trademark red cheeks make their unwanted entrance.

He smiled mischievously at me, then pressed one last, long kiss to my lips. Squeezing my hand, he leaned back in the seat as the Ferris wheel shook its way around and around. We sat in silence for the rest of the ride, and I couldn't even look over at him without blushing. I knew I must have had the most ridiculous grin on my face, probably bordering on maniacal, but I was well past the point of hiding it, and well past the point of caring.

I'd been waiting around for Frankie my entire life. I'd never dated anyone before his death, and I hadn't dated anyone since. Loving Frankie had been the only thing that mattered for as long as I could remember. Safe, comfortable, and almost normal for me. I couldn't see past it, and I didn't want to.

But now.

This moment. *This* kiss.

Perfection.

My first kiss was something I knew I'd never forget—that's a given. But somehow I couldn't imagine anyone's first kiss being like what I'd just shared with Toby. A kiss a girl waited for her whole life. I just knew it. I was determined to bask in it, and I was determined to get over whatever impossible feelings I'd been holding onto for Frankie. Loving Frankie was holding me back. I'd just never really known it.

As the Ferris wheel reached the top again, Toby kissed me once more. This time, his hands held my face and all feeling in my body seemed to rush up to meet his fingertips, to focus in on the places where his skin connected with mine.

As I relaxed into the kiss, I realized something bittersweet. No matter what, Frankie would never be able to kiss me like that.

He will never be able to make me feel like this.

$\mathcal{S}$*even*

When we pulled up and parked in front of our houses, my mom and dad were standing outside with their arms crossed. Waiting. Seething. *Shit*. Well, truthfully, looking at them a bit longer I could see that my mom was seething, but my poor dad just looked uncomfortable, like he was only standing there because she'd *made* him wait with her. He transferred his weight from foot to foot as if he was as nervous as I suddenly was.

"Shoot. What time is it?"

We looked at the clock on the dashboard in unison. It was only just after nine. I couldn't figure out why they were so angry. My curfew was ten on weeknights, and we'd really never set a curfew for weekends or Holidays since I never stayed out too late anyway, when I even bothered leaving the house. Either way, coming home after nine shouldn't have been a problem.

Toby got out of the car first and walked over to open my door. Even under the scrutiny of my parents' seemingly disapproving eyes, he remembered his manners.

"Hi, Mr. and Mrs. Van Ruysdael. Is everything all—?"

"Eleanor Victoria. Please, come inside. Good Night, Toby."

Oh no. That just happened. The first name I'd hated as long as I'd been able to pronounce it. Thanks to my mother, I would no longer be keeping *that* part of my life a secret from Toby. *Eleanor.* I looked at Toby with my eyes wide, mortified that he now knew the truth, but he wasn't focusing on that part. I could tell he was just as confused as I was about my parents' anger.

He mouthed "I'm sorry" as he watched me turn and walk up the driveway to my awaiting parents.

Once inside the house, I heard a car door shut, and the engine start up as Toby drove away. I was only able to briefly ponder why he wasn't just going inside his own house next door before my mom started in on me.

"Do you *know* how *old* he is, Ever?"

Oh. Well that hadn't taken long.

"Mom, wait . . . ."

"That boy is twenty-two years old! Twenty-*two*, Ever! *You* are seventeen! *Seventeen!*" Her voice was going up in pitch with each word flying out of her mouth. My dad slightly cringed each time.

"Mom, seriously, wait. I know I'm seventeen, but I'm also a *senior* in high school, and I'm leaving for college soon! How old do you think the boys will be in the fall, Mom? When I'm away . . . at *college?*"

"But . . . ."

My mom's open mouth slammed shut as the truth of my words sank in. I had a point, and she knew it. Seventeen or not, we had been discussing college for a while, and my parents were *supposed* to be prepared. I'd be leaving in the fall, and Jessie and I were going to be roommates. My parents had been okay with that idea. Or at least I'd thought they were. Somehow, they must have never even considered I'd be dating college-aged boys sometime in the near future.

Judging by the widening of my mom's eyes as she pondered this concept, I knew I was right—it had never even occurred to her. She looked up helplessly at my dad, who in turn looked to me for help.

Good grief.

"Mom. Dad. Seriously. He's twenty-two, not forty-two. I'm not a baby, and you have raised me well. I'm smart, okay? I'm not going to run off and have sex with the first guy who picks me up in a fast car, so relax!"

My mom's face paled just a tad at the mention of sex, but Dad seemed to see that I was right. He put his arm around Mom and looked at me with pride.

"Honey, you're right. You *are* a smart girl, and we *have* raised you well. There's absolutely no reason we shouldn't trust you." He gave my mom a squeeze, eliciting a little squeak from her. "You are mature beyond your years, Ev, and we know you will make the right choices for your life . . . don't we, Annabelle?"

My mom kind of nodded her head and smiled a confused grin. Another uncomfortable squeak escaped her lips, which I took as her way of conceding.

"Great. So that's settled. I'm going to go to my room now, okay?" I kissed them both on the cheek, told them I loved them, then wished them a good night. I grabbed a cold Cactus Cooler from the kitchen on the way to my room.

As I replayed the conversation in my head, I realized something that hadn't occurred to me before. To my parents, who had never tried to talk me out of it, my love for Frankie was *safe*. They'd never had to worry about me kissing boys or experimenting with sex. I'd never had my heart broken or come home crying after a particularly bad break up. I could see how they would find comfort in my loving a boy I couldn't possibly ever have. They were okay with my futureless feelings for Frankie because those feelings protected me.

I think it's why I was okay with those feelings as well. Loving Frankie was safe.

Huh.

I sat down, logged into Gmail, and found an excited email from Jessie. The subject line read "OMG EVER!" and I could almost hear the exclamation in Jessie's voice as I read it. She started off by chastising me for not calling her after my date yesterday or even today.

Shoot. I hadn't meant to forget, I'd just . . . not remembered. It was kind of like my issues with time. I wasn't really great with time *or* remembering things. Jessie knew me well, so after the quick reprimand, she began the interrogation about last night's date with Toby. I could just picture her face all lit up with curiosity as she wrote the email, the image made me smile. I was super excited to tell her about Toby. I began typing a response and then changed my mind. This kind of girl talk deserved a phone call. I took a sip of my soda and reached for the phone.

"That stuff will rot your teeth, Doll."

I just about flew out of my chair.

"Shit! *Frankie!* What are you doing in here?"

Frankie raised his eyebrows and put a finger to his lips in an effort to quiet me. He was right of course; this would be a bad scene if my parents caught wind of it.

Geez, luckily I hadn't been changing or something! I was somewhat irritated that he thought he could just waltz on into my room whenever he felt like it now, but I hadn't closed the door, so I guessed it was my own fault.

I remembered what was on my computer screen and suddenly felt insanely guilty about my two dates with Toby. The last thing I wanted Frankie to see was what I'd started to write in response to Jessie before I'd thought better of it and reached for the phone. I quickly sat back down and tried to square my shoulders so they would block my computer screen.

"What are you doing in here, Frankie? Mom will have a *cow!*"

He just smiled at me conspiratorially, and I rolled my eyes at him, turning back around to click out of my Gmail account.

Unsure of what to say to him, I asked the first question that came to mind. "Where have you been, anyway?"

"Well whaddya know, Dollface . . . I was about to ask you the same question."

I felt my face flush as I was flooded with guilt over being out with Toby. Then I remembered the kiss we'd shared, and my cheeks flamed up even more. I bet they were about as crimson as humanly possible, and I was glad to be facing the computer screen and not Frankie.

"I was out with Jessie."

Oh boy. I never lied to Frankie. *Who am I?* One minute I was allowing Frankie to join me in my bed, all the while practically *naked* in front of him, and the next minute I was lying to his face. What a mess.

"Out with Jessie, huh?"

In the reflection of my computer screen, I saw him tilt his head and look at me, twirling an unlit cigarette in his fingers. I felt as if he could see right through me, right into my soul. I felt like he somehow knew I was lying. I was sure my guilty conscience was to blame, but I felt it nonetheless. I may as well have branded a scarlet letter across my forehead for all the shame I'd been feeling lately. Like no matter what I tried to convince myself, or how innocent I knew I was, my heart still swore I was betraying Frankie. *Stupid heart.*

When he finished analyzing the back of my head, I watched his reflection in my dark computer monitor as he took a seat on the edge of the bed.

"Okay."

Phew. I'd freaked out for nothing. I mentally breathed a sigh of relief.

"Oh, by the way, I heard your mom and dad arguing about that new kid next door. It sounded pretty heated. Do you know what that was all abou—?"

"Fine!"

I threw up my hands and spun around in my chair to face him.

"Yes, Frankie, I was out with Toby, okay? Are you happy now? Ugh! Just . . . just *go*, Frankie. I want to go to bed."

His eyes practically bulged out of his head as I yelled at him, and he was clearly confused by my outburst. Well, that made two of us. I couldn't believe I'd just shouted at him like that, totally unprovoked.

"Wait, what? You were out with . . . but . . . I thought you said . . . ?"

The wounded expression on his face made me feel even *guiltier*, which in turn made me feel even *angrier*. It didn't make sense, but sometimes feelings just don't. His confusion should have softened me, caused me to rein myself back in. It didn't. Instead, it irritated me, confusing me further, if that's even possible.

"Yes, Frankie. I was out. On a date. With *Toby*. That hot new guy from next door. Okay? We had a *blast*. We kissed too, Frankie. Now run along and tell everyone about it. *Good night!*"

I emphasized each part of my story, unable to stop the words from flying out of my mouth. I'd gone too far. Like I was deliberately *trying* to hurt him.

He was gone instantly.

No comments. No theatrics. No puff of smoke. Nothing.

He was just *gone*.

I felt like someone punched me in the gut. *Why did I do that?* I was so beyond ashamed of myself—even more so than I had been about the date with Toby. I had never lied to Frankie, and I had *never* attacked him the way I just did. I would never forget the stricken look on his face.

I crawled into bed and fell asleep crying, though my sleep was again troubled. My subconscious continued to dissect my relationship with Frankie and my feelings for Toby, leaving me restless.

When I awoke in the night, I was again terrified and sprawled out on the floor. Like before, I was unable to remember a single thing about my nightmare, except my fear for Frankie's safety and my desperate need to find him. Frankie was back in my room, obviously responding to my calling out for him from the terrifying world inside my dreams.

He was squatting just a few inches away, leaning down over me, his weight resting on his fingers like he was about to play a childhood game of leapfrog. He was watching me intensely, his face twisted with distress. He looked frozen in place—like half of his mind was telling him to reach for me and the other half was dutifully reminding him he could do no such thing.

"Frankie."

"I'm here, Doll."

We stood at the same time and ended up almost nose-to-nose. My breathing began to slow as we stared at each other, and my fear eased slightly with every second. He licked his lips, and out of the corners of my eyes, I saw him begin to reach for me, only to see his fists clench in mid-air and land back at his sides.

I climbed back into bed, my eyes never leaving Frankie's, trying to grasp for something—*anything*—that I could remember about my dream. I couldn't come up with a single image or scene, aside from Frankie's face, and Frankie's name on my lips.

He walked over to the bed and looked down at me, his expression pained.

"Was I loud? My parents will come in . . . ."

"No, Doll, you weren't loud. I was pacing outside your door. I doubt they heard you all the way down the hall."

I don't know if it was the shame I'd felt earlier, the confusion of all the strange feelings I was having, or the leftover terror seeping out from my dream world, but hearing that Frankie was pacing outside my door brought tears flooding down my cheeks. I'd obviously really hurt him earlier if he found himself pacing outside my room.

"Shh, Doll, please don't cry." Frankie paced restlessly back and forth over the floor in front of my bed, his eyes remaining on me the entire time.

"I'm so sorry, Frankie. I didn't mean to be so rude earlier. I just . . . ."

"No, Ever. Please, don't cry. You don't have to apologize. You don't have to tell me what you do every single time you leave this house, and I shouldn't have asked you. It's not my business."

"But it is, Frankie. It *is* your business. You're—"

He looked at me expectantly when I paused, eyes intense, as he waited for the next words. As if he *wanted* me to say how I felt about him, who he was to me. Did he already know my feelings for him were so much more than they should be? Could I say them out loud?

You're my entire world.

"—you're my best friend, Frankie . . . and I . . . I just . . . ."

He flinched slightly when I said *best friend*, but I couldn't take it back, couldn't change the words without letting out the truth. The truth that he was so much *more* than my best friend remained unspoken. Where would that leave us anyway? *Nowhere. Absolutely nowhere.*

I had to move forward and see where this new thing with Toby would lead. I couldn't tell Frankie that I loved him any more than I could *continue* to love him.

"No. Shh. Really, it's okay. Go back to sleep, Doll. I'm not mad at you."

After I crawled back under the covers, chilled from the night sweats and exhausted from crying, he sat down on the edge of my bed with his back to me. He fit almost perfectly in the crook between my knees and my stomach, as though I was curled up around him. The pained look was still on his face, though he tried to mask it.

Before I drifted off, I saw that his hand was resting on top of mine.

But I couldn't feel it.

Days later, almost the entire week of Spring Break had passed since I'd seen or heard from Toby. It hurt. We'd been on two dates back-to-back, and I had really thought we'd hit it off. Maybe my lack of experience with boys was rearing its ugly head, because clearly, he'd been uninterested.

Mom and Dad had relaxed about Toby's age, which was perfectly ironic considering he'd burned me. I didn't tell them that though.

Frankie and I were pretty much back to normal, my unspoken secrets still tucked down deep, safely hidden away from exposure. It seemed my moment of insanity when I'd yelled at him was a distant memory.

I hadn't had any more nightmares, which also meant no more late night visits from Frankie . . . which sort of sucked, but let's face it, *what* on earth would have ever come of *that*? The fact that I *wanted* him in my room at all was big enough to deal with, let alone the intense feelings I had when he was actually there. His concern for me was adding fuel the fire. When I was trying to get over him by moving on with Toby, he was being all compassionate and showing up to comfort me in the middle of the night, thus totally confusing me further. So yeah, avoiding those late night situations was best. Or so I kept telling myself.

On Friday afternoon, Jessie and I were hanging out in the backyard, getting some sun, when she randomly started yelling at me.

At least, I thought the yelling was random. I was pretty sure it was the first I'd heard from her in the past hour or so. *I think. Shoot.*

Actually, now that I thought about it, I couldn't really recall if I had been ignoring Jess or not. Had she been talking?

"*Ever!* Do you even realize that you first *agreed to*, and then *allowed* me to paint your toenails pink? Pink, Ever! And not just any pink, oh no, I painted them the *brightest* pink I could find just to prove a point!" She waved the hideous pink bottle—which she obviously carried around in her purse—in my face for emphasis. "Right after I told you I was skipping college, moving to Las Vegas, and becoming a showgirl! A *showgirl!* This is spring break, Ever! The *last* spring break of my high school experience, and *you* have ignored me the whole time! Ugh! I should be off on a senior trip or something, meeting boys in Mazatlan and drinking cold drinks on hot sand, but oh no, I'm here with *you*. And frankly, Ever, you are being a little too *emo* for my liking."

The word was laced with disdain. *Emo* and Jessie had about as much in common as glitter and football.

"Will you snap out of it, Ever? As if your constant pining away for Frankie hasn't been enough to deal with all this time, but now this? Just go knock on his damn door and get it over with already!"

I was still trying to recall any bits of the conversation we'd most likely been having for the past hour, and barely processing her rant, when I looked down and realized my toenails actually *were* pink. *Oh my god. Have I been that out of it? Really? My toes are pink. Of all colors!*

"Or *I* will."

Wait. *What?* I looked up at Jessie and tried to process what she had just said. *Will what?* She was standing at the foot of my lawn chair with her hands on her hips, glaring down at me. Well, I assumed she was glaring, but the sun was behind her so all I could see was the dark outline of her body looming over me.

No, scratch that. I could actually *feel* the glare. Any normal person would have shrunk under the heat of Jessie's gaze, and I didn't have to see it to know.

"Did you hear me, Ever Van Ruysdael? I am going to go right over there and knock on his door if you don't snap out of this and enjoy the rest of this spring break with me!"

I jumped up, suddenly very aware of the close proximity to Toby's backyard, and hoped he and his dad were nowhere near enough to hear Jessie's ranting.

"Jess, shh. He'll hear you!"

"So? Let him hear me! *He* is the reason that my best friend has ignored me for four days! Four days! Do you hear me over there, *Tobyyy?* I will not allow some *guy* to ruin *my* vacation."

I was waiting for her to pump her fist in the air for emphasis, but her hands remained firmly on each hip. I slumped back down on the lounger, grabbed Jessie's pink, wide-brimmed floppy sunhat, and hid my face under it.

"Ohhh, no you don't. You are getting up and marching over there right now, or I am going to do it for you. I'm not kidding, Ever." She yanked her hat away and plopped it onto her head.

She was dead serious. I knew it. I knew she'd go over there, and I knew she'd make a scene, and I knew that somehow, at the end of it all, *I* would be the *only* one embarrassed. I also knew without a doubt, that there was no way in *hell* I was going over there myself. But I had to do something before she acted on her threat.

I got up, put on my crocheted bikini cover-up, then stared hard at her until she sat back down in her chair. Content that her tirade had worked, she happily coated her long legs with yet another layer of tanning oil and continued sunbathing like nothing had happened. She nonchalantly flipped through the latest US Magazine, sneaking peeks at me while I stood in front of her fuming.

I made my way through the house, pretending to head toward the front door. Yeah right! *As if I'm actually going to go over there and confront Toby for not calling me after our dates.* Please. I may not have known much about guys, but I was pretty sure they weren't into psycho stalkers, and I was *definitely* not the kind of girl to *grovel.*

Before I could even make it to the living room, Frankie stepped in front of me, startling me out of my thoughts.

"Don't go over there, Doll."

"What? Why?"

"That guy's not good for you, Ever."

"Oh god, not you too. *Why?* Because he's older than me? He's just a guy, Frankie. Just a guy who lives next door. Just a guy who took me out on two dates. *Two!*"

"Two? But I thought you—" He paused, and then shook his head as if shaking away confusion.

Ugh. He had only known about one of the dates. I closed my eyes. *Too late now.*

"Never mind. Look. This isn't about his age, Ever. It's more than that. Just don't go over there. Please."

He sounded strange. I knew he was holding something back from me which *should* have caused me to pause, caused me to question him. I *should* have talked to him like friends do, asked him what's wrong, but I couldn't get a grip on all the commotion in my head. I felt pathetic and silly after being dropped by Toby. Especially after only two dates. How could he even decide he didn't like me in such a short time? I didn't even understand.

Jessie had just totally yelled at me, which upset me *way* more than it should have, but now I was frustrated and angry and felt like everything was coming to a head.

Frankie's attempt to stop me from seeing Toby . . . well, it just set me off. I glared at his big, translucent eyes boring into mine, and realized my hidden feelings for him were at a boiling point. I was mad. At him, at Jessie, at Toby . . . and I was hurt.

Instead of telling Frankie the truth, that I had absolutely *no* intention of seeing Toby again anyway, or that I'd rather spend every day of the rest of my life here, in this house, with *him*, I fed a little fuel to the fire. Damn my stubborn streak.

"Why, Frankie? Tell me *why*. Or I'm going over there. Right now." I squared my shoulders, puffed up my chest, and crossed my arms, trying to give my best stubborn look while threatening him with my new neighbor. I'm sure I just managed to look like an angry toddler instead, but I was too annoyed to care.

Frankie's mouth opened, and I could tell he was about to say something. He stopped himself, his mouth shutting defiantly. I watched him, with my heart pounding in my ears, as a few different emotions crossed over his face. First pain—my heart pinched. Then . . . confusion, maybe . . . and then outright indignation settled tightly over his features. I saw that one plain as day. He could be as stubborn as me when he set his mind to it.

Well, we'd learned well from each other, and two could play that game.

I rolled my eyes, purposely dramatic. He was exasperating.

"Exactly. You've got nothing. Now, get out of my way, Frankie, and stay out of my life. I can see whomever I choose."

I stomped past him, surprised at my rotten attitude toward him and the terrible words that had just flown from my mouth, but I was too far gone to rectify it.

"Wow. He hasn't called you in four days, Ever. I just didn't know you were so"—he added a long pause, just to drive it home—"*pathetic*."

I stopped, inhaling quickly. The last word lingered in the air between us. It felt like he had just stabbed me in the back. He'd deliberately sounded out each syllable. *Pa-the-tic*. Coming from him, I couldn't imagine anything else hurting me worse. I slowly turned around to face him, my eyes already filling up with tears, but he was gone. The fire inside me fizzled out instantaneously, quickly replaced with sorrow, and I no longer cared to antagonize Frankie, argue with Jessie, or ponder the why's and what if's surrounding Toby.

I just wanted to be left alone.

I headed to my room, silently crying, and shut the door, content to cry and pout privately. It took Jessie almost an hour to realize I wasn't next door hanging out with Toby. Before long, I heard a knock on my door. I didn't respond, so she stuck in her head.

"Aw, Ever, I'm so sorry. I shouldn't have made you go over there. What did Toby say? You want me to go kick his ass?"

Though the thought of my sparkly best friend defending my honor had my lips trying to curl up into a smile, I didn't answer. I didn't want to tell her Frankie made me cry.

"I'm really sorry, Ev. Boys are *so* stupid. You know that."

"Really?" I looked up at her from my tear-streaked pillow, unable to keep the snark out of my voice. "You don't seem to think so."

She sat down next to me on the bed and smoothed my hair. "Only because I know how silly they are, Ever. I'm never serious about them. That's what's different about you and me. I know you aren't like that, and I shouldn't have ignored how hurt you've been this week. I'm sorry I made you go over there. Geez, Ev, I'm sorry I even pushed you to go out with Toby in the first place. I shouldn't have. I just . . . well, you're feelings for Fr—"

"It's not something Toby said. I never went next door."

"Oh. What? Why are you so sad then? Oh, is it me? I'm sorry; you know I was just giving you a hard time. I'm not really mad at you. I just want to have fun with my best friend, and you've been in such a funk lately."

"No Jess, it's not you," I said, wishing I didn't have to clarify the real reason I'd been crying.

"It's me."

We both turned quickly to the doorway, startled by Frankie's voice.

"Oh shoot, Frankie, you can't be in here! Shoo! Shoo!" She jumped up and made little shooing motions with her hands, trying to get him to head back out the door, but Frankie just stared intently at me as if Jessie wasn't even in the room with us.

"It's okay, Jess. Can you give us a minute?"

Jessie looked from me to Frankie and back again, pausing briefly each time, trying to make sense of the obviously tense situation between us, before finally deciding she might as well leave.

"Mhmm," she said with a suspicious tone in her voice. "Well, it's getting late, and I'm supposed to have dinner with Susan tonight anyway, so I'll leave the two of you kids alone." She turned back to me, pointing an accusatory finger in my face and whispered, "*You* better call me later. We have to talk."

With that she was out the door, dialing her cell phone as she made her way down the hall. Frankie held my stare, and we remained locked in silence while we listened to Jessie confirm her dinner plans with an obviously inebriated Susan, gather her things from the backyard, and then leave through the side gate. At the click of the gate popping back into place, I exhaled loudly, as if I'd been holding my breath since she'd left my bedroom.

"Can I come in?"

"Oh, you *ask* now, do you? Well, in that case, *no*. I don't want you to come in. You can stay right where you are."

I turned and lay down on the bed, my nose against the wall and my back toward Frankie. When he spoke next, he was right behind me, and I turned to see him sitting on my bed.

I tried to give him my best scowl.

"Oh, Doll, don't be mad at me. There's stuff I can't tell you, and things I can't talk to you about. But you have to believe me when I say that Toby isn't good for you."

"Seriously, Frankie? This is what you want to talk to me about? Here I was thinking you wanted to apologize for what you said earlier, but you just want to talk more about the neighbor! Big deal, Frankie! We went on *two* dates! And he hasn't even called!"

My voice faltered as I admitted to Frankie that I hadn't heard from Toby. Somehow, admitting to Frankie that I was a loser made it all the more real. My tears resumed their annoying flow from my eyes.

When I'd finally put myself out there, when I'd finally *tried* to get over my feelings for Frankie and had *some* semblance of a normal life, I ended up getting burned and crying to him. Look what moving on got me: a broken heart and embarrassment so thick I could almost taste it. I liked Toby. I really did. On top of that disappointment, my feelings for Frankie had become so convoluted, I had absolutely no idea which end was up. Half the time, I wanted to scream at him and drive him away, and the other time, I wanted to profess my love for him and run into his arms.

"I'm so sorry, Doll. I wish I could explain. And I am sorry for hurting you. I *never* want to hurt you. And I'm sorry he hurt you too, Ev. Really I am, but . . . it's for the best. You have to stay away from him."

"Leave me alone, Frankie. Go tell my parents not to worry about how old Toby is. I can't imagine I'll be seeing him again anyway. He's obviously not interested."

"Oh, I doubt tha—"

"Just *go*, Frankie. Please."

I grabbed my headphones and reached to turn on the computer. Once it was booted up, I clicked on Pandora, which was programmed to an old Jewel song list my mom had created in my account long ago. I left the poor-me station on, and as Jewel crooned about loneliness, followed by Sarah McLachlan singing that depressing animal shelter theme song, their sadness seemed perfectly fitting for my mood. I turned the volume up as loud as I could stand, and I didn't wait to see Frankie leave. Curled on my side with my nose pressed to the wall, tears streamed silently down my cheeks until I feared my tear ducts would dry up for good. That honestly wouldn't have been a bad thing.

I fell asleep listening to various women sing about broken hearts and shattered dreams, pondering how a person could go from no love life at all, to one as messed up as mine in just a matter of days.

And yet, it could still easily be classified as not even being a love life in the first place.

Frankie is right. I am pathetic.

My room was dark when I woke up, and judging by the time, I'd been sleeping for about five hours. It was just after eight in the evening.

I turned around to an empty room and took off my headphones, stretching after my ridiculously long nap to a chorus of growls coming from my stomach. I had slept right through dinner. Frankie must have told my mom I was upset because she hadn't tried to rouse me to eat. I looked over to my desk, to a note from my mom propped up against a plate of food. I glanced down at Gollum who'd been such a good boy—guarding the food for me while I slept. I patted him on the head.

"Good boy."

The note informed me that my mom and dad were out with the Robinsons, which meant that our neighborhood gossip—and my mom's best friend—Sharon, would get to hear all about my dates with the new boy next door, including his age. Maybe my mom would follow that shocker up with the fact that not only was he too old for her precious daughter, but he'd also totally burned her.

Super.

I knew I shouldn't be assuming that a group of adults had nothing better to do than sit around talking about me. I also knew better than to assume that my mom would discuss my private life behind my back. But hey, when you're having as good of a pity party as I was having, you just go with it.

Dinner was a turkey, lettuce, and tomato sandwich and some wavy Lay's potato chips. The sight of them triggered another rumble from my stomach. I moved to my desk and switched off Pandora—which had long been silent waiting for me to respond to the question of "Are you still listening?" I opened up Gmail to check if I'd missed anything life-altering. Just a few spam emails and a sale at my favorite online clothing store. I spent a few minutes absently browsing the spring clearance items and digging into my sandwich.

Halfway through inhaling my dinner, hungrier than I'd even realized, I heard a light rapping noise at my window. I looked up, startled to find Toby looking in at me. I felt both elation and anger. I swallowed my last bite hard, and it went down in an un-chewed lump. Luckily I'd been chewing the sandwich and not the chips, or I would have choked to death in front of him. I got up quickly and ran to my bathroom to check my teeth for any remaining chunks of sandwich. Nothing like a little piece of lettuce in your teeth to really turn a guy's head. My hair was a matted black mess, and I looked like I had just woken up, which was probably because I had, but there wasn't any time to fix it. I told myself I was going with a sexy tousled look. *Yeah right.* The puffy bags around my eyes were a clear indication that I'd cried myself out earlier. *Awesome.* Nothing sexy about that.

When I returned to my room, Toby had a confused look on his face, probably wondering why I had run away from him so strangely in the first place. I quickly shut my bedroom door, wishing I had a lock on it, and headed to open the window. Toby stepped back a bit, smiling at me expectantly, and his previous look of confusion was replaced with a look of satisfaction as his eyes roamed over me. I realized I was still in my black and white polka-dot bikini—with only my black crocheted cover-up on over it.

A very thin, very see-through cover-up.

Ha. Screw it. Still feeling angry and hurt, I decided I didn't mind. Let him see what he was missing. Again, I was stricken with a brazen confidence that was so unlike me. Or was it? I was beginning to wonder.

He had more of my favorite flowers in his hand, which this time wasn't strange since I'd since confirmed that anemones were indeed my favorite. The sight of the black and white flowers made those blissful butterflies return to my stomach—butterflies that clearly ignored the anger my mind was telling me to feel, going instead with the rhythm of my excited heart. *Stupid, stupid butterflies.*

I opened the window, and he started quickly apologizing for his absence the last few days. My defenses instantly melted away; damn them. Smiling from ear to ear, I quickly put a finger to my lips to stop him and then turned on my television, attempting to hopefully muffle the sound of our conversation. I didn't want my parents to hear me talking if they came home early. I also wanted to avoid attracting a certain other member of the household.

With a little help from Toby, I popped the screen off the window as quietly as I could then climbed down onto the grass. Before I was even all the way out the window, he'd dropped the flowers and his arms were around me, helping me down. Once on the ground, he didn't let go of me, and I felt the heat of his fingers on my back, one hand below the other, splaying openly as if to feel my entire back at the same time. I felt my own body heating up in response to those strong hands, regardless of my better judgment.

His eyes looked playful in the darkness, and he bit his bottom lip before kissing me.

With his lips on mine, he slowly pushed until my back was against the cold stucco wall of the house. Though I was a little caught off guard, my surprise only lasted a second, giving way to an intensely happy feeling in my chest. It felt far too good to be kissing Toby again, and I couldn't help but melt into it.

I could question his disappearing act later.

He didn't kiss me with the restraint or softness of our first two kisses. This time, he kissed me hungrily, clearly not holding back. The kind of kiss I'd only ever imagined, and I was momentarily stunned by the power of it. My heart pounded with relief—he'd missed me as much as I'd missed him. But wait. . . .

I wondered why he disappeared for four days if he liked me as much as he seemed to.

Stopping our kiss reluctantly, I put my hands on his chest and pushed him away from me. Toby's reluctance clearly matched my own, and he only allowed me to push him back a few inches, refusing to remove his arms from around my waist. We were still so close, and I felt his breath on my face, as uneven and fast as my own. My heart pounded excitedly, a deafening noise in my ears. All I wanted to do was resume the kissing.

But alas, I needed answers, and my heart lost the battle with my mind.

"Wait. Back to what you were saying. Where *have* you been, exactly?"

He absentmindedly played with a strand of my hair, curling and uncurling it around his finger. I tried not to notice, but I swear I felt as if every part of my body was on high alert around him. Even the tips of my long hair seemed to be aware of his touch, though *obviously* I knew *that* was impossible.

"I know. I'm so sorry. I should have called, and I wanted to, but I don't have your number—and I know I should have told you on Monday that I had to leave for work, but I forgot, and then your parents seemed so angry—and I just got back today, and I'm so sorry, Ever . . . forgive me?"

He inclined his head back in toward mine and took a little swipe at my bottom lip, grazing it lightly with a kiss. He had the most ridiculous puppy-dog look on his face, and I knew he was playing up the pout for my benefit, but I found that I just couldn't stay mad at him. I was too happy to be near him again to think of much else, especially being angry with him. I looked away, trying to grab a hold of my thoughts, but he mistook it as stubbornness and thought he needed to plead a bit more. I decided it didn't hurt to let him beg a little.

"Please forgive me, Ever? I brought you your favorite flowers . . . ." He reached down for them, letting go of my waist. He retrieved the flowers from the ground, but stayed down on one knee, reaching up to tickle my nose with them. He looked so silly on one knee, like a character out of a fairy tale.

I giggled a little and pushed them aside. As I did so, he grabbed my hand, and in one quick movement, pulled me down to the ground so I was sitting next to him. I shrieked in mock annoyance, but didn't resist him.

"Shh. Your parents will hear you! They hate me enough already."

We scooted back to the wall so we were leaning back into the shadows underneath my window. The grass was slightly damp and cold on my exposed legs and barely-covered butt. I tried to pull my cover-up underneath me as far as it would go. Which wasn't far. He didn't miss that part, and I watched his eyes roll over the length of my bare legs, blushing as he did so.

"They don't hate you; they just think you're too old for me. Thought. They *thought* you were too old for me. Not anymore. They're cool with it now. And they're not home anyway."

"Oh?"

He looked over at me, wiggling his eyebrows up and down animatedly, looking pretty ridiculous. I elbowed him lightly and laughed when he tried to elbow me back, but winced as his bare skin brushed against the stucco instead.

"So what did you tell them to change their minds about me? How smart I am? How good looking? My undeniable charm?"

I laughed and rolled my eyes.

"Ha! Please. I told them the truth, of course. I mean really, if they think twenty-two is old, they'd be amazed at how old you *actually* are . . . you know, in *vampire* years."

I looked at him then, smiling, waiting for a laugh, but the playfulness in his face was gone. *Maybe I'm not as funny as I think I am. Bummer.*

"No, seriously. What did you tell them?"

"What, why so serious? Oh please tell me you aren't *actually* a vampire, Toby."

With that he relaxed again and his smile returned with that knowing smirk I was beginning to really enjoy.

"Why? If I say I am, will you let me bite you?" He leaned toward my neck, causing me to suck in a breath, but stopped right next to my ear and whispered, "Too bad for you, I'm not." He gave my neck a quick nibble, right below my earlobe, sending shivers down my spine.

Mmm.

"Psssh! Whatever! Too bad for *you*." I pulled away from him and gave him another playful elbow to the ribs.

We sat in silence for a moment, shoulder to shoulder, my hand in his.

"Well?"

"Welll . . . what?"

"*Well*, what was it that actually *did* make your parents come around, aside from the now-known fact that I'm not a blood-sucking fiend?"

I explained to him how illogical their argument had been when they were about to ship me off to college—as if Jessie and I wouldn't be around older guys in just a few short months anyway. He pondered that idea for a minute, looking off into the distance with a look on his face that I couldn't quite place.

"They probably figure I'll be some quick fling, and you'll forget about me come fall, right?" He grinned wildly and added, "I mean, who knows, twenty-two is nothing comparatively. You could end up dating some *really* old guy . . . like one of your *professors*."

"Eeew! No way!"

We both laughed, and he leaned in again to kiss me. He still held my hand between us, but his free hand reached up and found a spot behind my neck that seemed to be specially made for his hand. It fit perfectly there, cupping my head and holding me to him. I let him kiss me, his mouth exploring mine, wiping most thoughts from my mind.

Maybe Jess has kissed so many boys because none of them have been like this. There's no way they've been like this. His hand moved to the side of my neck, resting just below my ear. His thumb moved back and forth over my jawline. More shivers travelled through me, the sensation of his hand on my skin an amazing feeling.

Or, maybe they've all been like this. Hmm.

After a few minutes of kissing, he pulled back to look at me. I was breathless and excited, wanting more, so much more. His eyes were so amazingly dark and unlike anything I'd ever seen before. I couldn't look away, even though I felt self-conscious under his intense stare. After a few long seconds of him studying my face and me trying to control my breathing, I broke the silence.

"So . . . what do you do anyway? For work, I mean."

He visibly tensed, and I wondered why. He sat back beside me, his hands holding one of mine in his lap again, absently playing with my fingers.

"I've told you just about everything there is to know about me, you know."

He looked over at me and smiled, nodding. "You have a point. Well, I travel a lot, obviously. We have jobs all over the place."

I waited for him to continue, but he didn't.

"Okay, and . . . ?"

"Well, I'm a collector. Of sorts."

"A collector? Oh, like antiques or something?"

"Sure. You could say that. I work for Ted, I mean, *my dad.* Sometimes we have to travel. It's cool."

"You call your dad Ted?" I'd never understood kids who refused to call their parents what they were—*Mom and Dad.* Except for Jessie of course; she had her reasons. Valid reasons at that.

"No, well, yeah. Sort of. I call him that when we're on a job. It's more professional than 'dad.' I guess I just get used to it, and sometimes it slips out."

"So, what do you do with the antiques? Do you guys have a shop or something? An EBay store?" My mom could lose hours searching for the perfect item at the perfect price.

"No, definitely *not* EBay." He said with a laugh. "I guess the best way to explain it is that we have jobs where we are sent to collect one thing in particular for the person we work for."

"And then *that* person sells them on eBay?"

He laughed at my insistence on referring back to eBay. "Yes, yes, okay, like eBay, but *not* eBay."

I could tell he wasn't going to elaborate further, but I kind of understood. eBay, but not eBay. Maybe flea markets were more his style. Or antique stores. That made sense. Some things were too valuable to sell on eBay, so they'd find their home in a fancy antique store instead. Maybe the people who hired Toby and his dad owned high-end antique stores.

He changed the subject shortly after that, and before I even realized it, we'd been talking about me and only me for hours. Just like during our previous dates, he managed to keep me talking and seemed to thoroughly enjoy learning every single detail about me, while I again learned nothing about him. He kept asking questions and digging, never leaving me room to turn the topic back to him. My life. My likes. My dislikes. My friends. My family. My dog. I don't think there was anything we hadn't covered between Sunday and tonight, except Frankie, of course. But somehow, it felt like I could continue talking to him forever and he wouldn't be bored.

My yawns were increasing in frequency and strength, however, and my eyes began to water with each one. Before I knew it, I'd stopped talking and was barely aware of the fact that I'd fallen asleep, the rhythmic rise and fall of his chest peacefully lulling me. I tried to tell myself to open my eyes, but nothing happened.

"Ever? I think you should probably go inside and get some sleep. It's pretty late."

"Hmm?"

"Ever? Wake up."

Half asleep, I pulled open my eyes and slowly stood, turning to crawl back into my window. Toby's hands on either side of my waist stopped me, and he turned me around to face him. He gently pulled my hair away from my face, tucking it behind my ears, leaving his hands there on either side of my face, his thumbs caressing my cheeks. He kissed me again, less needy than earlier, his tongue never entering my mouth. Though this kiss was much softer and gentler than our earlier kiss, my butterflies flew into a tizzy nonetheless.

So thoroughly focused on his kiss, I hadn't even realized he'd moved when I suddenly felt the heat of his hands on my back, *underneath* my cover-up, one hand between my shoulder blades and the other resting right above the top of my bikini bottoms. The hand on my lower back pulled me toward him and held me firmly in place. I was acutely aware of the fingers on that hand, their placement a little lower than my waist. All feeling in my body was centered there, in that small area just below my waistline where his fingers rested easily, an area that had yet to be touched until now.

My excitement burned, and I felt exhilarated. No longer tired, his light, easy kissing was suddenly not sufficient. I wanted more from him. I opened my mouth over his, exploring his mouth with my tongue, my body waking up from its brief slumber. He responded in kind, his hands tightening around me, and I felt my breath catch in my throat. I reached my hands up behind him and tangled them in his wavy hair. I was suddenly *very* fully awake, and *much* more aggressive than I'd ever imagined I could be. He pressed me back against the wall again and leaned into me. His hips crushed mine, and I was acutely aware of the pressure of his body in places that had never felt that kind of pressure before. My eyes wanted to pop open and widen at the thought of it, but I refrained. Instead, I continued to kiss him, my hands in his hair, and my hips pressing back lightly into his.

A few minutes later, he pulled away from me. I was breathless and slightly flustered. That amused grin was on his face once again, and his hair was slightly askew. *Wow*. I felt a chill from the night air touch my skin in all the places the heat of his body had just been pressed. Longing seeped through me, my body begging not to let him stop kissing me.

"Can I see you tomorrow?"

"Mmhmm." It came out as almost a moan, and he laughed quietly. *Geez! Get a hold of yourself!* I cleared my throat and tried again. "Yes, definitely." *Better.*

With my hand absently smoothing my hair, I smiled, pressing my lips tightly together to try to restrain the shit-eating grin bursting to get loose. *Holy mackerel! That kiss was amazing.*

"Cool. Tomorrow then. Eleven?" He paused, waiting for my response.

I nodded.

"Good night, Ever." He kissed me on the tip of my nose, turned me around, then lifted me back onto my window sill, all without my help since I was still half-dazed and useless from the intensity of the kissing. Behind me, I heard him reconnect the screen I had popped off earlier. "Sweet dreams, Ever."

When I turned around again, he was gone. A content and exhausted sigh escaped my lips, and I plopped down onto my bed without bothering to change into my pajamas. I fell asleep feeling happier than I could ever remember feeling. I was *really* looking forward to tomorrow. Or, well, not tomorrow exactly, since it was already three in the morning.

I hoped I would dream of Toby.

E ver, Ever, wake up."

With a gasp, I woke up to Frankie leaning over me. I was terrified. My eyes darted around the room, trying to make sense of my surroundings. I was vaguely aware I had been desperately searching for Frankie in my dream again. My heart thudded loudly in my ears as my eyes adjusted to the darkness. At the sight of Frankie's face, relief slowly pushed its way to the surface; the fear subsided, securing itself back into my dream world.

I sat up and reached out to hug him, so thankful he was there.

He quickly jumped back, away from the bed. I stopped myself mid-reach, suddenly realizing my mistake. I couldn't hug him. I would have fallen forward—*through* him—and off the bed. I leaned back against my headboard, disappointed once again that I couldn't touch him or reassure myself of his safety by holding him.

I was soaked with sweat, my pillow a wet, crumpled mess behind me, and my sheets scrunched up into a tangled pile again. My hair was plastered to my back.

After a few long seconds, Frankie sat down on the edge of the bed and slowly took in every inch of me. Looking down, I realized I must have stripped out of my cover-up sometime during the night. I was still in my bikini from yesterday, having been too exhausted earlier to change out of it. I looked around and found my cover-up in a ball on the floor next to my bed. I reached for it quickly, throwing it on over my head. Not that it covered anything.

Frankie smiled at me, amused by my haste, before his face turned serious. "Are you okay, Doll?"

"I was searching for you. But . . . but I can't remember why."

"Yeah, you were calling my name again."

"I can't remember anything about my dreams. It's really weird."

"It's okay, Doll. They're just dreams. You're safe . . . and look . . . I'm completely intact and right here." Noticing the slight tilt of my head and raised eyebrows, he realized the irony of what he'd said. Chuckling quietly, he stood and splayed his arms out as if saying *voilà*.

"Well, not *intact*, exactly, but *here* nonetheless."

His smile faded, and his tone became serious once more, "And I'm not going anywhere, Doll."

I smiled at him, finding comfort in not only his promise, but again in just his presence. It seemed everything was all right in my world when Frankie was around.

He sat down on the bed again, and I found myself wanting badly for him to lie with me. I wanted to wrap myself around him and never let him go. I'd never felt so safe with someone or so drawn to them—Frankie had been my entire world for so long. My safe place.

I was surprised to realize that I was simultaneously feeling that same strong pull toward Toby. I was either becoming totally *boy* crazy or totally *crazy* crazy. Either way, at that moment, my new feelings for Toby aside, I wanted nothing more than to be able to lie with Frankie, reassuring myself of his safety.

Somehow, as if he could read my thoughts, Frankie looked down, waved his arm over the bed, and raised his eyebrows as if to ask, '*you gonna make some room?*'

I scooted back against the wall like I had before, and Frankie lay down next to me. He didn't say another word, just stared into my eyes. I drifted off to sleep, knowing he was watching over me.

I woke up freezing cold from sleeping in nothing but a bikini and my scant cover-up, my sheets still in a tangled mess on the floor where I'd left them during the night. But sleep had come, and like the other times, something about having Frankie there was so soothing I'd slept soundlessly.

My bed was empty, and I quickly discovered that my room was as well. I felt an ache of disappointment that I quickly tucked away. What was I going to do with myself? *I can't keep having these feelings for Frankie, cannot be in love with him.* Next door lived a real flesh and blood guy—and super-hot flesh and blood at that—who actually wanted to take me out, and who could actually, potentially—*possibly?*—become my boyfriend.

Hopefully.

It was obvious that *something* had to shake me of the impossible feelings for Frankie.

I glanced at the clock. *Shoot! It's already ten!* I had a date with Toby at eleven. That left me with only one hour, which normally wouldn't be a problem, but I was so excited, I knew it was going to be another *What's in Ever's Closet? Fashion Show* kind of day. I decided to call Jessie to ask her to come over and help me find something to wear. Truth be told, her complete obsession with fashion could occasionally prove helpful.

As I dialed her cell phone, I started to pull possible outfit choices from my closet and lay them on my bed. I heard her phone ringing down the hall—if it could be called ringing. It wasn't actually a ring though. As usual, it was one of those musical ringtones that she was constantly changing to suit her mood—which was getting louder as it got closer to the other side of my door. This week the song was something about being sexy. It figured. She answered right outside my door.

"Finally! Geez, Ev. I thought you were going to sleep all day!"

"Jess? How long have you been here?"

"Oh, you know, Susan woke up and started her vomiting session around six this morning, so when I couldn't fall back asleep out of pure annoyance, I came over here instead." Jessie always tried to sound flippant about her mom's drinking binges, but I knew her well enough to know that she was here 24/7 because of how hard it was on her. Or because her mom had some random, equally drunk, guy at home. "I mean, I knew at least your mom would be awake, even if you weren't, but I don't think she's here. But judging by the way your kitchen smells right now, she made the most *sinful* banana bread I've ever imagined—"

"Wait, Jess? You've been here since *six?*"

"Of course not, Silly! First, I showered. Then, I got ready. Then, I went to Starbucks. Then, I met the most *amazing* guy waiting in line. Then, we exchanged numbers. Then, I came here."

I tried to calculate how long each of those things probably took, and I realized she hadn't been at my house all that long.

"So, you've been here, since . . . ."

"Just walked in the door," she said with a giggle. "And um, Ev? Why are we still talking on the phone? I'm coming in. I hope you're decent!"

The door opened just a second later, and Jessie's playful smile was almost instantly replaced with a look of utter horror as she noticed the bikini and cover-up from yesterday.

"Um, eew. So much for decency. Please tell me you aren't *still* in yesterday's bikini, Ever Van Ruysdael." She handed me a coffee, and I took a long drink before responding.

"I know, I know, I'm about to take a shower. I fell asleep in this last night." Jessie had probably already gone through three or four outfit changes since she'd left my house yesterday afternoon.

"Speaking of last night, what's up with you and Frankie? I mean, obviously I know what's up on *your* end, but he's acting pretty strange lately. And the way he was looking at you . . . care to tell me what *that's* all about?"

As she waited for my response—which would be a very *long* wait since I had no idea what to say—she looked around my room, surveying the mess I had already made of my clothes. I could practically see the light bulb flash on above her head when she put two and two together and realized I was getting ready to go somewhere. Luckily, that realization saved me from trying to put the weirdness between Frankie and me into words—I didn't actually *have* any words for it.

Also, knowing me as well as she did, she knew it wasn't just *anywhere* I was going. Not with such a large mess showing my indecision in choosing an outfit, and the flush of red on my cheeks when she looked at me with a question in her eyes.

"Oh my gosh, Ever! You have a date! Spill! Is it with Toby? Oh, of course it is, I mean, what am I saying, obviously it couldn't be with Frank—" Jessie paused when her eyes swept across the clothes on the bed. "—oh, *heck no*. Absolutely not. Please tell me you aren't planning on wearing *that*?"

She pointed at the outfit I'd settled on, making a disgusted face at my leggings and burn-out tank top and tossing them into my closet. After setting her purse and Starbucks cup on my desk, she turned back to the closet and rolled up the sleeves of her sweater, ready to get to work.

"Seriously, Ever, people are going to start thinking you're depressed if you don't start adding some color to your wardrobe. Never mind. It's clear I'm seriously needed here. Go shower, and I'll see what I can come up with"—she glanced doubtfully at my closet—"though I wish I would have known and brought reinforcements from my own wardrobe." She glanced down at her pink, satin mini-skirt and back to me with her eyebrows raised expectantly.

"Uh-uh. Not gonna happen, Jess."

"Suit yourself."

I started to close the bathroom door behind me when Jessie yelled after me, "Wait! How much time do we have?"

A quick glance at the clock told me we had less than an hour. Forty-seven minutes to be exact.

Deciphering the look on my face, she knew the answer. "Never mind. I don't even want to know. Just hurry up!"

When I got out of the shower just a few minutes later, Jessie had returned all my clothes to my closet, and it looked as though she'd completely rearranged it by clothing types. First tanks, then short sleeves, then long sleeves, and so on. I shook my head. She responded with a shrug.

"Since I have no choice other than black, black, or black—"

"Or gray," I said, pestering her.

She ignored me as if I hadn't even spoken the words out loud.

"—I did the best I could and came up with this." She waved her hands out over the outfit on my bed like Vanna White would showcase a prize on Wheel of Fortune.

A black tube top—price tag still intact—was paired with my stonewashed skinny jeans, a gray-cropped sweater, and my beat up old boots. I was nothing short of surprised to see them there since it was no secret how Jessie felt about them.

"My boots?"

"Yeah, yeah, I know. But he seems to have the same horrible taste in fashion that you do," she said with a wink, "So, I figured you might as well be comfortable. I'm sure he'll like the boots, and I skipped the leggings for obvious reasons."

Obvious to whom? I wondered. Not at all obvious to me, but I didn't argue. Why risk making her change her mind and forcing me wear something horrible, like . . . high heels? *Ugh. No thanks.*

"And you know what those jeans do to your J-Lo booty, Ev. He'll be putty in your hands by the time I'm done with you."

Jessie glanced longingly at her own butt in the mirror and sighed. I've always been self-conscious of my fuller figure, and she's always been envious. I guess the old saying is true; people really do believe the grass must be greener on the other side. But seriously, what I wouldn't do for smaller boobs and a much smaller butt.

I dressed as quickly as I could, tucking the sweater into my purse since it was too warm to need it just yet. Jess loosely braided my wet hair, and demanded that I put on more make-up than usual. I gave in to appease her since she'd given in and was letting me wear my boots. Fair is fair.

Jessie called the guy she'd just met at Starbucks and planned a little date of her own. I always thought you were supposed to wait awhile before calling a guy, but normal dating rules never seemed to apply to Jessie, and we knew my dating knowledge was limited at best. Listening to her on the phone with him, I wondered if I would ever come across as confident and sure of myself as she did. With a quick peck on my cheek and a huge smile, she was out the door, heading home to do her own primping. I promised I'd call her after my date with Toby so we could exchange details. This elicited a slight glare from Jessie because I'd forgotten to do it the last time I'd gone out with Toby. *Never living that down.*

Within a few minutes, I was ready and waiting by the door. It wasn't even eleven yet. As I watched Jessie's car turn the corner of my street and disappear out of sight, I noticed Toby was watching me from his perch on the hood of his Mustang in the driveway next door. *Damn.* And there I was all proud for being early.

When our eyes connected, he smiled, and my heart skipped a beat. Or two. Possibly more. He slid down the hood of his car and started walking toward my front door.

I was secretly thankful I hadn't seen Frankie. Or my parents. I was in a *really* great mood and didn't want anyone dampening my spirits by trying to talk me out of seeing Toby. I also wanted to avoid any guilt-ridden feelings that seeing Frankie would most definitely induce.

Unfortunately, a quiet exit wasn't going to happen. The sound of my parents coming in from the garage stopped me as I was about to run out the door to meet Toby.

I groaned in defeat . . . inside my head, of course.

"Oh good! You're up!" Noticing I was about to leave, my mother continued. "Ever, honey, before you go . . . we've decided we'd like to meet Toby. We didn't give either of you a chance, and we're very sorry."

"Um, well, can it wait? We're about to go somewhere."

"It really won't take long, Ev, we're not going to interrogate the boy, are we Love?" My dad flashed an evil grin, but began laughing unabashedly when my eyes widened.

"Ever, relax," he said around bouts of laughter. "Mom and I promise we won't embarrass you. *Too* much."

"Oh geez. Okay. Let me at least give him some warning before you pounce, alright?" I started to turn for the door when I realized something. "Hey, guys? Please make sure Frankie stays out of sight!"

Toby was waiting for me on the porch. He didn't say anything when he saw me; he just put his arms around me and pressed his face into my neck, inhaling deeply. Though I was completely overjoyed to be in his arms, I was a bit uncomfortable knowing my parents were on the other side of the door. I imagined them with their noses pressed against the wood, fighting over the tiny peephole.

Mmm, I thought, breathing him in. He smelled fresh . . . like Irish Spring soap.

He moved his face up and found my mouth, closing over it with his own in a slightly restrained kiss. When he stopped and pulled away, I was happily breathless.

"Well, hello to you too," I said with a giggle.

"Hey." He kissed me again, but this time just a quick peck. "You look *especially* amazing today."

I ran my hand over the braid hanging over my shoulder, twisting the bottom of it in my fingers. "Um, thanks," I managed to get out through my huge smile and red cheeks. I was giddy all over again, the butterfly frenzy in my stomach becoming a usual occurrence now. I'd have to get used to that. Not that I was complaining.

He was wearing dark-washed blue jeans and a black and white ringer. His faded black boots had been replaced with black Chuck Taylors. I was sure Jessie would be glad to know we weren't *totally* matching, but the converse made me think of Frankie, sending a pang of guilt through me. With a deep breath and a quick shake of my head, I pushed the guilt aside and made myself focus on the guy in front of me instead of the ghost in my house.

"So . . . it turns out my parents want to meet you."

His eyebrows rose slightly, but he smiled.

"Okay. Is *now* good? I mean, I can only be out in the sunlight for so long, you know."

I laughed at his vampire reference and gently shoved him, grabbing his hand to head inside. When we entered the house, I was pleasantly surprised to see that my parents weren't standing on the other side of the door. Instead, they were sitting at the kitchen table, and my mom was brewing a fresh pot of coffee. When they saw us, my dad stood and shook Toby's hand, while I introduced him to them both.

"Toby, this is my dad, George, and my mom, Annabelle. Guys, this is obviously Toby."

After that, I just stood there. I had absolutely no idea what to say after the introductions were made. Luckily, my mom quickly went into hostess mode, getting everyone a cup of coffee and placing some banana bread on the table.

"Well, Toby, you and your father are antiques dealers, is that correct?"

Toby glanced at me curiously before he smiled at my mom, diving into a similar explanation as the one he'd given me.

Funny, I didn't remember telling my mom about Toby's profession.

My dad, clearly much less impressed or curious about Toby's work, interrupted the story smoothly and changed the topic to one about cars.

"Say son, what year is that black stallion you've got parked outside?"

My mom clucked her tongue at my dad for interrupting, but did so with a smile, and I knew she was just pleased to see him joining in the conversation with Toby.

"Nineteen sixty-five, sir. Want to take it for a spin?"

And that's when Toby won my dad's heart. Their mutual knowledge and adoration of classic cars made for a very easy conversation between the two of them. My nervousness faded away. The four of us took a few quick spins around the neighborhood, my dad smiling like a circus clown the entire time.

About an hour later, pleased with both my choice in boys *and* my easy-going parents, I kissed my mom and dad goodbye and headed out for my date.

"Well, that wasn't so bad. You're parents seem pretty cool."

"Yeah, I guess they are, aren't they?"

It had gone *really* well in fact, and luckily, I hadn't seen even a trace of Frankie while we'd been inside.

"So, where are we going?"

"It's a surprise. There's somewhere I'd really like to go, and I'm hoping once we get there that you can show me around. Ready?" He hurried in front of me to open the door to the Mustang.

As we pulled out of Toby's driveway, I noticed his dad standing in the window of their living room. My mom's gossip mill information had been correct—he *was* insanely handsome, although a bit young looking. I deduced it was where Toby's good looks came from. My appreciation of him ended abruptly, as did my sense of relaxation after the smooth meeting between Toby and my parents, when I caught his dad's fierce stare. The way he was looking at me sent a chill down my spine.

I shuddered. *What the hell?*

Toby looked over at me and followed my eyes to the front of his house. When he saw his dad standing there, his jaw hardened, and he picked up speed. We practically burned rubber getting out of the driveway.

"Whoa. Easy there, Speed Racer. You okay?"

"Yeah, I just . . . never mind. Yeah, I'm fine. I'm just excited to spend the day with you, that's all."

I knew there was more to it but didn't push him further. I had already concluded that Toby would rather talk about *anything* than his home life and his family, and I was okay with that. He'd tell me when he was ready. Plus, he had just endured over an hour of talking with my parents, and even though it hadn't been nearly as torturous as I'd thought it would be, it couldn't have been the greatest way for Toby to start his day.

But as we drove away, I couldn't shake the strange feeling his dad's stare left me with.

After a little over twenty minutes of driving, I realized that the *somewhere* he'd like to go was the Queen Mary in Long Beach. I hadn't been there forever and didn't really think of it as a *date* type place. But I was open, and seeing the ship looming up in front of us turned out to be a bit more exciting than I would have expected. The ship was massive.

Toby quickly came to my side of the car, opening the door for me and taking me by the hand. His fingers intertwined with mine, and he gave my hand a squeeze that sent sensations throughout my body. I was falling fast, and falling hard, and I hadn't thought about Frankie in—well, that's not necessarily accurate, but I was *trying* not to think about Frankie. That's really the best I could do, and more than I'd done before.

The ship was bigger than I even remembered. Once onboard, we headed to lunch at the Promenade Café. The hostess sat us at a table near a wall of windows overlooking the harbor. The day was beautiful and sunny with very little smog, so the view was amazing.

The restaurant gave me the same feeling of stepping back in time that the rest of the ship did, with carpet that had an art deco pattern in shades of blue, mustard, cream, burgundy, and black, and large circular lights popping out of the ceiling like portholes looking in, not out. Amid all the architectural details from the 1930's, I felt as though I was actually a part of something larger than myself.

We ordered our meals and waited, reading through various pamphlets while we did. As soon as the plates were on the table, we simultaneously removed the dill pickle spears from our plates. We noticed ourselves doing it at the same time and laughed.

"I hate pickles," he said, grinning around a mouthful of burger.

"I only like Bread and Butter pickles."

We talked a bit during the meal, and I told him everything I knew about the Queen Mary . . . which was very little. Our server, after overhearing us and helping herself to a seat at our table, began telling us about a couple tours we could take, rambling on and on about the haunted tour while absently rubbing one of her old, callused heels with equally old and callused fingers.

She proceeded to tell us about the people—*ghosts*—who resided aboard the Queen Mary, which of course made me think of my own ghost. Feeling annoyed by my thoughts, I tried to push him out of my mind and listen to her stories.

One couple in particular, who you could occasionally—*supposedly*—see swimming in the pool, was the focus of her story. Apparently, these were the ghosts that she'd personally had contact with. She explained to us that she'd been on the deck by herself after her shift just a few weeks ago, when the man waved to her from the water, smiling and beckoning for her to join them. Toby and I looked across the table at each other with amusement in our eyes, and poorly hidden smiles on our faces.

I was fighting a very strong urge to kiss him. But I decided that doing so right in front of our waitress might be frowned upon. *Especially* while she was mid-story. Still, the desire to do so was there nonetheless.

"You don't believe me, do you?" she accused, noting our smiles. "Well, that's fine. I know what I saw. You two aren't too scared to check it out for yourselves now, are you?"

Um, no. Our server definitely had a few ghost stories of her own, but I knew her *experiences* had nothing on mine. I just smiled at her and shook my head, not knowing how to answer, when what I'd really like to do was invite her over to dinner. Not only would my ghost smile and wave at her, but he'd sit right down next to her and strike up a conversation. I had no doubt that his slightly crooked smile, big brown eyes, and casual ease would charm the pants right off that tired old waitress. She winked at me, as if following my thoughts, and turned back toward the kitchen.

After we paid our tab, we did a little exploring. We passed a door with a sign that read Stairs to Engine Room, and Toby grabbed my hand, pulling me through the door. Once on the other side, the door closed behind us, and we descended the stairs. Toby was smiling mischievously all the while, like we were doing something we shouldn't be doing. I just laughed and allowed him to lead me further down the narrow, metal staircase.

After a few turns, and going through a door or two along the way, we were in one of the inner stairwells of the ship, between the engine room and lowest visitor-accessible decks, when he pulled me quickly out of sight. We ducked under a burgundy velvet rope with a sign hanging from it stating *KEEP OUT.* I let a little shriek escape me, though I wasn't really scared, and followed Toby through another door.

Once inside, I looked around at our strange surroundings. We were in a warm, dark room with walls that looked like they were sweating. I glanced around and realized they were wet from steam. The sound of gears turning and machines clicking was an overwhelming noise. I knew these weren't the actual engines for the ship since the Queen Mary hadn't departed Long Beach Harbor in decades and those particular engines wouldn't be running. But it must have been some sort of machinery room that helped run the hotel and restaurants above us.

Toby pulled me tightly to him and kissed me, pressing me back against the wall with his body. He had both hands on my hips, and one hand moved slowly up my waist. My nerves shot into overdrive as his fingers lightly grazed the side of my chest on their ascent to my hair.

"Finally," he whispered between kisses. "I haven't been able to stop thinking about kissing you all afternoon."

I giggled, and he pulled back to look at me.

"What? What's so funny?"

"Oh, nothing . . . I . . . I've just been thinking the exact same thing." I giggled again, embarrassed by my honesty.

He smiled broadly and resumed kissing me, his right hand cradling my head and his other hand resting on my hip, thumb hooked into one of my belt loops.

A few minutes later, we heard a door open and close, followed by footsteps that stopped just on the other side of the huge metal tanks we were standing behind. Toby looked at me and put his finger up to his mouth in a silencing motion. I held my breath, praying we wouldn't get caught.

I felt the hand on my waist begin to move as he unhooked his thumb from my belt loop and slowly slid his hand up under my shirt. My breath caught in my throat, and I bit my lip, trying to keep quiet. My nerves were going crazy, and all the blood in my body seemed to be rushing toward the places where his fingers met with the bare skin of my belly. He looked at me, staring deep into my eyes, and my heart rate increased even more. I wondered where his hand would move to next, and when he started to lean in again for a kiss, I opened my mouth to inhale a breath and . . . .

He tickled me.

Laughter flew past my lips before I could stop myself, and Toby started laughing too. He grabbed my hand, and we pushed past the stout security guard and out the door we had come in through.

He started to follow us, his angry voice a booming threat that echoed off the steel walls behind us. "Kids! Hey, you two! Stop! I knew I saw you come in here! The sign says *Keep Out!* Can't you kids read these days?"

We ran out onto the deck and headed to the front of the ship, never looking back. When we got there, the security guard was nowhere to be found, so we stopped to catch our breath.

The rest of the day was like that. I felt like a little kid, running from place to place, letting Toby chase me for kisses, stopping only to laugh and catch our breath. I couldn't remember ever having this much fun.

We were walking back through the ship and stopped to check out a small replica of the Titanic when I realized we weren't alone. I felt the hair on the back of my neck stand on end, as if someone had run a cold finger up my spine. I shivered and turned around quickly.

A pale, ghostly woman stood off to the side, well out of the way of any foot traffic. She wore a long, flowing white dress that moved around her ankles as if the wind was blowing the light fabric. We were inside. There was no wind. She watched us with a sad, wary look on her face. When I made eye contact with her, her eyes widened as though she was as shocked that I was seeing her as I was. She looked from me to Toby and shook her head from side to side, as if she was telling me no. I felt a shiver go through me.

Toby realized I wasn't looking at the display anymore and turned. Seeing the haunted look on my face, he squeezed my hand.

"Babe? What's wrong? You're all pale."

He followed my gaze to the corner of the great room, and then looked back at me, obviously seeing nothing.

He can't see her.

"Ev? You look like you've just seen a ghost. Are you okay?"

Ha. A ghost. I've just seen a ghost. I'd never seen another ghost before. I was *not* okay.

We rode home in silence. I didn't have much to say. I'd never seen a ghost besides Frankie. I guess I just figured I could only see him. The fact that I'd just seen another one was really weird. Why had I seen her? Would I see more ghosts now? *Whoa.* That thought was disturbing.

Toby parked in his driveway and made his way around to my side of the car, again opening my door for me like a gentleman. He took me in his arms and looked down at me. His eyebrows were drawn together.

"Ev, seriously, are you okay?"

"Yeah, yeah, I'm sorry. I'm just tired I guess. I think I'll just go to bed early tonight."

Obviously as unconvinced as I felt, Toby's eyebrows rose.

"Seriously, I'm fine. I'm sorry. I'll see you tomorrow, okay?"

He leaned down and kissed me gently before releasing me. He watched me walk inside, a sad look on his face as he did so. I wished I could explain it to him. *All of it.*

I said goodnight to my parents who were sitting on the couch, watching TV, then headed down the hall.

I was hoping to see Frankie, but I didn't. I really wanted to talk to him. What would he think? Did he see other ghosts, too? Frankie suddenly appeared out of nowhere in the hallway in front of my room, scaring me half-to-death.

"Oh!"

At the sight of his angry face, my mood plummeted even further.

"Hey, Doll. Where've you been?"

"Hey, Frankie."

I just stood there dumbfounded by his apparent anger, not knowing what to say, my inability to lie rearing its ugly head. I wanted to tell him about the ghost but couldn't do so without telling him I'd been with Toby all day, and Frankie was clearly mad. *What is going on with him?* I looked at the floor and played with my braid. *Dammit. Say something!*

"Um . . . ."

"Were you out with him again?"

My silence was all the answer he needed.

"Oh, Ever." The words were said on a sigh, so quiet I barely heard them. His disappointment in me was loud and clear. Painfully clear. It reminded me of the ghost shaking her head at me. I looked up to his face but he was gone. He didn't give me a chance to defend myself, or defend Toby, or even ask *why* he cared so much *who* I dated, or where I'd been.

That was the worst part: *why* did Frankie suddenly care so much?

It didn't matter though. Frankie didn't have a say in what I did, and I didn't have a say in anything he did. Not that his options were very great.

I decided to tuck the ghost story away. The Queen Mary was known to be haunted. Surely I was just like anyone else who'd ever stumbled across an old Queen Mary ghost. Just like our waitress from lunch.

I tucked the strangeness between Frankie and me away as well. *One* of us had a life to live, and I needed to actually *live* it. Crying over Frankie, or dwelling on feelings that were ridiculous, or dreaming of a relationship that could never happen, were all a waste of time, and they were all keeping me from the life that was meant for me.

I had to *live*. Really, truly *live*. This meant taking chances, like seeing where things were going with Toby.

I fell asleep telling myself that no matter what, I would no longer let my feelings for Frankie take away from my feelings for Toby. I told myself that if the night brought me nightmares again, I wouldn't let them dampen my happiness.

I wished for dreams about Toby, knowing that *he* could *never* be the subject of nightmares.

I'm running through the corridor of what looks like a high school hallway. I vaguely register that it's Jessie's school before I realize it isn't a school at all . . . .

It's a mall. An outdoor mall. The Block in Orange. The lockers covering the walls from floor to ceiling, slowly melt away to reveal storefronts, closed doors and metal bars indicating that they're closed for the night. There are no lights on, and the dark is eerily consuming.

The shadows reach and curl toward me as I run . . . .

Suddenly I'm on a ship.

No, not just a ship; the Queen Mary.

The storefronts I ran past just seconds before are now staterooms. The hallway is long and narrow and seems to go on forever, like a carnival funhouse illusion. The carpet I remember liking when I had been awake now makes me feel nauseated. Its colorful, art deco pattern morphing and changing under my feet, reaching for me as the shadows did only seconds before.

The lights on the walls flicker and flash . . . .

The woman in white stands idly by, watching me run . . . .

She shakes her head again and whispers something I can't hear . . . .

My breath pushes out of me in ragged puffs, and my lungs squeeze in exertion. I feel like I've been running for miles.

There he is. Finally.

Just a few yards in front of me.

Frankie. My Frankie.

My heart pounds at the sight of him, threatening to fly out of my chest and go to him. Relief floods me. I have to reach him. Everything will be okay if I can just reach him.

Faster.

His outstretched arms welcome me. I pick up my pace. I have to get to him, have to run into those loving arms, have to be near him, with him. I know that I can save him. I just have to make it to his open arms.

Save him!

But wait . . . save him from what?

The dream shifts again, and Frankie is standing in front of my house, arms still outstretched and reaching for me.

"Hurry," he silently whispers inside my mind.

I run harder, faster, my legs and arms pumping, my breath whooshing in and out, in and out.

I can't get to him.

I push harder. Run faster.

I still can't get to him. I scream out in frustration.

His welcoming, loving smile turns down at the corners, and his arms flap limply to his sides. I realize why I can't reach him.

Something is holding me back.

Someone.

The hand on my shoulder tightens.

"Stop running, Ever. You can't save him."

I know that voice. I begin slowly turning around to face the source of it, but everything shifts again.

Before I can see his face, he is gone. The front yard and my house are also gone.

Everything is white now, a blinding whiteness shining painfully bright from every inch of my world. It hurts. I want to hide my eyes.

Something catches my attention before I can squeeze my eyes shut to avoid the glare.

Still separated by those few frustrating yards between us, in the middle of all that blinding whiteness, Frankie lies in an unnatural heap on the floor.

The scene shifts again.

I stand over him now. Frankie's lifeless body. Red is the only color I see against all that blinding white.

Blood. So much blood.

Frankie's body is splayed out, his arms and legs bent around him unnaturally. Blood covers his torso, drops of it crusting on his neck and jaw line, drying into his dark hair.

I'm dreaming. This has to be a dream. Wake up!

I crumple to the floor. Cradling Frankie's head in my lap, I scream out in agony.

"Get up Frankie! Get up!"

My tears fall, splashing onto his face. They mix with the blood and cause pink rivers to flow over his alabaster skin.

I sob and sob, screaming in agony as I hold him.

He doesn't wake up.

"Ever."

There it is again. That calm voice I know so well. The voice that once made my heart flutter in anticipation.

I look up to Toby's face—once a thing of beauty—now something . . . else. There is emptiness in his eyes.

His hands—hands that once held me—are covered in red.

Frankie's blood.

He reaches toward me, his fingers wet with the crimson liquid. He runs his hand along my face delicately. I can feel Frankie's blood on my cheek.

When he speaks, his voice holds the icy emptiness of his eyes.

"You can't save him."

I woke up screaming. Tears streamed down my face as every horrific detail stayed with me well into waking. I didn't know how long I'd been screaming, but my throat hurt, and almost as soon as my eyes were open, my mom was rushing into my room, my dad close on her heels.

"What is it, baby? What's wrong?" Her voice was frantic, her gaze darting around the room as she ran to me. She threw herself onto the bed to hold me while my dad turned on the lights and checked the window, making sure it was securely locked. Then he stuck his head inside the closet—as if the closet monster had jumped out and scared his little girl. I was surprised he hadn't gotten down on all fours and checked to see if the boogeyman was hiding under the bed . . . until he did that too.

"It was just a bad dream, Dad."

"I know, Evvie, but it doesn't hurt to check. Just humor your old man."

"What was it, baby? Do you want to talk about it?" She pulled my hair away from my face, wiping my tears and my sweat-covered forehead with her sleeve.

I caught a glimpse of Frankie pacing outside the doorway to my room. He couldn't come in with my parents there, and I knew it was killing him not being able to comfort me. I also knew I couldn't tell Frankie about my dream, which meant I couldn't tell my mom while Frankie was in earshot.

"I . . . I don't really remember much of it."

"Oh, baby, it was just a dream. It's okay. Everything is okay. Mama's here." She was rocking me in that way she always did when I was a little girl, which was soothing, but I wanted to talk to Frankie. After seeing him dead in my nightmare, I wanted to see him alive. Or . . . well . . . not *alive* exactly . . . .

"I'm okay, Mom. I'm tired. I'm just going to go back to sleep."

"Are you sure? I could sleep in here tonight, or we could go into the kitchen and have some hot cocoa?"

"No, Mom. Go back to sleep. I'm okay. I'm sorry I woke you guys."

After I'd convinced them I was okay, which took a while and made me realize I must have really been screaming bloody murder—no pun intended—they left me alone.

Frankie appeared moments later. His face was tense, but it seemed even more tense than usual, like more than just concern had him disturbed.

"You lied to your mom. You can remember that one."

I didn't answer.

"Yeah, I thought so. Care to tell me about it?"

He sat down on the bed next to me and waited for me to explain. I couldn't find the words. How could I explain that I'd just dreamt such a monstrous nightmare? What did it say about *me* that I could see such a violent, vivid scene in my dreams? What did it say about *me* that my boyfriend killed my best friend in my sleep?

Again, I said nothing.

"That's okay, Doll. You don't have to talk about it."

Soon, my eyelids grew heavy with exhaustion.

Frankie waited for me to fall back to sleep, and in the safety of his protective presence, I slept.

Ten

hen the phone rang the next morning, Frankie and I were sitting on my bed, talking about nothing in particular—Frankie just trying to distract me from my thoughts, and me unable to think of much else.

"Ever," Mom called down the hall. "Toby's on the phone!"

We both jumped up at the sound of her voice, but probably for totally different reasons. I assume Frankie was worried she'd find him in my room, and he disappeared without another word. The mention of Toby's name is what did it for me. I slowly made my way to the phone on my desk, regarding the receiver as if it might bite me. *Get a grip,* I scolded myself. It was just a dream! I picked up the receiver and said 'hello' slightly relieved that it hadn't actually bitten me. *Ridiculous.*

"Good Morning, Beautiful."

At the sound of his voice, the horrid details of my nightmare flooded back to me.

Blood everywhere. Frankie's blood. Frankie's blood on Toby . . . .

With the images bombarding my thoughts, I was momentarily shocked into silence.

"Ever? Are you there?"

I shook my head, trying to shake away the pictures. *It's not real. It's not real.*

So much blood . . . .

"Yeah, yeah. I'm here."

"Is everything okay?"

"Yeah."

"Oh, okay. Can I see you tonight?"

Tonight. He wants to see me. My first response was no, but I couldn't think of a valid reason to give him. *Um . . . shoot . . . um . . . .*

"Ev? Seriously, is something wrong? You don't sound very good, and after yesterday . . . do you want me to come over or something?"

"No!" *Shit.* "I mean, no, no, I'm okay. Honest."

"Okay." He paused, clearly having trouble believing me. "So? Tonight then? Around eight?"

"Yeah. Sure."

"Great. See you then. Have a good day."

"Yeah, bye."

I hung up the phone with a sigh. I should have been excited for another date with Toby, but instead, I was worried. I didn't know how I would feel when I saw him again if the sound of his voice alone had brought back all that gory vividness of my nightmare.

Gah! It was just a dream!

But I couldn't help playing it over and over in my head when I thought about Toby or looked at Frankie.

Frankie could sense it; he could always sense my moods. He came back a few minutes later and stayed by my side as much as possible the rest of the day. My fear slightly eased around him but never fully went away. He didn't ask me about the nightmare again, which I appreciated, knowing it was difficult for him. He didn't ask me about my phone call with Toby, which again, must have been incredibly difficult for him.

As we spent Sunday morning together, waiting for the time to come for me to head to work—later than usual because Jo finally decided the early bird adoptions were pointless—Frankie talked about normal everyday stuff, like cars, music, and movies. He talked about my school stuff, and the animal shelter, asking me questions I knew he already knew the answer to, just to keep me occupied.

As irrational as it was, I couldn't shake the horrible foreboding that had filled me since awaking from my nightmare. Still, even more irrational than that was the fact that I feared Toby because of what I feared he would do to Frankie. It made *zero* sense.

You can't save him.

As I walked out to my car to head to work, the words from my dream echoed through my mind for the thousandth time since waking that morning.

You can't save him.

I couldn't save him. Frankie who couldn't be killed. Frankie who was *already dead*. I tried again to decipher my crazy dream as I drove the short distance to work, annoyed at how ridiculous it all was.

Jessie wasn't at the shelter when I arrived. She was *always* there before me, but her pink bug was not in its usual front row spot. Still, I searched the lot and surrounding areas, thinking maybe she'd decided to park somewhere else. *Not likely.* With a shrug accompanied by a little bit more of that foreboding feeling I couldn't seem to shake, I headed inside.

The door was locked which meant that I had to use my key to get inside for the first time in all the time I'd worked there. A quick check of the voicemail informed me that Jo had a family emergency and wouldn't be coming in at all today. I relaxed at that knowledge, happy that Jessie wouldn't get penalized for being late even though it unfortunately meant I had the task of getting the whole front office ready for business—which was Jessie's job and something I was completely unfamiliar with.

I dialed Jessie's cell number from the office phone, and then her house number, getting no answer at either one.

I'm sure it took longer than it would have if Jessie had been there, but eventually, after checking on the few employees in the back kennel and getting someone to cover for me, I headed to the front window, flipped the cardboard sign over to announce that we were open, and sat down to wait for the day's customers. I was completely unsure of what to do next, so as I waited for something to happen, I returned to trying to sort out my love life. *Ha.*

An hour later, no further in my thoughts than I'd been when I started, a huge, bright yellow Hummer with tinted windows and an obnoxious roll bar pulled up. Blocking both handicap spaces, the monstrosity idled in front of the shelter.

Annoyed, I stood up to head out the door, determined to suggest the driver park in a proper parking space. Before I could get outside, Jessie's long, pink-covered legs descended as she jumped down to the ground from the passenger side. Relief flooded me at the sight of her, and I instantly felt silly. I don't know what I'd thought had happened to her, but irrational or not, I'd been worried. Her platinum hair was not in its usual sleek bob, hanging perfectly at the sides of her face, but instead was pulled back into a clip that would normally *horrify* Jessie.

Though it wasn't the hair clip that really shocked me.

It was the USC sports jersey she wore over her pink maxi skirt. Never mind the fact that it wasn't pink, or that it was three sizes too large. As if those things weren't enough, seeing her in her most hated college colors was a huge shock. There was one thing I knew for sure in life and that was that you were either UCLA or USC. *Never* both. And if you were one, you *hated* the other. It was just . . . I don't know . . . the way it was I guess. My eyes were wide, and my jaw was on the floor when she walked in.

"Oh, Ever! I'm so sorry I'm late!" She quickly looked around as if trying to locate our boss. "Where's Jo? Is she *so* pissed?"

She walked right past me and sat down in the chair I'd just vacated, instantly turning to the computer screen and looking busy—

as if it was totally normal that she was an hour late. *And wearing a USC shirt that clearly doesn't belong to her.*

"I totally overslept!"

"It's almost four in the afternoon, Jess." I'd finally found my words.

"Oh, Ever, I wasn't *really* sleeping." She giggled and winked at me like she was letting me in on an extra special secret. I couldn't keep from smiling even as I chastised her.

"Jessie!"

"Shh! Jo will hear you!"

I shook my head, laughing. "Jo's not here, Jess. *Where* have you been?"

"She's not? Oh phew!" She looked around, smiling devilishly, and rolled her chair over to where I stood.

"Sit! Sit!" She motioned to one of the lobby chairs. "Oh my *gosh,* Ever! Remember the guy I met yesterday at Starbucks? I think he's *the one.*"

She said *the one* with such emphasis and complete seriousness that I couldn't help but laugh.

"What? He is! His name is Greg, and he's a sophomore at USC. Can you believe it? I told him we're going to UCLA next year, and he doesn't even care. He joked about us being star-crossed lovers. Can you imagine it? I'll be a freshman already dating a Junior! Eek!"

She was so excited that I couldn't possibly crush her spirits by telling her to slow it down, but I knew that so many things could happen between now and then. I mean, it was only April, after all.

We spent the rest of the day in the front office, and I learned every single thing there was to learn about the love of Jessie's life— whom she'd only known for 24 hours, but who's counting?

On the way home, we stopped at Jessie's so she could pick up a few things before I drove her to her car. She'd apparently left it at Irvine Spectrum where she'd met up with Greg the night before.

The beat-up F-350 in the driveway indicated that Susan had someone over.

The Confederate flag hanging off the antenna and the *'Guns don't kill people, I kill people'* bumper sticker indicated that that *someone* was probably a real winner. The plastic balls hanging from the rear bumper didn't help either.

"Ugh. Come in with me?"

"Of course."

When we opened the door to the house, the smell of cigarettes and marijuana wafted out. We just looked at each other and, rolling our eyes, braced ourselves for what we'd probably find inside.

Jessie's mom was lying on the couch in nothing but panties and an oversized NASCAR t-shirt, her legs draped over a shirtless man in his late thirties or so. Of course, by his weathered smoker's skin and unkempt facial hair, it was anyone's guess how old he actually was. He could have been in his twenties for all I could tell.

He let out an appreciative whistle when he saw us, pushing Susan's legs aside to stand.

"Ow! Hey!"

"Well *you* must be the daughter," he growled as he looked Jessie up and down.

"Oh *gross*," Jessie said, her lip curled upward. "Get real, *dirtbag*."

"What in the *hell*? Get back here, you little bitch!"

Jessie was already down the hall, but I was a bit slower in my retreat, shocked that he'd spoken to Jessie like that. Shaking myself out of my stupor, I just shook my head at Susan and started to turn to head down the hall after Jessie. My mom would have *never* let anyone speak to me that way.

"What? Don't you shake your head at me like that *Eleanor*. And you tell my little bitch of a daughter to watch her mouth. That's not how we treat company in this house."

"Eleanor, hmm? Well, well, look at the rack on you."

My eyes widened in disbelief, and I crossed my arms over my cursed chest. I quickly made my way to Jessie's room, Susan's and her boyfriend's mocking laughter following me down the hall. I heard

Susan trying to lure her boyfriend back to the couch, her sweet, *trying-to-be-sexy* tone giving me the creeps.

Jessie was already returning from her room, a hastily packed duffle bag dragging behind her, and we almost collided in the hallway. She shook her head and walked past me.

"I'm sleeping at Ever's tonight," was all she said as we headed outside, the screen door clanging shut behind us. Once in the privacy of the car, she let out a long sigh. I gave her arm a squeeze, knowing she probably didn't want to talk.

I definitely did *not* tell her about the comment the guy had made about my 'rack.'

Eleven

T oby knocked on the door promptly at eight, but of course I was running late.

This time, however, I wasn't late because of difficulty picking out an outfit, wasting too much time enjoying the hot water in the shower, or even my dawdling for no apparent reason. This time my nerves had me moving slowly.

I was scared of seeing Toby. Irrational? *Yes.* Ridiculous? *Definitely.* But scared nonetheless. I couldn't shake last night's nightmare, or the strange sense of foreboding it left me with.

Frankie was as intact as a ghost could be, pacing the hallway outside my room. He hadn't said a word to me, but I knew he was mad I was going out with Toby again. As long as I knew where Frankie was, I could handle his anger. At least I knew he was safe.

Safe. What a ridiculous thought. How lame is it that I was even worried for his safety in the first place? *He's dead!* Shaking my head at myself, I said goodbye to Jessie, who was lounged out on my bed watching TV and texting with *the one.* I took one last glance in the mirror, grabbed my purse, then headed out to meet Toby. Once outside my bedroom, Frankie stopped me, clearly unable to stay quiet any longer.

"Don't go, Doll."

His pleading mirrored my own irrational thoughts, but I couldn't tell him that. I also couldn't delay any longer with Toby obviously waiting for me outside.

"Frankie," I said with a sigh, "You know I'm dating Toby. Please don't make this difficult for me. I want to be happy. I . . . I want to have a boyfriend."

Frankie shook his head eerily reminding me of the ghost on the ship, and disappeared. This time as I approached the front door, the butterflies in my stomach were fluttering for totally different reasons.

Fear, confusion, trepidation . . . until I opened the door and saw his face.

Seeing the familiar amusement curving his lips into a gorgeous smile, my defenses were instantly stripped away. My fears and my nightmare were suddenly the furthest things from my mind. *What is on my mind, however, is kiss—*

My thoughts were cut off when he pulled me into his arms, his lips covering mine in a strong, hungry kiss. My stomach grew warm, the butterflies kicking up their frenzy, and my skin feeling as though it was lit on fire.

Wow.

Clearly, a kiss had been the first thing on his mind as well.

"I missed you," he said as he pulled away from me, his arms still around my waist.

"Hi," I said, slightly dazed.

"Hi yourself. Ready to go?"

He led me to the car, holding my hand and again opening my door for me. I stopped abruptly when I heard the loud diesel engine coming down the street, accompanied by tire screeching. I looked up, even though deep down I already knew. Toby's gaze followed mine. Sure enough, the rusted old F-350 came tearing down the street, stopping in my driveway with a spray of grass. Well, *partly* in my driveway. It was partly in my yard as well.

"Where is that little bitch? It's time for a lesson in manners."

Still shirtless, Susan's boyfriend hopped out of the driver's side, gripping a Budweiser Tallboy in his hand. Susan was stumbling out of the passenger side of the truck, crying, a look of terror on her face. She still didn't have on any pants. Neither one of them had bothered to put on shoes.

Toby looked down at me; his brow creased in alarm.

"Meet Jessie's mom," I whispered, not taking my eyes off the approaching figures.

Jessie made her way outside and stood next to me, eyes narrowed and defiant, showing only a hint of fear behind them. Toby protectively positioned himself in front of us. My mom and dad were walking out the front door and soon joined us on the lawn.

"Susan, honey, is everything okay?" My mom's voice: ever calm and collected, even in such moments of stress. Her hands were up in front of her in an almost calming, surrendering stance, as she tried to diffuse the strange situation.

"Oh, don't you worry about her," the guy spat as he motioned toward Jessie's mom. "She's just fine, ain't 'cha, honey?"

"Ye—yes, but . . . let's just go, okay?" Her words were slurred, of course, and her large travel cup of *who-knows-what* sloshed around in her hand.

"Mom, please. Just go. I'm staying here tonight."

Susan looked at Jessie with pain in her eyes and then looked back at her boyfriend.

"Please, Roy, let's go home. I've got some frozen pizzas—"

"I don't want no god dammed frozen pizzas. Your girl here needs to know . . . I don't take too kindly to people disrespectin' me. This here's a lesson only I can teach. She needs to learn respect like you had to, honey." He licked his lips, reaching for his waist. As I watched him unbuckle his belt, my eyes widened and my heart rate picked up. *Oh my* god. He's not actually going to . . . .

Toby stepped away from us, his shoulders rigid, and his fists clenched tightly.

"Oh, look at this, Susie, a little hero. What'cha gonna do, hero?"

"It's time for you to go. You don't want to cause any trouble." Toby's body was tense, and his voice was strong with an edge to it I hadn't heard before. But it was obvious that this guy wasn't about to back down.

"Oh, don't I? Don't I want to cause any trouble?" He exhaled a cloud of cigarette smoke in Toby's face, and I swear Toby was just seconds away from hitting him. But instead, he just cocked his head and continued standing in that protective stance between us and Susan's boyfriend.

"It's time for you to go. I won't ask again."

My dad was standing next to Toby now, and I have to admit, he wasn't nearly as intimidating with his glasses and his hunched over shoulders from so many years in front of a computer. But I was beyond proud of him anyway.

"Well, look at this. You gonna fight me too, old man? I just came for what's mine." He looked past my dad and Toby at Jessie standing next to me. "C'mere, you little bitch. Daddy wants to teach you a lesson."

My dad and Toby were both ready to fly off the handle after Roy's latest remarks, but somehow, Jessie managed to push past them, venom and rage shooting out of her like sparks.

"*You* are *not* my *daddy*, you disgusting piece of trash." Jessie's voice was slow and deliberate, anger emphasizing each syllable, and her pointer finger poking Roy's chest with each word. Then she pointed her finger in Susan's direction without taking her eyes off Roy. "*She* is *barely* my mother, and *you* are just some *nasty* thing she picked up in some *nasty* bar."

Her hands clenched into tight fists and dropped to her sides. I watched her take a deep breath, and time slowed to a crawl as I watched what happened next.

"Oh! Get your hands *off* me—" Jessie's words were cut off as her mom's boyfriend reached out and grabbed her arm with one hand, punching her hard across the face with the other.

Everything was a blur after that. My mom and I were down on the ground, helping Jessie up and trying to get her inside the house. Jessie's nose was bleeding, and tears poured from her wide eyes. My dad was yelling something to us, but I couldn't tell what it was over the drunken sobs coming from Susan. Susan, who didn't rush to her daughter's side, but instead just stood by the truck, wailing and screaming indecipherably.

As we headed for the door, I looked back in time to see Toby dodge a swing from Susan's boyfriend, quickly responding with a punch of his own. Clearly having the upper hand, and not at all hindered by alcohol, Toby's fist connected to its target with a loud *crack!* Whether Roy was hit hard enough to go flying, or his drunken state made him clumsy, Susan's boyfriend flew back into the truck and crumpled into a heap on the driveway, unconscious.

My dad grabbed Toby, pulling him back toward the house.

Susan ran to her boyfriend's side, trying to rouse him from his slumber.

"Roy! Honey, honey! *Get up,* baby! Oh my God! What is *wrong* with you people?" Susan shrieked at us. "Look what you've done to him!"

As if it was our fault.

As if we were the ones who just showed up on *her* doorstep looking for trouble.

She was more concerned about the asshole who just hit Jessie than she was about Jessie. I was once again disgusted and amazed by this sorry excuse for a woman. This sorry excuse for a mother.

She doesn't deserve Jessie.

Twelve

B y Friday afternoon, Jessie's black eye was on the mend, though no amount of makeup could truly cover up the strange yellow tint of her healing skin. After a long discussion with my parents Sunday night, Jessie had insisted that they not call the police and had convinced my mom and dad that she didn't want to press charges against her mom's boyfriend. Reluctantly they agreed, but they went to have a chat with Susan first thing that next morning. Once Susan sobered up, she was distraught over the situation and swore that she would never see that man again. Yeah. I guessed we'd just have to see if her word was as good as her choice in men.

Toby had been out of town since Monday morning, so I could barely get through the afternoon, knowing I would see him again soon. I couldn't help myself—I kept checking the clock and looking over at the fence between our backyards in anticipation.

Jessie and I were lounging in my patio chairs, enjoying the sunshine, looking through newspapers, magazines, and the Pennysaver. Since we had decided not to live on campus, we were trying to find the *best* apartment for the *least* amount of money—which could be a crapshoot in Los Angeles.

Jessie paused to look at me, a question in her eyes.

"What is it, Jess? I know that look."

"Well, you know, Ever"—she closed the Apartment Guide, briefly glancing over to the fence before turning her full attention to me—"you never really tell me anything about Toby."

"What? What do you mean? Of course I do."

"No, actually you don't. I mean, sure, you talk about Toby *all* the time—which tells me how head over heels you are. And the way he stood up for me Sunday night shows how *chivalrous* he is, which totally makes me love him . . . but you never actually tell me anything *about* him. But he seems to be away a lot, and"—she paused, and I could tell she was trying not to sound *too* concerned, but I knew she wasn't happy about how frequently Toby was absent from my life—"well, you know, you don't tell me much. Like who he is, what he does, what he likes, et cetera."

An image of Toby standing over Frankie's lifeless body flashed through my mind. I shuddered and pushed it aside. After how amazing he'd been on Jessie's behalf Sunday night, I'd told myself I wasn't going to dwell on my silly nightmare.

So much blood. Frankie's blood.

I couldn't possibly tell her that I didn't actually know anything about Toby, so I tried to recall everything I did know.

"He's twenty-two."

"Wow, that's really unique and shocking, Ev. You've overloaded me with information."

Okay, um . . . "He likes the Black Keys."

"Well, that's easy enough. Doesn't *everybody* like the Black Keys?"

"Does Greg?" I already knew he didn't from Jessie's very first email about him. She had been shocked and traumatized that *the one* didn't like her favorite band. *That's it,* she'd typed, *I can never see him again!*

She'd gotten over that *real* fast.

"Well, well, touché Ever, you do have a point. Okay, so he has stellar taste in music, cars, and he likes black as much as you do. Maybe even *more* than you do." She made a disgusted face and scrunched up her nose.

"He works with his dad. That's why he's away so much."

"Oh geez, Ever, I *know* that. Tell me something I don't know. I can't imagine he's as mysterious as he seems. That's so cliché."

I looked down at my hands, trying to think of all the things I knew about Toby. I felt strange—unable to recall more than what was already common knowledge. How could I be so into someone I hardly knew?

So much blood.

"Dammit!"

"What? Geez, Ev, relax."

I looked up at Jessie, realizing I'd cussed out loud and trying to figure out a way to explain why. *Shoot.* I didn't know what to say.

"Well then, it seems you need me. Don't worry, Ev. That's what best friends are for. I'll investigate Toby, and you can investigate Greg! Ooh, this will be so much fun! And Greg totally wants to meet you!" She paused, looking off into the distance briefly. "Tonight. We'll meet up tonight. Sound good?"

"Wait, Jess, I don't know what Toby has planned tonight so—"

"Oh, Ever, *call* him, silly! Tell him that your very best friend in the whole wide *world* wants to hang out with him. I'm sure he'll understand. And who knows, maybe he and Greg will hit it off and become best friends, too. Wouldn't that be fantastic?"

As she gathered her copies of our apartment hunting materials and was getting ready to leave, she added, "Meet us at the Block, at . . . Fridays? I could totally go for some Green Bean Fries. Say, what, like five o'clock?"

She kissed me on the cheek and was out the door, clearly not waiting for an answer.

I hadn't even talked to Toby since he'd gotten back, so I had no idea what we were doing yet. I hoped he didn't have anything planned because I knew I wouldn't be able to get out of a double date with Jessie and Greg now that she'd set her mind to it.

I headed inside to my room and picked up the phone on my desk to call his cell.

"Hey, babe."

"Hey." I felt myself blushing. I explained the situation to him, and he reminded me that our date was *my* choice tonight. That part out of the way, I figured I should give him a heads up about the best friend inquisition he was about to experience so he could mentally prepare himself.

He just laughed. "Okay, sounds good."

"Are you sure? I mean, I can cancel—"

"You make it sound like she's going to attack me or something."

"Well . . . ."

"Right. I can't imagine someone who dresses like a cotton candy machine could pose much of a threat, but I'll take my chances."

I was relieved he was so agreeable to the idea of a double date. I was looking forward to meeting the guy who finally got Jessie to commit to something serious. I assumed he must be pretty special. I looked at the clock and realized I was running out of time, so I jumped in the shower and got ready as quickly as possible.

When I stepped outside that evening, I noticed that Toby wasn't waiting for me as he usually was. *Ha! I'm finally ready before him!* A silly victory, yes, but I allowed myself to celebrate. Until I looked at my watch and realized that I was actually about twenty whole minutes early. *What?* How had I managed that? I made a mental note to check the clock in my bedroom for accuracy when I got back later.

I crossed over our two yards with a cocky smile on my face. Ridiculously early or not, I was just happy I wasn't late for once. I reached up to knock but stopped when I heard his father's shouting coming from inside. My hand was suspended in the air, just inches away from the door. I knew I should either knock or go back to my own house and pretend I wasn't twenty minutes early for our date, but I couldn't help myself. I listened. *I'm a terrible person.*

"You are interfering, Tobias! You have a job to do! Or have you forgotten?"

"I'm well aware of that fact, Ted, you don't let me forget—"

"You are not some ridiculous lovesick *boy*, Tobias. You are wasting precious time. Can you even imagine the repercussions that could come of this little romance?"

Romance? Are they talking about me?

Curiosity killed the cat, I chided myself. *Go home, Ever. This is none of your business.* But my feet didn't move, and I didn't turn away.

"She is getting in the way of our priorities."

"*Our* priorities, Ted? Or *your* priorities?"

"It's time to end it. I've allowed this silliness to go on for too long already. You were supposed to get yourself inside her *house* . . . ."

My house? My questioning thoughts were cut off when he finished his sentence.

". . . *not* her pants.

I'm sorry, what? Did he just say what I think he said? Fury bubbled up within me. *My pants?*

"You know how badly I need this, Tobias."

"You're right. I do know that. You've made it *very* clear on *numerous* occasions. What I don't know is *why*. *Why* do you need this so badly? Why *this* family?"

This family? This was just getting weirder by the second. *It's your own fault. I mean, who does this?* I mentally chastised myself again for my eavesdropping.

"I . . . I can't tell you why. Just get the job done, Tobias."

"I just need a little more—"

"A little more *what*, Tobias? More *time*? Oh, now I've heard everything! There is no more time!"

His father was laughing at him now, and I couldn't believe the menace in his voice. Maybe this was why Toby never wanted to hang out at his house or talk about his family. His dad sounded like a total jerk. And a crazy one at that. I mentally crossed inviting the two of them over for dinner off my list of things to do.

"You have until the end of the week to get the information I need, or coming here will be a complete wash. Get rid of that child, Tobias."

Child? I had never even met his dad officially. Heck, I'd only even seen him that one time. How could he dislike me so much? If I was being honest, it hurt my feelings. I had never been so disliked by anyone—at least, anyone that I knew of. And knowing is half the battle.

"Oh, and Tobias? One more thing. I've already called in Gregor."
Gregor? What's a Gregor?

I was startled out of my puzzled thoughts by the door opening and Toby almost running right into me in his haste to leave the house. He stopped in front of me, nose to nose, our toes almost touching. I smelled his familiar scent of Irish Spring soap and light cologne. His eyes blazed with anger, their dark blue shade intensified.

"Ever. What are you doing here? What time is—?" He glanced at the time on the screen of his cell phone. "How long have you—?"

As Toby swung the door shut behind him, I caught a quick glimpse of his father glaring out at me. *Wow. If looks could kill.* All the hairs on my body stood on end under that stare, relief pulsing through me when the door slammed shut between us.

Toby saw the confusion on my face and must have assumed I'd heard part of their conversation, because he went right into trying to explain what he thought I'd most likely heard, grabbing me by the hand and leading me to the car. I got in and sat down, too stunned to say anything or even buckle up.

What was that all about?

I couldn't shake the terrible feeling I'd gotten from his dad's stare down.

"See, Ever," Toby began once he was settled in his seat, "you don't understand Ted—I mean, my dad. You don't understand my dad. He doesn't see the point in me dating and spending so much time with a girl."

"Oh. I see. He wants you to date *lots* of girls."

Toby reached over and took my hand. "No, no. It's not like that at all. He doesn't want me to date *any* girl. Period."

"Oh," I answered, not really knowing how to respond. And then it hit me. "Oh. Since your mother left?"

He paused halfway through backing out of the driveway, his hand going slack in mine, and looked over at me. I realized my mistake—*he'd* never told me about his mother leaving. I had heard it via the neighborhood gossip mill, but *he* had never told me. In fact, it may or may not have even been what happened.

Oh no.

He considered me through slightly squinted eyes for a long few seconds before leaning over and kissing me, just a brief, tender sweep of his lips against mine. I admit that wasn't what I had been expecting him to do. He lingered there, just inches away from my face.

"Yeah. Since my mom left. He just doesn't see the point anymore."

"I'm sorry, Toby. I shouldn't have said anything. I know you don't want to talk about it. You don't have to. I get it. I shouldn't have brought it up. I'm sorry. I don't like to talk about certain things either, like my sister, and—"

Shit.

His eyebrows rose slightly. I was rambling. I was feeling so awkward over what I'd just said about *his* life, that I almost went way too far into my *own* family history. I was about as eager to tell him about my dead sister as I was ready to tell him about Frankie.

"You have a sister?"

There it is. The question of all questions.

"Had. I *had* a sister. She died before I was born."

Toby's eyes widened ever so slightly. "Oh, I'm sorry, babe. I didn't know."

"Yeah, well, I don't talk about her, so . . . ." I shrugged. No big deal. It's not like I'd known her.

He kissed me again and turned his attention back to driving, not pushing me further, as if knowing I didn't want to go there. That's the last either of us said about his dad or my sister. I guessed I'd have to wait for the details. I was okay with that. He'd tell me more when he was ready. And one day I'd tell him about my sister. *If we're still together in August,* I thought to myself. Yeah, I'd tell him then. We celebrated her birthday every year.

"So, tell me how to get to Friday's from here. It's off Katella, right?"

"No, no, it's off the 22 freeway."

I directed him to the Block, which was pretty crowded, being a Friday night. We had to walk a little ways to the restaurant from our parking spot. When we got there, we surpassed the large group of people waiting to be seated as Jess waved us over to a table in the corner where she and Greg sat waiting for us.

Where Toby was tall and lean, Greg was bulky and muscular. He had the body of a football player, and he wore a college letterman's jacket in those familiar rival colors. I knew instantly what had drawn Jessie to him and it wasn't his massive chest, chiseled jaw, or cheesy Hummer . . . the letterman's jacket sealed the deal. Who cared that his alma mater was USC instead of UCLA? A letter was a letter. His hair was dark brown and cut short. His eyes were hazel, and his nose was strong and chiseled like his jaw, with the telltale bend of a nose that had been broken once or twice—probably on the football field, I imagined. He was quite a few years older than us, and I assumed he was probably nothing like the boys Jessie had dated before. She must have been in heaven.

Jessie made the necessary introductions as a frazzled looking waitress herded us into the booth so we'd get out of the walkway. She took our drink orders and quickly hurried off. I picked up a menu, opening it to see what I wanted to eat, and reached down for Toby's hand. When I found it, I was surprised to find it balled into a tight fist at his side. I looked up at his face and noticed his jaw was rigid and tense, and he was staring hard at Greg. *What the heck?* Jessie was engulfed in her menu and hadn't noticed the tension coming from

Toby. I looked next to her at Greg who seemed to have the same intense look in his eyes, returning Toby's heated stare.

What the heck? Do they know each other? This was way too weird.

I gently nudged Toby's hand to get his attention. My touch seemed to snap him out of his funk, and he broke eye contact with Greg and turned his head in my direction. I shrunk back reflexively when the full heat of his stare was directed at me. Seeing the confused look on my face, he slightly shook his head and smiled at me, his playful side back again. He snatched my menu, breaking the tension.

"Hey!"

"Oh whoops! The waitress only gave us two for the whole table. Guess you don't get one." He held it just out of my reach and then whispered, "I'll trade it for a kiss." He nibbled my ear before pulling away, sending a happy feeling down into my toes.

I gave him a brief kiss on the cheek, not being one for public displays of affection, and he frowned at me.

"That's not what I meant."

I knew, but I just smiled my biggest smile, and he gave in, holding the menu between us. Jessie pushed her menu between her and Greg, and we all sat in silence for the next few moments, the strange intensity between the two guys fading away.

The strain of the fight with his dad had left Toby extra quiet, and without him to prompt me, I wasn't incredibly talkative either. As if not having much to say wasn't already bad enough, I occasionally caught something weird passing between Greg and Toby. I'd see a look from Greg that resulted in Toby's body growing tense again. Or I'd see a tightening in Toby's jaw, followed by a smirk from Greg. It was all very strange, and it made for a slightly uncomfortable evening, though somehow, Jessie remained completely oblivious to it. I wondered if I could possibly be imagining things.

About halfway through the meal, Jessie apparently had enough of the strange silence and began talking up a storm, telling stories and asking questions. Before long, *newscaster* Jessie arrived, and we were all actively engaged in the conversation.

"So, Toby, how many girlfriends have you had before Ever?"

"Oh my gosh! Jessie!"

Eyes wide from shock, I looked over at Toby. He'd tensed up, and his jaw was tight again. I couldn't believe Jessie had asked him that. Wait. Yes I could. We're talking about Jessie after all. Always the reporter.

"What? It's not that hard of a question, Ev. I mean, it's not like I asked him boxers or briefs." She looked at Toby expectantly and batted her long lashes.

"I've only had one serious girlfriend before Ever."

Greg scoffed, and I looked up at him quickly, but he ducked his head. I felt Toby's hand tighten ever so slightly on mine. *What is up with these two?*

"Only one, huh? What was her name?"

"Oh my god, Jessie! *Stop!*"

"What? It's not like we'd actually know her, right? I mean, he just moved here from Idaho. Let Toby answer the question."

"Montana, actually. And you wouldn't know her."

Jessie finally caught on to his tense reaction to this line of questioning, and I watched her eyes glisten from the hint of a story.

"Ooh, touchy subject. Was she a psycho?"

I could have sworn Greg scoffed again at that.

"Yeah," Toby answered, "It's probably pretty safe to say that."

"I'm sorry, Toby. I don't know what's come over my friend here." *Yes I do. It's Jessie. She can't even help herself. You'll get used to it.*

PS. Your ex was a psycho?

Toby leaned over and kissed me on the nose, and then whispered quietly so only I could hear him. "It's cool, babe. Cotton candy, remember? I think I can handle it."

He leaned back, and I was pleased to see his familiar smirk was back in place on his face, and his eyes were less tense. He turned the conversation back to Jessie, and within minutes, she was talking to

Greg and ignoring us completely. Toby and I were sitting back and watching quietly, relieved to no longer be in the spotlight.

With Jessie's prompting, I managed to learn a little bit about Greg, like where he went to school, where he worked—small stuff like that. He seemed like a good enough guy, but I was having trouble ignoring how strange Toby acted when he'd first seen Greg, and the uncomfortable tension that still slightly lingered between them.

After we'd ordered dessert, Jessie excused herself to the bathroom, and her not-so-stealthy nod to follow her was hard to ignore.

"Wow, Ev, I can see what you see in him. He's so quiet and mysterious, but you can tell there's *so* much going on inside that head of his. It's like he's watching and analyzing everything. He's like a puzzle just waiting to be solved! And he's *so* your type. I totally give him my 'best friend stamp of approval.'"

She giggled and turned her attention to her reflection in the mirror. I hadn't known I had a *type* since it had always just been Frankie, but I was glad she approved. Plus, I had to agree with her; he was pretty fantastic.

"I'm just happy to see you've focused your attention elsewhere. You know, away from—"

"Yeah, Jess. Thanks for bringing him up." I shook my head, staring at her in the mirror.

She had the dignity to look apologetic and change the subject.

"So, oh my gosh, can you believe Toby's ex was a psycho? I wonder what *that's* all about. Like, do you think she was just a stage five clinger, or like . . . an *actual* crazy person who chased him down the street with a candlestick?"

"Easy there, Jess. This isn't a story waiting to be discovered."

"Fine. You don't let me have any fun." She turned back to the mirror and puckered up. Halfway through reapplying her pink lipgloss, she added, "Well?"

"Hmm? Well, what?"

"Geez, Ev, what do you think of Greg? Isn't he *amazing*?"

They've already sent Gregor.

Toby's dad's words randomly floated through my head. *No. It couldn't be. Could it?* That would just be way too weird. *Greg. Gregor.*

"Helloo, Earth to Ever? Is anyone home?"

Whoops. Of course she wanted my 'best friend stamp of approval' as well.

"Oh, yeah, Jess, he seems pretty cool. And *he's* definitely *your* type."

"I know, right?"

Pleased with my response and my approval, as lackluster as they were, she gushed about Greg for the next five minutes before we finally made it out of the restroom and rejoined the guys. The tension was still there, hanging in the air between them, but Jessie was oblivious to it again as she slid back into the booth next to Greg. *Gregor?* I looked at him then, *really* looked at him, trying to put the pieces of the puzzle together. If they were even supposed to fit together in the first place. I was probably just being silly.

I turned away when Jessie grabbed his face and pulled it to hers for a kiss—a very uncomfortable kiss to witness. I briefly wondered why she had bothered reapplying her lip-gloss.

Toby, sensing my discomfort, distracted me by tickling my side, and then the dessert arrived, saving me from anymore of Jessie and Greg's PDA's.

After the bill was taken care of, we said our goodbyes and went our separate ways.

Once the distraction of Jessie and Greg was gone, we were left to our thoughts, and we spent the rest of the evening in silence. Fortunately for us, movie theaters are the perfect place for that, though I had a hard time concentrating on the movie.

Toby was probably still reeling over the fight with his dad, and frankly, I was too. I tried multiple times to figure out a way to ask him why his dad disliked me so much, but I couldn't come up with anything that didn't sound insecure or narcissistic. *Or an alarming combination of the two,* I thought dryly. *No thanks.*

Maybe his ex was an insecure narcissist.

On top of the issue with Toby's dad, I couldn't stop thinking about Toby's weird reaction to Greg. I mean, nothing had happened or anything, and nothing had even been said, but there was no mistaking that I'd seen *something* pass between them. I just couldn't shake the feeling that they knew each other, and what they knew was *not* pleasant. Not to mention the mysterious 'Gregor' that Toby's dad referred to earlier. Of course, I wasn't supposed to have heard that, so I couldn't say anything. I wouldn't want Toby to think I'd been eavesdropping that long. And yet again, I reminded myself of his psycho ex. *Super.*

By the time the movie was over, I'd decided that I'd make myself crazy if I continued trying to analyze it all myself, so I'd be better off leaving it alone. Maybe Toby would choose to tell me what was going on when he felt ready to. Maybe nothing *was* going on. *Maybe it's none of my business.*

Walking back to the car, my curiosity finally beat out my better judgment. As it often did.

"Toby?"

"Mhmm?"

"Um, do you know Greg from somewhere?"

He stopped walking and turned to face me, a confused expression on his face. "What? No, I just met him tonight, you know that."

"Really? Because the way you were looking at him . . . it was . . . I don't know, I could have sworn you didn't like him. I mean, I could probably even go as far as to say you were pissed to see him tonight. Like, angry. *Really* angry."

"What? Really? That's weird. Nah, he seemed like a pretty cool guy. And Jessie seemed to like him. Why, do *you* not like him?"

"No, no, I mean, he's fine, and you're right about Jessie—I've never seen her like this over a guy."

"Good. She should be happy too, right?" With that he picked me up and twirled me around, making me laugh as I squirmed, trying to get down out of his grip. He stopped spinning me around and lowered me to the ground.

"You're happy, right, Ever?"

"What? Yeah, of course. Why would you ask that?"

"No reason. I've just . . . well, *I've* never been this happy."

I stretched my neck up to kiss him, a smile making its way quickly across my face. *He's never been this happy?* I barely registered the rain drops sprinkling on my head during our kiss, but I was far too thrilled to care. What was a little rain when I'd just found out my boyfriend had never been this happy?

Of course, by the time we stopped kissing and got to the car, we were sopping wet.

Maybe there was a bit more than a *little* rain.

After what was probably the most wonderful date in the history of the world—the strange parts of the evening purposefully forgotten so I could focus on our *mutual* happiness—we were driving home from the movie theater, holding hands between us, both of us content in our silence. I kept catching him staring at me and had to remind him to pay attention to his driving.

"Ahem. Eyes on the road, please."

A police car zoomed past us, lights and siren on full blast.

We continued heading down Chapman, and just after we passed the roundabout in the center of the Orange Circle, we had to pull off to the side to allow a second and third police car to whip past us, an ambulance trailing closely behind them.

Slowly, we pulled back onto the road and proceeded a little further.

Toby reached over and squeezed my hand, just as my stomach turned over and I felt an unfounded tightening in my chest. I looked over at him, and his lips were pressed tightly into a grim line, his brow furrowed in concentration.

"*Shit*," he cursed under his breath.

What's going on?

The accident was about half a mile up ahead of us. We were just close enough to see the glare of the lights and the commotion in the street. The rain made the flashing red and blue lights glisten and dance in the darkness.

Toby slowed down, glancing worriedly over to me and then back at the road in front of him, never making full eye contact. He pulled off to the side of the road and parked, much to the annoyance of the cars behind us, who honked as they drove past.

Toby put the Mustang in park and turned in his seat to face me. He took my hands in his. The radio was off, and all I could hear was the rhythmic swoosh-swoosh sound of the windshield wipers, and the click-click of the hazard lights he'd turned on when we stopped.

"Why are we stopping? What's going on, Toby?" I couldn't control the high pitch in my voice as the look in his eyes told me something was terribly wrong.

"There's an accident up ahead."

Well, that much is apparent.

"It's not good, Ever."

"What? What do you mean, Toby? What's going on?"

He leaned over and tried to pull me toward him, but I looked past him and saw my dad standing on the other side of the street.

"It's my dad!"

"It's your dad."

We said the same words, simultaneously, though how Toby could see what I was seeing, I had no idea. I didn't stop to ask *how* Toby knew my dad was standing on the street behind him. In a flash, I was out of the Mustang, racing to the other side of the street through moving cars and curious onlookers who stood in the rain under vibrant-colored umbrellas.

My dad had also been standing in the rain, but he hadn't had an umbrella, and . . . he hadn't looked wet. He hadn't smiled at me when he'd seen me in Toby's parked car. He'd just stood there, staring at me, a sad look in his eyes.

And where is he now? I searched the street, but he was nowhere to be found. Suddenly, Toby's arms were around me, and he was telling me something. *Get back into the car,* maybe. *I'm sorry,* I think he said. I didn't know what he was saying. There was a pounding in my head that I couldn't seem to shake. The thumping became louder, like a drumbeat picking up tempo. The next thing I knew, I was out of Toby's arms, running at full force, rain splashing down on my face. I heard Toby shouting my name behind me. My jacket was in the car, so within seconds, my jeans and my sweater were soaking wet and plastered to my skin.

When I reached the area where the emergency lights were flashing, all I could see through the hordes of onlookers and passerby were fire trucks and emergency response vehicles. Police officers donning bright yellow raincoats were spaced out in a loosely formed circle, trying to control the commotion of the surrounding crowds.

I pushed my way through the crowd, elbowing the nosy onlookers who stood in my way. The pounding in my head matched the thumping of my heart. It was maddening. I ignored the grunts and snide remarks from the people I shoved aside, with one thing on my mind. I had to see something. I had to see. . . .

It's not my dad. It's not my dad. It's not my dad.

From the front of the crowd, I saw the entire accident scene. A fire hydrant had been hit and was spraying water with full force, like a fountain shooting water up into the heavens. An elderly woman sat on a stretcher nearby, her burgundy Oldsmobile half on the curb and half on the street, its front end busted from the collision with the other car.

An overturned silver SUV.

No, not just any SUV, a Honda CR-V.

My dad's car.

It's not my dad.

A wail escaped my lips as I told myself again that it wasn't my dad, knowing with every ounce of my being that it was.

I pushed past the caution tape and was grabbed by someone. My fists pounded blindly into the chest of the police officer who tried to restrain me. I shouted repeatedly, words that may or may not have made any sense. Eventually, realization hit him, and his face softened as he looked at me. His brief hesitation was all I needed to push past him.

I ran to the body-shaped lump in the middle of the intersection.

It's not my dad.

Raindrops beaded up on the surface of the plastic covering before quickly streaking down the sides.

It's not my dad.

I was vaguely aware of voices shouting around me and people running toward me as I reached down to lift up the yellow tarp.

It's not my dad. It's not my dad. It's not my dad.

He was covered in blood and a deep gash ran down the length of his face, from his forehead down through his temple, and ended in the beard stubble on his chin. His graying hair was mottled with blood and glass. His glasses were still on his face, though cracked and bent beyond repair. His eyes were open, but they didn't see me.

They would never see me again.

Daddy!

Blackness crept up around my vision, as if a dense fog was spilling into my eyes. I heard screaming nearby and wondered who could be so upset about my dad that they'd be crying so horribly loud. *They don't even know him!* The blackness continued to creep into my vision until I had only a tiny pinhole to look through. I stayed there, squatted next to my dad's body, rain pelting down on me, my hair plastered to my head, and that awful screaming blaring in my ears.

Why won't they shut her up? Please, please shut off that awful screaming!

Toby's arms were around me when I collapsed.

As my eyes closed, giving into the blackness claiming my vision, the awful screaming finally stopped.

My screaming.

It was quickly replaced by another scream.

My mom's.

Thirteen

W hen I woke up, I was in dry pajamas, tucked snuggly into my bed. It was light outside, so I knew I'd slept through the night. I looked around and saw that Frankie was in the chair at my desk, watching me intently. His eyes were sad, and his lips were pulled down into a small frown. I stretched my limbs and cringed. My body felt as though it had been folded into a pretzel and stuffed tightly into a cocoon. Since Frankie was there, I realized I must have had another nightmare. It was weird though, because I didn't feel any of my usual fear or worry, and I didn't remember waking up in the night searching for him, or calling out his name.

"Was I screaming again, Frankie?"

"No, Doll."

Okay. That's weird. I briefly wondered why he was in my room if I hadn't been calling for him, but then he spoke again.

"I'm so sorry about your dad, Ever."

My dad?

Oh god.

With Frankie's words, the awful memory of what happened came rushing back to the forefront of my mind. The car . . . the fire hydrant . . . my dad's broken glasses . . . it all flooded back to me with such force that it felt like a herd of elephants had just rammed into my chest. I could barely breathe. *Oh my god. Oh my god. Oh my god.*

Seeing me begin to panic, Frankie came to sit by me on the bed. Looking up at his translucent form, a thought occurred to me. A thought that to anyone else would have been downright *crazy*. But to me, it made perfect sense. My anguish was quickly replaced with an intense feeling of *hope.*

Oh! Of course! I jumped up and ran from the room, leaving Frankie behind.

"Dad? Dad!" I called his name, running from room to room, frantically looking for him. "Dad! Where *are* you?"

As I entered the kitchen, my mom reached for me and swallowed me up into a firm embrace as she cried into my hair.

"He's dead, baby. Daddy's dead."

I pushed away from her. "Mom, I *know* that! But where *is* he?"

She paused, a quizzical look on her face quickly being replaced with understanding, then making way to pain as she slowly realized what I was thinking.

"Oh, honey. I see. Daddy's not here, Ever. He passed on."

He passed on.

With those three words, my heart sank, and my knees grew weak. I dropped to the ground.

"But . . . but I *saw* him. I saw his . . . *ghost.*"

"No, baby. You're confused. Daddy's gone."

"No! I *saw* him! You weren't there!"

"Crisis apparition."

Toby's voice startled me, and I quickly turned around to make sure Frankie wasn't standing behind me in the doorway to the hall.

"You saw him when I pulled over, didn't you?" Toby asked.

"Yes." My voice sounded soft, far away. I almost didn't even recognize the sound.

"I think it's what they call a '*crisis apparition*'. It's like when a person is close to death, the 'ghost' of this person can appear to a loved one. In this case, your dad appeared to you."

I shook my head. He didn't know about Frankie. He didn't know that *my* ghosts stay with me. *My dad has to be here. He has to be.* I looked up at my mom. Surely *she* understood. Surely *she* knew. But she looked at me with pity, tears streaming down her face.

"No, baby"—she got down on the floor with me and lowered her voice so only I could hear her—"Daddy's in heaven with Estelle now."

My dad was dead. And he was gone. *Really* gone. Like my sister, he didn't want—or need—to stay with us. My dad was gone. Forever.

Once again, the realization of his death consumed me. My mom cradled me in her arms as I broke into a million little pieces. She sobbed into my neck as she rocked me back and forth.

"It's okay, baby. It's going to be okay," she said as she soothed me.

But I wasn't the one crying. Not anymore. I wasn't the one needing to be soothed. My anguish was slowly being replaced with . . . with nothing. Empty space. Numbness.

After a few minutes, my mom realized I wasn't crying and composed herself again, her sobs ebbing momentarily. She explained briefly what happened to my dad. Toby came to sit with me on the floor, and I leaned into him, suddenly exhausted.

My dad had been driving home from the mini market, after getting some olive oil that he and my mom had forgotten at the store earlier in the day. A quick trip that he'd made *many* times before, but somehow, *this* time had been different.

The old woman hit the hydrant. Then she hit him. He wasn't wearing his seatbelt. My dad. Wasn't wearing a seatbelt. I couldn't even fathom it. It seemed like the worst kind of irony ever.

Mr. Responsible. My dad wasn't wearing his seatbelt. Of all people.

"Oh, Ever, I'm so sorry you saw that. I'm so sorry we *both* saw that." She choked out a sob and began crying again.

This time I soothed her, rubbing *her* back and telling *her* it would all be okay.

"It will be okay, Mom." *No it won't. It won't be okay.* "Shh, Mom. It's okay." *It will never be okay again.*

My dad is dead. And he's gone.

Fourteen

Eleven days.

That's how long it had been since my dad died.

Dead. Gone.

Between my mom, Jessie, Frankie, and occasionally one of the neighbors, I hadn't been left alone for very long unless I was sleeping. And even then, who knew? Even my showers were interrupted frequently by a knock on the door, or someone poking their head in—*not* Frankie, by the way. Everyone had been hovering around *poor Ever*, worried that if left alone for too long, I might hurt myself or do something crazy.

I wasn't crying over my dad's death.

Apparently, that was cause for alarm.

I didn't care either way. Crying wouldn't bring back my dad. In fact, I hadn't cried at all since the night it happened. I was completely numb. I couldn't feel much of anything. It was weird, not feeling anything.

I guess my blank stare pegged me as the suicidal type or something. I was practically on twenty-four hour suicide watch, tucked safely away—a 51/50 in my own home. It was totally ridiculous, but I didn't have the energy to tell everyone to leave me alone. *I* knew I wouldn't kill myself.

Right now, my mom and Jessie were dealing with the dozens of concerned friends, neighbors, and random strangers who appeared out of the woodwork for the memorial service. Frankie had been keeping out of sight all day and Mom had been so smiley she reminded me of The Joker from Batman—all toothy grins and crazy eyes. I didn't know *what* that was all about.

Everyone gathered in my living room, offering their condolences, sipping free wine, eating cheese balls and Jell-O molds, and telling my mom how much they'd absolutely *adored* my dad, or how very, *very* sorry they were. That one was my favorite. *Sorry.*

Why? Did you *kill my dad?*

I only said that once in the days after my dad's death, before I realized the statement was pretty inappropriate. Okay, that's a lie. I didn't have to *say* it to know it was inappropriate, but sometimes you just can't help yourself. And *ugh*, people kept saying it! Seriously, just don't say anything. Because saying *nothing* is better than apologizing for something you had nothing to do with.

I'd managed to make it through the entire funeral service and burial without saying one word. Not a single word or sound. It was a game I was playing with myself, mostly because I was bored, and partly because I didn't think anyone was really listening to me anyway. At the cemetery, I just smiled and shook hands with each person in the condolences line, allowed them to hug me and pat my head, and then I would nod, smile, or frown when it seemed the response they were looking for. Toby stood by me the entire time, holding my hand, and I swear he was the only reason I kept it together.

Back at the house, my game continued.

However, if another person told me they were 'sorry for my loss'—as if my dad was *lost*, as if we had just *misplaced* him—I knew I'd explode. I was quickly getting to the point of needing to scream at everyone which was quite a stark contrast from not saying a word all day—talk about your opposite ends of the spectrum.

Maybe I was a head case after all.

The one time I was left alone for even a second, Toby found me cornered in the kitchen, being *consoled* by one of my dad's old friends from high school. He stood a little too close to me, his breath smelled a little too much like Budweiser and pepper jelly, and his fingers lingered dangerously close to my chest.

He leaned into me as he spoke, shamelessly glancing at my chest every few seconds. Just another awesome curse of large breasts. His finger was lightly grazing my arms as he prattled on, arms which were crossed in front of me in a sort of "back off" stance that he was either oblivious to or simply ignored.

I was about to lose it. Toby must have seen it in my expression as he entered the room. He stepped in front of me, putting some distance between my dad's 'friend' and me. Though the look in his eyes was anything but kind, Toby politely excused us and waited for the guy to take the hint. He stared Toby down for a long second, a silent challenge, before finally walking away. After he left, Toby took a deep breath and turned to me, kissing the tip of my nose. He grabbed my hand and led me down the hall to my bedroom. I followed behind him in a daze, relief flooding me as I left the mass of *mourners* behind, focusing instead on the gorgeous savior in front of me.

Dressed all in black—a black button-down dress shirt and black slacks, his trademark boots laced up underneath them—he was a welcome sight. I followed him into my room, closing the door behind us, wanting nothing more than to shut the day away.

For the first time since it happened, I was alone in my room with Toby. Well, actually, this was the first time I'd *ever* been alone in my room with Toby.

"*Fuck.* That was too much."

Clearly shocked by my colorful choice of words, his eyebrows shot up and he laughed.

"What?" I replied, a slight edge to my voice.

"I just think it's funny that you chose *that* word to be the first thing you said all day. Come here."

So he *had* noticed my little game. Of course he had.

He sat down on my bed, cross-legged, after dropping his boots on the floor. I crawled into his open arms, leaving my black boots next to his. *His and hers.* No one had forced me to ditch the boots today— I'd worn them with my dress and dared anyone to comment.

I let him curl me into him, holding me tightly while I finally cried for the first time in weeks. Feeling his protective strength around me unlocked the flood-gates, and all the pain I'd been hiding was unleashed on him—leaving tears and snot streaks on his chest, probably ruining his nice shirt. I must have looked and sounded terrible, but he didn't loosen his grip in the slightest bit, and we sat there for what felt like an eternity. I just cried and cried while he held me.

Eventually I was sufficiently cried out, with only an occasional sniffle. I looked up at Toby. He pulled his head back to look into my eyes, still not letting go of me even as he repositioned himself. With a pained expression on his face, he tucked my hair back behind my ear and gently stroked my cheek where the tears had no doubt left ugly mascara tracks. Since I hadn't cried since the accident, I hadn't worried about waterproof mascara while I'd gotten ready for the service this morning. An oversight I was likely paying for now.

He kissed the tops of my cheeks, leaving a trail of kisses where the tears had been. When his lips gently found my mouth, a jolt of life coursed through my body, making the rest of the world—the funeral, the people, the pain—melt away.

I didn't want him to kiss me gently or tiptoe around me as if I might break at any minute. I didn't want him to look at me with concern or pity in his eyes or worry that I might soon fall apart. I didn't want to be babied like a little girl whose daddy had died. I was *tired* of the way everyone had been treating me.

I wanted him to treat me like an adult who could handle anything. Like a woman who was very much *alive* and anything but fragile. Maybe if he treated me that way, I would *be* that way. I wanted to grow up right *then*. With *him*.

Maybe I was having some strange reaction to the gloom and death that had lingered in the house for days. Maybe it was my way of feeling alive after the consuming numbness I'd felt since the night of my dad's death. Maybe I was searching for a way to fill the emptiness threatening to swallow me whole. Whatever the reason, I was suddenly kissing Toby without restraint.

I tangled my fingers in his hair, and I pushed him back on the bed so we were lying down together. His arms still held me tightly, reassuring me all the while that I was safe with him, though I already knew.

He stroked my back with strong hands, switching between pressing his fingertips into me one moment and lightly grazing my skin. I stopped to look at him, taking in the beauty of his dark eyes, his tanned skin, his perfect lips, all flush from our kissing. *He is so beautiful.* I leaned down and kissed him in the nook where his throat met his collarbone and then left a trail of kisses up his neck, leading back to his mouth.

My legs tangled with his, and I repositioned myself so I was lying completely on top of him, my legs straddling him on either side. I had never behaved like this with anyone before, and I felt powerful and wonderful and *frightened* all at the same time. My inner voice was screaming at me. *Stop*, it said. *Slow down*, it warned.

I don't want to stop. I don't want to slow down.

At that moment, I didn't want to be responsible. I didn't want to be careful. I didn't want to be *that* Ever—my dad's Ever—the one who everyone knew would be good and kind and wise, and would always, *always* make the smart decision, would *always* do what was right.

I turned off all thoughts and focused on kissing Toby.

Before I'd noticed, Toby had my dress up and over my head, lying in a heap on the floor beside our boots, leaving nothing to cover up my bra and panties but a sheer black slip that I had borrowed from my mom.

We resumed kissing, and my brazen, irresponsible side took the reins. I felt my hands touching Toby as if they were driven by some other force, moving of their own accord. They seemed to want to touch all of him at once, though from my position on top of him, they were currently focusing on his shoulders and his lean arms, or tangling again in his hair.

Toby stopped me, pulling my head away from him and holding my face in his hands. He looked up at me as if to ask if what we were doing was okay. He was slightly breathless, and I could see his chest rise and fall with each breath. When he opened his mouth to form the question into words, I answered him by moving my body into a sitting position on top of him and beginning to unbutton the first few buttons of his dress shirt. His eyes widened and I laughed, as surprised as he was by my brave actions.

After the first few buttons were undone, I opened up his collar to expose the top of his chest, my breath catching as I did so. Covering the entire left side of his chest was a darkly lined tattoo. I only saw about half of it with how few buttons had been undone, but I saw what looked like some sort of tribal tattoo, but with the tip of an angel's wing poking out above it. When I went to pull his shirt further aside, he reached for my face and pulled me back down to him, covering my mouth with a kiss. I completely forgot about the tattoo.

Kissing him felt amazing—as it always did—but I had another brief thought that we should stop. That we should slow down. But I told myself to *go on, keep going, you can do this, you* want *to do this.*

It occurred to me that I was about to go all the way with Toby. The idea excited and terrified me. I couldn't believe I was doing this. I'd only known Toby a short time, and he was the first guy I'd ever even kissed. *This is crazy!* What if my mom opened the door? I quickly pushed that thought aside and told myself that it was *so absolutely worth the risk.* I *wanted* to go all the way with Toby.

I love him.

I think.

It didn't matter. In that moment, the only things that mattered to me were the warmth of Toby's body against mine, the taste of his tongue in my mouth, and the spark of life I felt inside me for the first time since . . . since . . . .

Shit. I'm crying again. I hadn't meant to, and I wasn't crying loudly, but I think Toby must have felt my tears on his face. When we pulled apart, his eyes were dark with concern. He smiled a sad smile and gently wiped my tears with his hand. *What a mess.*

I lay my head on his chest, listening to the soothing rhythm of his heartbeat. He pulled the covers up over us, and I instantly felt less self-conscious. He didn't say a word and didn't try to continue what I had ended so abruptly, though I could tell by his quickened breathing that it must have been difficult to show such restraint.

We laid like that for a long time, his hands rubbing my hair and my back, not saying anything, just listening to the hushed conversations down the hall and the front door opening and closing each time a guest left the house. By my calculations, there weren't many remaining.

"Ever. I'm so sorry."

I groaned at his poor choice of words. "I know, Toby. But please don't say you're sorry. I hate that." I sat up, starting to feel anxious and upset again. I wondered if I'd go from content to upset all the time now, or if the ups and downs of my mood swings would soon fade away. Maybe I'd be numb again soon. I hoped so. Numb was easier.

"I just don't understand! Why? Why did this happen? My dad is so careful! So responsible! He's driven that road a million times!" I realized what I'd said. "*Was.* My dad *was* careful."

"I know. I know. I'm so sorr—" The look I shot him made him stop before he said the dreaded words again. "It wasn't supposed to happen."

Wait. What did he just say? It wasn't even the words, strange as they were. It was the way he said them.

"What?"

"Nothing. Never mind. It's just that he was so young."

A knot started forming in my chest, a tightening of my stomach following suit.

"Toby, I heard what you said. What do you mean *'wasn't supposed to happen?'* That's kind of a weird thing to say, and honestly, I've heard all of the weird things people say to someone whose dad died."

I pushed out of his arms and grabbed my dress, suddenly feeling *very* exposed. I paced the floor. I couldn't understand what he was saying or why I was so freaked out by it. Of course, *I* thought it wasn't supposed to be my dad who was never coming back. Of course, *I* had the purely selfish thoughts, the dreams, and the moments of wishing it could be *anyone else's* dad but mine.

But the way Toby said it . . . *'it wasn't supposed to happen'* . . . the words were innocent enough, but his tone, and the meaning behind them . . . something wasn't right. I knew it deep down in my gut.

Something else came crashing into my mind. I was back in the car with him the night of the accident. I could clearly see Toby's face, his concern . . . and I could hear his words.

'It's your dad.'

How had he known?

"Ever, please calm down. Stop pacing."

I stopped pacing. I stood in front of him, arms crossed. I knew there was a look in my eyes that dared him to tell me again to *calm down.*

"Explain, Toby. And I mean explain *everything.* How did you know it was my dad that night?"

His jaw clenched, and his face went hard. It was brief, but I caught it. Then he sighed. There was a pained expression in his eyes. I watched curiously as it slowly changed from pain to confusion . . . to something else entirely. *Resolve*. Stone cold resolve, free of any other emotions. His sudden determination left his eyes dark and seemingly without feeling. My heart dropped in my chest.

He got up off the bed and put on his boots before turning back to face me.

"This isn't working."

Holy shit. What? That's the last thing I'd expected him to say. Just minutes ago we'd been making out and . . . and I had even thought I was about to go all the way with him . . . and now he was . . . *is he breaking up with me?*

"Toby, what? What do you mean?" I felt myself tense up, an angry heat spreading through my body.

"I mean exactly what I said, Ever. This isn't working. This. *Us.* You and me. I don't want to be with you anymore."

"*Why,* Toby? Tell me *why*." My words were sharp, direct—the opposite of how my heart felt. *Oh my god. This isn't happening.*

I felt my composure slipping away piece by piece, but my eyes stayed dry. Maybe I'd cried out all of my allotted tears for the day.

"It's not you, Ever. It's—"

"Get the hell out, Toby."

"Wait, Ever, I—"

"Yeah, yeah, I know. Seriously though? How freaking *typical* can you get? It's not you; it's me. Maybe we can still be friends. You're a really nice girl. I've been hurt before. Yeah, yeah, yeah. Save the bullshit, Toby. Just because I haven't had a lot of boyfriends before doesn't mean I'm a complete moron. I've seen the movies. Read the books. You're just as textbook as the rest of them. I ask you a question that you don't want to answer, and you *run.* Well, I'll save you the trouble of letting me down easily. Get the hell out of my house, Toby. *Run* away."

He flinched at my words, or maybe it was my tone of voice that cut him. I didn't really know, and I didn't really care. I was *not* about to be nice about it. He'd completely blindsided me, and I'd be damned if I begged him to stay or tried to change his mind. I'd rather be alone forever than become *that* girl.

My thoughts raced through my head. My heart screamed. I remembered the night he said he'd never been this happy before. I recalled the way he'd always been so interested in learning about me. I thought back to just a few minutes earlier—kissing him, touching him. I had almost given him the most important thing I could ever give a man. *Myself.*

That thought angered me beyond repair. What if I had gone through with it? What if I hadn't started crying? Would we still be standing here? Would he still be breaking up with me? Ugh! How much worse would I feel then? I was so angry; I was beginning to sweat.

And he's just standing here! Why is he still here? He was just staring at me, his eyes pleading. The hurt look on his face completely at odds with his devastating words. I swear I could feel each little fissure forming in my heart. Each little crack spreading, consuming. The pain tightened in my chest, the anger making it hard to breathe. His presence was infuriating!

Toby had just broken up with me. Yet he stood there, staring at me, looking as if I was the one causing all the pain. He was not saying a word, the look on his face reminiscent of a lost puppy. How could *he* be looking at *me* that way? *He's the one who did this. What the heck is going on?*

Our gazes locked. With one look into that beautiful blue abyss, I felt the last bits of strength seep out of me. I opened my mouth, but words wouldn't come. My survival instinct kicked in, telling me I had to get away from him. *Fight or flight. It's now or never.*

I punched him.

I don't know what overcame me, but one minute I was standing there staring into his eyes, feeling myself get sucked into them again, and the next minute Toby was stumbling backward out the door of my bedroom, rubbing his jaw.

When I spoke next, my voice sounded strong and firm, and so unlike how broken and small I felt inside.

"I said *get out,* Toby."

I shut the door to his shocked expression, put on my headphones, and crawled under my covers, pulling them up over my face so I was completely engulfed in darkness. I didn't cry. There really just weren't any tears left.

I woke up a few hours later, a sweaty mess of sheets and matted hair welcoming me back to the world of the living. The black satin slip was plastered to my body, and the underwire on the right side of my bra had busted through the lace and was digging into the skin of my chest.

Frankie was standing in front of me, and I could vaguely remember searching for him in my dream. But, like all the others, that was the extent of the memory.

"I'm here, Doll. Go back to sleep now. It was just another dream."

But I didn't want to go back to sleep. I didn't want to fall back into the realm of nightmares I couldn't remember. Nightmares in which my panic and dread would follow me into wakefulness along with images of blood, but nothing else. Just that cold, relentless fear gripping me, and telling me that Frankie was in danger.

Nightmares about Toby's bloody hands, most likely.

"I punched Toby."

Frankie's eyebrows flew up, and a small smile crept over his face. I watched him trying to hide it, trying to look serious without much luck, and I busted out laughing. He joined me, and after we'd had a good laughing fit, he sat on the bed and tried again to look serious.

"Is your hand okay?"

"Yeah. Thanks. It hurts really bad, but . . . ."

"Are *you* okay?"

I looked at him. His eyes were dark abysses like Toby's, but for totally different reasons. They used to be dark brown, with golden flakes of caramel in a sea of chocolate. I'd stared into them so many times, wishing for him to *see* me. Now, they were just a hollow, translucent abyss. Death stripped him of the vibrancy in his eyes, his skin, his life. Everything was just shades of gray now where Frankie was concerned.

Yet it was suddenly obvious to me that there were no shades of gray between *us*. There was just love. I felt it hanging in the air, saw it in his concern for me. I knew I wasn't imagining it. The way he looked at me now . . . *he finally sees me. Finally.*

But it was too late.

"Yeah, I'm okay, Frankie. We broke up, but . . . I don't know. Something tells me I'll be okay. And it felt really good to punch him."

"You've definitely got spunk, Dollface."

"Yeah, well, you just better watch yourself around me. I'm not above punching a ghost. I'd just have to work out the logistics of it."

"Right, right. Noted."

We laughed again, and something occurred to me. Something I was confused about. Maybe Frankie had some answers.

"Frankie? Did you see my dad when he died?"

He bowed his head.

"No, Doll."

"Oh."

"I heard what Toby told you—that it was a *crisis apparition*. I don't know much about that, and I don't know why I'm still here and your dad isn't. I wish I had answers for you. But I don't."

We talked about my dad then, long into the night. It felt good to talk to someone who knew him so well. Someone who missed him as much as I did. Well, *almost* as much as I did.

Spending time with Frankie was the perfect remedy for what I'd just been through.

My heart would heal in time.

Fifteen

Four weeks had slowly crept by since I'd seen or heard from Toby.

Four *miserable* weeks.

I kept waiting for him to knock on my door and apologize or say *something* to fix what happened, but . . . nothing. He hadn't even fought for me. Hadn't tried to make it right. My boyfriend dumped me on the day of my dad's funeral. I was angry and hurt and so mad at myself for allowing him into my life in the first place. I felt like a bit of a loser at times, but mostly I was just pissed off.

And I'd be lying if I said I didn't miss him terribly.

He was out of town again. Or so I assumed. I hadn't seen his car in at least a week. I knew I shouldn't monitor him, now that we clearly weren't together, but I couldn't help myself. It would be so much better if he didn't live right next door to me. Of all the luck.

My nightmares ceased, leaving me a bit confused about their existence in the first place, as well as leaving my room free of ghostly visitors.

Frankie kept his distance from me, knowing I was dealing with the death of my father and the death of my relationship. I knew he must have been pleased Toby was out of the picture, which angered me greatly, the longer I stewed about it. My misdirected anger was ridiculous, but being angry at Frankie was easier than being in love with him, so whatever. Unfortunately, it didn't get rid of those feelings completely, and my love for him remained a background noise. I pushed the noise aside, allowing myself to be mad instead. I knew it was wrong and slightly childish to blame Frankie for the failure of my relationship with Toby, but what could I say? Sometimes people acted irrationally in love.

My mom was a total mess, which helped me avoid any motherly inquiries regarding Toby's sudden departure from my life and my decision to delay college—though any lectures on that subject would have been pointless because I'd made up my mind—but my worry for her was a lot to handle. So was the sudden onset of responsibilities. My mom didn't even get out of bed most of the time. It was like, as soon as she was no longer worried that *I'd* kill myself, she allowed herself to feel the grief *she'd* been ignoring.

And then, she allowed that grief to swallow her whole.

With only one parent in the house, and that one parent on hiatus for an undisclosed amount of time, I had to step up and make sure things got done around here. I didn't have to worry about bills, luckily, as my dad's life insurance took care of those for a long while, and Sharon came over weekly to monitor our financial status and keep it all up to date.

I had to do all the *other* stuff. Since my mom could no longer cope with day-to-day life, I was stuck doing the housework, yard work, and errands. Oh well, they were all good distractions.

I finished up my morning chores and threw on a black maxi dress and flip flops. I was finished with all my school stuff and was officially out of high school. *Whoopity doo, a high school graduate. Big deal.* Jessie still had a week left, so I had spent my time at the library when

I wasn't busy at the shelter, doing household chores, or taking care of Mom.

Sometimes I checked her breathing, just to make sure there still *was* breathing.

I bent down and kissed my mom on the head, leaving a glass of water and some pretzels—she still didn't have an appetite—on her nightstand. I didn't even bother opening the blinds. I knew she wanted it dark, and the daylight only reminded her that it was another morning without my dad. Gollum had taken on the important role of caretaker, and he curled up at the foot of her bed. I patted him on the head, silently thanking him for keeping watch over her. I hoped his presence was at least somewhat soothing.

I glanced over at the rocking chair in the corner. It had been in my dad's office prior to his death, but since my mom's decline, I'd moved it into her room . . . in case . . . in case he came back. He'd have a place to watch over her.

He's not coming back.

I grabbed my purse and headed for the library, stopping momentarily to drive through Starbucks for an iced latte along the way. My appetite still hadn't returned one-hundred percent either, but I filled myself up with coffee most of the time. Too bad if it stunted my growth. I didn't really believe that anyway.

Silence greeted me at the library, and I was thankful that most people were still in school. I just wanted to sit and read without interruption. I walked over to the young adult fiction section to grab a thick hardcover by one of my favorite authors. I found myself a beanbag chair in the children's section and dragged it over to a dark corner of the room, away from windows and hopefully out of the path of foot traffic.

I was a little over halfway through the book when a soft voice startled me out of my imaginary world.

"Excuse me?"

I jumped, causing the lid of my latte to pop off, and melted ice and latte remnants spilled onto my dress.

"Darn it!"

"Oh, excuse me. I'm so sorry. I didn't mean to sneak up on you, but you seem to have dropped this book."

I looked up to see a girl—no, a *woman*—standing over me. Her eyes were big and round and . . . yellow. *Yellow eyes.* They were so hazel they were almost yellow, and I'd never seen a shade like that in anyone but my mom. I'd been less lucky and gotten my dad's brown eyes. Her long black hair was twisted into a loose knot on top of her head, and she wore long ivory feather earrings that skimmed her shoulders. She had on a pale blue peasant-style shirt that hung off her shoulders and tight fitting jeans that she'd tucked into knee-high, brown riding-style boots. They had buttons running up the length of them, reminding me of something out of the Victorian era. She looked like she just stepped out of a fashion magazine or a clothing catalogue, except that she had on no makeup that I could tell.

Of course, that only added to the natural beauty of her face. I felt small next to her. And slightly chubby, if I was being honest.

She reached down, handing me a large green book with tattered edges and writing I couldn't quite read. As she leaned toward me, I smelled the slightest hint of Irish Spring soap. *Toby.* My stomach turned over as the familiar scent triggered memories and pain. I found myself staring at this stranger in front of me, without actually seeing her, as my mind plummeted back into memories I'd tried to forget.

As I daydreamed of Toby, I noticed the girl's eyes tighten a little—just enough to snap me back to the present. Embarrassment quickly caused my cheeks to flush as I realized that in my reminiscing, I hadn't been staring off into space, but staring directly at the girl in front of me. *She must think I'm crazy. Sorry, I'm just hanging out, daydreaming about the beautiful guy who dumped me. You smell just like him.* Yep, pretty crazy. And pathetic too.

I shook myself, and looked down at the cover of the book she'd handed me, trying to make out what it said. It was too smudged with age, and I couldn't read the writing.

"I'm sorry, but it's not mine. Someone else must have dropped it." I looked back up at her and smiled courteously.

"Oh, I'm sorry. My mistake. I'll just go ahead and return it to the librarian. Enjoy the rest of your day."

She forced a smile, curling up the corners of her mouth with what almost felt like disdain. Then I realized I was either completely imagining it or I probably *deserved* disdain for staring at her like a total creep.

As she turned to walk away, a piece of paper slipped out from the book and drifted down to land at my feet. It was plain white paper, folded in half one time. Probably someone's notes or references to pages in the book.

"Wait! Excuse me? Something fell out of that book!"

I grabbed the sheet of paper and stood up to chase after her, but she was already gone. *Hmm, that was quick.*

"Um, *okay*," I whispered.

I picked up my purse and the book I had been reading before the interruption, then headed to the front of the library to see if I could find her there, but again, she was nowhere in sight. While glancing around the room searching for her, my eyes grazed the clock. *Shoot!* I was momentarily stunned at how much time had gone by since I'd arrived at the library. It was well past dinnertime, and I had wasted the day away, my nose in a book.

Without thinking, I shoved the folded piece of paper into my purse, checked out my book at the computer, then ran to the car. I had plans with Jessie in an hour, and I was going to be late. As usual.

Jessie planned to drag me out to an end-of-the-year summer kick-off party, and I wasn't exactly thrilled. I liked parties and socializing, but I hated going places where I didn't know anyone. Since this was a party at one of the senior's houses from her school, chances were that I would know only a small handful of people—especially since I'd never gone to the same school as Jessie, even before homeschooling.

I kept hoping Toby would show up and surprise me, begging me to come back to him and saving me from the horror of being the third wheel with Jessie and Greg, but no such luck.

Clearly, I'd read too many love stories. I shouldn't have wanted him back at all.

I had only a few minutes to change and reapply my makeup. Jessie was promptly through the door at seven, Greg following closely behind her. She was all glitter and sequins, in a bright-pink tube-top and shiny, black cuffed shorts. *Black?* She had on strappy black wedges, and her cropped blonde hair was pulled back on one side with a pink rhinestone clip in the shape of a bow.

I looked down at my black jeans and faded fitted tee knowing Jessie was going to make me change before she even said a word. I knew there was no way she'd allow any of it—especially my Havaiannas. I silently cursed my spilled latte, wishing I could have just kept on my maxi dress.

I held up my hands in surrender when she made a face. "I know, I know. I'll go change."

"I'll be right back, Greg!" She said the words loudly, letting Frankie know someone else was in the house so he didn't make an appearance in the living room, scaring the bejeezus out of Greg. He gave her a funny look, probably wondering why she was yelling at him, and she followed me down the hall.

"Black?" I said, motioning to her shorts.

Jessie smiled widely before responding. "Greg thinks black is *so* sexy."

Of course, it would be because of a guy. I'd been trying to get her to accept black as a valid color option for years.

"Well, welcome to the Dark Side."

"Oh my gosh, Ever, speaking of sexy, did you see how *hot* Greg looks tonight? I could just die."

I agreed with her, naturally, and watched as she rummaged through my closet. Greg was hot, no question. But he wasn't Frankie.

Or Toby.

160

And now I'm thinking about Toby again. Damn.

Jessie finally decided I'd wear a dark red racer-back tank and a black denim skirt, my black lace bra straps showing just enough to be—as she called it—*sexy, but not trashy.* I disagreed completely, but there's just no arguing with her about fashion. To save my dignity, I grabbed a black hooded sweatshirt from the hamper, making Jessie frown. I raised my eyebrows at her in a silent challenge and won— she didn't push me to ditch the hoodie. She made sure I didn't zip it up, mumbling something about my cleavage. She ran out to her car and grabbed her black bow ballet flats for me. She *tsk-tsked* me as I looked longingly at the black Havaiannas flip flops by the closet door.

"Uh-uh."

"Fine." I didn't feel like arguing with her.

Before we left the house, Jessie grabbed my oversized gray purse and exchanged it for a tiny, black glitter wristlet she'd given me this past Christmas. She didn't mention the price tag that still hung from the clasp. She dumped the contents of my purse onto the bathroom counter and grabbed my lip-gloss, powder compact, driver's license, and keys, throwing them into the clutch as she pushed me out the door.

The party was at a huge house in an upscale neighborhood in Anaheim Hills. How this kid went to Jessie's high school all the way in east Orange, I had no idea, but I knew the school was known for their sports teams, and people often lied and used other addresses to get their kids in.

When we pulled into the neighborhood, we realized there were no places to park long before we even found the house. We ended up having to walk at least half a mile. Jessie's shoes were already bugging me, and I assumed she'd gone half a size smaller than she should have. Again. She had a weird thing about wearing size seven and a half even when she knew she was easily a size eight. Seeing as how I was *definitely* a size eight, my toes felt the pain of Jessie's strange shoe quirk.

People were everywhere. Discarded red party cups lined the street. Music blared from the back of the house, an almost deafening sound, and not because of the volume. A live band was playing, but they didn't sound familiar and definitely didn't sound good.

Greg and Jessie walked ahead of me, hand in hand, and I knew this was a really big deal for Jessie. To have a serious boyfriend, who didn't go to her school and who was quite a bit older than the boys she'd dated before, was something I knew made her extremely happy. I had always wondered about her perpetual dating—now I had my answer. It wasn't what she'd *really* wanted at all. This Jessie, the Jessie in a serious relationship—*this* was the happiest Jessie I'd ever seen. She practically vibrated with excitement.

And honestly, Greg was a pretty cool guy. With Toby out of the picture, I'd been around Greg a lot more frequently and saw a side of him that was the opposite of that tense night at T.G.I.Friday's. He was relaxed and open, and he had been pretty supportive of my mood swings—even when they annoyed Jessie. He'd also helped around the house since my mom's decline, and I'd be forever grateful for that.

I followed them through the house and tried to look like I was into the party, but it was difficult to do. Being the third wheel sucked. A lot.

Though the music became louder as we got closer to the backyard, it did *not* get better. I knew I'd have a raging headache by the end of the night.

We followed the trail of red cups to the kitchen where a keg was set up in the corner. I looked around and imagined what my parents—sorry, *parent*—would do if she came home to this scene. I was picturing my mom's face when a man in his mid to late forties walked in, slapped a few of the guys on their backs, then proceeded to do a handstand on the keg. While drinking out of it. I'd never seen that before.

I know my mouth must have been open as I watched, but it fell to the floor when he finished and one of the high school boys said, "Yeah Dad, that was *awesome!*"

Dad?

All the guys whooped and hollered, and the dad walked away smiling triumphantly . . . and a little sloppily. I guessed it hadn't been his first moment of impressing the kids tonight.

The guy whose dad had just finished impressing the crowd saw Jessie walk in, and his face lit up at the sight of her. He pushed through the crowd to greet us, irritating a few of the female partygoers as he left them behind to come to us. I saw their glares directed at Jessie and imagined she probably dealt with them at school on a daily basis. He stopped dead in his tracks when he spotted Greg—who was, of course, still holding Jessie's hand. He looked familiar as if we'd met at one party or another before this one.

"Hey, Jess. I'm glad you came. Who are your friends?" He gritted his teeth behind a forced smile, and I could tell he struggled to be polite. And when he said '*friends*,' he wasn't looking at me, just Greg.

"Hey, Scottie! Great party! This is my boyfriend Greg—"

Greg extended his hand, but Scottie ignored it, looking down at me as if just realizing I was even there. He stared at me for a split second before recognition dawned on his face, and he smiled—a real, genuine smile—not the scary smile Greg received.

"—and you remember my best friend Ever, right?"

"Yeah, yeah, your lesbian lover, if I remember correctly?" He laughed and winked at me, which made me laugh too. I still found it quite funny that Jessie's school thought she'd been coming out of the closet when she brought me to her prom last year. Jessie smiled awkwardly and glared at me, pissed that people still joked about it. She'd never seen the humor in it like I had. Greg turned to Jessie, a smile on his face and his eyebrows raised in question.

"Lesbians, huh? I can get down with that." Greg put his arms around both of us and laughed.

Jessie glared at me again. "Oh, Ever. Do you see? It *never* ends." To Greg she said, "And, *no*. Don't get any ideas, Greg. It's not *that* kind of party."

They both laughed, and Jessie dragged him over to the keg, leaving me trapped in the corner with Scottie.

"Ever, huh? Cool name. I remember you from prom last year."

Yeah, I'd figured that much out by the lesbian comment. "Thanks. So, was that your dad just now, Scottie?"

"Oh, yeah, but he's not usually like that. It's just been . . . different . . . since my mom died. And it's just *Scott*. I don't know why Jess insists on calling me Scottie like we're still in third grade."

"Oh, don't worry; she sometimes calls *me* by my *full* name. I'd take a third grade nickname over *that* any day." He opened his mouth to speak, but I stopped him. "Uh-uh, don't even go there. I won't tell you what it is."

"Okay. Okay. I get it." He laughed and lifted his hands in surrender. "You can tell me when you're ready."

Which will be never.

A large group of kids gathered around the pool, chanting, drawing our attention outside. Scott's dad was at the center of the group, beer bong in hand, standing on top of a rock slide in just his boxers. Scott rolled his eyes and groaned, turning his attention back to me.

"See?" He motioned toward the backyard and shook his head. "First keg stands, and now this. My mom would flip if she could see him right now."

"Yeah. That's um . . . cool, I guess."

"You don't have to lie, Ever."

"So, I hope you don't mind me asking, but . . . you said your mom died? Was it recently?"

"Yeah, just last month actually."

He leaned in closer, his momentary displeasure toward Jessie and Greg no longer apparent on his face. I could tell by the sudden glint in his eyes that he had set his sights on me. It happened at every party I went to with Jessie. Something about being the mysterious girl who no one knew was apparently hard to resist. The elusive homeschooled chick. *Yeah, I'm irresistible all right.*

Oh well. Whatever takes my mind off Toby.

"Wow, I'm sorry. I mean, I know *'sorry'* sucks to hear, but . . . well, I understand. My dad died last month as well."

"No shit, really? Man that sucks. Well then, I guess I'm sorry too. Should I say I'm *'sorry for your loss,'* or does that bug you as much as it bugs me?"

We both laughed at that and moved on to compare stories about all the people who had said stupid things in their attempts to console us. We talked about how our parents died—the funerals, the time leading up to the funerals, and the way our remaining parents changed since the death of their spouses. Turns out it wasn't just my mom who'd drastically changed, though our parents changed in opposite ways. Where my mom curled up inside herself, Scott's dad decided to live every second like it was his last. From skydiving and rock climbing to tonight's being a kid again—*and* the life of the party.

We were sitting at the kitchen island, a freshly poured beer in front of each of us. I played with a Sharpie, doodling on the side of my red cup instead of actually drinking its contents.

"You're not much of a drinker, are you?"

I smiled, my cheeks flushing just a bit. "So, it's obvious?"

"Yeah. I'd say so. But hey, it makes a great art project." He motioned to my doodling before standing up and heading to the fridge.

"Okay, there's Coke, Sprite, Red Bull, and . . . oh, Cactus Cooler, too."

Ah, perfection. "A Cactus Cooler would be perfect."

When he returned with my drink, he sat so close to me that our knees touched. I reflexively moved my legs away, not wanting to be that close to another guy, but after quick consideration, I put them back. Scott was sweet, and I enjoyed talking to him. The distraction was welcome, and my mind was almost completely distracted from thinking about that other person—or, those other *people*.

We'd been sitting in the middle of the kitchen, talking for almost three hours, when he reached a hand up to run through his unruly blond hair, and I noticed how cute he was.

He caught me looking at him and paused. The hand absently taming his hair slowly made its way to rest on top of my thigh, and his other hand reached up and settled on the back of my neck. My body tensed up—little did he know I'd only kissed one other guy. He leaned in to kiss me, and my heart skipped a nervous beat. My head screamed at me to *run away!*—or maybe that was my broken heart screaming at me—but I ignored it. I had to move on with my life. Frankie was a *ghost*, and Toby was an *asshole*. He was obviously not interested in me anymore. Toby suddenly coming back to me was as likely as Frankie suddenly *not* being a ghost anymore. Pining for either of them was pointless and silly and had caused me nothing but pain. *Lots and lots of pain.*

I closed my eyes and leaned toward Scott, anticipation and a little bit of guilt making my nerves jittery. *Guilt! What's wrong with me?* I parted my lips slightly, and when his lips connected with mine I was . . .

Disappointed.

I'd hoped I would feel the same spark I felt with Toby, but . . . *nothing.* I was doomed. I once thought no one would ever be able to kiss me the way Toby had. Turns out that was a safe assumption. *Damn.*

Kissing Scott wasn't terrible. It wasn't even bad, really. It just wasn't . . . Toby.

Or Frankie. Not that I would ever know what *that* felt like.

Wow, I am pathetic.

Jessie walked up right then and interrupted us by clearing her throat. I'll admit it: I was a bit relieved. I felt horrible for feeling that way, but I couldn't help it. My heart was already torn between two guys—there really wasn't room for a third.

Jessie tried to hide a look of utter horror with one of her trademark million-dollar smiles, but I could tell something was wrong. *Shoot. She can't be mad at me for kissing Scott, can she?*

"Jess, what's wrong? Are you okay? Where's Greg?"

"Um, yeah, Ev, everything's fine; it's just time to go, that's all. Hey, Scottie, thanks for the great party. See you at school on Monday." She grabbed me by the hand and started pulling me toward the front of the house.

"Jess, wait—you aren't mad that he kissed me, are you?"

Scott caught up to us, grabbing our arms to stop us.

"Wait! Why are you guys leaving? Ever? Stay awhile. I'll drive you home later. Jess, I'll drive her home, okay?"

Looking at Scott's pleading face, I knew he couldn't actually drive me home because of how much beer he'd likely had to drink, but I did want to stay. Sort of. I had finally been feeling somewhat *normal.* I was carrying on a normal conversation and had even laughed a little. I liked the way Scott looked at me, and the kissing aside, I liked the way Scott make me feel: not *as* broken. It was nice to have my mind on other things for a change, and I figured if we kept talking *and stopped kissing*, I could go back to being distracted from my thoughts about—

Toby.

When I saw him, it was like the wound in my heart reopened and all the pain rushed back out to the surface. Like I was bleeding internally. *What is he doing here? Why can't I just have a night out and finally feel good again?*

Greg walked toward us, leaving Toby sitting on the couch with a stricken look on his face. Greg's face was angry, and I knew they must have just had some sort of argument.

Then I saw that Toby was with someone. *Oh my god.* Greg must have been defending me or something.

Next to him—no, scratch that, she was practically draped *on top* of him—was the girl from the library. I couldn't believe it. Toby's eyes met mine, and I froze in place. She was oblivious to me and didn't even seem to see that Toby had stopped paying attention to her, his gaze locked on mine, his body tense like mine. Clearly unfazed by whatever Greg had just said to Toby, the girl continued running her fingertips up and down his arm and talking away, smiling to herself at whatever clever thing she was saying. I watched Toby's fists clench, clearly angry at seeing me here. *Oh god, he hates me.*

My heart pounded, and my eyes burned. A pain formed in my stomach, and I couldn't stop looking at them, even though it killed me inside.

I knew I couldn't just stand there and stare at him in shock, but now that he'd seen me too, I knew I couldn't run away either. Could I?

I quickly sorted through my options. Option one: confront him. I imagined marching over there and screaming at him and making a scene, throwing my drink on her, possibly even . . . no, too dramatic. Option one was out. Option two: say hello and act like I didn't care that he was with someone else. I knew that would be incredibly painful and close to impossible. Or, option three—the easiest and most attractive option: run like hell in the other direction. *Yes. That's the one.*

"Ev," Jessie whispered, "why are you nodding your head?"
Whoops.

Unfortunately, I couldn't take my eyes off Toby, which meant I wasn't likely to run away either. So, I chose option two. Because clearly, I hated myself and enjoyed inflicting pain upon my heart.

I grabbed Jessie and walked over to where they sat on the couch. I tried to look happy when I approached him, but the tears were knocking right behind my eyes, and I knew it was only a matter of time before I lost all composure. I'm sure my forced smile looked more like a painful grimace, but it was too late to choose option three. Greg stood behind us, one hand on my shoulder, lending support. I tried to muster up all the nonchalance I could. I pictured Toby's carefree stance outside my house that first day I met him and tried to copy it, but picturing him on that gorgeous day only made my heart hurt more and my grimace tighten.

Toby stood when I approached, sparing a quick, angry glance at Greg. Toby was probably mad Greg didn't stop me from coming over here. *What an asshole.*

I felt Scott come to stand next to me before I heard him speak. He looked from Toby, to Jessie, and then to Greg, before looking back at me, trying to assess the situation. I could tell he was searching my face for some indication of what was going on, but I couldn't take my eyes off Toby.

Scott reached out and grabbed my hand, and my stomach tightened. Toby's gaze locked on our clenched hands, and he narrowed his eyes. I couldn't tell what he was thinking.

Scott leaned over and whispered, "Hey, Ever, what's going on? Are you okay?"

"She's fine. Who are you?"

Oh, hell no. He's kidding, right? Does he really think he can speak for me?

I scoffed at Toby, unable to keep my mouth from falling open. I turned my attention to Scott, whose face was reddening. I could tell he was offended that this *stranger* would stand in *his* home and have the audacity to ask *him* who he was.

"Yeah, I'm fine, Scott. I should probably go."

I looked back at Toby, locking eyes with him, daring him to speak on my behalf again. A million feelings and thoughts flooded my mind, anger leading the pack. I swear I saw relief in his eyes. *Is it relief that I'm leaving? Geez, what did I ever do to him?*

"Hey," was all he said. *Hey? Is he serious right now?* After not seeing Toby for *four weeks* and then seeing him there, with *her* . . . all he could say to me was 'hey?' It seemed so casual, so careless . . . so . . . .

Oh.

It is casual.

He's over me.

The knot in my stomach twisted tighter.

The girl from the library stood next to Toby and laced her fingers in his, prompting my stomach to do a somersault. I'd only had half a soda, but I felt like that little bit would be making a comeback soon. I dropped Scott's hand, unable to inflict the same pain in Toby as this girl inflicted in me. Whether he cared for me or not, I could be the bigger person. Toby pulled his hand away then shoved it in his pocket.

The girl stuck out her now-free hand. I tore my eyes away from Toby's and found myself staring at her long, red-tipped fingers as if they were attached to an alien. *Which they very well could be.* I shuddered. I was suddenly very aware of the chipped black polish on my nails as I reluctantly returned her handshake.

"Hi! I'm Ariadne. Are you guys friends of Tobias'?" She addressed all of us, but her eyes never left mine.

Tobias. She said his name like they'd known each other forever. I'd only overheard his dad call him Tobias. I felt that ball of jealousy churn a little more in my gut, growing ever larger and harder to ignore as I looked at her standing in front of me, holding Toby's hand. The hand I should be holding.

Used to hold, Ever. Past tense. The hand I used *to hold.*

With her hair down, I saw it mirrored mine in length and color. But that's where the similarities stopped. It was beautiful and lustrous, that perfect blue-black shining like it had just been polished. It hung elegantly over one shoulder, every hair in place—with not a single flyaway or broken piece that I could see. I felt my hand reach up to smooth my hair, my self-conscious habit popping up at the most inopportune time. She had perfect skin so pale it reminded me of a porcelain doll. It was so beautiful next to her dark hair and yellow eyes.

I hate her.

Her lips were big and full, which I hadn't noticed at the library— probably because I'd had no need to analyze her then, not knowing she was *with* Toby. *Ugh.* Tonight she had on a dark, glossy red lipstick that gave her mouth a look of pouting, but not in a bratty toddler way. Oh no, this was a very sexual pout.

I really hate her.

I found myself comparing the two of us. It's only natural. Looking back at Toby, I wondered what he ever saw in me.

Jessie's elbow connected with my side, reminding me that the girl had been speaking to me. I tore my gaze away from Toby and looked back at her, trying to recall what she'd said. She was looking at me with a glint of curiosity in her eyes, her amusement apparent. *What had she asked me? Friends of Tobias.* Her voice floated through my mind. *Oh yeah. Friends.*

"Well, no, I guess not. We *used* to be, um, *friends*. Not anymore." I snuck a sideways glance at Toby when I said it but didn't linger on his face for long. Looking at him was too painful.

She had a good five years on me, I could tell—a good five inches, too. She stood with pride, as if she knew everything there was to know about life—and about Toby too, I imagined. Her confidence, much like Jessie's, was almost palpable.

I am so out of my league.

"Um, anyway, hi. I'm Ever."

"Oh! Is this *the* Ever!? I've heard so much about you! It's such a pleasure to finally meet you!"

The words were pleasant enough—if not completely confusing— and her voice was sweet as she spoke them, but there was something unmistakable in her eyes, an anger lurking just beyond the surface. *She must know I'm his ex, then.* I wondered if it was any coincidence I'd run into her at the library earlier, but I wasn't going to be the one to mention it. She'd probably been checking me out to see if I was competition. Seeing her now, all done up for her date with Toby, I highly doubted she had anything to worry about.

"Um, well it's nice to meet you, too, Ariad—"

"*Air-ee-add-knee*," she said, pronouncing each syllable as if I was some kind of idiot.

"Yeah, I got it. You're named after a Greek goddess or something, right?"

Of course she is. How terribly fitting.

"Oh great! Most people have *no* idea how to pronounce my name. It's so frustrating! I'd rather have a simple, easy name like yours. Is it short for something?" She paused, waiting for a response, but I gave her none. "Well, anyway, you can just call me Ari. That's what Tobias calls me, and since you're a friend of his . . . ." She trailed off then, looking at him and nuzzling her nose against his neck.

His jaw twitched slightly, and my stomach churned.

"You look so familiar, Ever. Have we met somewhere before?"

She was toying with me now, the glint in her eyes daring me to talk about our chance meeting at the library. What I didn't know was *why*.

I stood there like an idiot, not knowing what to say. I was getting really good at that.

"So, did you guys like the band? I've known the drummer for ages."

Ah. So that's why they're here. Just my luck that I'd go to a high school party with a bunch of high school kids I didn't know, and Toby—who was definitely not in high school—would just happen to be there with his hot new girlfriend because she would just happen to be friends with the band. Of course.

PS. Your friend's band sucks.

I watched her reclaim Toby's hand in hers as she nuzzled closer to him. The muscles in his jaw tensed again as she did so, and I figured he was at least a *little* uncomfortable in front of me.

Good. Asshole.

As angry as I was trying to be, that ball of pain and jealous energy was grinding away at my insides, and I felt myself start to waver just a bit, my knees growing weak. I couldn't take my eyes away from his eyes boring into mine and threatening to swallow me up into those beautiful sapphire pools. Jessie must have sensed it because she grabbed my hand and pulled me back the way we'd come. As we walked away, she turned back to Ariadne.

"Well, it was just *fantastic* to meet you, *AU-ree-ANNA*. But we were just leaving, so we will just *have* to get together some other time. Enjoy the party!" Purposely mispronouncing her name, Jessie left her with the most deliciously evil smile I'd *ever* seen her turn on anyone. Moments like this were why I adored my best friend.

She pulled me through the crowd, stopping only once—to watch with wide eyes as a side of me she'd never seen before pushed its way to the surface . . . I grabbed a freshly poured beer out of the hand of one of the partygoers and chugged it until it was gone.

Yuck. I don't know what I was thinking.

I don't even know what happened to Scott after that—I didn't look back the whole time. Heck, I was barely even looking forward. I let Jessie lead me to the car, Greg's hand resting supportively on my back the entire way.

Once we were inside Greg's yellow beast, Jessie let all her anger out in a rush.

"Oh. My. God! Some people! It's only been *four weeks* since you guys broke up! *Four weeks!* What a *dirtbag!* And he hasn't even called you! Oh my god! I am *so* pissed right now! What a *dick.* And I can't believe he would show up to a high school party! I mean, gross, how old is he? And how old is *she?* Like *thirty-five* or something? Who cares if you know the band! Ugh! Did you even see what she was wearing? I mean, my gosh, have some class—"

"Jessie, *stop.* I'm sure Ever would like to ride home in peace, babe."

Ah, thank you, Greg.

I *did* want to ride home in peace. I appreciated Jessie's anger, but sometimes . . . sometimes you just don't want to hear it. Sometimes you just want to . . . wallow in your misery. Quietly.

Alone.

And for the record, I *had* seen what she was wearing, which only fueled my insecurities about my curves. She was tall and thin with legs for days like Jessie, and if I thought her outfit at the library screamed high-fashion magazine, the purple dress she'd worn tonight showed off her insanely long legs and screamed *Victoria's Secret Catalogue*. Or maybe *Frederick's*. I imagined Toby running his hand up one of those legs . . . and then I imagined them wrapped around him . . . *Ugh*. Thanks to my vivid imagination, and the whole cup of beer, I was definitely going to be sick soon.

I didn't say a word the rest of the ride home, and thankfully, neither did Jessie or Greg. They also spared me from their usually frequent displays of affection.

Thank God for small favors.

Sixteen

When we pulled up in front of my house, there was a car in the driveway that didn't belong.

Ugh.

Seeing the car when I did, and coming to the same conclusion as I was, Jessie turned around to face me in the back seat.

"Hey, Ev, do you want to come out with Greg and me for a while instead? Maybe get some late-night pie at Denny's or something? Or, we could just go to my house, just you and me? Have a sleepover?"

Though I appreciated my best friend's attempts, I wanted nothing more than to be alone. Why oh why did my mom decide *this* was the night to suddenly wake up from her depression and have friends over? I hoped that Frankie wasn't hiding out in *my* room while my mom's visitors were there. I didn't really want to see him.

I just shook my head in response to Jessie and got out of the car. Jessie rolled down the window before they drove away and shouted, "Call me later, Ev. Seriously, *any* time, okay? I'll come back if you want me to."

"So will I," Greg shouted from behind the wheel.

I waved my hand behind me as I walked toward the house, too drained to respond with words. A glance to the side showed me that Toby's driveway was still empty and his house was dark. *Maybe he's never been out of town after all. Maybe he's been here all along and I just haven't seen him coming and going. Maybe he's been staying somewhere else, with Ariadne.* That thought made my stomach turn over again, and I stopped to take a deep breath, tears silently cascading down my cheeks once more.

When I looked inside the front window of my house, I saw Bonnie and Sharon—our neighbors, and my mom's two closest friends. Mom was crying, and both women had matching looks of concern and pity on their faces as they rubbed her shoulders and drank their tea. I figured they were trying to pull her out of her funk, and I was happy about that. Well, as happy as I could be when my own funk was all I could think of.

I decided that the last thing I wanted to deal with was my mom and her friends questioning me about my tears. They would probably assume it was because of my dad's death, which would then lead to trying to console me, which would then lead to making me even more upset. And probably also annoyed.

Even if I *could* somehow make it through the house undetected by my mom and her friends, if Frankie saw me . . . saw my face like this . . . and my tears . . . .

No, I definitely had to avoid seeing any of them tonight.

So, I headed for the side yard and hoped I could sneak into my window undetected. I'd seen Toby pull off the screen and figured it couldn't be *too* difficult.

Once I was adequately frustrated by the near-impossible task of replacing the screen from the inside, I finally gave up, sliding the glass part of the window closed. Sure there was some trick to it but too irritated to care, I sat down on my bed, pulled my knees up to my face, and cried.

All this time I'd been hoping Toby would come back, that he'd apologize and everything would be okay, that he'd tell me he loved me and we'd go back to the way we were before the accident. I'd talked myself out of my anger—well most of it anyway—and I just wanted a boyfriend again.

And all this time, he'd been with someone else.

How could I be so stupid?

She was so much older than me and so pretty—so confident. It was really no wonder. To make matters worse, they had obviously talked about me.

"Oh, is this the Ever?"

So what had he said about me? Was his relationship with me just a big joke that they liked to laugh about?

"Oh Ari, remember that little girl I dated before you? She was such a loser!"

"Hahahahaa, Tobias! How could you even stand it?"

I was heartbroken. And embarrassed. And confused.

And Toby was at my window.

I heard the light rapping on my window at the same moment I saw his face looking in. *God he's gorgeous.* Even in my anger, my stupid heart skipped a beat at the sight of him. I wiped my tears on the sleeve of my hoodie and walked over to open my window. I didn't know what to say, so again, I just stood there like an idiot.

"Can I come in?"

I snorted. *Very attractive.*

"Why, *Tobias? Why* do you want to come in?"

"I want to talk to you, Ever, please?" I watched as he started to climb into the window. I should have stopped him, I know, but I didn't.

"You've had a month to talk to me, Toby. A *month.* What could you possibly say to me now? After all this time? After . . . ." *Her.* I was going to say, *after her.* But I didn't say it.

I stayed calm and kept my voice soft, but I felt like screaming at him. Why was he suddenly *here?* Was it because he'd seen me with Scott? Was it the age-old *'if I can't have you, no one can?'* Because that's bullshit. The tears continued to roll silently down my cheeks.

With a light *thump*, he was inside my room, standing in front of me. His hands cradled my face. His thumbs wiped my tear-streaked cheeks.

Before I could protest, his lips were on mine. A sob escaped me, muffled by our mouths pressed together. He pulled me closer to him. With my body pressed to his, all the pain and need I'd felt for the past month began drifting away, my own weak body betraying me as I melted further and further into his kiss.

After a few long—*amazing*—moments, I stopped him. Pulling back, I placed my hands firmly on his chest and pushed him away from me.

"What the *hell*, Toby? You can't just come in here and kiss me like that! Like nothing happened! Like I didn't just see you at that party with *another girl*!"

"Please, Ever, it's not what you think—"

"Oh, really? It sure *looked* like what I think."

"I know what it looked like. I know what Ariadne *made* it look like. But it is *not* that way. Please, believe me when I tell you that we aren't together like *that*, Ever. We haven't been together since—" He paused.

Oh. I get it. An ex-girlfriend. That explains the familiarity between them. And the use of his full name. *Tobias.*

Was she the *ex-girlfriend? The psycho?*

His hands rested on my outstretched arms, his thumbs rubbing little circles on the insides of my wrists that made it very hard to concentrate. The same sparks I used to feel with him were here again, and with every touch of his thumbs, I felt more and more alive. It was making my anger a very confusing and muddled feeling. But I held on to it anyway. *I have to remember why I'm so mad. I have to be strong.*

"You know what? It's not my business, anyway. You aren't *mine* to claim, Toby."

I stood there, arms stiffly extended in front of me, pushing him away, waiting for him to argue. Waiting for him to tell me he *was* mine to claim. *Please, let him say something.* I'd waited for this moment for so long now, the moment when he returned and everything was *fixed.* But in none of the scenarios I'd imagined in my head had I ever pictured myself walking into a party and seeing him with *someone else.* That thought caused a pained groan to slip past my lips. *So much for composure.*

He winced at the sound.

"I haven't seen Ariadne in years, Ever. Honestly. She's here for work, and she's convinced herself that she and I will get back together. It's not going to happen. I don't want Ariadne. I want *you,* Ever. I left the party and came straight here. I *want* to be yours to claim. Please, tell me how I can fix this."

My heart fluttered at his words. He wanted to fix this, fix *us.* I wanted to let him. But I couldn't give in yet, and I was briefly shocked when my mouth opened and I said the words I *should* be saying, not portraying any of the excitement I was actually starting to feel.

"*Fix it,* Toby, really? Fix it? I *needed* you. My dad had just—" I stopped myself, unable to finish. "Toby, you haven't called or come over in a *month.*"

He lowered his head and sighed. "I know. It's been . . . it's just . . . I know I should have called, Ever. I *know.* I should have been here for you. And I should have done something—*anything*—to find a way to make it work between us. But then, a few days passed, and I felt so guilty . . . and pretty soon it had been another few days, and I just didn't know how to fix it . . . I don't know what to say, Ever. I screwed up."

"Yeah," I scoffed, "That's putting it mildly, Toby. But . . . I don't understand what happened. *Why* did you do it?"

"I . . . I thought it would be best, Ever. For you. I saw how much pain you were in, and I knew I could never take being the cause of that kind of pain. I freaked out. So I left."

"Toby, what you did . . . *leaving* me when you did . . . *that* caused so much more pain than you can even imagine. That . . . you . . . ." I shook my head, unable to say the words aloud.

You broke me.

I kept that part to myself.

"I told myself I didn't deserve you. I figured that if I left right then, you'd be mad at me for a minute, maybe even hate me, but then you'd get over it. You'd see how wrong I was for you . . . you'd move on and—"

"Move on?"

I haven't moved on at all.

"I'm so sorry, Ever. I'll do anything to make it up to you. I made a huge mistake. Please. Please, forgive me. Let me back in."

His apology still didn't explain why he hadn't called, or come by, or even fought to keep me. How could he have gone this whole month without seeing me? Was he in pain all this time? Had he been hurting like I had been?

I must have relaxed my arms while I was thinking because there he was again, his breath in my face and the lingering smell of his soap on his skin, playing with my senses. I was weakening, and my anger was subsiding. I fought to hold on to that anger, to hold on to what little control I had.

"I love you, Ever. God, I love you so much. I've been crazy without you."

And there it went. All of my control was gone in an instant.

He loves me.

I inhaled a quick, ragged breath, and more tears streamed down my face. Toby began kissing my cheeks. Relief flooded me, and I just continued to cry. I was letting go of all the pain of the past month without Toby, and I realized that more pain from my dad's death was slowly creeping its way to the surface again as well.

Toby led me to the bed and held me while I cried. Just like that last night we'd been together in my room. And just like that last night, I soon became very aware of Toby's body—so close to mine— and I wanted to feel *all* of him. The heat from the points where our skin connected swam through my body, and before long, I was crawling on top of him, hungry for more of his kiss and wanting nothing more than to lose myself in him. It was as though a hunger took over me and I *had* to make up for all of that lost time.

He pulled me down on top of him and held my face to his as he kissed me in that powerful, no holds barred way of his. Weaving his hands through my hair, his kisses grew passionate, needy. Slowly, he moved his hands from my head, down my back, and up under the hem of my shirt, giving me goose bumps all over and sending a quick shiver through my body.

"Are you cold?" he whispered, glancing over to the open window.

I giggled—my goose bumps had absolutely *nothing* to do with temperature—and kissed him some more. His hands continued their exploration under my shirt, and after a small struggle, my bra was undone. *Oh!* He didn't do anything more than that though. He splayed his fingers across my bare back, feeling my naked skin under his hands, sending more shivers and heat through my veins.

He slowly turned us over, so I was lying on my back with him halfway on top of me, one of his legs positioned in between both of mine. He was propped up on one elbow, and his free hand slowly traced the features of my face. He stayed like that for a few moments, touching my face and looking into my eyes. His eyes were so dark and blue they reminded me of deep lagoons.

"I'm so sorry, Ever. I can't believe what an idiot I was. I'll never let anything like this happen again. I promise I will *always* fight for you."

He traced the shape of my lips with his fingers and kissed me gently, slowly teasing my mouth with his. He gently nipped at my lower lip with his teeth, sending another welcomed chill through my body. I tangled my hands in his hair and brought his mouth down harder onto mine. I had so much lost time to make up for that I wanted to stay like that for days—our mouths pressed together, our legs tangled up, our bodies so close I felt the heat of his body through our clothes.

Pretty soon, his hand wandered again, slowly feeling the curve of my hip, down over my thigh, and up again, eventually finding its way underneath the hem of my shirt once more.

When his fingers crept their way toward my chest, exposed underneath my shirt since my bra had been unfastened, I tensed, sucking in a quick breath. *I want this. I do. I want him.* But I was nervous and scared—my broken heart warning me to be careful. He must have felt my body tense up because he slid his hand back down to my waist, resting it in the curve above my hip.

So many feelings bombarded me. Happiness at having him back in my life. Fear of letting him in again. Fear of losing him. Resentment. Excitement. Anticipation.

Anger too, but less and less as each second ticked by.

Then there were the *physical* sensations . . . wonderful and exciting, regardless of my responsible inner voice.

The way his hand felt on the bare, sensitive skin of my waist . . . the way his mouth moved with mine . . . the way my belly burned with expectation . . . the nervous beat of my heart . . . .

A knock on my door interrupted us, and we froze. *Oh no!*

"Ever?" My mom's voice carried softly through the door. "Are you home, sweetheart? I want to talk to you. I'm so sorry for how I've been behaving lately, honey . . . ."

I jumped up in a panic that elevated as I noticed my bra hanging haphazardly underneath my shirt. I knew I couldn't fasten it very quickly without taking it all the way off and turning it around, so I grabbed my hoodie from the bed post and threw it on.

As I was worrying about my appearance, Toby had obviously been wise enough to realize that of all the things going on, my bra was probably the least of my worries. My mom was about to find a guy in my room. By the time that all dawned on me, however, Toby had already tiptoed to the window and was halfway out. He looked back at me with a devilish smile on his face, then turned to leave.

Luckily, my mom had been talking the whole time, so focused on her apology that she hadn't heard my movements, or Toby's escape efforts, and apparently hadn't thought to just walk right in like she normally did.

I opened the door, and her relieved grin told me she really needed to get this apology off her chest. I soon realized how relieved I was, as well. My mom's grief-stricken funk had really taken a toll on me—more so than I had even realized before now. She had always been so cheerful and happy, and I knew that though she'd never be quite the same as she was with my dad, I really, *really* wanted to see her smile again.

And sure, avoiding the motherly talks after my break-up with Toby had been nice, but was that really what I wanted? To deal with it completely on my own? No. I hadn't wanted that at all.

I missed my dad—more than I could begin to put into words—but I didn't want to miss my mom anymore.

The surprise visit from Sharon and Bonnie had been just what she needed to break out of the depression that I couldn't help her break out of.

I didn't care what or who it was that finally made her snap out of it; I was just grateful that she seemed ready to move forward.

"It will be hard, Ever, for both of us, but Daddy wouldn't want either one of us sulking, and he surely wouldn't want you to have to take care of me. I'm the mother here, and I need to be what you need me to be. That's what Daddy would want. No more role reversals here."

"Mom, you've always been a good mother, and I understand that you needed some . . . um, time . . . away from life. It's okay, really. I didn't mind taking over the chores and stuff."

"Well, I appreciate that, honey, but it stops now. Well, not completely, of course—I mean, all kids need *some* responsibility, right?" She winked and smoothed my messy hair a bit.

My cheeks heated up as I thought about *why* my hair was so messy right now.

"By the way, how's that boy from next door? Toby, right?"

I was weary of her quick subject change, my guilt flaring up and making me feel like she could somehow sense he'd just been there. Before I could shake myself of my momentary stupor, she continued.

"Are you two still . . . dating?"

I knew the word "dating" was difficult for her to get out, seeing how uncomfortable she'd been from the beginning of my relationship with Toby, but what shocked me wasn't her struggle with the word, but the fact that she was completely unaware that he'd been out of my life for the past month.

"Um, well . . . it's sort of . . . um . . . *complicated* right now, Mom."

"Well yes, complicated. I understand. That's how it is when we're young. You'll figure it out." She gazed off into the distance, and I could tell she'd expended her energy for the night. It would probably just come back in little spurts for a while now anyway.

I hugged and kissed her goodnight, relieved she was beginning to find a way out of her funk. I closed the door again, then walked to the window. I looked outside, squinting at the darkness, hoping Toby was nearby waiting to crawl back inside. I still felt the excitement of having him back in my life and wanted to feel the warmth of having our bodies so close together again, so I was disappointed when I didn't see him waiting outside my window.

With all the different emotions running rampant inside me, I didn't think I'd be able to fall asleep any time soon. I sighed and turned back to my bed, only to jump at the sight of Frankie sitting on it.

"Shit! Frankie! What are you doing in here?"

"I think the question, Ever, is what were *you* doing?"

The characteristically playful tone of Frankie's voice was gone, as was his familiar pet name for me. No *'Hey, Dollface'* tonight. He looked at me, unflinching, and I grew uncomfortable under his accusatory stare.

"What? Nothing. None of your business, Frankie. Please, leave my room so I can change. You shouldn't be in here anyway; my mom was *just* here."

"I know. I waited 'til she was down the hall. She'll be asleep soon anyway. It's *late*." His glare intensified ever so slightly with that last word.

"Still, I'd like you to go. We can talk in the morning, Frankie."

He chuckled as if I'd said something humorous.

"In the morning, huh? Nah. Right *now* works for me."

I was shocked by his tone and the menace in his words. He'd never spoken to me that way before. In fact, I'd never heard Frankie speak to *anyone* that way. Least of all, *me*.

"You know that guy's no good for you, Ever, but still you wait for him. Now he's back and you're all excited like an ignorant toddler waiting for Santa Claus. But Santa's a myth, Ever, isn't he? A *myth*. So what gives?"

I did *not* like being compared to a toddler, and I was especially angry that he had the audacity to call me *ignorant*. What was even worse was that Frankie was coming in here—to *my* bedroom—with more negativity toward Toby, when I had just *finally* gotten Toby back. Never mind that he may have had a point. I mean, yeah, I *had* pretty openly accepted Toby back into my life, very few questions asked. But that was *my* business. And I planned to talk to Toby about the past month. I *would* talk to him about it. Soon.

"That's enough, Frankie. You have no right to tell me who to date, and I don't appreciate the way you're talking to me right now." There. That sounded direct and strong, didn't it? *No toddler tantrums here, thank you very much.* I was pacing the room but halted when Frankie jumped up from the bed and rushed me.

He stopped inches away from me. My heart raced. If he'd been human, I would have felt his breath hot on my face, smelled the cigarettes he carried with him at all times. His next words came out so angrily that I probably would have felt spit fly as well.

"Dammit, Ever! Wake up! You really are pathetic, you know it? That guy is bad news, Ever! Where's he been for four weeks? Huh? Did he tell you that much? Did you even bother to *ask*, or did you just jump straight into bed with him?"

Excuse me? Now *that* was going too far. What he implied . . . I took a few deep breaths, trying to calm myself before I spoke. My fists clenched and unclenched instinctively as anger flooded me. I took another deep breath. I didn't want my mom to hear us and come back down the hall. How on Earth would I have explained this angry, confusing passion between Frankie and me?

"How *dare* you, Frankie?" My words were cool, calculated—so unlike the fire in my chest or the fever in my cheeks. "How dare you say something so . . . so *cruel?* If you think I just jump into bed with random guys, then you don't know me *at all*. You have to leave now, Frankie."

"Huh. So you *weren't* just in bed with him?"

My mouth dropped open. I *had* been in bed with Toby, but . . . geez . . . not in the way Frankie implied. Not *quite* anyway.

What could I say, though? Frankie had clearly made up his mind about me.

For a few excruciating moments, we stood nose to nose, his head bent down toward me. His lips were just inches away from mine, his mouth a tight line. His anger I could handle, but his obvious disappointment in me was the worst part.

"You shouldn't be with someone like him, Doll. He's no good for you. You deserve"—his shoulders slumped, defeated—"You should be with someone like . . ."

As his words trailed off, he turned his back to me and headed to the door. His arm reached out for it, not because he could physically twist the knob and open it—he tended to just go *through* doors—but because every so often an old habit reappeared, an old habit like opening a door by hand or reaching out to touch me.

"With someone like who, Frankie? Someone like *you?*"

My voice was softer, my anger quickly fading as I sensed the pain in the words he didn't speak out loud. I heard myself falter, my voice cracking just enough to show that my thoughts mirrored his. He was right. I *should* be with someone like him. Someone who cared about me no matter what. Someone who knew me, understood me.

Someone who accepted my quirks, my insecurities. Someone who loved me beyond my faults.

Frankie. Frankie loves me like that. He has all along.

He slowly turned to face me again, the anger almost completely gone from his face. His eyes were sad, wistful, his voice a near-whisper. "Yes, Doll. *Someone. Like. Me.* Is that so hard to imagine?"

No. It isn't hard to imagine at all. He was beautiful and funny and kind and always knew what to say to make me smile. He was my best friend, my rock. And so much more than that. He was a savior when the nightmares struck, making me feel safe and loved, and . . . *I love him.* It was as simple as those three words.

I'd always loved Frankie.

Yet, none of those things mattered. I had no choice but to push my feelings for Frankie away, tuck them deep down inside, and continue to focus on my life. Frankie could never be what I wanted or needed him to be. I had to move forward with Toby.

My feelings for Frankie . . . *Frankie's* feelings for me . . . they were completely irrelevant.

"You're dead, Frankie."

He was gone before the words even left my lips.

I stood there quietly after those last heartbreaking words, waiting for something to happen. I didn't know *what* I was waiting for, but nothing happened.

My words hung conspicuously in the air, and I wished I could take them back. I stripped out of my clothes then threw on a pair of plaid cotton shorts and a black tank top. I climbed into bed, knowing I was way too upset to sleep. I was mad. At Frankie. At our circumstances. At the confusion now surrounding my once-easy feelings for him.

But then, there was Toby. Very much *alive* and right next door. Regardless of my feelings for Frankie, I couldn't just lay there all night thinking about how impossible a future with Frankie was. I'd been thinking about *that* for too long to note, and *nothing* had changed.

Nothing.

Seventeen

After lying in bed for an hour or so, too restless to close my eyes and *try* to sleep, I took a chance and hopped out the window. I don't know what made me decide to do it. Maybe I was so mad at Frankie that I wanted to shut off my feelings for him by being with Toby. Maybe I was crazy and pathetic after all and didn't make sound decisions anymore. Either way, for whatever reason, there I was tiptoeing through the night, slinking across our yards, the grass cold and wet on my bare feet.

I didn't know which room was Toby's, but I hoped it wasn't Frankie's old bedroom. I practically grew up in that house, in that particular room. I almost stopped myself, knowing I shouldn't be going over to his house in the first place, but feeling even guiltier about it because it had once been Frankie's house. I had to stop to take a deep breath, steeling myself before continuing.

Figuring I had nothing to lose, aside from someone actually catching me sneaking around in the middle of the night, I headed to the other side of Toby's house, hoping luck was on my side.

The first window I came to was open, and the blinds were drawn. The screen was removed and leaning against the wall below the window, which was the first indication that this was the right room, and led me to believe that Toby used this as an entry/exit point as he did with my bedroom window.

Why he should need to escape quietly from his window at twenty-two years old, I had no idea. But his dad *was* pretty scary, so . . . .

The room was bare, with only a few things on the walls, and not much to go by as far as deciphering whose room it was. The plaid wall border still lined the room from when it used to be Frankie's dad's office. The memory was hard to swallow. It occurred to me I'd completely avoided this house since Frankie's dad moved away, divorced and suddenly childless. For a moment, I tried to remember the last time I'd been inside. Shaking my head, I tried to let go of the memories.

That was a different time, a different life. *A different me.*

I leaned into the room to get a better look. I didn't dare climb in though—my courage went only so far.

As I scanned the room, my eyes passed over a neatly made bed with simple forest green bedding and a couple black throw pillows tossed on top. Next to it was a small table with an alarm clock, a lamp, and a couple magazines—but I couldn't tell what they were from where I stood. There were a few clothing items tossed about, and Toby's black boots sat on the floor at the end of the bed, giving me all the proof I needed.

He was exiting the bathroom, towel drying his hair when he saw me and stopped in his tracks. A wry smile played at the corner of his lips, and I knew my being there shocked him.

Somehow though, he'd managed to shock *me.*

I was momentarily stunned by the beauty of him. His chest was strong and sculpted but lean, that same beautiful tanned color of his arms, with a small patch of golden hair right in the middle that looked like it was sun-kissed. The way the muscles in his chest moved with each breath sent nervous chills through me without our skin even connecting. His tattoo was massive—a beautifully intricate angel wing reaching up and over his shoulder.

Below his belly button, the muscles began to form a 'V' that ended somewhere under the waist of his . . . .

Towel.

Oh. My. God. He's in a towel.

He was wearing a towel, nothing more. Heat rushed to my face as I blushed, realizing where I was staring. I looked away, hoping he hadn't noticed. I ran my fingers through my hair, a nervous and unavoidable response. *Oh my God, this is so embarrassing.* I think I heard him chuckle, but I closed my eyes so I couldn't see if he was smiling. *I* was smiling awkwardly of course, my nerves getting the best of me.

When I opened my eyes again, he was standing right in front of me. I gasped. With the height of the window and the slant of the lawn, I was eye level with his waist. *Oh my God.*

Standing this close to him—*in only a towel*—I was so embarrassed and feeling so awkward. I knew my cheeks must have been crimson, and I was tempted to run away right that very instant. *What was I thinking coming over here in the middle of the night!?*

I should leave.

Instead of leaving though, which would have been the responsible thing to do, I found myself slowly looking up at him, his smile making my stomach flutter uncontrollably. He reached out for me and helped me climb inside.

I should leave.

Before my feet were even on the ground, his lips were on mine, and the fresh scent of his clean skin overwhelmed my senses, bringing that welcomed warmth back to my veins. Before long, I was right back to tangling my hands in his hair and kissing him hungrily, as if the interruption earlier hadn't even happened.

Damn. Clearly, I have zero self-control.

"Well, this is a surprise," he said when he stopped kissing me to take a breath.

I didn't respond. *Couldn't* respond. Tongue-tied was an understatement.

I slid my hands down from his hair, feeling the curve of his shoulders, the muscles in his chest, the strength of his arms. Suddenly *very* brave, I traced my fingers along his tattoo, the bottom feathers of the angel wing dipping below his left nipple, and the three tips of the lines of the dark tribal design stretching up over his shoulder. He was unlike anyone I'd ever seen—not that I had much to compare to—and I just couldn't fight the urge to run my hands all over his skin.

He stood perfectly still, watching me study him, his breath catching when I ran my fingers over certain more sensitive areas.

He led me to his bed, easing me down on my back, and slowly lay down beside me. His towel remained on—*thank goodness*—because I didn't know if a red exists that would be able to describe the color of my face if he were to strip down before my eyes. I was barely keeping it together as it was. I could have busted up laughing from my crazy nerves any second.

The kissing resumed, softly at first, his lips and tongue teasing mine in that sexy way of his. His legs stretched out around me, one of them nestling firmly between mine. His hands left my face, and he ran them over my body, slowly and firmly feeling every inch of me.

I was *so* nervous . . . but so *completely* excited. I was a jumble of emotions. I felt so *ready* to be with Toby, but I was terrified at the same time. What if I did something wrong? What if it hurt? What if I didn't like it?

Oh geez, what if he doesn't like it with me?

What if he breaks up with me again?

What about Frankie . . . ?

To shut off the millions of terrified questions in my head, I spoke. "Toby . . . I . . . I've never . . . ."

"Shh. It's okay, babe." He smiled a reassuring smile. "I'm perfectly happy doing exactly what we're doing right now." To make his point, he kissed me again, pulling me closer.

Then he sat up, leaning back to look at me. My heart kept skipping beat after beat as I watched his eyes roam over me. My arms instinctively moved to tug my shirt down over my belly, and my cheeks flared up bright-red from embarrassment. I'd never had anyone just *look* at me like that before.

"You have absolutely *nothing* to be embarrassed about, Ever."

He smiled appreciatively and took both my hands in his, kissing the tops of my knuckles one by one before laying my hands back down at my sides. He leaned down and, starting with my shoulder, left a trail of kisses all the way across my collarbone to the other shoulder. He brought his face down further, lifting up the hem of my shirt just enough to expose my belly, and resumed his kisses, dropping them randomly on my rib bones, then my belly button, and then stopping right at the top of my shorts. I shivered with each one, goose bumps covering my body and embarrassment over my exposed stomach making me blush. With the last kiss—the kiss closest to the uncharted area beneath my clothes—I giggled from both nervousness and because it tickled. He ran a finger lightly across my lower belly, tracing the line of my shorts from hip to hip. I silently cursed my stupid aversion to sit-ups.

He brought his face back to mine and kissed me gently once more.

"I'm glad you surprised me."

I had worried that he would want to push the sex issue, but he just lay down on his side next to me, curling me into him 'til my back was pressed tightly into the curve of his body. He reached past me and turned off the light on his desk.

"Sweet dreams, love."

We lay like that for a while. I found comfort in the feel of his body wrapped around mine, and the knowledge of having him back in my life. The past month would need to be discussed, I knew that, but for now, I was happy to leave it alone. Being near him was all I'd wanted for the past month, and there he was. *Finally.* His pillow smelled just like him, and I was overwhelmed with the happiness that being with him brought me. I dozed off in his arms, breathing in the scent of him and listening to his breath near my ear.

When I awoke from my nightmare, Toby was propped up, peering into my face and rubbing the sweat-matted hair away from my eyes. I turned onto my back to look at him, confused and disoriented.

Blood everywhere. So much blood.

Once again, I remembered only all the blood and fear, nothing else carrying with me from the dream but my concern for Frankie's safety. *Frankie!* My gaze quickly darted around the room, looking for him, and I realized I wasn't *in* my room.

"Shh, babe. I'm here. It was just a bad dream."

I was still at Toby's house. The sky outside his window was a dark purple—the color of early dawn.

"Shoot! What time is it?"

"Almost four."

I decided I should hurry back to my room before my mom figured out I'd been gone. Toby put his arms around me and nuzzled his face into the crook of my neck. His closeness slowly eased me out of my nightmarish world, his body comforting mine.

He held me and comforted me in a way Frankie never could, but it still wasn't as comforting as seeing Frankie would have been.

"I don't want you to go," Toby said, as he left a trail of kisses just underneath my chin from ear to ear.

"So, come with me." *Oh! Where had that come from?* The look on his face told me it was too late to take the words back. I averted my eyes so Toby could throw on some flannel pajama pants, and we quietly snuck back across the yards and into my room.

As soon as we were inside, I opened my door to listen for any noise coming from the rest of the house. It seemed quiet enough—as it should at that time of morning—so I closed the door and turned back around only to have the life scared out of me when I came face to face with a *very* angry ghost.

Frankie stood directly in between Toby and me, pure disgust clear on his face.

I was completely devastated by the situation and totally confused as to how to explain Frankie to Toby.

Worse than that, how would I explain *Toby* to *Frankie?*

"Shit," I whispered.

Toby heard me and came to stand next to me, walking *through* Frankie in the process. I realized that Toby couldn't see Frankie. Somehow, Frankie was invisible to Toby. I didn't understand it, not even the slightest bit, but that part was irrelevant.

Why Toby couldn't see Frankie didn't matter.

Because Frankie could see *Toby.*

The initial shock of seeing Frankie there quickly turned to embarrassment as I realized what he must have thought of me. I had two guys in my room, and I was pretty sure I had just seriously damaged my relationship with one of them.

I suddenly felt embarrassed and ashamed, and my heart broke as I watched Frankie disappear from the room, his disgusted expression slowly replaced with one of pain.

"Oh, god."

"Hey, what's wrong? Come here." Toby pulled me over to the bed with him, covering us both with my blankets, then kissed me gently on the forehead. "Are you still upset about your nightmare? It was only a dream, Ev. Why don't you try to get a little more sleep?"

If he only knew. I wish it had been only a dream. The nightmare I had already forgotten—as always—but the look on Frankie's face . . . the look on Frankie's face I would *never* forget.

Toby fell right back into a deep sleep, his arms cocooned around me. I couldn't go back to sleep after that, however, and I lay there in Toby's arms, listening to his breathing, torn between my feelings for him and my feelings for Frankie.

There was no denying how much I had fallen for Toby and how much I should have been enjoying this time with him—the closeness of his body next to mine, the warmth of his breath on my neck as he slept. I should have been in heaven. It was everything I'd been wishing about for the past month. Toby was back. And he *loved* me.

But it was clear, now, that Frankie loved me too.

Somewhere along the way, Frankie's feelings had grown to mirror my own, and just because we couldn't actually *act* upon those feelings didn't make them any less real or any less painful. I knew that without a doubt. I'd lived it.

I had broken his heart tonight, breaking pieces of my own in the process.

I would never forget the look on his face.

As I lay in Toby's arms, I watched the clock tick off the minutes through the early morning. 4:13, 4:14, 4:15 . . . 4:57, 4:58, 4:59 . . . when I finally woke up, it was 7:54, and I was alone in my bed.

The little sleep I had helped my mind make sense of what happened. I loved Frankie, and probably always would, but no matter what we felt for each other, whether one-sided or mutual, we'd never be together. I sighed and rolled over, wishing Toby was still lying with me.

When the phone on my desk rang, I jumped out of bed. *Who's calling this early?* I picked it up, said hello, and smiled broadly when I heard who it was.

"Hey, babe."

"Hey. Where'd you go?"

"I didn't want to be there when your mom woke up. I tried to wake you, but you were out, so I let you sleep. I'm sorry."

"It's okay. Was I snoring?"

"No," he answered way too quickly and then laughed.

Damn. I'd for sure been snoring.

"Meet me outside at nine?"

"Sure!" I answered. "Where're we going?'

"You'll see."

We hung up, and I sighed. A long, cheesy movie sigh.

Toby was back in my life. Everything was okay. I chose to move forward with Toby. I pushed everything else aside and hoped that my feelings for Frankie would eventually go away.

I got into the shower, refusing to think about him, but his face kept popping into my mind, breaking my thoughts into little fragments of nothingness that floated around his dejected expression. That expression would haunt me for a very long time.

By the time I was ready to meet Toby, my heart still ached for Frankie, but the concern was slowly being replaced by my excitement.

I was *finally* back together with Toby.

Eighteen

I checked on my mom a little before nine. She was sound asleep on the couch, still in yesterday's clothes. She must have fallen asleep there after she'd said goodnight to me. I had a quick pang of worry and contemplated staying to see if she needed me, but in remembering her words from last night, I stopped myself. She had made the decision to snap out of it, so instead of staying with her—and in turn *mothering* her—I left a note with Toby's cell number, adding that if she needed me, I would come back home right away.

I was relieved not to see Frankie on my way out of the house, not having the slightest clue what I would say to him. I knew I couldn't avoid him forever, but for the time being, I just wanted to enjoy my day with Toby.

Toby wasn't outside, but since it was so early on a Saturday morning, I didn't want to knock on the door in case his dad was still sleeping. I'd hate to get chewed out by *him* first thing in the morning. I walked over to the driveway and leaned against the passenger-side door of the Mustang.

"So. You want to play games, do you?"

At the sound of her voice, I turned around to see Toby's psycho ex—*Ariadne*—walking out the door of the house. Toby's house. *What the hell?* She was wearing a very skimpy navy-blue nightgown with ivory lace trim and lavender ribbon accents that I am *sure* would show her panties if even the slightest breeze kicked up. *If she's wearing any.* Was this seriously what she slept in while visiting her *ex*-boyfriend—and his *dad?*

Slut.

I couldn't help thinking it, but I didn't allow myself to say it out loud. I do have some restraint.

Instead, I said, "I'm sorry, *what?*"

"You heard me. You saw us together last night, *Ever*. You know I'm *with* Tobias. So if a game is what you're looking for, consider this your warning: I don't play well with others."

My initial reaction was one of hurt and doubt. Then it occurred to me where Toby had been all night.

"You don't play well with others, huh? That's a real shocker. Speaking of last night, Ariadne, where *did* Toby go after the party?"

Her mouth smacked shut and she glared at me, her silence being the only answer I needed. I'd struck a nerve.

That's what I thought. I guess I don't play well with others either. I smiled and looked down the street at the approaching figure walking our way.

He carried two huge Starbucks cups, and my heart skipped a beat at the sight of him. I wondered if I'd ever *not* get butterflies when I looked at him.

Ariadne turned her head in the direction I was looking and, following my gaze, noticed Toby coming down the street. He hadn't noticed her yet, as she was hidden in the shadows of the porch covering.

Lowering her voice so he wouldn't overhear her, she continued trying to intimidate me. "Look, little girl, you may be his plaything for now, but mark my words: he *will* leave you. And when he does, it will be *my* name on his lips." She lowered her voice even more, "And by the way, game *on*."

"Hey babe, sorry I'm late—" He stopped short when he saw her standing outside his front door, and his face went from an expression of pleasure to something dark. "Ariadne. What are you doing here?"

"Good morning, Tobias." She spoke with almost a purr and turned her sexy, pouty smile to him. I swear I saw her inch her nightie up to expose more of her long legs.

"I was coming out to get the newspaper"—a quick glance revealed there wasn't any newspaper in the driveway—"when I saw Ever here. We were just having a friendly chat. Right, hon?"

I rolled my eyes and shook my head, turning my attention to Toby.

"Yeah. I bet. *Go inside*, Ariadne. Pack your bags like I instructed you do last night and be gone by the time we get back."

He handed me my cup of coffee. "Good morning, Beautiful." With his free hand, he pulled my face to his and kissed me—a bit longer and more aggressively than I would have normally allowed with an audience nearby. But this wasn't a *normal* audience, was it?

"And get some god damned clothes on before the whole neighborhood sees you."

I knew I was blushing when I got in the car, but that kiss was amazing, and the sour look on Ariadne's face was priceless. Toby had obviously gone the extra mile playing up the kiss for her benefit, but hey, I sure wasn't suffering because of it.

"Well, that was quite the 'good morning.'"

"I'm so sorry, Ever. I don't know what that chick is thinking most of the time."

"I wasn't talking about Ariadne, Toby—though she's definitely a piece of work—I was talking about that kiss."

My cheeks blazed red again, even though I was the one who'd said the words.

"Oh, yeah? Well, there are plenty more where that came from."

As we pulled out of the driveway, Toby's dad walked outside and put his arm around Ariadne's shoulders. As he glared at me with that dark, menacing stare I'd seen before, I noticed how protectively he held Ariadne. It was almost fatherly. *Um, okay. If she's that close with Toby's dad, they must have been pretty serious.* My petty green monster reared its ugly head.

A few minutes later, when Toby's tension eased a little and we were stopped at a red light, he leaned over and kissed me again, just like he had before. *This* time the performance was all for me. The kiss helped me let go of some of those feelings of jealousy I'd been having toward Ariadne.

A honk from the annoyed driver behind us ruined the moment. The light had changed.

Blushing from the heat of his kiss, I ran my hand through my hair nervously.

"Ah, there it is. I've missed that."

"What?" Confused, I looked out the window, trying to locate what he was talking about.

"That." He grabbed my hand out of my hair and brought it to his lips. "I love the way you run your hand through your hair when you're nervous."

"Oh." More heat rushed to my cheeks.

"That, too." He pointed to my cheeks, making me blush even more. "*God* I've missed you."

He set my hand down on his thigh so he could shift gears, and we rode the rest of the way in happy silence. He occasionally picked my hand up to kiss my palm before setting it back to its resting spot on his leg. I was happier than I had been since my dad's death, the past month of being without Toby—and its cause—a distant memory.

We were driving down Ball Road, and I was about to ask him where we were headed, when he turned into the Disneyland parking structure. I was almost jumping up and down like a little kid by the time we parked and walked to the gate. I hadn't been to Disneyland in *years*. A big part of my childhood, Disneyland reminded me of all that I'd lost recently. Memories of my dad flooded my mind, and I felt a strong sense of longing at the thought of him. Shaking my head, I tucked the memories and sadness away. Dad would want me to have fun.

Once inside the park, I threw my arms around Toby's neck, kissing him and thanking him profusely. "Thank you, thank you, thank you!"

He laughed, kissed me back, then slowly removed my arms from their chokehold around his neck. He turned me around so my back pressed up against his chest, put his arms around my waist, and whispered in my ear.

"Happy Birthday, love."

"What? How did you—?"

He placed one hand on my jaw and turned my face to the side, where I saw Jessie and Greg approaching.

"Oh my God!"

I tore away from Toby and ran to Jessie. She was wearing a brand new, bright pink Minnie Mouse t-shirt that was about three sizes too small—which was doing remarkable things for her figure. Only Jessie could pull off sexy while wearing a little kid's shirt. She grinned from ear to ear. Greg had one of those strange, tense expressions again as he approached us. I looked at Toby and saw that his smile was a bit forced now that Greg was there. *What is the deal with these two?* I knew I had to get to the bottom of it, but now wasn't the time. *Later,* I told myself. For now, I was just going to enjoy today. My birthday.

"Happy Birthday, Ever!" Jessie threw her arms around me, lifting me up in the air an inch or two off the ground. "Are you surprised?"

"Um, yeah, I think it's pretty safe to say I'm surprised! When did you guys plan this?"

"Oh, you'll never believe it! Toby here was at Greg's door at seven this morning! He told us all about what a *huge* mistake this past month has been. I told you he'd regret that! Then he told us what a huge *bitch* that chick from last night is—the understatement of the year—and well, I might have let it slip that it was your birthday, and"—she waved her arms out to show our surroundings—"here we are!"

"This is perfect, you guys!"

"You're not mad? I know you'd mentioned not wanting to celebrate this year . . . ."

"No, Jess, this is perfect. Honestly." I squeezed her hand reassuringly.

Greg picked me up in a huge bear hug, a genuine smile on his face as he wished me Happy Birthday. He took Jessie's hand and said, "Well, Ev, you're the birthday girl; lead the way."

The park was crowded, it being a Saturday in the middle of summer, but we grabbed Fast Passes as often as possible, which helped us bypass some of the worst of the lines, and somehow, we managed to get onto just about all of my favorite rides.

When we were somewhat alone in the Haunted Mansion, concealed by the walls of our buggy seat, Toby pulled me close to him and kissed me. I felt that same amazing buzzing feeling I always felt with him, and I once again thanked my lucky stars that he was back in my life and that he was *mine*. I couldn't fight the grin slowly pulling at my lips.

"What are you smiling about?" He leaned back a few inches from my face, trying to see me in the darkness of the ride.

"I'm just glad you're back."

"I should have never left. I love you, Ever. I won't leave you again."

I kissed him again, unable to return his words. Something in me held back. I hoped he didn't realize I hadn't said it back to him. I just wasn't ready yet.

And no one needed to know my heart was torn.

When we came to the last part of the ride, and a ghostly apparition was projected into our buggy, I couldn't help but think of Frankie again. Well, truth be told, I had thought of him quite a few times during the ride—the irony of its theme not lost on me.

As right as I felt when I was with Toby, and as happy as I was that he was back, I wondered if the part of me that loved Frankie would ever be able to truly love Toby.

If not, would I ever be completely happy?

I didn't have long to ponder that question before Toby grabbed my hand and pulled me onto the moving platform, Jessie and Greg following behind us. We exited the ride, quickly moving to the next, only stopping to listen to a jazz band in New Orleans Square.

As far as birthdays go, it turned out to be one of my better ones. I had a blast; though, spending the day at Disneyland had its bittersweet moments as well. At one point, I was struck with emotion when I saw a little girl on her daddy's shoulders. They were so happy, and I couldn't help but think about my dad and all the times he'd taken me to Disneyland in my childhood.

But I knew life would always have those bittersweet moments now that my dad was gone, and I had to get through them without falling apart. With a reassuring squeeze of my hand, I was reminded now that I had Toby back, I'd be okay.

After a long and exhausting day at the park, followed by dinner at a bread company in Downtown Disney, we pulled into Toby's driveway around eight. Jessie planned on spending the night at my house, so she and Greg followed behind us in Greg's ridiculous yellow hummer, parking at the curb.

The windows revealed the inside of my house was dark, so I figured my mom was either feeling depressed again and hiding away from the world under the covers in her bedroom, or she was down the street at Sharon's. I knew my mom's decision to snap out of it would take time, and I could be patient with her for as long as she needed. I had only known Toby for a short time when we'd broken up, and I had been devastated without him—I couldn't imagine what my mom must have felt after losing her soul mate.

Toby and Greg parked the cars and walked Jess and me to the door to say goodnight. I barely had the key in the lock when my mom threw open the door and yelled "Surprise!"

Oh no.

She hadn't done anything like this since my tenth birthday, and that time I'd been just as thrilled.

Nineteen

Now, when I said 'surprise party' I mean some colorful balloons, a few streamers here and there, and my mom standing in the middle of the living room with her friends, Sharon and Bonnie. I was willing to bet I could blame one of them for this little idea.

Except that I already knew who to blame.

"Jessie."

"Don't be mad, Ever. It wasn't me, I swear."

With Toby's hand in mine, I walked into my house, bracing myself for whatever was in store. If I was lucky, it would all be over shortly so I could get to bed. If they were lucky, I'd somehow manage to stay awake for the whole thing.

When the door closed though, I knew I was wrong: there would be absolutely *no* luck tonight. Toby's hand tightened around mine as our eyes simultaneously took in the other person in attendance. Off to the side of the room, previously blocked by the open front door, stood—

"What in God's name is *she* doing here?" Jessie practically spat the words into my ear.

Ariadne was in my living room. Inside *my* house.

"Oh, honey, are you surprised? Come in. Come in! Hey, Jessie! How was your day? Did you kids have a nice time? What did you go on . . . ?" My mom rambled on and on, more animated than I'd seen her in a long time. Either she had really taken recovery to a whole new level, or she'd completely lost her mind. I didn't know what to say.

Yes. I am definitely very surprised.

I just stared at Ariadne, our eyes locked in a battle that would make even the best staring contest champions jealous.

All four of us stood in the open doorway. I didn't know if they were all as tense as I was, but I was completely shocked, and my body was rigid.

What the hell is Ariadne doing in my house?

". . . and this is . . . well, Toby, you already know her, obviously, but, Ever . . . Ev? Honey? Come in! Why are you still standing by the door?"

My mom walked over, ushering us inside so she could close the front door behind us.

"Did you hear me, honey? This is Toby's—what did you say you were? Cousins, right?—Aree—I'm sorry sweetheart, how do you pronounce your name again?"

"*Air-ee-add-knee,*" she said, pronouncing each syllable clearly for my Mom but never taking her eyes off me. Her grin was wicked at best.

Mom went to stand next to her, and the uncanny resemblance between the two of them struck me. Something wasn't right.

"Oh, yes, that's right; I'll get it. Did I tell you what a beautiful name that is? Ever? Why don't you sit down? You look like you've seen a ghost!" She giggled then, realizing the irony of her statement.

I wasn't laughing.

Toby snapped out of his shock before I did and managed to pull me over to the couch. I plopped down, and he sat down beside me, never letting go of his death grip on my hand.

Jessie and Greg sat down on the loveseat across from us, and though Greg looked tense—again making me question if there was any coincidence I was missing here—Jessie looked downright evil. She was not pleased to see Ariadne in my house, and man oh man, if looks could kill.

"Jessie? Want to help me with the cake?" Jessie tore her eyes from Ariadne and reluctantly followed my mom, Sharon, and Bonnie to the kitchen, shooting an accusatory glance at Toby on her way.

I looked over at him and whispered, "What the *hell* is going on here?"

He shook his head, his eyes dark with anger. A muscle twitched in his jaw. "I don't know, but I intend to find out." He looked at Ariadne, disdain in his eyes.

"What the *hell* is this, Ariadne?"

Ariadne hadn't moved from her spot in the corner yet, but when Toby addressed her, she smiled a sly, sultry smile, and slowly walked toward us. She had on a black mini dress—if you could call it a dress—with an overlay of black sheer fabric hanging to the floor. *She didn't have to get dressed up on my account.* The sheer fabric caressed every curve of her body as she walked, and she took her time, deliberately giving Toby and Greg a show. As she approached, I saw the tip of a tattoo sticking out above her low-cut dress, thick black lines that were strangely familiar. I tensed up even more, reaching into the back of my mind for the bit of information I was having trouble grasping. Toby put his arm around my shoulders and pulled me close to him in response to her approach. There was something about her tattoo. . . .

Before Ariadne could answer Toby's earlier question, or I could demand to see if her tattoo was what I thought it was, a loud crash came from the kitchen, accompanied by a scream from my Mom. I ran into the kitchen with Toby right behind me, vaguely registering Ariadne's words behind us.

"Ooh!" she squealed with delight, "I think your mother just found your birthday present."

I took in the scene in the kitchen with a quick sweep of my eyes, before I realized the cause of my mother's scream.

Sharon and Bonnie were standing by the sink with matching looks of confusion on their faces, startled by my mom's scream more than anything else. My mom stood by the dining table, her hands covering her mouth as if holding in the rest of her screaming. Jessie stood next to her, gripping the back of one of the wooden chairs. Her knuckles were white, and her mouth was open in shock. My birthday cake and my mom's favorite cake plate lay in a shattered mess on the floor.

My breath caught in my throat—a quick hiss of sound accompanying the intake.

My birthday present. Ariadne's words crept through my head.

"Oh my God."

Toby tried to grab me, but I was quickly out of his reach, making my way to the other side of the room.

Standing in the hallway to the kitchen was Frankie.

But not in ghost form.

He was solid, real, *whole*. I saw all the definition in his face. I saw my reflection in his black framed glasses once again. His dark hair was shiny, the perfect comb lines visible and defined in his pompadour. Things that had been translucent and fuzzy for so long were suddenly clear and *tangible* again. His eyes met mine as I approached him slowly, cautiously, like one might approach a wild animal.

"Hey, Dollface."

"Frankie." It came out barely a whisper.

Frankie's eyes quickly darted behind me, and his face tightened. I turned to follow his gaze as Ariadne slowly walked into the room. She sashayed her way past Toby, stepping over the mess of birthday cake on the floor. She stopped next to Frankie, lacing her fingers through his. I heard Jessie gasp behind me.

Why is she touching him?

My thoughts were wild and frantic, trying to make sense of the situation in front of me but unable to believe it—even though I was seeing it with my own eyes.

I looked from Frankie to Ariadne, then down at their entwined hands.

This isn't happening.

I shook my head and looked back up at Ariadne, who had cocked her head condescendingly and now watched me with bitter amusement on her face.

"Happy Birthday, Ever."

And then she kissed him. Frankie. *My* Frankie.

Everything went black.

Two sets of arms reached out to catch me.

Toby's arms.

And Frankie's.

Twenty

E ver! Ever! Wake up!"

I opened my eyes, and Jessie's face was all I could see. She hovered over me, eyes wide with worry. A cold washcloth was pressed to my forehead, and I was lying on something cold and hard.

"Jess, I'm awake, I'm awake. Stop shaking me." I took a quick look around to get my bearings. I was still in the kitchen, and the cold, hard thing I was lying on was the kitchen floor.

"Oh, geez. I passed out?"

"Um, yeah, I'd say so! Are you okay?"

"Yeah, I guess so . . . what happened?"

She made a face, her mouth pinched in concentration, trying to figure out what to say. And then, I remembered. *Oh, god. Frankie. Real, solid, alive. Ariadne kissing him.* My stomach turned over. But wait . . . maybe I'd been dreaming that part. Maybe my birthday hadn't even happened yet.

"Jessie, what day is it? Where's Frankie?"

Jessie shook her head, probably still trying to make sense of the evening. "June fourth, Ev. It's still your birthday."

Oh. So much for that idea. It hasn't been a dream after all.

"Frankie's in the living room with Toby and Greg . . . and that bitch Ari—"

Jessie stopped mid-sentence as we heard the voices carry in from the living room. We stared at each other as we listened.

"But I did this for you!" Ariadne shrieked.

"*Me?* You did this for *me?* What the *hell* is *wrong* with you, Ariadne?"

I held my breath as I listened, the anger in Toby's voice something I'd never heard. Not even when he was fighting with his dad that day.

"I thought you'd be happy, Tobias. I thought you'd be pleased." Her voice was meek—not the confident purr she usually carried— and it sounded like she might even be crying. *Good.* I couldn't help but feel good about that, even though I knew I should never find pleasure in someone else's pain. But boy did she have it coming!

"Happy?" Toby spat, disdain lacing his words. "You think I'm *happy* that you've done this? What you've done to Ever . . . to my *girlfriend* . . . this makes me far from happy, Ariadne."

"But, now we can be together." She sounded timid and unsure, like a scared little girl.

Together? What is she talking about?

Greg was speaking to someone in the background, and I briefly wondered if it was Frankie. "Yeah, you need to get over here right away. Yeah, she's here. But get here quick—Toby's about to kill her."

He said goodbye, and I realized he must have been on his cell phone.

"This is some pretty messed up shit, Ariadne." Greg spoke with a combination of disgust and anger. "Even for you. The ramifications of this . . . shit . . . I don't even know."

So they do all know each other. I knew it.

Just a few short seconds later, the front door opened and my eyebrows rose, mimicking Jessie's questioning expression. We shot up off the ground, anxious to see who else was coming into my house, the sudden movement making me dizzy. My head pounded, and I leaned on Jessie for support, still weak from passing out. We stood still for a second while the fogginess cleared from my head. I had to see what was going on with my own eyes. I had to see Toby. I had to see Frankie again.

And I seriously needed to punch Ariadne.

We quickly made our way into the living room, just in time to hear the door slamming shut once again. Only the three guys remained, so punching Ariadne would have to wait. *Damn.* Greg stood off to the side of the entertainment center, arms crossed, and Frankie sat next to Toby on the couch.

Frankie. Is. Sitting. Next. To. Toby.

I had trouble processing that part. My boyfriend and my biggest secret . . . sitting next to each other in my living room. It was all too surreal.

"*Where* did she go?" I demanded, my fists clenched and ready to fire.

At the sound of my voice, Toby and Frankie both leapt up to come toward me. Frankie stopped midway as if only then realizing Toby was my boyfriend, not him, and Toby was responding as such.

"She's not here, babe. She just left with Ted."

Toby took me from Jessie and walked me to the couch, sitting down beside me. Jessie sat down across from me on the loveseat she'd been sitting on with Greg earlier. As I watched her stare at Frankie, a mix of horror and wonder on her face, I noticed a thin veil of sweat on her skin. She was pale. I hadn't noticed it before because I was so out of it after fainting . . . and too focused on the conversation in the living room. The perspiration, combined with her blank expression, told me that she was clearly as shocked as I was by the situation, possibly even more so. She tucked her legs up underneath her and absently played with a loose thread in one of the decorative throw pillows.

"Frankie?" I had to talk to Frankie. I'd worry about Jessie in a minute.

Frankie still stood halfway between the couch and the kitchen, but when I said his name, he came forward, stopping directly in front of me.

"Hey, Doll." He was calm. The understanding I saw in his eyes alarmed me. He didn't seem shocked by any of this.

I stood and reached out to him, tentatively at first. I touched his face. He closed his eyes and sighed softly as I traced the lines of his cheek and jaw with my fingertips. *He's real. Frankie is real again.* It was . . . it was just too much to believe. Suddenly our arms were around each other, holding tightly. I was scared to let him go, scared to find out it was all a dream. My Frankie was finally real again. Without hesitation, he pulled me even closer, ignoring the people around us— and the fact my boyfriend was among them. With his face in my hair, Frankie breathed me in, inhaling the scent of me as if he had to use all of his senses to greet me. I knew the feeling.

"What's happened?"

Frankie pulled away and glanced to Toby. They both said nothing, instantly irritating me. This was no time for them to be tongue-tied.

"Toby? One of you has to explain. I don't know what's going on here," I tried to muster a stern, demanding tone, "but we have a right to know. So I don't care which one of you it is, but someone is going to tell us what the *hell* is going on."

Frankie looked at Toby again, his repeated looks for approval telling me Toby was at the bottom of this. I turned to him as well, searching his eyes for any indication that he would tell me the truth. I knew he *had* to know what was going on. The question was: would he tell me?

It was a shock when it wasn't Toby or Frankie who spoke, but Greg.

"Where to start. Okay, well, Jess, I know you're going to be mad, but—"

213

"Greg?" Jessie's voice was small, timid, and her eyes were closed. "Please, don't. It's obviously bad, so just . . . just don't say it." She shook her head, and I saw that she'd decided she didn't want to know.

I watched Jessie fall apart before my eyes, and it angered me.

Greg walked over to us and stood at the end of the coffee table. He threw his arms up in surrender. "Look, this is not how any of this was supposed to happen, Jess, but we're here now, so let's all agree to be open-minded, okay?"

"Open-minded!" I shot up to my feet, angered by the relaxed way Greg acted, angered by the detached look in Jessie's eyes and the silence coming from Toby and Frankie, when we *clearly* deserved answers.

"What *exactly* do we need to be *open-minded* about, huh, Greg? Or should I call you *Gregor?*"

It was a shot in the dark, sort of, but when Greg's face paled, I knew I'd hit the nail on the head with my assumption. There *was* some sort of correlation between this Greg—the Greg who dated my best friend—and the Gregor who I overheard Toby and Ted talking about.

Toby stood then, taking my hand and turning to face me. He looked at me sweetly . . . almost *condescendingly.*

"Babe? Why don't we go to your room? You should probably get some rest. It's been a long day. We can talk about all of this tomorrow."

I scoffed. *He can't be serious.*

"Don't patronize me, Toby. You can't just shoo-shoo me off to bed when you don't want to talk about something! I'm not eight-years old! I want to know what the *hell* is going on!" I paused, turning toward Frankie. "Frankie?"

"I'm sorry, Doll."

I gaped at them, my mouth open in shock. Had they lost their minds? There was so much to be discussed! Not only did my boyfriend and Jessie's boyfriend know each other—and had never even told us they did—but they both also knew about my ghost, and on that note, *he* wasn't even a *ghost* anymore! They thought sending me to bed was the answer? I felt like I'd woken up in a mental hospital!

Oh shit. Maybe I have.

"Jess?" I pleaded.

Jessie just sat there, eyes closed and her head barely shaking from side to side, as she tried to wrestle the events of the night into a neat little explanation. Like *that* was going to happen. I couldn't believe I was watching Jessie struggle with this so badly. She was the one person who had *always* argued on the side of *accepting* the possibilities of the existence of otherworldly beings. But turn one ghost back into a human and all hell breaks loose.

What am I saying?

Greg placed a hand on Jessie's shoulder. "I'll take Jessie home. Toby, we'll be back in the morning."

I was speechless. But only for a second.

"Oh, *hell* no. You're not taking her anywhere." I felt like I was the only one capable of making sense anymore, and then I realized my mom wasn't there. *She'll know what to do!*

"Wait a minute . . . where's my mom?"

At the mention of my mom's name, Jessie let out a little squeak of a whimper.

My stomach turned. I didn't want any more shocks tonight.

"Toby? Frankie? What's going on? Where's my mom? Where are Bonnie and Sharon?"

"They left after you . . . well, after you passed out, Doll." *Geez, how long had I been out?* "And your mom, well—" Frankie paused, clearly searching for the easiest way to say whatever he was about to say. I had a funny feeling it wasn't good, and his long pause proved me right.

Toby picked up where Frankie left off, direct and to the point as usual. "Your mom is in her room, Ev. She's having a hard time . . . coping."

Coping? Crap.

As I tried to process whatever the *heck* that meant, Greg helped Jessie off the loveseat and I watched them walk out the door, shaking my head in disbelief. Jessie was clearly in shock, and my mom was in her bedroom, hiding from the world again. Having trouble *coping.*

How was I the only one keeping it together?

Well, aside from the whole fainting thing, but I was past that.

Frankie mumbled something about going outside for a smoke, leaving Toby and me alone in the living room. I let go of Toby's hand and started heading down the hallway. When he followed me, I put a hand out to stop him and spoke without turning around to face him.

"No. I'm going to check on my mom."

"Okay, babe. I'll be here when you get back," he said, and I heard the couch squeak when he sat back down. I had the strongest urge to tell him *not* to be there when I returned, but I bit my tongue. I continued down the hall to my mom's room, wondering what I would find.

The lights were off, but the soft glow of the hall light illuminated enough of the room that I could see a lump in her bedding. She was completely covered up, hiding from the situation just as I had imagined. I'd seen the behavior before. Just recently, in fact. We were right back to the dark, gloomy solitude of the past month, her momentary desire to *survive* gone in a flash. I sat down on the edge of the bed and realized she looked like she was probably in the fetal position. She'd slept like that often in the days since my dad had been gone—clutching tightly to his pillow or one of his favorite flannel shirts. I wondered briefly if that stuff even still smelled like him, and my heart pinched.

No time for that now.

I gently nudged the part of the lump I assumed to be my mom's shoulder.

"Mom?"

Light snoring answered me. I looked to the bedside table and saw her prescription bottle of Ambien. I sighed heavily. *Back to that again.*

She'd be dead to the world for at least another eight hours. I considered waking her, shaking her and *demanding* that she face this with me, but I couldn't do it. I briefly considered taking a few of her *Mommy's Little Helpers* but I couldn't do that either.

We'd talk tomorrow. Maybe she'd be ready to *cope* after a good night's sleep.

I hoped.

I didn't want to spend another minute in my mom's dark cocoon of a room. I already felt like I was suffocating, and I'd only been in there for a few minutes. I quickly headed back to the front of the house, frustrated that I couldn't do anything to help my mom.

Toby stood as he saw me enter, coming toward me with open arms. I looked up at him, wondering if I could really be with someone who could cause this much chaos in my life, and my tears silently streamed from my eyes. My throat tightened, and my chest pounded. I felt like I couldn't draw in a breath.

I inhaled, but my lungs didn't expand like I needed them to.

I ran past him, desperate to get outside, desperate to fill my lungs with fresh air.

I flew out the front door, gulping in the cool night air, suddenly unable to get enough of it. I was *thirsty* for it. I inhaled and exhaled, over and over, until I was feeling lightheaded. Toby came up behind me and closed his arms around me, pulling me into a tight embrace.

"I'm so sorry, Ever," he whispered into my hair. "I never intended any of this to happen."

And with *that*, I was reminded that we had so *very* much to discuss.

I pushed out of his arms, turning around to face him. I wiped my tears, resolved to be strong and face this situation head on, even if my mom and Jessie couldn't. Or maybe *because* they couldn't.

"Yes. About that. What *did* you intend exactly?"

I sat on the edge of the stoop and waited.

Toby closed the front door, then sat next to me. The closeness made my skin burn to touch him, but I ignored it. I had a strange feeling in my gut telling me *that* part of our relationship was gone.

He put his elbows on his knees and his head in his hands. "Okay. I have to tell you something."

"No shit, really?" I said, sarcasm the only emotion I had a solid hold on.

He turned and looked at me with his eyebrows raised.

"Sorry. By all means, *do tell.*" I waved my hand, signaling him to continue, my polite words tainted with more sarcasm. But hey, what could he really expect from me?

"Okay, well, you know how I told you I was a collector of sorts?"

"Yeah, antiques, not for eBay, I get it. But what does that have to do with—?"

He put his hand out as if to stop me and continued, reaching for me in the process. I yanked away from him, and his hand stayed extended in mid-air for a few long seconds before he tucked it back under his chin.

"Please, just give me a minute; I've never told anyone this before . . . okay, look . . . I lied to you, Ever. I *do* work with Ted, I mean, my dad . . . well shit. Okay. He's not really my dad. I want to be honest with you, Ever, I do . . . but . . . well . . . we aren't in antiques."

There was something off about the tone of his voice, and I could tell he struggled with what he was saying. He was always so smooth and confident when he spoke, so hearing this new hesitation from him unnerved me. He paused to find the right words.

"Okay, here goes. I . . . well, *we* . . . we're . . . soul collectors."

Oh, okay. What? "*What* did you just say?"

It took everything I had in me to stay sitting next to him when all I want to do was get away from him. *I didn't just hear that, did I?* This couldn't be happening. I was cursed. I'd cared about two guys in all my life. One of them is—*was*—dead, and the other turned out to be a psychopath. Of course. Toby was a total nutcase. A dreamy and beautiful nutcase, yes, but I had to look past that part and focus on the craziness.

"I know this is a lot to take in, and this is not how I planned on telling you—*at all*—but after what Ariadne has done . . . well, you have a right to know." He paused, taking a deep breath and turning to look at me before he continued. "I'm a soul collector, though *collector* isn't quite the right word. We're more like guides. I find souls that are lost—or misguided—and help them find their way; though, it's not as simple as that. I didn't start out this way . . . ."

I don't know if I heard the rest of what he said. Maybe the information registered somewhere deep down in my subconscious, but he'd pretty much lost me with those first few words.

Soul Collectors?

I sat there staring at him, eyes wide and jaw open in disbelief. My thoughts screamed wildly through my head.

What the hell is he talking about?

I must have hit my head on something when I passed out earlier . . . .

I'm obviously hallucinating.

Soul Collectors?

Yes, hallucinations had to be the culprit. Or I was actually *still* passed out on the kitchen floor. I sure as heck didn't want to believe that my boyfriend was a psychopath. *Or a soul collector.* No, neither of those would do. When I found my voice, as soft and muted as it was, I asked the first question that came to my mind.

"Are you even from Montana?"

He just looked at me.

Seriously? Of all the things to ask him, *that's* what I came up with?

"No. I'm originally from Seattle. That's where I was raised, at least."

Seattle. Huh. "So you lied when you said you'd never seen the ocean?"

He raised his eyebrows at me before nodding his head, clearly surprised by my silly questions when something much more serious was going on. I was surprising even myself, but hey, I could only process so much craziness at a time.

Oh, wait. This has to be just another one of my nightmares. I desperately hoped I wouldn't remember this one. I'd take bloody nightmares any day over my whole world being flipped upside down.

Only one thing to do then . . . I pinched myself. *Ouch!*

"What are you doing?"

"Oh, nothing. Just pinching myself."

I pinched myself again. *Ouch!* "It's not working."

"I know. It's because you're not dreaming, Ever. I know this is hard to understand, but *you* more than *anyone* should be able to be open-minded about this."

"*Open-minded?*" I screeched at him, "Did you really just say that, too!? Is that all you guys can say? As if it isn't weird enough that my boyfriend just told me he's a freaking soul collector, now he wants me to be *open-minded?*"

I jumped up to get away from Toby, but he stood almost as quickly and grabbed my arms at the elbows, holding me in front of him. He turned me to face him. I looked straight ahead, instead of at his eyes, anywhere but those blue eyes. He let go of one of my arms, and with his free hand, he turned my chin toward his face, forcing me to meet his gaze. I closed my eyes.

"Look at me."

I straightened my back and squared my shoulders, trying to give the illusion that I meant business. I tightened my closed eyelids. All the while, it felt like little pieces of me were breaking apart inside. His hand on my face still made me weak, the warmth and closeness of our bodies sending my body signals I didn't want to receive. Either someone was playing a really screwed up joke on me or this was all true.

Truth or not, I did *not* want to end up in the fetal position like my mom. No way.

"Look at me, Ever."

I opened my eyes to his sapphire gaze. As he stared at me, I frantically searched his face for any indication that he was joking—or lying—or anything.

But he wasn't.

He was as serious as I'd ever seen him. I looked longer, searched harder, waiting for a smile to crack his serious expression. But it didn't.

"Please, Ever. I didn't want to tell you like this, I swear. But now that you know . . ."

Something strange happened. It was like everything sort of fell into place in my head. Something inside me actually *believed* him, as crazy as that was. That same something inside me started to carefully put the pieces together—the little things I'd ignored along the way.

The strange conversation with his dad—I mean, Ted—about getting inside my house. I had pushed it aside, ignoring it because I just wanted to be with Toby.

The fact that he knew my dad was dead, before we had even seen the accident. Impossible. No matter *how* you looked at it.

Frankie no longer in ghost form. More than impossible, but I'd seen it with my own eyes.

"Are you . . . are you even . . . ?" I couldn't say the word. I looked down at the arms holding me. I couldn't ask. I *should* ask, but . . . I couldn't find the strength to do so.

"Human?"

Shit. He said the word I was trying to ignore, quietly, as if he was also afraid of it. As if he was also afraid of the answer.

"Look at me."

Ugh. *Why does he keep making me look at him?* It's like he knew my defenses weakened when I looked into his eyes.

He took my hand and placed it on his chest. I knew the angel wing tattoo was right beneath my fingers, as was his beating heart. I could feel it, thumping away as quickly as mine was. I looked back up into his eyes. *A heartbeat.*

Human.

My boyfriend was a soul collector. The rational side of my brain tried to remind me that I didn't believe in soul collectors. But then, there had also been a point in my life when I hadn't believed in ghosts either. Speaking of ghosts . . . .

"Wait a minute. How long have you known about my ghost, Toby?"

He looked down at the ground, avoiding my eyes.

"It's why we moved here, Ever."

Oh. So it wasn't just a beautiful coincidence that he had moved in next door.

"Could you see him in my room last night?"

"Yes."

Oh.

"But, I couldn't do it. I know what you're thinking, Ev, but it's not what it seems. I didn't know how I would feel about you. I didn't know I would—"

"Wait. What are you saying . . . ?"

It hit me. *Oh, god.* Not only was his moving here no coincidence, but our entire relationship had been a lie. He didn't really love me after all.

He doesn't love me. It's not real. I'm just a foolish little girl, and he tricked me. He tricked me into loving him and letting him in . . . and it was all just to get to Frankie.

"Oh my god."

I pushed out of his grip and began pacing the length of the driveway. This was just too much to consider while standing still. And *way* too much to consider while his hands were touching me.

"Please, Ever, please, believe me. It wasn't supposed to be like this. I didn't know I would love you! I would have never agreed to come here!"

"Stop, Toby. *Please.*" I turned, coming back to stand in front of him, anger replacing the hurt. "What about Frankie?"

Toby shook his head. "It's . . . it's not . . . ."

"Stop. *What. About. Frankie?* Have you come for his soul?"

"Yes."

"Oh, god." I didn't know what to say. My world seemed to be spinning out of control right before my eyes. Frankie. *My Frankie.* In danger. His soul . . . .

"But wait. Then why is he *alive*, Toby?"

Toby bowed his head again, clearly troubled by what he had to tell me.

"Ever, Frankie was never *supposed* to be alive again. That's not the way it works. What Ariadne has done, it's . . . it's . . . unheard of. Unnatural. And it's *wrong*."

"What? What do you mean by *wrong*?"

"Ever, Ariadne warned me that she would do whatever it takes to get me back. She thinks she's *giving* you Frankie. She's just messed up enough to believe that this is a trade you would agree to."

"What?" It seemed to be the only word I could muster. My mind was spinning too fast for anything else. *A trade?*

"She thinks that if Frankie is alive, you'll choose him and I'll be free to be with her. Before Ted came to grab her earlier, she told me she'd done it for me. She doesn't care that it's not what *I* want. She doesn't care that I'm in love with *you*. She doesn't care that there will be repercussions for Frankie—"

Yeah, yeah, I'd heard all that. But . . . .

Repercussions?

"What?" I snapped. There it was again, the only word I could manage. "What do you mean when you say *repercussions*, Toby?"

He took my face in both of his hands, forcing me to look at him again, forcing me to look into those gorgeous blue eyes I loved so much.

I knew I didn't want to hear what was coming. I just knew it. *Felt* it even.

But I listened anyway. Always such a glutton for punishment.

"Ever, Frankie's soul belongs to Ariadne."

Twenty-One

I'm going to be sick—"

I pushed past Toby and ran into the house, making a beeline for the bathroom, then locking the door behind me. I could barely hear Toby's voice through the door, my heaves were so loud. I didn't even have time to be embarrassed that he could hear me retching; the pain of his betrayal and the shock from this new information about Frankie took center stage in my mind.

There were so many unanswered questions, and the scope of it all made me sicker.

"Go *away*, Toby!" I yelled, my voice echoing in the toilet bowl. I fumbled with the toilet paper, trying to grab some to wipe my face.

"Ever, I'm so sorry. Please, let me in. Please, talk to me."

"Leave!" I shouted between heaves.

Frankie's soul belongs to Ariadne. Toby's words were like a broken record playing in my head. *Frankie's soul. Ariadne.* The information was just too much for my body to handle. I vomited violently, worse than I could remember from even the most unforgiving stomach flu.

I don't believe in soul collectors.

Maybe if I said it enough times, it would stick.

I don't believe in soul collectors.

But who was I kidding? I'd lived with the reality that I shared my home with a *ghost* for the past two years—so was this realization really any different?

After emptying my stomach, and heaving a few more times just for good measure, I closed the lid and rested my head. The coolness of the ceramic was soothing on my cheek, so I ignored the fact that my head was resting on a toilet. I had been through far too much to care. I stared at the side of the faux wood-finished cabinet, without actually seeing it, until minutes later, when something caught my attention.

The tiny corner of a piece of paper was sticking out from between the cabinet and the trashcan. I reached for the paper and realization dawned on me. The library. The day I'd met Ariadne. *Ugh.* My stomach made a slight gurgling sound, and my mouth watered, but nothing else happened. Luckily, my stomach had nothing left to give. It had only been a few days, but I'd forgotten all about the book and the piece of paper. I'd chalked up Ariadne's appearance at the library to reconnaissance, the typical *new girlfriend doing an investigation of the ex-girlfriend* type thing. Everything happened so quickly since then, that I hadn't given it another thought. The paper must have fallen behind the trashcan when Jessie dumped the contents of my purse out that night.

I listened to the other side of the door, but it seemed Toby had finally given up. Maybe he'd gone home. I *hoped* he'd gone home. I needed time to process everything. Or just wallow in my confusion for a while. I unfolded the paper, assuming it was notes for a test or something else a library patron might leave behind.

I was *completely* unprepared for what I found on that neatly folded page. It wasn't notes at all.

It was an image, a drawing, black and bold, the thick lines clear and concise.

An angel's wing. But not just *any* angel's wing. It was an angel's wing with three thick, curved lines going through the center of it.

Toby's tattoo.

I gasped.

What the hell was going on? Things just kept getting more screwed up! Why was Toby's tattoo on a sheet of paper that had fallen out of a random library book?

I paused. *Random?*

Ariadne.

Oh. I knew without a doubt that there was probably *nothing* random or coincidental with Ariadne. Everything she did, she did with ulterior motives and precise purpose. I shook my head in disbelief. I've heard about crazy ex-girlfriends, but this had to take the cake.

I looked back down at the piece of paper with Toby's tattoo on it. Something was bothering me. Something I couldn't quite grab hold of yet. I stared at the image, urging the reluctant piece of the puzzle to fall into place, but nothing did. There was just a tickle in the back of my mind that wouldn't come forward, taunting me just out of reach. I wasn't fully connecting the dots.

Finally, exasperated and tired of sitting on the bathroom floor, I got to my feet and flung open the door, startling Toby, who had apparently been leaning against it. He hadn't left after all. He fell backward quickly, then righted himself and stood to face me.

"*What* is this?" I demanded, waving the piece of paper in his face.

He looked at the piece of paper in my hand, then back at me. He looked at the piece of paper again, and his eyebrows pinched together.

"Where did you get this?" He stared at it while speaking to me, as if expecting to get the answers from the paper itself.

"Are you *serious*? *Where* did I get it? Who cares, Toby! *What is it?*"

"It's my tattoo."

"Really? Wow, I hadn't figured that out at all! Seriously, Toby, answer me."

226

"We—"

Ah, there it was. *We.* I remembered the piece of the puzzle that had refused to fall into place. It finally settled in comfortably with the other pieces. And what a *screwed up* puzzle it was. I interrupted him before he could finish, my own thoughts bursting to get out.

"Ariadne has the same tattoo, doesn't she? In the same place even?"

"Yes."

"Wow." I felt like I'd been punched in the gut, and not because of the vomiting episode. What a fool I'd been! "She's more than just a silly ex-girlfriend, Toby. Nobody gets matching tattoos with someone they aren't serious about."

"No, Ever, it's not what you—"

"Oh, please. No more of the *it's not what you think* bit. And seriously, is this some sick attempt at angel of death humor?" *Gross,* I thought to myself. And so *not* funny. "Ugh, just go, Toby. Seriously. I need some time away from you."

It was pretty safe to say I did *not* want to hear his explanation, whatever it was.

I was so grossed out by the idea that he could have once been *that* serious—maybe even in *love*—with someone like Ariadne. How could he love someone like *her* . . . and then love someone like *me?* The thought bothered me to no end. I didn't want to look at him while I pondered what it said about *me.* Was I more like her than I realized?

But wait. Toby never really loved me. I reminded myself that our whole relationship had been a sham, and it didn't make me feel any better, but it did make me stop comparing myself to *her.*

"Go, Toby. Please."

I pushed past him and headed for the hallway.

He followed me to my room. "Please, Ever . . . please let me explain everything. There's so much you don't understand."

There's just something about someone telling me that I don't understand. It's got to be one of the most infuriating things in the world.

"Oh, *please*, Toby. I think I understand just fine. And if I don't, then let's just assume I don't want to understand *more*. Now *go*."

I shut the door in his face then turned on the TV, cranking up the volume to a painful level. I sat down on the bed, not sure of what to do next. Truthfully, I didn't understand at all. Not even a little bit. But the last thing I wanted to do was continue looking at Toby. I needed to think.

A little while later, I turned the TV down—I wasn't exaggerating; it actually *was* painfully loud—and as soon as I lowered the volume, I was startled by a knock on the door.

"Oh god, Toby! Go home! *Please!*"

"It's me."

Frankie. My heart jumped at the sound of his voice, and my breath caught in my throat.

So many feelings rushed to the surface. Love, happiness, confusion, fear . . . half of me wanted to throw open the door and fling myself into his arms, and the other half of me wanted to yell at him to leave me alone.

"Please, go, Frankie. I need some time to think."

Open the door. Let him in. Touch him. Hold him.

No.

I didn't do it. I needed to think, and I couldn't let anyone distract me. Not even Frankie.

Part of my brain cried out that I didn't know how much time I had with Frankie in his physical form, but the other half of my brain told me it didn't matter. I couldn't just continue behaving like a lovesick little girl. I had to figure out this mess.

I heard his forehead hit the door with a light thump. "Okay, Doll. I'll be . . . in the kitchen, I guess." His footsteps retreated down the hall, and my heart ached to be with him. But I stayed.

I pulled on my pajamas then sat down on the bed, intending to think. Even the best intentions can go to waste when you are as exhausted as I was, and I soon found myself drifting off to sleep. What a long, crazy day.

My birthday.

It was still my birthday. And what an eighteenth birthday it was. Adulthood welcomed me with quite a bang.

This was definitely one birthday I would never forget.

Twenty-Two

Falling.

I'm falling fast down a slick tunnel, wet with blood.

I reach out to grab for anything that can catch me, but my hands just slide down the wall, the blood smearing as I fall.

So much blood.

Now I'm in that white room again. Blinding, glaring whiteness surrounds me.

Nothing but whiteness. Except for all the red. The blood.

Frankie's blood.

I slowly make my way to the center of the room.

As I walk, painstakingly slow as if I'm trudging through quicksand, a figure appears in front of me. A beautiful, graceful figure.

A woman.

She is dressed in red, a long flowing frock clinging to her body. At her knees, it fans out like a mermaid's tail.

Who is she?

I walk further, closing in on her, trying to make her face come into focus.

Ariadne.

I stop. She's immediately in front of me, those yards previously between us gone in a heartbeat.

As I stand before her, I realize her gown isn't red at all.

It is white. Had *been white.*

White silk, ruined with blood.

So much blood.

She smiles and looks down at the source of all the blood.

"You can't save him, Ever." Toby's words, but Ariadne's voice. *"He is mine now."*

I follow her gaze.

Frankie.

When I woke up screaming, Frankie was there again. But this time, solid hands shook me awake. Solid, warm, *living* hands.

I opened my eyes, and Frankie's face was only a few inches above mine.

I threw my arms around his neck, terrified I was going to lose him, terror still gripping me from my dream world. As I held him, the fear didn't fade as it usually did upon waking. Instead, it grew as I quickly recapped what I'd just been through.

Frankie. In solid form.

Ariadne. Trying to win Toby back.

My mom. Dead to the world.

Toby. A soul collector.

Frankie. In solid form. Being this close to him—to a *solid* Frankie—was strange and unfamiliar. And yet, completely natural. I pulled back, my hands flopping down to the bed on either side of me. I felt awkward, as if hugging him was wrong, or I was overstepping some invisible line. We stared at each other for a few very long moments, and I watched as realization hit him.

The sudden closeness.

The possibilities.

A hungry intensity filled his eyes. I bit my lip, scared of what I might do if I didn't. My heart rate increased, and my thoughts raced. I actually *felt* his breath quicken with mine. I felt each of his quick exhalations on my face, his mouth just inches away from mine. The fear eased. The awkwardness ended. Something else filled me entirely.

Need.

He licked his lips and brought his hand up to my face. His thumb lightly brushed my bottom lip. I closed my eyes. My mouth parted on a quick intake of breath, and the impossible happened. He kissed me. A fevered, hungry kiss that sent shivers through my body. A kiss that I had told myself over and over again would never, *ever* happen. A kiss that had for so long been . . . *impossible.*

A kiss that was impossible no longer.

My lips ached with the pressure of his mouth, and my body screamed with joy. My arms ached to hold him, so I wrapped them around his neck once more, pulling him closer to me, reveling in a moment I'd waited so long for. It was almost too good to be true. A tear slid down my cheek.

He wrapped his arms around me in return, holding me the way he'd never been able to before, and my heart rate sped up even more, excitement filling me. He slowly crawled on top of me, his body crushing mine, the thin sheet between us. Everything I'd ever wanted was mine. Finally. He pulled back for a second, looking into my eyes, and then his mouth was back on mine. Electricity shot through me. Our tongues tasted each other, a caressing, playful game, and I didn't want to stop kissing Frankie for as long as I lived. I'd waited far too long for this moment.

He sat up, pulling away the sheet. He pulled his shirt up over his head, and my breathing picked up rapidly. His body was just as perfect as I remembered—lean with lightly defined muscles, his alabaster skin a beautiful contrast to his dark hair. I couldn't help myself—my hands had ached to touch him for years. They had no restraint now as they explored his chest and arms. He slowly lay down again, half on top of me, our legs tangling together, his body melding with mine like two halves of a whole.

Without the blanket between us, I felt the warmth of his skin where my tank top had slid up, exposing an inch or two of my stomach. It wasn't enough. I needed to feel more of him.

As if hearing my private thoughts, Frankie's hand slid down to my waist and up underneath my shirt. He didn't stop kissing me—never breaking contact with my mouth—assuring me that he'd waited as long as I had for this moment to happen. His hand slowly explored my chest, his touch eliciting sensations I'd never experienced. It had me both nervous and excited, those sensitive parts of me never having been touched before. He tugged at my shirt, and my arms lifted in response, acting on their own accord once more. Slowly, he slid my shirt up over my head. I'd never been this naked with anyone before, and yet, I was completely comfortable. I was not afraid. He looked at me like I was the most beautiful girl in the world. When he lay back down, our chests pressed together, and I reached up to hold him to me. We turned slightly, both of us now lying on our sides, pressed tightly together. This closeness, this heated moment, our bare skin touching . . . it was *everything* all at once. Happiness, fear, lust, love . . . .

"I love you."

I gasped. The words just came out of my mouth. I hadn't meant to say them. *Shit.* I'd ruined the moment. *What is wrong with me?*

His eyes widened ever so slightly, and he brought his mouth back down on mine. His kiss was even hungrier than before, if that was possible. He slid his hand down my body, settling on my hip. Tightening his grip on me, he pulled me closer. One of his legs slid between both of mine, and the pressure of it brought an intense heat to my body. The warm feeling started in my stomach and moved outward, inching its way through my veins. I was overwhelmed with the closeness of him, this guy I'd loved for my entire life.

He leaned away from me slightly, breaking our kiss long enough to look me in the eyes and smile that slightly crooked smile I adored.

"I love you, too, Doll. I've loved you since that day you fell out of my tree house."

"What?" The memory of that day flew to the front of my mind. I could picture it like it was yesterday. My cheeks flushed. "You laughed at me. You called me a baby."

"I was nine. What do you expect?"

"You love me?"

"More than I could ever put into words."

I couldn't help it. Tears streamed down my face, pooling on my pillow. He wiped them, but they didn't abate. *He loves me.* He resumed kissing me. My tears continued to slide silently down my cheeks— happy, relieved tears of absolute joy. I wrapped my arms around him once more and dove into his kiss. The skin-on-skin connection between our bodies was unlike anything I'd ever felt before. His kiss—the way it sent shivers and heat through my body simultaneously—was unlike any of the kisses I'd . . . .

Toby.

My mind whispered the name to me, my conscience determined to ruin my life. I tried to ignore it, but my heart pinched at the thought of him. This wasn't me. I wasn't *this* girl. I couldn't go any further with Frankie—no matter how long I'd wanted to, or how much I loved him—when I was still technically with Toby. Our relationship hadn't been real, I knew that now, but I could still be the better person.

Ugh.

Angry at my own conscience, but unable to ignore it any longer, I stopped the kiss, putting my arms between us and pushing Frankie back just a little.

His lips were red and flushed from the pressure of our mouths pressed together, his breathing coming fast and heavy. I wanted to kiss him again. I wanted to say *'to hell with right and wrong!'* I wanted to hold him forever, now that I finally could.

I'd wondered if he felt the same way for me all this time. I'd begun to think so, but now I had my answer. And it didn't matter. Not yet anyway. There was too much to figure out. I couldn't just rush into making out with Frankie and ignore all the things I'd learned in the past twenty-four hours. I couldn't ignore the fact that just last night I'd been in bed with Toby.

"It's him, isn't it?"

Damn. "Yes, Frankie. But it's not . . . it's not what you're thinking. It's . . . it's *all* of this. I just need some time to sort through everything."

He sat up and slid away from me, sitting a little further down on the bed, putting distance between us for reasons I imagine mirrored my own. The closer we were, the more we'd need to touch each other. The distance left my arms aching to hold him, but I restrained myself. I reached for my shirt then slid it back on, catching the slightest hint of a frown play at Frankie's lips.

"Okay," he said, and I knew he understood me as always, and that he'd be patient. He knew me better than anyone.

I looked at the clock. It was almost morning. I'd slept a few hours, and I knew I should sleep more but didn't think I could.

Picking up as if we hadn't just been half-naked together—a fact I found incredibly difficult to ignore with his lean chest still exposed— Frankie asked about my nightmare.

"Can you remember this dream, Doll?"

I nodded.

"Care to share?"

I wanted to. I did. But when I tried to form it into words inside my head, it sounded so crazy. First it was Toby who killed Frankie. Now it was a dream about Ariadne killing Frankie. It just didn't make sense. Especially now, when Ariadne had done the exact opposite of killing Frankie; Ariadne somehow *gave* him life. And aren't dreams supposed to be metaphorical? Weren't these just the silly conflicted nightmares of someone who was struggling with her feelings for two different guys? Like, subconsciously my mind was telling me that by being with Toby, I would lose Frankie.

It sounded pathetic in my head—or crazy—and I didn't want Frankie to think either of me.

I shook my head. I couldn't tell him.

He just nodded, always so understanding. It was time to change the subject.

"Frankie? What happened?"

I didn't have to clarify. It was the elephant in the room, after all. Frankie sighed and turned, both of us now sitting cross-legged on the bed and facing each other. He picked up a pillow and smoothed the creases on it, searching for the right words to begin. I had no idea what I would learn when he finally found the right words. Would he tell me how he met Ariadne? *When* he met Ariadne? Would he tell me how long he'd loved me?

"What has *he* told you?"

My stomach turned at the thought of repeating Toby's earlier admission, and since I hadn't eaten anything since last night's vomiting episode, the bile burned. I realized that maybe—just maybe—I didn't want to know quite yet. Maybe I just wanted to enjoy Frankie's presence a little while longer.

Maybe I was being a coward.

I had a strong feeling that learning the truth from Frankie, and soon learning more of the truth from Toby, would shake my world to its core. And I figured that could wait a little bit longer.

"Never mind, Frankie."

He looked up from his repetitive pillow smoothing.

"Can you just hold me for now? We can talk tomorrow."

He exhaled a relieved sigh. "Absolutely, Dollface. *Absolutely.*"

We lay down together, my back to his chest, and his body curled up around mine. His face was pressed into the top of my head, and I had the feeling he was breathing me in again.

Somehow, even after everything I'd been through, sleep managed to find me once more.

I fell asleep under Frankie's watchful eyes as I often had before, but this time I fell asleep in his protective embrace as well. The arms that held me felt safe, familiar. As if I was finally home.

Twenty-Three

I was alone the next morning. That much I felt before even opening my eyes.

My room was empty, and it was well after ten. My stomach churned, but it was from hunger, not anxiety. The few additional hours of rest helped me feel better both physically and emotionally, and I was ready to tackle the task at hand.

Well, at least a *little* bit ready.

There was a note from Frankie on my desk, telling me he was going to the store. I imagined what he must be feeling leaving the house for the first time in so long, and I tried to ignore a little pang of sadness that he hadn't wanted me to come along. I wished he had woken me up.

Something else struck me as odd: I hadn't seen his writing in so long. He had neat writing—his mom used to get so mad at him for writing in all caps. She worried his teachers would chastise him for it. She'd eventually given up.

Seeing his familiar penmanship was such a trivial thing, but a flood of emotion accompanied it. There were suddenly all these little things to notice about him, things that had been lost while he was in ghost form. Things I took for granted before that were now new again, exciting in their very existence. Like the faint smell of cigarette smoke in his breath in my face last night . . . the tight safety of his arms . . . the warm pressure of his lips when we kissed . . . the taste of his mouth on mine . . . .

Whoa! That's enough of that!

I had to focus. I had a huge mess of a puzzle in front of me, and I had to get to the bottom of it. There were questions—*so* many questions—and it was safe to assume they were not going to answer themselves.

There was also the nagging issue of Toby. I wasn't ready to see him yet. My anger was too fresh, too overwhelming. What he'd done . . . what he'd brought into my life . . . and the lies . . . I didn't know if I could forgive him. I needed to stay away from Frankie for a little while as well, though moving forward in my quest for answers seemed daunting without him by my side. But he and Toby were distractions, and if I thought it had been bad before, now that I'd kissed them both, I was really in a heap of confusion.

What a mess.

In addition to being distractions, I was a bit scared to hear what they'd have to say. Or, more honestly, what they possibly *wouldn't* say, either in the name of soul collector secrecy—*geez, that sounds so ridiculous!*—or to protect me. I really wouldn't put it past either of them to hide some of the truth if they thought it would protect me. So, the thought occurred to me that it might not hurt to find out a little on my own before I went to them. If that was even possible, of course. Only time would tell.

But first things first. *Coffee.*

My research could wait until I'd at least had my coffee, right?

I quickly checked my emails, slightly surprised to note that it really was only June 5th—the day after my birthday. How could it feel like so much time had passed when it hadn't even been twenty-four hours since I'd come home from Disneyland? How could so much happen in such a small window of time? I felt like a different person. Who knew my entire world would change on my eighteenth birthday? Certainly not me. Most people expect things to be different, only to be gravely disappointed when they aren't. Yay me.

I threw on a comfy gray sundress and a hoodie, then left my room, my body auto-following the scent of coffee coming from the kitchen. As I made my way down the hall, I heard my mom's voice coming from the dining room. I was surprised to hear her, but relief flooded me. If she was up and out of her room, then she must have woken up refreshed and ready to deal with life—craziness and all. I could mark off her mental health from my list of things to contend with for the day. I breathed a sigh of relief.

Then I heard Frankie's voice and groaned. *So much for avoiding him for a while.* I mean seriously, was this really my luck? Two guys I needed to avoid for a minute, and one of them actually lived in my house, the other right next door to it. Both of which made avoiding them for any extended periods of time absolutely impossible. I groaned again. *Ugh.*

I guess I *could* avoid Frankie, at least for now . . . if I avoided the kitchen.

Hmm. I debated with myself only briefly. Nope. Avoiding my morning coffee was definitely not an option after the night I'd had. I needed fuel.

So, I entered the kitchen.

Mom sat at the table with Frankie, chatting away about neighborhood gossip. I paused to really look at her. I noticed happily that she seemed to be in a good mood, a smile on her face. I admit I'd been hesitant still, even after I'd mentally crossed her off my checklist. But maybe she'd be okay after all.

My gaze caught on Frankie's hands, wrapped tightly around his coffee cup, and it was just one more thing I noticed about him. His hands: solid, real, and not going *through* the coffee cup he held. The memory of his hands on me last night popped into my brain, and my cheeks burned. *Focus. Breathe.* He was still in the same fitted white t-shirt and blue jeans as yesterday, and I mentally made a note to take him shopping after I'd tackled my list of things to do. Well, I guess it wasn't so much a list of *things* to do, per se, more like *one* thing to do: find the truth. Not too crazy an idea, I hoped.

I watched Frankie for a minute, soaking him in. His hair was starting to fall out of the almost-perfect pompadour it'd been styled into for the past two years, now that the hair grease was real again. I mentally noted that we'd need to get him some of his favorite hair stuff later as well. My stomach jumped around at the thought of it. All of these little things on my mental to-do list—the clothes, the Suavacito hair putty, the new Chuck Taylors—they all meant Frankie was finally home again. *My Frankie.* I didn't know whether to be terrified that the impossible had happened or ecstatic. But I was mostly ecstatic, which made it really hard to focus.

Especially since he'd kissed me last night, and the moment was repeating in my head on loop.

I turned my back to my mom and Frankie, and I tried to rein in my thoughts. Staring at Frankie was doing nothing but make me blush, which was *exactly* why I wanted to avoid him for a little while.

Damn. The carafe was near empty, with only about two sips left in it, so I set to making a fresh pot. Which totally sucked because waiting for the coffee to brew meant waiting in the kitchen, with Frankie, and I knew that I'd find myself staring at him again.

"Well. It's about time you woke up. I wish I had the luxury of sleeping all day."

I almost dropped the coffee can. The sharp sound of her voice sent a chill through my body, my muscles rigid in defense. I closed my eyes, inhaling deeply, and wishing her away.

"Good morning, Ever."

Well that wish didn't work. Seriously. What had I done to deserve this? I turned around, trying to mimic her faux pleasantry, but finding myself unable to offer even a forced smile. I hated her.

"Ariadne. What are you doing in my house?"

"Well, I should think that's obvious. I'm having coffee with Annabelle and Frankie. I'm sure even *you* can figure that out."

She said it all with a smile, that sickeningly sweet smile she tossed around so flippantly. I wanted to punch her. *Maybe I will.*

"Get out," I said, through tightly clenched teeth. I wasn't one to sling fakeness around the way she did. It wasn't who I was. It took everything I had in me not to grab her by her hair and pull her right out of that chair and out the front door. I didn't care if she was taller than me. I had body mass on her skinny ass, and I wasn't afraid to use it.

"Ever! That is no way to treat our guest!"

My mouth fell open, gaping in shock at my mom. How could she welcome this . . . this *monster* to our table? How could she . . . *ugh*. She was even sitting in my dad's seat.

"No, no, Annabelle. Don't be upset with Ever." She reached over, patting my mom's hand and smiling her evil smile. "She's had quite a shock, haven't you, Ever?" She winked at me before turning back to my mom. "I have to be heading out anyway. Thank you so much for the coffee."

She glanced back at Frankie as she left the room, and her smile reminded me of a shark—all teeth, power, and appetite. I think I might have growled at her.

I closed my eyes again, trying to get the image of Ariadne the Shark out of my mind. My heart raced, and I was already sweating. She really rubbed me the wrong way. I really wanted to punch her.

After I heard the door close behind her, I turned back to filling up the coffee filter. Conversation picked back up between my mom and Frankie. After a few minutes of focusing on the painstakingly slow drip of the coffee, the conversation behind me began registering in my brain.

I turned around to look at them, my brows pulled down in confusion.

"Are you guys *serious* right now?"

Both of them looked at me—my mom with pleasant confusion, and Frankie's face determined, his eyes boring holes into mine. Was I missing something?

"What do you mean, honey?" My mother answered me in a sweet voice that matched her quizzical, doe-eyed expression.

"Um, well," I started, sure that the look on my face was blatantly perplexed and slightly irritated, not sweetly quizzical. "I guess I'm just a *teensy* bit confused about how Sharon's begonias being trampled on could trump what's going on in our *own* home." I waved my hand in Frankie's direction and then toward the empty seat Ariadne had only recently exited to emphasize my point.

Frankie looked at me pointedly and then quickly shook his head, as if telling me to stop.

"What?" *I'm definitely missing something.*

Frankie cleared his throat. "*Ever*, your mom had just been telling Ariadne and I that it wasn't just *anyone* who trampled your neighbor Sharon's flowers . . . it was *Bonnie's dog* that trampled the begonias." Frankie spoke slowly, widening his eyes and emphasizing some of his words, subtly urging me to understand.

I didn't understand at all. *Bonnie's dog? Begonias? What the hell?* I just blankly stared at him before glancing down at my own dog lying on the floor at my feet, as if he could help me understand the connection. I swear Gollum looked back at me with pity in his big brown eyes.

I played it over in my head. Bonnie's dog. Sharon's begonias. *Yep, still nothing.*

My mom, eager to get back into her normal everyday gardening activities—she'd avoided them since my dad's death—began rambling on and on about her flowers and how she hoped Bonnie would keep her dog on a leash from now on, and how she hoped that the friendship between the three women wouldn't be ruined. She kept talking as if Frankie and I were both staring at her and listening intensely. We were not, of course, as Frankie was watching *me* intensely and I was *intensely* confused.

Frankie came to stand next to me in front of the coffee pot, slowly turning me around so my back was toward my mother once again. As he fiddled with pouring my creamer and making my coffee—a task he handled perfectly I noticed happily—he explained the situation in a voice quiet enough that only I could hear him.

"Your mom seems to . . . not want to . . . well, *shit*, Doll, how can I say this . . . she doesn't seem to be *ready* to acknowledge what happened last night. More directly, what has happened to *me*." He waved his hands toward his body, acknowledging his new physical form.

"Oh." *I don't get it.*

It took me a second to catch on. I *really* needed that coffee. I grabbed it from Frankie's outstretched hand, took a generous sip, and waited.

Oh!

Oh, geez.

'Not ready to acknowledge what happened.' Then Toby's choice of words from last night floated back into my mind: coping.

Having. Trouble. Coping.

Frankie looked at me and smiled a sympathetic smile. My shoulders fell in defeat.

"Hey, hey, don't worry, Doll," he whispered, "I'm sure she'll be fine. Maybe we should just give her a day or two to come to terms with it. She's been through a lot, you know."

My jaw tightened.

As if I haven't also been through a lot? As if my dad didn't just die. As if my boyfriend isn't the one who turned out to be a soul collector. As if my ghost isn't suddenly standing three inches away from me, begging me to touch him.

Or, well, maybe not *begging*.

But seriously. As if this whole situation wasn't happening to *me*. As if it wasn't *me* who brought Toby into our lives. *Me* who ignored my dreams. Dreams that were obviously—somehow—*warnings*.

Me. This was all because of me.

Maybe *I* wanted to check out of reality, too. Maybe *I* wanted to have a meltdown and crawl back into bed, cocooning myself up for a few days or focusing on gardening like gardening actually mattered. Maybe *I* wanted to *choose* to ignore what was happening right in front of my face! Had anyone thought of that? Had anyone thought about how *I* might be feeling?

I didn't voice those thoughts, keeping my immature ranting to myself.

I stared at Frankie for a long moment, unable to find something relevant to say, and finally turned to head to my room.

Frankie began to follow me, and I shot him a glare over my shoulder. "No. Not right now."

It wasn't that I didn't *want* to be with Frankie, I did, but I had to take charge of this situation and get some information out of *someone*. I no longer had time to nurse, or even think about, my emotions or feelings. It felt like I'd suddenly grown up overnight. My dad's death and now my mom's apparent vacation in crazy-town had left me with very few options.

So. I became an adult at eighteen after all. It was awesome, adulthood.

I settled down in front of my computer, powering it up and waiting for the screen to welcome me back. I opened up my browser then turned on Pandora, deciding on a little Lana Del Rey to start things off. Something about *'Kinda Outta Luck'* was very fitting for my mood.

I opened Google. I put my fingers on the keys. And then . . . *nothing*. I just stared at the screen. What was I looking for, anyway?

Soul collectors? Hot guys who trick you? Ghosts that have become human again? Get real!

I racked my brain, trying to come up with something *somewhat* logical to look for.

When that didn't happen, because let's face it, there was nothing logical about my life now, I entered the first words that had originally come to mind.

Soul Collectors. I felt foolish typing them, but whatever.

The first few websites were about some cheesy TV movie from the 90's.

There was a shoe website called . . . wait for it . . . The Sole Collector. Shoe soles. I shook my head at the ridiculousness of it.

Then I found something worth looking into. A website about soul collectors, believe it or not. It was worth a shot.

It started out pretty promising.

'Here you will find info on the soul collector . . . .'

Okay. I was listening.

'. . . or as some call him, The Hat Man . . . .'

Resisting the strong urge to slam my head into my desk took a lot of energy. *Hat man?* I tried to picture Toby being called a 'hat man'. *Ugh. Stupid.* I'd never even seen him wear a hat, though I assumed the nickname was probably some sort of metaphor anyway. But I continued reading, if only in hopes that I'd at least be entertained for a few minutes by delving further into this nonsense. I had to be doing *something* because sitting there would just drive me crazy. Or drive me to seek out one of the two people I was currently trying to avoid, which I was sure would be a mistake. Plus, there was also the solid fact that I had absolutely nothing else to go on.

I soon discovered that the website's owner had nothing else to go on either. The website wasn't even finished. *Great. Thanks for nothing, Hat Man.*

The website had a link for pictures, and I was half-tempted to ignore it, for the simple fact that if I clicked on it and saw a picture of Toby, I'd probably pass out. I clicked on the link reluctantly, holding my breath and cringing while I waited for the bomb to drop.

Nothing. Just a blank page.

Thank god. I was relieved. That's silly, I know, but I was relieved nonetheless.

I also felt completely ridiculous. I mean, what kind of people hung out on these websites anyway? Certainly not levelheaded people like me.

After that website, there were a few band websites—Soul Collector was apparently a very popular choice in band names—and a few book links and gamer sites. Three or four pages into my Google search, I discovered that there was absolutely nothing to discover. Super.

I decided to try to find something on Toby and Ariadne's matching tattoos. *Gag.*

In my frustration, my heart tried to tell me to go ask my boyfriend my questions, but I sternly reminded my silly little heart that Toby wasn't really my boyfriend—not if he'd never truly loved me and our relationship had never been *real.*

My heart then tried to convince me to call Frankie into my room and ask *him* my questions. But my heart was so *trusting,* which made it completely *untrustworthy.* Clearly, my heart didn't want to accept the fact that I was pretty much on my own in this, and that was just too bad.

After I'd searched Google images for angel wings . . . and angel wing tattoos . . . and angel wing *tribal* tattoos . . . and Seattle tattoos—seriously? What was I thinking with that one?—and tattoos with three lines—*that* one was even more ridiculous than the previous search for 'Seattle tattoos'—I was completely annoyed, and nowhere closer to finding anything out. None of the images was what I was looking for, even though the list of word combinations was endless, as were the images.

My patience, however, was not endless.

After an hour or two of searching and coming up with no results, I gave up.

What to do next . . . ?

My next thought was the library, but then I reminded myself that without a point of reference to start from—and I couldn't just ask for a book about soul collectors if I wanted *non*-fiction—I'd end up with the same frustrating results Google gave me.

I stared at the wall for a few minutes, wishing for the idea to come to me. *Begging* it to come. But when it did, it wasn't good.

Dammit.

Be careful what you wish for, whispered a little voice in my mind. I swear the voice was mocking me.

No way. I don't like this idea one bit. I stared at the wall for a few more minutes, willing something—*anything*—to come to me. There had to be a better plan. *Ugh.* I turned off the computer, reluctant to act on my idea, but unable to come up with a better one.

Maybe, if I played it just right, I'd slip and fall when I stepped into the shower, cracking my head on the tile and bleeding out before I had to actually *act* on my next idea.

Maybe a house would land on me when I walked outside.

I showered slowly, unable to rush because I knew what I had to do. I threw the gray sundress back on, because I'd only worn it for a few hours anyway, and called Jessie. I wasn't about to do this alone.

When she answered her phone, I could hear that she'd been crying. *Oh, no.* She'd taken the shock worse than I'd figured. Of course, if she was crying, I realized, she hadn't checked out completely like my mom had. The silver lining of the storm cloud that was now my life.

"Jess? What's wrong?"

"I broke up with Greg, Ever!"

Oh, geez. Why had all of this happened? Anger filled me again, and most of it was directed at Toby. He brought these people into our lives, and whether he had *intended* all of this was beside the point. Like it or not, it *had* happened, and more than just *I* was affected by it.

"Oh man, Jess. I'm so sorry."

"Do you know what he *told* me, Ever? He told me he's a soul collector." She paused, waiting for my shocked reaction. "A *freaking* soul collector, Ever! Did you hear what I just said?"

Oh, geez.

"Yeah. I know, Jess."

"You *know*? So what, you *believe* them, or something?"

"Yeah, Jess, I guess I do. I don't understand it—*at all*—and I don't know what it all means, but I intend to find out. And wait a minute—

aren't you the one who's been telling me to open my mind to the possibilities?" She couldn't see my hand, but I'd added air quotes to *possibilities*.

"Oh, Ever. I wasn't serious!" Uh-huh, sure. Whatever. I dropped it.

"Okay, well—"

"He used me." Her voice had gone down a few octaves, and my heart broke at the sound of it. "He used me to get to you."

"Jess. Maybe he—"

"Forget it, Ever. It's no big deal. There are a million guys just like him who would die to date me. No biggie. What's your plan?" And with that, she'd moved past it. Or at least pretended to.

"Well, I'll tell you when I see you. I'll be at your house in twenty minutes."

"Don't bother; I'm almost at your house. I just parked around the corner because I didn't want to accidentally run into Toby. Or Greg. Or that bitch Ariadne. *Ugh*. I'll be there in a few. Oh, and bring me some clothes and stuff."

"Clothes?" I asked, but she'd already hung up the phone. I grabbed the toothbrush she kept at my house, a tube of toothpaste, and a hairbrush, a gray and black striped maxi dress, and my black gladiator sandals. She'd have to just deal with the color choice today because I didn't own anything that even closely resembled pink.

Moments later—after escaping through my window to avoid seeing Frankie or my completely detached mom—I was buckled into Jessie's bright pink VW, and the two of us were ready to take on the world. Or figure this thing out. Or at least eat a really big, fattening lunch, because that's where we were headed. I might have been delaying the inevitable, but my stomach was growling, and I wasn't one to argue.

Jessie had on the pink Minnie Mouse shirt she wore to Disneyland yesterday, so I imagined she'd had even less sleep than me. I wondered how long she'd stayed up talking to Greg.

"Don't even look at my outfit right now, Ever. After we got to Greg's house last night, I passed out. I don't know if it was shock, or what, but when we woke up this morning, I freaked out on him, and then, after what he"—she paused, shaking her head slightly, brow furrowed—"what he *told* me, I got in my car and drove straight to your house. I've been sitting down the street all morning not knowing what to do next."

"Oh geez, Jess, why didn't you call me?"

"I don't know"—her stomach rumbled loudly, breaking up her words—"I was sort of just . . . scared, I guess. And now I look disgusting."

She didn't look disgusting by any means, but Jessie was Jessie. She made a face when I handed her the clothes, crinkling her nose at all the black. "Well, I guess it *does* go with my mood. All dark and grumpy."

We ended up at Islands, deciding that a basket of Cheddar Fries could make even the very *worst* situation better. With bacon of course, because *everyone* knew that bacon definitely made *everything* better. Jessie headed to the bathroom to change and wash her face, and I ordered our food and drinks.

Jessie came back to the table and began applying her makeup, trying to camouflage the puffiness from all her earlier tears. I blankly stared into space. I knew what I had to do next, and I didn't want to do it alone, but I also knew that Jessie was going to be pissed.

"I can't believe I just brushed my teeth in the bathroom here. People probably think I'm a hobo." She paused to look around for anyone nearby, and, satisfied that she looked the best she could look under such dire circumstances, she closed her compact, turning her full attention to me.

"All right, Ev, *soul collectors*. What's your big plan?"

Delaying the inevitable again, I gave her the back-story. I explained to her that I'd been on the computer all morning, searching for anything that would help us, and I'd come up empty handed. Then I told her about my plan—which was a *far* better idea than going to Greg or Toby with our questions—but you wouldn't guess that by her reaction.

You'd think I'd asked her to off someone for me.

"*What?*"

Three women dining at a nearby table turned their heads in unison at the sound of Jessie's shriek.

"Are you freaking kidding me right now, Ever? Is there something *wrong* with you? Freaking *Ariadne*? Of all people? *Ariadne?*"

"I know, I know, but hear me out."

"Yeah. Okay. I'm sure you have something *amazing* to tell me. Something earth shattering that will justify going to *that* horrible bitch for help. Do you know she hooked up with Greg? Ugh. That chick's a major stain. I can't even believe you right now, Ever."

My eyes widened. *Greg, too? Slut.* I shook away the thought. Ariadne's lack of character, or why Toby and Greg had apparently *both* hooked up with her, was not what was important right now. And frankly, it kind of made me sick to think about.

"Jess."

"Fine." She waved her hands in mock surrender. "Go ahead. I'm all ears."

"You're right, Jess. She *is* a *major stain*, whatever that means. I hate her as much as you do. Trust me. What she did . . . to us . . . to *Frankie* . . . well, crazy bitch status aside, she's at the bottom of this whole mess. I'm not ready to talk to Toby. You're obviously not ready to talk to Greg." I waited for her to argue, but she conceded by averting her eyes. She didn't want to admit that I had a point, and frankly, neither did I. But that wayward house I'd wished for never fell on me when I walked outside earlier and I didn't die in the shower, so as of now, this mess was still my life. "And you know what, Jess? I have a pretty good feeling that both Toby *and* Greg will hide the truth from us, or at least some of it. So screw them. We're going straight to the source."

"Your plan sucks. I hate that chick."

"I know. You've said that. But can you think of a better idea?"

"Yeah, I can. What did Frankie have to say about all of this?"

At the mention of his name, my cheeks flushed. Heat rushed into them without my consent, and I looked down at the napkin in my lap, trying to make my hair fall forward to hide my blushing.

"Oh my gosh, Ever Van Ruysdael. What is that?" She pointed to my red cheeks.

"What?" I tried to answer her nonchalantly with a casual shrug and a blank look on my face, but I knew my cheeks were giving me away as usual. I looked anywhere but at her, my head still slightly tipped forward. I tried to play it cool, all the while knowing it was a lost cause. I'd never been able to keep anything from Jessie. I took a long sip of my Passion Fruit iced tea, hoping that somehow it would magically cool my cheeks. *Yeah, maybe if I rub the ice directly on them, or pour the tea over my head.* She'd think I was crazy, but at least that would draw the attention away from talking about Frankie.

"Oh no you don't. Look at me."

I looked at her, my lips twisting into a smile beyond my control.

"Oh, Ever, you *slut!* You hooked up with Frankie, didn't you?"

The slut reference stung a little, but *only* because of my shameful conscience. I knew Jessie didn't really think I was slutty. God knew *she'd* kissed a lot more boys than I had.

"Jessie, shh!"

The waitress delivered our gooey, cheesy mess of fries at that very moment, and my cheeks flushed even hotter, as if *she* also knew that I'd kissed two boys in as many days. Jessie waited for her to leave and then lowered her voice to a conspiratorial whisper, speaking around a mouthful of fries and ranch dressing. Her eyes were wide with anticipation.

"Spill."

I told her how Frankie woke me up during the night, after another one of my nightmares. I began to describe the way it had felt to see him there, to finally *feel* his hands on me—

"Wait . . . *what?* What do you mean *another* nightmare?"

Oh. Shoot. I hadn't told her. I wanted to, plenty of times, but we always got to talking and we never finished one story before we'd started another one, and there were *always* so many other things going on—most prevalently her new, exciting relationship with Greg, and my often-confusing relationship with Toby. And somehow, *somehow*, I had neglected to tell my best friend about my nightmares.

This meant, unfortunately, that I'd never told her about Frankie's visits to my room at night. As I began to tell her about all of the nightmares I'd had, and the subsequent nights spent with Frankie, I saw in her face that I'd hurt her. She tried to mask it with her interest in my story, but it was there. Plain as day.

Ugh. I hadn't meant to hurt her, really I hadn't. But it was too late for that now.

"Jess, I'm so sorry. I mean, I *meant* to tell you, but—"

She shook her head lightly and waved her hand in the air, silver bangle bracelets clanking around her wrist.

"No worries, Ev. It's all a bit to take in, yeah, but I can't even imagine how weird it was for *you*. I mean, being with Toby all that time, but loving Frankie too, and then . . . and then Frankie was coming into your room at night to comfort you!" She paused and licked her lips. "It sounds like such a great episode of Gossip Girl! Or 90210! But . . . you know . . . like a *Halloween* episode or something . . . since Frankie's a ghost." She paused again, and her eyes widened slightly. "*Was* a ghost. Whoa. That's weird." She shook her head. "Okay, so anyway, enough about your secret little affair with Frankie."

Her words had me feeling slightly disappointed that she didn't want details about my kiss with Frankie, when it was something I'd anticipated for so long.

Obviously able to decipher my feelings from the expression on my face, she continued, "Oh, Ever, relax. Of course I want to hear all about how amazing of a kisser he is. Just, not right now. Seriously, stay focused. Tell me about the actual dreams. You said you never remembered them—except for one, right?"

Hearing Jessie tell *me* to stay focused was funny all in itself, but add to that the fact that she was trying to *not* talk about boys . . . our lives really *had* changed.

"Well, *two* technically. I can remember two dreams now. I can remember the one from last night. Or, this morning I guess. Whatever."

"Okay, so what were these *two* nightmares about?"

I had no problem relaying every detail, as each nightmare was still vivid in my mind. First, the nightmare with Toby standing over Frankie's bloody, lifeless body . . . and his words, the words that still haunted me: *'You can't save him.'* Then, most recently, Ariadne standing over Frankie's body, her beautiful white dress ruined with his blood, taunting me with those same unforgettable words.

'You can't save him.'

The words ran through my mind again, followed by an image of Ariadne kissing Frankie. I shivered. I realized Jessie's face had paled considerably since I began describing the details of my nightmares.

"Jess?"

She swallowed hard, placing both hands palm down on the table. Her napkin was under one of her hands, and I noticed that she had shredded it into tiny pieces as she listened to my story. She inhaled deeply.

"Oh, Ever, don't you see?" she whispered. "Your dreams . . . they were warnings. About Frankie's *soul*. It's . . . it's all . . . it's all *real* then. Greg was telling the truth." She swallowed again, and her face paled even further. She was almost a pale greenish-blue color.

"Jess, hey, they're just *dreams*," I said, even though I'd already come to the same conclusion about them. "Eat some more of your salad. Drink some tea. Do *something*. You look like you're going to be sick. We'll figure this out. I know we will."

I reached across the table and squeezed her hand. It was ice cold.

"Jess? It will be okay. I promise."

Something in my mind tried to tell me not to make promises I couldn't keep, but right at that moment, I had every intention of *keeping* that promise.

For both of us.

Twenty-Four

A *riadne.*

I couldn't believe I was doing it, but as we walked up to Toby's front door, and I watched my fist reach up and knock three times, I realized it was really happening.

I was going to Ariadne for help.

Beside me, Jessie tightly crossed her arms, and she tapped her pink toes in annoyance. Or nerves. But we'll stick with annoyance. She exhaled a loud sigh, deliberately letting me know her strong opposition to my plan. I looked at her and shrugged. Too late to back out now. The door was opening.

"Oh. What a pleasant surprise. Have you come to thank me, or apologize for your less than hospitable hospitality earlier?"

"Oh my god, Ever. This is a mistake. Let's go before I show Ariadne what *my* hospitality looks like."

I placed my hand on Jessie's arm and tried to ignore the smug look on Ariadne's face. She was already winning by getting a rise out of Jessie. I ignored Jessie's words and responded to Ariadne's. "Neither. We have questions, and you owe us answers."

"Do I now? How do you figure?"

"Look, Ariadne. Cut the crap. Will you let us in and talk to us, or do we have to keep playing games like we're at the school lunch tables?"

"Well, I *did* warn you that I don't play well with others." She stepped aside and waved us in.

I had to practically drag Jessie inside. She was trying to play it cool, but I saw her gaze darting around, looking for Greg. Apparently Ariadne caught it, too.

"Relax, blondie. Your boyfriend isn't here. In fact, neither of them are. They're off with Ted somewhere. It's just us girls. Who wants to paint my toenails?" She sat on the couch and raised the long hem of her maxi dress, wiggling her toes at us.

Jessie sat in the chair across from the couch, as far as she could get from Ariadne, which left me two options: sit down next to Ariadne on the couch or stand.

I chose option number three and paced the floor.

"Oh relax, Ever. Seriously, I'm not going to bite. You." She winked at Jessie, and Jess looked up at me with pleading eyes. She was normally the one with all the moxie, but Ariadne really set off something in her. Maybe it was the connection to Greg. I looked at my best friend and realized she'd really felt something for Greg. I mean, I'd *known* she really liked him and that she was more serious about him than any other guy before him, but now I realized just how much she loved him. Being around Ariadne would make anyone uncomfortable, but Jessie's agitation went far past uncomfortable. In fact, it seemed to match my feelings toward the girl.

Reluctantly, I sat next to Ariadne. *Only* because pacing wasn't helping me organize my thoughts into actual questions. "Look, Ariadne, Toby and Greg have told us a little bit. We know you are . . . soul collectors."

"Why, Ever, your pause tells me you have trouble believing that." She tilted her head as she examined me. "Do you not have your own little secrets? How can you doubt what *we* are when you've been keeping a ghost as a pet for two years?"

"Hmph." Jessie's scoffing was quiet, as though she didn't want to join in on the conversation but wanted me to know she agreed with Ariadne—at least on this one innocent statement. Jessie's little way of saying 'I told you so,' after trying in vain for years to convince me to broaden my beliefs, was hardly consistent with her reaction to all of this. I mean, last night I was scared for her sanity. But I ignored the bait. Jessie's beliefs—or disbeliefs—were not important right now.

"So, yes, we are soul collectors. That part is correct. What else did *my* boys tell you?"

Jessie cringed, her lip curling up ever so slightly.

"Well, I don't know about Greg, but Toby explained it to me a little bit. Like, I guess you guys find souls that haven't passed on, and you . . . I don't know . . . guide them?"

"Indeed. To heaven or hell, depending."

"On what?" I couldn't help but ask with Frankie's soul being the one in question.

"Don't worry, Ever, your Frankie was a good boy. You should know that—I mean, you've been obsessed with him for . . . what . . . your entire life, haven't you?"

"What about now?" Jessie asked.

Whoa. I wasn't yet ready to know about Frankie's soul's current status, so I quickly changed the subject. "So, you *guide* souls to their final destination. I guess I understand. Sort of. Why do souls get lost in the first place?"

"Not lost so much as stubborn. Frankie isn't *confused* about where he's headed. He's just too stubborn to go." She looked at me with mock adoration, batting her eyelashes at me. "He didn't want to leave you. Aww."

I got that she was making fun of me, but I continued anyways. No need to let her know she was making me want to punch that fire-engine-red pout of hers. That lipstick would probably stay on my knuckles for days. So I ignored the bait.

"You guys came here for Frankie?"

"Yes. In a roundabout way."

"Ugh. Seriously? What the hell does that mean?"

"Oh, Jessie. I forgot you were here, hon. Well, what I *mean* is that Toby and Ted came here for Frankie. Greg came here because Ted called him. Apparently Toby was losing his focus." She looked directly at me. "*I came* for Toby."

She made my skin crawl. Literally. Had it not been attached to my body, it would have crawled away from her. I was on edge just being near Ariadne. Her double entendre was tacky at best, but still managed to get on my nerves. Now, she looked at me like she was going to eat me, and I couldn't help but squirm. Ariadne the Shark had returned. Fan-*freaking*-tastic. I got up and paced the floor again, ignoring the satisfied look on Ariadne's face. She'd gotten a rise out of me. Fine. But she still hadn't won the battle.

"So, Ted and Toby came for Frankie. Why two of them? Why not just one person, or . . . I mean, just *one* soul collector?" My slip of the tongue reminded me that I'd have to eventually ask her if they actually *were* human. A question I was not looking forward to asking.

"Ever. Don't think I didn't catch that. We are people. We're just people with an actual purpose. Unlike yourselves."

"How do people like *you* become soul collectors?" Jessie asked. "Did you do something especially nasty, because that I could believe."

"The how's and the why's of it are unimportant. I think Ever has much more pressing questions for me, don't you, Ever?"

"Why did Ted come?" Yes, I know, I was avoiding the big question. I couldn't help but delay it for as long as possible. I was too scared of the answer.

"I don't begin to know why Ted does what he does. And I don't question him. He's here, and he must have a reason for it. I'm sure we'll all find out in due time. But to answer your question, Toby could have handled Frankie on his own. Had *you* not gotten in the way, of course."

Me. So, had I not gotten involved with Toby, Frankie may have just disappeared one day and they'd both be gone. I looked at Jessie, her wide eyes matching mine.

"Aha. I see the two of you aren't as dense as you look. Had you stayed away from Toby, he would have been in and out in a matter of days. Frankie would be adjusting to his new home, and Toby would be off to the next town, actively meeting his quotas and staying focused. But he just couldn't resist that silly little innocence thing you've got going on. He's a sucker for wide eyes and zero world experience. You fit the bill perfectly. All naïve and clueless."

"Ha! Listen up, *bitch*. Ever obviously has something *you* don't have. And I'm not talking beauty, brains, or *class*, because those go without saying. I'm talking about the one thing you want most in the world. *Toby.*"

Jessie was standing now, staring down at a very irritated Ariadne. I felt the tension building between them, and Ariadne had a weird twitch going on in her left temple. Jessie struck a nerve, and I could tell it was about to come to a head between the two of them. One point for our team, I guessed, but I wanted to prevent the two of them from coming to blows in Toby's living room.

"Okay, okay, Jess. Thanks for defending me, but let's all try to stay focused." I was tempted to add that, for the record, Toby didn't *have* me, but I withheld that bit to let Ariadne stew in it a little longer. Toby as leverage was the only upper hand we had. "So, Toby got distracted or whatever, and Ted called Greg. What was he supposed to do, come get Frankie?"

"Yes. And how hard could *that* be, right? Then he meets the bubblegum fairy over here and that plan goes to shit, too. I swear, it's like the two of you dimwitted morons have magical powers or something." The insults flew right past Jessie. I saw by the glimmer of hope in her eyes and the slight tilt of her head that all she'd heard was that she'd been the cause of Greg's plan 'going to shit.' It gave me hope that even if my relationship with Toby had been ruined, maybe Jessie and Greg stood a chance at working things out.

"Somehow, both Toby *and* Greg came to get Frankie, and neither one of them succeeded. Because of us." I found that strange, being the more insecure of Jessie and me, but I continued. "Why didn't Ted just do the job himself?"

"Like I said, hon, no one knows why Ted does or doesn't do things."

"Then you showed up. Why?" I already knew the answer, but I wanted to hear her say it. *Because I'm a glutton for punishment.*

"I came for Toby. I didn't care why Toby was here—his jobs have nothing to do with me. I had some free time between gigs, and figured I'd seek him out. When I arrived . . . ugh. I couldn't believe he was so hung up on you. I had to see you for myself, see what was so amazing about you. I followed you to the library that day. I watched you for hours, trying to figure it out. I couldn't, obviously." She waved a hand in my direction, as if it was so obvious that there was nothing to be hung up over. "And then I think, 'hmmm, maybe she's surprisingly intelligent.' So I come a little closer, check out your reading materials. Is it Jane Eyre? Moby Dick? Or even Hamlet? No. It's a freaking book about *vampires* going to a private *vampire* school." She paused again to look up at me. "You do know there is no such thing as private vampire schools, correct? Ugh. I can't even begin to tell you the horror of finding him all hung up on someone as simple as you.

"So, I'm sitting there watching you for hours—which you have to understand is excruciating—and I finally decide Toby's lost his mind, and it's my job to fix that. It would have been fine. I would have had him focusing on me again in no time, if you hadn't shown up at that party."

Toby and Ariadne getting back together was not the important part of this story, nor was it the reason we were there talking to her. But I couldn't help but take the bait. She'd gotten under my skin, and a girl can take only so much.

"You know, Ariadne, I'm pretty sure Toby finds you repulsive. Whether I'd been in the picture or not, you didn't stand a chance at getting him back. That ship, as they say, has sailed. And sunk. And is currently rotting in the bottom of the metaphorical ocean."

She didn't move. Only her eyes showed she was listening; they narrowed into tiny slits. Then her mouth curved up into a sly smile.

"Had you been in his bedroom with us that morning before the library, Ever, I think you'd have seen that his *ship* was very much *not* at the bottom of the ocean. His *ship* was indeed sailing. Full mast."

"Ugh! You are disgusting, Ariadne. And frankly, I'm not surprised that you have to use your *body* to get a guy to pay attention to you. Your personality is as appealing as a pile of dog shit. But really, we don't have to listen to this, and you clearly aren't planning on giving us any useful information. Come on, Ev."

"Hmm. Seems I struck a nerve with our sweet, innocent Eleanor here."

"Ever?"

The morning before the library. As I was taking care of my mom. And my house. And my broken life. Toby and Ariadne were having sex in the very house next door. *Having sex.* And then he came back into my life. He apologized. He told me he loved me. He . . . .

Oh, god. I almost had sex with him. Just hours after he'd been with her!

"Hon, did you really think he hadn't been with anyone else? I mean, you two *were* broken up. And we *do* have a history, so . . ." she paused, waiting for me to say something. "Oh. That's sweet. You actually had thought that. Your naivety has no end, does it?"

"Ev, seriously, let's just go. We don't need to talk to Ariadne. She's not giving us any information we don't already know."

Jessie's hand was on my arm, and I looked at her standing next to me. She pleaded with her eyes, urging me to give up this silly quest for answers. She was right. Ariadne was just using this time to hurt us both. But if I wasn't ready to go to Toby with my questions before, I was even less ready now.

I took a deep breath, steeling myself to continue, and sat down next to Ariadne on the couch. So what if she'd hooked up with Toby again? It wasn't my business any longer. I'd decided the fate of my relationship with Toby, and he was no longer my concern. Setting that decision aside, I focused on the task at hand. I cleared my throat, preparing my voice *not* to crack and give away my distress, and continued. "You turned Frankie human. Tell me why."

"You know why, Ever. Don't be coy; it doesn't suit you."

"I want to hear *you* tell me why."

"Well, I should think that it's obvious, but whatever. It was your birthday, and I didn't want to be the only one at the party without a gift. Seeing as how you have terrible choice in clothing *and* literature, I asked myself, 'what would be the next best thing?' Naturally, I came to Frankie. So, surprise!"

"You wanted Toby back, which clearly wasn't going to happen unless you fought dirty. So you brought out the big guns. Because clearly, if Frankie were suddenly an option, I'd leave Toby and you'd have him back to yourself. What you failed to calculate is the fact that he finds you disgusting and desperate and whether or not I'm in the picture, you will still be the pathetic ex-girlfriend who whores herself out to get what she wants."

I looked at Jessie and headed to the door.

"We're done here, Ariadne. You win. Toby is no longer spoken for. But mark my words; he will never be yours. You lack the one thing needed to get him back . . . a *soul*."

Ariadne's laughter stopped me in my tracks, my hand frozen on the doorknob. Jessie practically ran into me.

"Soul." She said the word slowly, tasting it, feeling it in her mouth as if it was new and foreign to her. "Your choice of words amuses me. I may not have Toby *yet*, but don't think you've won."

I wanted to laugh in her face, but I refrained. Must have been this new *adult* me, but it felt like a victory taking the moral high ground. I began to open the door.

"You didn't really think I'd just give you something for nothing, did you? Like we're such good friends?" The hardness in her voice pulled at me.

I turned and looked at her beautiful, ruthless face.

"Awww, you did! That's just adorable."

"You didn't give me anything," I said. *Oh, wait. Frankie.* "Well, *technically* you gave Frankie back his life . . . or a chance at a new one . . . but—"

"Exactly."

She rose from the couch. Every step she took toward me was deliberate. Every word she spoke was as sharp as a knife to my soul. Her sexy pout was now a hard line.

"I can take that gift back any time I want."

She was baiting me again. I didn't want to stay, but I was unable to convince myself to open the door and leave. Something tugged at me, an unknown truth about to be revealed. So I waited. I tried to return her hard stare, tried to look as determined and ruthless as she was.

"Now that I have your attention, little girl, I'll explain *one* thing. You came here for answers, and I'll give you just this *one*. I gave Frankie his life back. I gave you a gift. But I am far from selfless, and my gift comes with a price. You're just naïve enough to think that Toby is the price for my kindness. Guess again, hon."

Jessie quickly sucked in a breath, bracing herself for what we were about to hear.

I knew we should leave. Leaving would have protected us from the terrifying words I knew Ariadne was about to say. But again, my feet were reluctant to move. Jessie placed her hand on my arm and gave me a squeeze, knowing I was as afraid as she was.

"Here's a lesson for you. Consider it my second gift. You don't get something for nothing. Not in your world, and not in mine. You get to keep Frankie now. But what will you give me in return?" She paused, letting the words sink in and waiting for the information to click in my brain.

I sucked in a breath, knowing what she was going to say before she even said it.

"An eye for an eye, Eleanor."

Twenty-Five

J essie had always been the bubbly, confident one. The girl with the sharp wit and million-dollar smile, who shines like a hundred-watt light bulb. I'm somewhat of the opposite—not dark per se, but a little darker than Jessie. I'm a little more into black than most, a little quieter than some, and slightly prone to the occasional outburst of punching someone. Jessie has never hurt anyone with more than smiles and flattery.

So I'm sure anyone would understand why I was a bit surprised to find myself in my kitchen, sitting with her while she nursed her bruised hand.

"That bitch had it coming. I am *not* apologizing."

"No one is asking you to, Jess. I'm just wondering if maybe we should have held off on the punching until she'd actually given us something to go on."

"Eff that. She's not going to give us any information, Ever. Come on."

"Well, since we have absolutely no idea what any of this means or what will happen next, I think we need to go back over there."

"What? Oh, Ever, you can't be—she looked at me, realizing I was dead serious—"*No.* I'm not kidding, Ev. I won't apologize to her."

"Fine. Then I will apologize for you, and you can stay here."

"Yeah right. Like I'm going to let you go back over there by yourself." She removed the Ziploc baggie of ice and stretched her swollen hand, slowly moving each finger. "My hand hurts."

"Huh. I can't imagine why."

"Oh, like you weren't about to do the same thing. I saw your face."

"Yeah, she's lucky the guys came back when they did. Between the two of us crazy bitches, she wouldn't have known what hit her."

"Exactly. But now I'm the only one with a swollen hand. It's throbbing like its having its own little heart attack. Is that normal?"

"Yeah. Sorry. But thanks for coming to my defense."

"Please. It was nothing. Oh, hey, I forgot to ask you how your mom was this morning. She okay? We were all kind of um . . . *shocked* last night."

Oh. My mom.

"Well, last night she was a mess. She took a few sleeping pills and curled up in the fetal position."

"Oh, geez."

"It gets better. This morning, she has absolutely no idea what's going on and is acting like everything is completely *normal.* Like, I walk into the kitchen and they're all sitting at the table. Frankie, who is very obviously no longer a ghost, my mom, who's all smiles and sparkle, and . . . you'll die . . . guess who else was there? Ariadne."

"*What?* How did you not tell me this sooner?"

"I know, I know. I'm sorry. So there they all sit, in *my* kitchen. She's even sitting in my *dad's* chair."

Jessie's mouth dropped open, rightly so.

"They're all drinking coffee and talking about how Sharon's flowers were trampled on by Bonnie's dog. As if *that* has any importance compared to what's going on in *our* own home. My mom's just sitting there, happy as a clam."

It sounded even more ridiculous saying it all out loud, but Jessie's expression turned dark. She closed her eyes and shook her head.

"Oh, Ever. Your poor mom. I can't even imagine what she's going through. After your dad . . . and now this?"

"I know."

"What are you going to do?" She looked at me expectantly.

I was unfairly irritated by her question, but I couldn't help but feel annoyed. Why did everything have to fall on *my* shoulders? Why did I have to take care of my mom? Why did I have to find all the answers? Why *me?*

"What is it, Ever?

"Nothing, Jess. I'm just frustrated, that's all. This whole thing is such a mess."

"I know. So what now?"

"I don't know, Jess. I don't know."

"Well, I for one could stand a little distraction. Let's go out tonight."

"Seriously? Our boyfriends—"

"Ex," she clarified for me adamantly. "They are our *ex-*boyfriends."

"Well, I haven't *officially* broken things off with Toby."

"Ev, I think it goes without saying, don't you? I mean, after everything he's caused!"

"Yes, Jess, but you get my point. We just found out that Toby and Greg are soul collectors, which in itself is a huge thing. On top of that, Frankie is no longer a ghost, and my mom has completely checked out of reality. Oh! And my soul is up for grabs or something. You think *now* is a good time to go out?"

"Actually, yes. I think it's the *perfect* time to go out. First of all, you can't change what Toby and Greg are. Or whatever the hell is going on there. You certainly can't change what happened to Frankie . . . unless you kill him, of course, and I definitely don't see you doing that. And third, you can't help your mom face this stuff, Ever. She has to come to grips with it on her own."

She had a point. But a night out? Seriously? It just didn't seem like the right thing to do.

"Actually, I have an idea."

Uh oh.

"When's the last time Frankie went out, Ev?"

"Um. That's kind of rhetorical."

"Exactly. We're taking Frankie out tonight. There's a party in Costa Mesa."

"Did I just hear you girls say you're taking me out tonight?"

"Frankie! Yes!" Jessie's eyes lit up as she turned to watch him come in from the garage, hands full of shopping bags. "Oh look, you went shopping! Perfect. Go get dressed and meet us back here at seven. Ev, I'm running home. See you guys in a few hours!"

"But—"

The look she gave me on her way out the door could have cut glass.

To say I was reluctant to go out for a night of fun amidst all the chaos of my life was putting it mildly. But when I saw Frankie's face light up at the prospect, I couldn't deny him. I was sure Jessie had known that would be the case. *Fine. I'll play along.*

But there was something I had to do first.

I told Frankie as little as possible, then headed outside. He could probably tell by my voice or the somber look on my face, where I was headed. He didn't question me.

Thinking twice about knocking on the door and risking catching the wrath of Ariadne, I snuck around the side of the house. I was almost to Toby's window when I heard his voice.

"Please, just let me try to fix things with her first."

His words carried through the open window, and I paused, afraid he and whoever he was talking to would see me. I knew I should leave, and I was shocked at myself for staying to spy on Toby *again*. But I couldn't seem to make myself leave. Something kept me there, hiding outside his window in broad daylight. I felt like maybe I'd learn one of the truths I was searching for. Like maybe by eavesdropping, I would learn more than Toby would tell me himself.

I would *not* be ashamed. I needed answers.

"It's done, Tobias. As soon as I have this mess sorted out, we're leaving. The time that takes is all the time you will have. My priority is fixing this situation with Ariadne, not worrying about your love life. This has gotten far too out of hand."

"You don't think I know how out of hand this is? Give me some credit, Ted! What Ariadne did . . . well, I can't even wrap my mind around it. She's completely psychotic!"

"Is she now? What about you, Tobias? Have you not also lost sight of your work, made the wrong choices when it comes to this girl? I don't see much difference between you and Ariadne right now."

Me. They're talking about me.

Someone walked to the window, and I held my breath. I heard Toby sigh. Then, remarkably, Ted sighed as well.

"This is my fault, Tobias." He was calmer, more relaxed. He sounded almost sympathetic.

I tilted my head, my brow crinkled in confusion.

"I shouldn't have brought you here. I should have known what would happen."

"What do you mean? How could you possibly—?"

"Just believe me when I tell you that I'm sorry. For *all* of this. But I can't allow you to stay here any longer than necessary, Tobias. Tell the girl what you will; I won't ask you not to. But as soon as I've fixed the mess Ariadne has created, we're gone."

"I can't leave."

"I know."

After a few long seconds passed, I began to wonder if they had left the room.

"I love her." Toby's voice was quiet, almost timid.

"You *can't.*"

When the door slammed shut, I heard Toby cuss under his breath, his frustration evident. I knew he was alone, and I could reveal myself to him, but I couldn't find the courage. I actually *had* learned something by eavesdropping.

Toby loved me. He truly did.

A part of me loved him too.

But I also knew I loved Frankie—and that Toby was a soul collector.

I had to end things with Toby.

Regardless of my feelings for him or his feelings for me, he caused all of this pain in my life. He'd brought these people—could I even call them that?—into my life, and chaos ensued. Ariadne connived and cheated, and Frankie was now human again, his soul belonging to her—whatever that meant. Greg used Jessie as a way to get to me, and now my best friend nursed not only her confusion but a broken heart as well. My mom—well, my mom was a mess. There was no pleasant way to put it. My mom had completely checked out of reality, and frankly, I had no idea what to do or how to help her.

To make matters worse, *my* soul was possibly in jeopardy . . . or whatever crazy thing Ariadne hinted at when she'd said *'an eye for an eye'*.

And it was all because of Toby.

So it was clear. I had to end things with him before anything worse happened. The choice was out of my hands.

I took a deep breath. *I can do this.* The tears started to fall, silently weaving a trail down my cheeks, proof that my decision was breaking the part of me that loved Toby. Pooling all of my strength, reaching down as deeply as I could to find it, I prepared to confront him.

He jumped out of the window and landed just a few feet in front of me. I shrieked, quickly pressing my hand to my mouth to muffle the sound.

He whipped around to see the source of the sound.

"Ever? What are you doing here?"

After the initial scare wore off, it was replaced with pain—heartache to be precise. Looking at him standing there, his messy hair, his gorgeous face . . . it was hard to believe what I was about to do. But I didn't have a choice. This wasn't just about me anymore. This was about everyone I cared for.

"Why are you crying, babe?"

He quickly closed the space between us and wrapped his arms around me, spreading light kisses on my neck and up to my earlobe. My heartbeat picked up pace, and my eyes overflowed with more tears. He felt my stiffness and realized after a few seconds that I wasn't returning his embrace. He leaned back to look at me.

I found I couldn't bring myself to look up at him.

He lightly traced the tears on my cheeks with his fingertips. "Ever? Look at me."

No. I can't.

"Babe?"

I swallowed, my mouth suddenly pasty and dry. I forced myself to meet his gaze. His eyes—*god I love those eyes*—were dark and pained, and I knew he *knew* what I was about to say before I even composed myself enough to speak the words.

"Don't, Ever. Please don't."

More tears fell as Toby's half of my heart shattered a little more.

"I know you're upset, and I'm so sorry. I'm trying to find a way to fix it, I promise . . . but please, Ever. *Please,* don't do *this.*"

I have to, I reminded myself. *This isn't about me. And it isn't about Toby. It's about my Mom. And Frankie. And Jessie.*

He pulled me back to him, crushing me in a fierce embrace. His lips closed over mine, hungrily kissing me, claiming me, urging me to change my mind with the passion of his kiss.

Without words, he almost convinced me. I almost gave in. I wanted to. I loved him.

But I loved my mom. And Jessie. And Frankie.

I loved Frankie. How could I love them both so much? So differently and yet . . . so *equally?* So *intensely?* A muffled sob escaped me, and he pulled back.

"I'm so sorry," I sobbed.

I pushed out of his arms and, unable to find any more words, I ran back into my house, barely seeing anything through my tears. Right into Frankie.

"Oh!"

"Hey, Doll, I'm sorry, I just—" One look at me and he stopped talking, closing his arms around me tightly.

"What has he done?" he practically growled.

"Nothing, Frankie. He's done nothing. I . . . I just broke up with him." I slowly collected myself, realizing I didn't want to cry to Frankie about the end of my relationship with Toby.

"Oh, Doll, I'm sorry."

"It's okay. I had to do it. It was over between us. I can't . . . what he's done . . . and you . . . ."

I looked up at him, and the part of my heart that had always belonged to Frankie swelled with warmth. As I looked at him, I knew that with time, and with Frankie, the parts of me hurting right then would heal. I knew I'd made the right choice.

"Do you want me to leave you alone?"

No. I didn't want to be alone at all, but could I really ask Frankie to comfort me while I cried over another guy? What kind of girl would I be if I did that?

He reworded his question, speaking softly. "Do you want me to go?"

I couldn't find the words to tell him to leave me alone. More tears made their way silently down my cheeks.

He sat on the couch, pulling me down next to him. "Are you sure, Doll?"

He knew me too well.

I shook my head.

He pulled me into his arms. "I'm here for you, Doll. I'm always here for you. I did this for you."

Another sob escaped me. *What?* I looked up at him, confusion and a small dose of fear fighting for center stage in my mind. "What did you say?"

"I did this for you, Doll. I love you." He said it so matter-of-factly, like it was normal, obvious even. "It's always been you."

It's always been me.

I cried more, letting it all out, unhindered by anything. I just needed to cry. I was confused, scared, happy.

Frankie was holding me, comforting me. I loved him, and he loved me.

And nothing else mattered now.

I had never wanted anything so badly in my life. Just Frankie.

Finally Frankie.

Twenty-Six

A few hours later, after a *very* long shower, I was finally ready to go. I met Frankie in the living room just as Jess came inside. Frankie looked practically edible in his new jeans and Chucks. My heart skipped a few beats at the sight of him.

"Hey, Doll."

"Hey, Frankie. You look . . . ."

I trailed off then, searching for the right word. I couldn't possibly say *edible* out loud.

"Yes, yes, we all look fantastic. Unfortunately, if we stand here too long, no one else will get to appreciate us. And, Ev, your cheeks match your shirt, B.T.W." She giggled as I flushed more. "Oh, geez, come on, lovebirds."

"Jessie."

"Oh, Ever. Like he's not looking at you the same hungry way you're looking at him. Seriously, this is like *the* worst third wheel status ever."

"Jess, you are not the third wheel. We are three friends going out to a party, nothing more."

Although, while saying that last part, I had to look down at the ground. It was a total lie. It felt even more like a lie when Frankie reached for my hand and I dodged it by pretending I'd forgotten something and running back to my room. What was I doing? I'd just broken up with Toby, and now I was already starting something with Frankie? Was this even right?

There's a name for girls like me.

"Relax," I said to the reflection in my bathroom mirror. "Relax. Enjoy your night."

As I stood in the bathroom, trying to collect myself, I reminded myself that I should be getting answers. I should be *confronting* Toby, not just breaking up with him and calling it a day. I should be questioning Ariadne. Possibly even finishing up where Jessie left off. *Anything* but going out and acting like everything was normal. There was nothing *normal* about my life, and going out to some pointless party seemed like the exact opposite of what we *should* be doing.

"Ever? You coming?" Jessie was in my doorway.

I quickly looked past her.

"He's in the car, Ev. What's up?"

"What are we doing? What am *I* doing?"

"We're going to a party, Ev. No big deal. And look, you've been in love with Frankie for how long now? A *really* long time. You've only known Toby for what—a few months? And honestly, he's caused *all* of this mess. So, I don't fault you for wanting to gobble up Frankie now that he's in human form again. I mean, look at the guy. He's practically begging for it!"

I laughed at that and wondered briefly if Jessie *could* read my mind. After all, the first word that had popped into my mind had been *'edible.'* I took a deep breath.

"Seriously. Forget about Toby for one night. I'm not saying you need to go rip off Frankie's clothes, but just . . . let's just try to enjoy ourselves. This mess will be here for us in the morning, unfortunately. Toby will still be next door. Ariadne will still be a total bitchface. Your mom will hopefully be better, but if not, we can deal with that, too." She paused to take a breath. "I, for one, am totally over this whole thing, and I'm going out. Screw Greg and Toby and their soul collector nonsense!" She grabbed my hand and pulled me back down the hall.

I felt better.

Sort of.

Jessie was right. A night out would probably do us all some good. And it was nagging at the back of my mind that Frankie needed a night out more than any of us. Who was I to deny him something he'd missed out on for so long?

Yeah, this is for Frankie, I told myself. *Like a favor for Frankie. That's all.*

And then it hit me. Frankie couldn't possibly go to a party! What was wrong with us? Someone could recognize him! Oh my god. We'd almost just made the biggest mistake in the history of the world.

"What is it, Ever? You look like you've just seen a gho—" Jessie giggled.

"Jess, we can't take Frankie out . . . to a *party*. What if someone sees—?"

"Oh! Oh my god! You're right!" She gasped. "What were we thinking?"

I shook my head and sat on the bed. She sat next to me. When Frankie finally showed up in my doorway a few minutes later, I'm sure we both looked like we'd been shocked—eyes wide, and confusion on our faces. We'd narrowly missed a catastrophe.

"Girls? What's going on?"

"Frankie, we can't take you out to a party tonight. What if . . . ?"

"Oh."

Clearly, he hadn't thought of it either.

"Well, that sucks."

"Well, maybe not, I mean, you guys didn't even go to my school. And the party's all the way out in Costa Mesa. So . . . ."

"Jessie, you can't be serious. Think about it!"

"Wait a minute. She's right, Doll. No one will recognize me. It's been over two years, and we probably won't know anyone anyway. And even if someone *does* recognize me, they aren't really going to believe what they're seeing. Right?"

I thought about it. He kind of had a point. Plus, most of his friends were probably in college by now, so not likely hanging around at high school parties. I hoped. Frankie's eyes pleaded with me, and my defenses fell. Apparently so did my better judgment, because before long, we were in the car, driving to the party. I couldn't seem to deny him.

Luckily, I didn't have to sit by him, which would have made it incredibly difficult not to stare at him for the entire ride. I was still not fully used to his solid form, and he was pretty damn good looking in the flesh. I'd have been helpless sitting next to him. Not to mention the incessant need to touch him. By the time we arrived at the house where the party was, I felt ten times better.

Of course, getting out of the car meant I had to actually *look* at Frankie again, and walking up to the party meant I had to actually be *near* him. Unless I wanted to act like a total weirdo and walk a few yards away from them. When he grabbed my hand, I felt nervous and childish, my cheeks heating up and giving me away. But I didn't yank it away this time.

The three of us walked inside, and I felt like we stuck out like sore thumbs. Though I know we didn't, the feeling that the whole world was looking at us didn't go away. There was no way anyone could know that Frankie had been a ghost for the past two years, unless they knew him while he was alive. No one could know that my feelings for two guys had me feeling like the worst person to ever walk the earth. No one could know that Jessie and I had both recently been dating soul collectors. And no one could possibly know that just the feel of Frankie's hand in mine had me feeling warmth in ways I shouldn't have been.

Still. I felt like flashing lights and screeching alarms were going off around us nonetheless.

We made our way through the house, Jessie stopping to say hi to friends and introducing Frankie and me to various people along the way. I knew a few of them already, from various parties and such, so seeing familiar faces eased my tension a little bit. But I still felt like I was on display. In the backyard, we came across a cooler of miscellaneous beer brands, and Frankie's eyes lit up at the prospect of a cold beer. He found himself an ice-cold original Coors, and you'd think he'd just found bars of solid gold the way he looked at it. I didn't get the excitement, but I guess for someone who enjoys drinking, having a cold beer after two years of having nothing to drink at all might be pretty nice.

He almost drank the whole thing in one sip. He noticed Jessie and me staring at him with our eyebrows raised, then donned a slightly embarrassed smile and shrugged.

"Sorry. It's just been *so* long."

We giggled at him and headed out in search of our own beverages. There had to be soda *somewhere* at this party, right? Once inside, we were standing in front of an open fridge door, feeling only slightly guilty to be looking at someone else's fridge contents—but hey, not everyone drinks beer—when a voice stopped me mid-search.

"Ever? Jessie?"

"*Shit,*" I whispered to Jessie as we turned around to the source of the voice.

Scott.

Honestly, I'd forgotten all about him. It had only been a couple days since I'd kissed him at that party at his house, but *so* much had happened since then. Scott was at the very back of my mind. When I saw the look on his face, I could tell the opposite was true for him. I was still *very* fresh in his mind. When he reached for me, I froze. Frankie was standing just a few feet away with an odd expression on his face. I didn't know what to do. I probably had only seconds before Scott pulled me into a hug, and I couldn't possibly risk the chance that he might kiss me.

"Hey, Scottie! It's good to see you!" Jessie reached forward, lightly pushing me aside and squeezing Scott into a massive bear hug, intercepting the embrace that had been intended for me.

Phew. The confused look on his face was priceless, but I didn't have long to look at it. Frankie pulled me outside, and Jessie pulled Scott toward the living room.

"What was that all about?" Frankie laughed, obviously aware that the moment had been a bit awkward for me. Could I tell him I'd kissed Scott only days before? *'Hey Frankie, by the way, you're the third guy I've kissed in as many days. Cool, huh?'*

No. Not a chance. I had to lie. Again. Who was this girl I'd become?

"Oh, that's just some guy from Jessie's school who has a little thing for me." Not a *total* lie. Right? Just not the total truth either. *Damn.*

A few minutes later, Jessie came outside to find us, and commotion erupted all around.

"Cops!"

The partygoers were yelling the warning almost in unison. A few guys hefted the cooler of beer inside, while other frantic people trashed their drinks and scattered.

"I guess that's our cue!" Jessie said, as she quickly headed for the side gate of the yard.

Frankie looked at me and smiled, the light in his eyes giving away the fact that he was clearly excited by the prospect of having to run from the cops. I guess when you haven't had *any* excitement for as long as he hadn't, possible minor-in-possession charges were exciting. I shook my head and followed Jessie to the car.

After the party, we ended up at Starbucks. Not nearly as exciting for Frankie as cold beer and possible arrests, but who could resist a good latte? Not me, that's for sure.

Jessie dropped us off around ten or so, stating she wanted to sleep at her house. I figured she was worried about Susan again, and quickly wished that Jessie didn't find her with another asshole like that last one.

I checked on my mom, who was in her bed reading a book about gardening, Gollum curled up at her feet.

"Oh! Hi, kids! You're home early! Frankie, honey, I made up the guest bedroom for you, and there's a fresh pitcher of water next to the bed, along with some magazines and a CD player."

Just the typical houseguest procedure. No big deal. I sighed, and Frankie reached out to squeeze my hand. Once outside her room, he whispered, "It will be okay, Doll. You'll see. She'll come around."

"I hope so. This is just too weird for me."

He reached out and gently ran his fingers across my chin, his thumb grazing my lip. He was only inches away from me, and in the darkness of the hallway, with my mom's door closed blocking her from sight, it was easy to imagine we were the only two people in the world.

I wanted to imagine that. If only for just a second.

He licked his lips and looked into my eyes. My cheeks heated up. I ran a hand through my hair, trying to figure out what to do next. *God* I wanted to erase everything else. Every*one* else. I wanted to be alone with Frankie. Just him and me. No Mom. No Toby.

I turned away from Frankie, but he followed me to my bedroom door. The tension and heat from being so close to each other all night was near the bursting point. Well, at least for me it was. I either had to get as far away from him as possible—*immediately*—or turn and throw myself at him. There was no gray area tonight. It was either Frankie's kiss . . . or spontaneous combustion.

I stopped at my door, took a deep breath, and turned to face him. *Oh!* He was closer than I realized.

I was going to tell him we needed to move slowly. That was the responsible thing to do. Move slowly. But with his lips pressed to mine and his arms crushing me to him, it was growing increasingly hard to think. Even harder to speak.

Gripping me tightly, he pushed gently until I was crushed between his body and my closed bedroom door. He moved one hand up the length of my ribs and over my shoulder blade to where it could rest comfortably on my neck. Holding my head in place, he kissed me hungrily. I lost all coherent thought.

It was just me and Frankie and his *kiss*.

I melted into him, our mouths moving in a rhythm almost too natural to be real. It felt like I'd been kissing Frankie for years, like we knew the next move the other person was going to make before they made it. At the same time, kissing Frankie was unfamiliar, the excitement and the thrilling feeling of finally kissing him, new and exotic. My heart pounded, thumping loudly in my ears. Every part of me wanted more of him.

The sound of my mom's door opening abruptly ended our kiss, and Frankie flew to the opposite side of the cramped hallway. I swear I could see the red heat between us, hanging in the air, but like everything else going on around her, my mother was blind to it.

"Frankie, before I forget, there are clean towels for you in Ever's bathroom. Good night, kids! Love you both!" She shot us both a smile and went back into her room.

I shook my head. My dad would have seen the lusty heat between Frankie and me in a heartbeat, and I probably would have gotten a nice boring lecture on boys. My mom, however, was completely oblivious. I sighed.

Frankie stared at me intently, and I ached to touch him again. But unfortunately, my mom's behavior cooled the heat in my veins and reminded me that there was so much more at stake here. So much more to do before I could even *consider* moving forward with Frankie.

"I have to go to bed, Frankie. I . . . I can't do this right now."

"I know, Doll. I'll see you in the morning."

Of course he knew. Of course he didn't try to argue. He always knew exactly what I needed. I closed my bedroom door behind me then slid down to the ground. I heard a rustling on the other side of the door as Frankie did the same thing.

"Frankie?"

"Yeah, Doll?"

"What are you doing?"

"No idea."

"Do you want to come in?" My voice was a whisper, and half of me was surprised by the words. As if they hadn't fully had my permission to come out.

I stood and opened the door to him. He was already standing, and before I'd even opened the door all the way, he was kissing me again. I heard the door shut softly behind him. Then both of his hands were on me, and he was leading me to the bed.

He slowly laid me down on my bed, and before long, he was on top of me. We were both breathing quickly, our hands franticly touching each other. Our clothing came off next. First my shirt, then his. Eventually his jeans. As if it wasn't new or awkward at all.

Lying with Frankie, with only his boxers and my denim skirt between us, I wasn't afraid. There was no doubt in my mind that I was safe with Frankie. My body, my heart—he would never hurt me. As we kissed and his hands explored my naked chest again, I knew without a doubt that I was going to lose my virginity to Frankie tonight.

I couldn't imagine anything feeling more right.

I reached down between us, slowly at first, and slightly nervous even though I'd made my decision. I began to tug at my skirt, but it was awkward while his weight was on top of me. Feeling what I was doing, he slid to the side of me. His eyes were dark, the caramel brown a rich sea of hunger now.

He slowly drew circles around my belly button, and goose bumps broke out over my bare skin. I resumed trying to remove my skirt, but Frankie reached down and stopped my hand. He set it by my side and sat up.

Slowly, with his hands on either side of my waist, he slid my skirt down my legs. I felt exposed and vulnerable, but the way Frankie looked at me—with so much love—my worries quickly faded away again.

This is right.

He lay down on top of me again, and without my skirt to restrain me, I wrapped my legs around him. He groaned deep in his throat, and something sparked inside me in response. Our kissing intensified, his tongue actively searching my mouth, his hands firmly feeling every inch of me possible. I felt the pressure of him between my legs—an intense and strange feeling that brought pleasure and fear, dangerously laced with anticipation.

His hips moved, slowly at first, and feelings I can't even describe shot through my body. A sound I'd never heard before escaped my lips. Frankie answered it with another groan deep in his throat, and then he stopped kissing me, his breathing fast and heavy.

He looked into my eyes, an unspoken question between us.

Is this okay?

Yes. *Yes.*

He reached down to his jeans on the floor and pulled out a small foil package. For a second, I didn't know what it was. Then it occurred to me, and my cheeks flared up. *Holy shit!*

"Frankie!"

He sheepishly looked away.

When did he buy condoms? What was he planning?

"I'm sorry, Doll. I know this looks bad. But . . . after last night . . . after we . . . I just . . . I just wanted to be prepared. I swear. Please, don't think I'm a creep, Ever. I just wanted to be prepared."

He looked at me then, eyes slightly ashamed, and his cheeks slightly red. I laughed in spite of myself. He wanted to be ready. He wanted this as much as I did. I smiled at him, shaking my head slightly at how uncomfortable the situation had just become. I reached for him and pulled him back to me. We kissed again, and my heart flapped around wildly in my chest.

Yes. I was going to go all the way with Frankie.

The boy I'd loved for my entire life.

Feeling uncharacteristically brave and sure, I wrapped my legs back around him, silently giving him permission to continue. Within moments we were naked, the feel of our skin connecting in so many new places an unfamiliar and exhilarating thing. I didn't worry about what I was doing or if I was doing it wrong. I didn't worry about my stomach or how skinny or fat it was. I didn't worry about how I was moving or if I was supposed to be moving differently. I didn't worry about *anything*. Because with Frankie, I just *was*. I saw myself the way he saw me—the way he had always seen me—and I wondered how I ever doubted his feelings.

He'd loved me his entire life.

Nothing could have been better than this moment.

It was just me and Frankie and our love.

Finally.

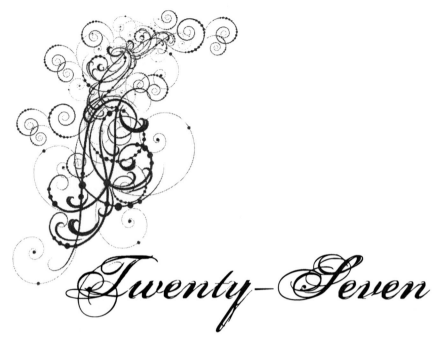

Twenty-Seven

Just days after Toby and I broke up, I found myself reluctantly crossing over our yards again. Frankie, Jessie, and I had decided it was time to get some *real* answers to our questions.

I had made the trip plenty of times, but this time I felt even *more* butterflies than I used to feel. This time, I wasn't coming to Toby as his girlfriend. This time, I was coming to him as his *ex*-girlfriend whose new boyfriend was standing beside her. I didn't want Toby to know Frankie and I were officially together yet. I didn't want to hurt Toby, or for him to think poorly of me. But I felt like he was going to see it between Frankie and me. Like somehow he was just going to *know*.

But Toby's feelings aside, we needed answers. We *deserved* answers. We'd gotten pretty much nowhere on our own, so this was the only option we had left. Even though it felt strange for me to have to see Toby again so soon after breaking up with him, we were out of options. The three of us were going to demand answers to all of our many questions, regardless of how those answers—or the time spent face to face with Toby again—affected me.

And affect me it did.

Toby answered the door, and his face lit up when he saw me. My heart clenched, and my eyes did that weird tingly thing they do before I'm about to start crying like a baby. I felt Frankie's body behind mine, like there was an invisible thread pulling us to each other. I hoped Toby couldn't see it.

Jessie squeezed my hand, knowing how difficult this was for Frankie and me.

"Hey," Toby said, with a relieved smile.

"Hey," I said back to him, my voice cracking to give away my discomfort, clearly not as strong and pulled together as I'd thought I was. *Damn.* I pushed past him into his living room and sat on his couch, Jessie and Frankie sitting on either side of me.

"You three seem like you mean business." He addressed all of us, but his attention was intently focused on me.

Frankie stiffened next to me.

Toby caught the slight movement, and his gaze traveled back and forth between us. As if responding to Toby's silent question, Frankie put his hand on my thigh. Staking his claim, I imagined.

I took a deep breath.

"We do mean business," I said. The strength in my voice surprised me. "Sit down, Toby. We want answers."

He sat on the floor with his back leaning against the high-backed chair opposite us, and his legs spread out in front of him, crossed at the ankles. "I'll tell you anything you want to know. Anything."

I sure hoped he was telling the truth. We had so many questions.

"Okay, um . . . ." I had no idea where to start.

"Well, Toby, for starters, what *is* a soul collector exactly?"

Ah, thank you, Jess. At least she wasn't struck dumb, sitting in her former boyfriend's living room with her current boyfriend by her side, and thus, able to form a coherent question. She also managed to sound like a professional newscaster, and I pictured her with a microphone in one hand and a cameraman close by.

Ariadne sauntered into the room before Toby could answer, and both Frankie and Jessie stiffened beside me. My gut coiled. *Ugh.* She sat in the chair behind Toby, slowly stretching her legs to either side of him, so his head was practically in her lap.

He tensed.

She smiled her sweetest smile and winked at Frankie. Though the darkness around her eye had faded significantly, the proof of Jessie's outburst was still apparent. Jessie smiled, and I knew her thoughts mirrored mine. I seriously *loathed* her very existence and wished *I'd* been the one to punch her.

"Oh, look. It's Ever. Hello, *Ever*," she purred.

My fists ached to connect with her pouty lips, and Frankie must have felt it in my arm muscles because he reached for my clenched fist. His thumb rubbed soothing motions on my skin, and I relaxed my hand.

Toby and Ariadne watched the gesture, and Ariadne laughed. A heartless, icy laugh.

"Well, well. You've decided to accept my gift after all. You don't move slowly, do ya?" She cocked her head and stared hard, analyzing me. "Oh!" Her eyes widened. "Well. I'm a little surprised you moved *that* quickly. I'll admit it though . . . I'm a little impressed, too." She winked at me, like suddenly we were in cahoots.

Not likely.

Below her, Toby tensed, and she ran a hand down his chest in a soothing motion. Though I knew she had no desire to soothe him. Otherwise, the next words would have never left her lips.

"So? What was it like? A girl's first time can be so . . . awkward."

Toby shot up and turned on her. Staring down at her with his back to us, I could only imagine the menace from his stare. She shrank back under the heat of it.

"That is enough, Ariadne." Toby's words were forced through gritted teeth and dripping with anger.

"Oh, calm down, Tobias. I'm only having fun with our little friends here. I mean look at her; she practically oozes with sex. It's such a change from her angelic purity bit."

I watched the muscles in Toby's back tighten and his fists clench.

"Why are you still here, Ariadne?" My words were forced through gritted teeth as well. *If only I could get in one swing. Just one tiny swing. What could it hurt?*

"Oh, didn't Toby tell you, hon? We're leaving tomorrow. *All* of us." She emphasized the word *all*, no doubt enjoying the pain she was inflicting on Jessie as well.

"What?" I was stunned.

I wasn't with Toby anymore. I didn't want to be with Toby anymore, and I definitely didn't have a right to want him to stay. I'd wished he'd leave so many times over the past few days. But to hear he was actually leaving? That was another thing entirely.

And we still needed answers. What about Frankie's soul? What about mine?

When neither one of them explained further, I asked again. "What does she mean, Toby?"

"Thanks a lot, Ariadne."

Toby briefly glanced between Frankie and me, at our clenched hands. Frankie squeezed my hand, subconsciously claiming me again. Or possibly consciously. I didn't know. I saw pain flit across Toby's face, and my heart broke. I didn't want to hurt him, regardless of anything that had happened between us, or any pain he'd caused my friends and me.

"Ever, I—"

"You're leaving?"

"I don't want to leave. I'd stay here forever if I could. I'd wait for the rest of my life for you to change your mind"—he glanced at Frankie again—"if I thought you would." He sighed and bowed his head. "But I know you won't. I know you *can't*. After all that's happened, I just—"

"It's okay. You're right, Toby."

But was he? I didn't know for sure. Would I have never changed my mind?

It didn't matter. He was leaving. I had Frankie. Where Toby and Ariadne ended up was none of my concern.

"Oh! Enough of this! Stop making a fool of yourself, Tobias. You're pathetic."

Ariadne's words cut deep. I remembered what it felt like when that word was used on me.

Jessie had enough as well. She stood and faced Ariadne, barely holding in her disdain. "Look, bitch. You said the other day that Ever owed you something. An eye for an eye. What did you mean by that?"

Toby groaned, and I looked at him. His gaze met mine, and a silent apology passed through his eyes. *Oh shit.*

"Oh, you're still stuck on that? Well, it's easy, really. Ever has until she's—"

"Stop!"

Everyone's heads shot up in unison to look at Toby.

"Don't, Ari. Please."

Ariadne softened for just the slightest second, then her eyes narrowed and she looked back at me, the full force of her wounded pride pointing at me like a weapon. Her lip curled slightly, distorting her pretty face.

"You have one year, Ever. I will come collect your soul in place of Frankie's when you turn nineteen. It's really a pretty fair trade and much more than you deserve. See, I'm nothing if not fair."

Thank You For Reading.

Curiosity Quills Press
http://curiosityquills.com

Please visit http://curiosityquills.com/reader-survey/ to share your reading experience with the author of this book!

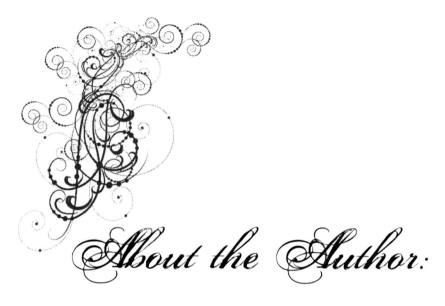

About the Author:

An unashamed super fan of all things *paranormal romance*, Jessa Russo reads, writes and breathes paranormal YA, rarely straying from her comfort zone. When not writing or reading, Jessa enjoys making memories with her awesome family and amazingly supportive friends, while secretly planning her next trip to New Orleans. She's won a few flash fiction contests and had a short story published, but feels her greatest accomplishment is raising

the coolest kid ever – a little girl with a Tim Burton obsession and a desire to save every animal she sees.

Jessa will always call Southern California home, where she lives with her husband Jon, their daughter Faith, Bronco the Great Dane and Lola the Chihuahua.

Acknowledgments

Anyone who has written a book – or even *attempted* to write a book – can tell you that as solitary as it may seem at times, it is anything but. I have been blessed with an extremely tolerant and ridiculously supportive group of people that I could not (and will not) live without.

My *beta* or *first draft* readers have watched EVER change so many times it probably made them dizzy. Yet they read and reread my story with passion and fervor, and have always – *always* – cheered me along in my journey. I believe in myself because they believe in me. So thank you *Melissa Purkey, Mat & Michelle Magaña, Kathleen Kubasiak, and Nanette Pitts* - you're all wonderful friends and amazing betas, and I don't deserve you. Many other people have read EVER along the way as well, and your enthusiasm for my writing has been priceless. There are too many of you to name, but I cherish all of you and I hope you know who you are.

Mom – I can't imagine that anyone has a cheerleader like you in their corner. You have always believed I can do no wrong – even when I'm doing it. You have given me something irreplaceable – my drive to keep on keepin' on. Thank you for loving me unconditionally and always believing in me – even when I don't believe in myself. You're probably responsible for my massively inflated sense of self, and for that I am eternally grateful.

My critique partner *Tamara Mataya* – I can't even properly express how important you are. Even more valuable than your critiquing, is your ability to push me when I want to quit, or pull me down from that pesky tree of self-doubt. Whether it's a surprise bouquet of flowers, or a picture of a sloth scratching its butt, you *rock* at saving me from myself. I'm so blessed to know you and call you my friend. Your friendship means the world to me. *Shiny Critique Partners FTW!* *fist pump*

A HUGE thank you goes to my editor, *Krystal Wade*. Not only did your belief in this book turn my dream into a reality, but your friendship has proven invaluable. I owe you so much more than gratitude and I hope I can pay you back some day.

To everyone at *Curiosity Quills* – thank you for believing in me, believing in EVER, and being the most supportive group of the coolest people to ever grace the planet. I am thrilled to be a part of the CQ family! Thank you for welcoming me so warmly.

My family deserves endless praise for putting up with this all-consuming passion of mine. *Jon* – I love you more each day – even when you're teasing me about my imaginary worlds and fictional boyfriend collection. You're stubborn and hard-headed like me, and I can't wait to grow old with you. *Princess Bella* – I know that at times it was frustrating, and for a long time you didn't understand my constant need to write. I hope that in the end, you are proud of me. Most of all, I hope that I have taught you to finish what you start, and always chase your dreams – no matter how old you are, or how unreachable those dreams may seem. *You can do anything.*

Last but not least, thank you to YOU – the person reading this right now. Whether you love this book or hate it, I hope you *feel* something when you read it. EVER is my firstborn word-baby, and the fact that you are reading her story means more than I could ever put into words.

So, thank you.

Fade, by A.K. Morgen

When Arionna Jacobs meets Dace Matthews, everything she thought she knew about herself and the world around them begins to fall apart.

Neither of them understands what is happening to them, or why, and they're running out of time to figure it out.

An ancient Norse prophesy of destruction has been set into motion, and what destiny has in store for them is bigger than either could have ever imagined.

Wilde's Fire, by Krystal Wade

Katriona Wilde has never wondered what it would feel like to have everything she's ever known and loved ripped away, but she is about to find out: her entire life has been a lie, and those closest to her have betrayed her.

What's worse, she has no control over her new future, full of magic and horrors from which nightmares are made.

Will Kate discover and learn to control who she really is in time to save the ones she loves, or will all be lost?

Wilde's Army, by Krystal Wade

"Hello, Katriona." Those two words spark fear in Katriona Wilde and give way to an unlikely partnership with Perth, the man she's been traded to marry for a favor. Saving her true love and protector Arland keeps her motivated, but the at-odds duo soon realizes trust is something that comes and goes with each breath of Encardia's rotting, stagnant air.

Now, Kate must unite her clashing people, and form an army prepared to fight in order to defeat Darkness. When so many she's grown fond of die along the journey, will she still be Katriona Wilde, the girl with fire?

Worlds Burn Through, by Vicki Keire

Chloe Burke has nightmares of a world burned to ash and the strange boy who saves them both. Underneath the dreams lurks a deeply buried reality; Chloe and a handful of others are survivors of a decade old apocalypse that burned their home world to the ground.

Now their ancient enemies hunt them again. To keep their adopted world safe, Chloe must undergo a ritual of blood sacrifice that will have life-long consequences if she survives. Her lethal protector, Eliot Gray, must keep her alive long enough to do it. Together they will uncover even more dangerous secrets buried in the past's deepest, darkest ashes.

Automatic Woman, by Nathan L. Yocum

There are no simple cases. Jacob "Jolly" Fellows knows this.

The London of 1888, the London of steam engines, Victorian intrigue, and horseless carriages is not a safe place nor simple place…but it's his place. Jolly is a thief catcher, a door-crashing thug for the prestigious Bow Street Firm, assigned to track down a life sized automatic ballerina. But when theft turns to murder and murder turns to conspiracy, can Jolly keep his head above water? Can a thief catcher catch a killer?

The Department of Magic, by Rod Kierkegaard, Jr.

Magic is nothing like it seems in children's books. It's dark and bloody and sexual – and requires its own semi-mythical branch of the US Federal Government to safeguard citizens against everpresent supernatural threats.

Join Jasmine Farah and Rocco di Angelo – a pair of wet-behind-the-ears recruits of The Department of Magic – on a nightmare gallop through a world of ghosts, spooks, vampires, and demons, and the minions of South American and Voodoo gods hell-bent on destroying all humanity in the year 2012.

CPSIA information can be obtained at www.ICGtesting.com
Printed in the USA
BVOW082247170912

300557BV00001B/16/P